"Marcus Grodi weaves the web of story with consummate skill and interweaves the threads of theology with seemingly seamless ease. His new novel warms the heart, informs the head and invigorates the spirit."

—Joseph Pearce, author
Literary Converts and *Tolkien: Man and Myth, A Literary Life*

"Readers of Marcus Grodi's earlier work will recognize immediately the special touch of this writer, namely, a narrative which, grounded in the common stuff of our mortal life, with all that this means of happiness, sorrow, perplexity, doubt, struggle, and fulfillment, brings the reader on through to what T. S. Eliot called 'The Permanent Things.' *Deo gratias* for that great Pillar and Bulwark."

—Dr. Thomas Howard, author
Evangelical Is Not Enough and *Lead, Kindly Light*

"A rather famous storyteller once said that fictions are 'God's grandchildren.' Marcus Grodi knows this truth, and his drama follows the lines of the art that made the world. Here, in *Pillar and Bulwark*, is providence, with all its patterns and surprises, drawing lives together even as it seems to push them apart. God's drama keeps us turning the calendar pages from day to day. That rare novelist who successfully imitates God will also keep us turning pages. This book is a page-turner."

—Mike Aquilina, author
The Fathers of the Church

"Marcus Grodi, a Christian man for all Seasons and all Media, has written another thriller set in the world that he knows intimately, the world of spiritual struggle in the setting of Family and Faith that does not leave space for easy choices. You the reader may well find yourself in this compelling novel."

—Rev. C. J. McCloskey III, fellow, Faith and Reason Institute,
Washington, D.C.; author
*Good News, Bad News: Evangelism,
Conversion, and the Crisis of Faith*

"Marcus has written an engaging story with a vital message. The characters will come alive because they reflect in a novel manner the real experiences of real people! Rather than spoil the story for you, let me just urge you to buy and read a copy. Like me, you will enjoy it so much you will want to pass it along to a friend."

—David B Currie, author
Rapture: The End-times Error that Leaves the Bible Behind

"*Pillar and Bulwark* is beautiful narrative of conversion that weaves together elements of Truth in a captivating vision. A story of love and sacrifice, it captures the experience of many who find themselves on a journey to the fullness of faith."

—Dr. Kenneth J. Howell, senior fellow,
Newman Center, Univ. of Illinois, Chicago; author
Ignatius of Antioch & Polycarp (Early Christian Fathers)

"The Psalmist asks, "When the ancient foundations are being destroyed, what can the righteous do?" In a masterwork of fiction, Marcus Grodi gives us strong Christian men and women whose long-held traditions are being shaken to the very core. Listen to their inner-most thoughts as they struggle to answer life's most vital questions. Only a 'Pillar and Bulwark' will stand-up to the attacks they must endure. A riveting read!"

—Rob Evans
The "Donut Man"

"Here is a story that is full of life even though it starts in a graveyard. It captures the mindset of a huge cross-section of America that gets swept away by apocalyptic and anti-Catholic hysteria. And yet the book offers its lessons gently and warmly. You will understand why anyone who sits down with Marcus Grodi immediately feels comfortable."

—Dale Ahlquist, president, American Chesterton Society; author
G.K. Chesterton: Apostle of Common Sense

"Marcus has done it as few others can. He has woven top-notch apologetic lessons with a riveting story. The read is so good, you sometimes don't realize how much truth you are learning."

—Dr. Ray Guarendi, psychologist, radio show host, author
You're a Better Parent Than You Think!

PILLAR &
BULWARK

ALSO BY MARCUS GRODI:

Journeys Home
Thoughts for the Journey Home
How Firm a Foundation

MARCUS GRODI

PILLAR & BULWARK

CHRESOURCES

Zanesville, Ohio

CHResources
PO Box 8290
Zanesville, Ohio 43702
740-450-1175
www.chnetwork.org

CHResources is a registered trademark of the Coming Home Network
International, Inc.

Library of Congress Cataloging-in-Publication Data

Grodi, Marcus.
Pillar and bulwark / Marcus Grodi.
    p. cm.
Includes bibliographical references.
ISBN 978-0-9830829-5-8 (softcover : alk. paper) -- ISBN 978-0-9830829-4-1
(hardcover : alk. paper)
I. Title.
PS3607.R629P55 2011
813'.6--dc23

                    2011042765

Cover photos: Image Focus/Shutterstock.com, Travel Bug/Shutterstock.com,
Crystal Woroniuk/stock.xchng, Konstantin L/Shutterstock.com, Ethan Boisvert/
Shutterstock.com, Sean Pavone/Shutterstock.com, Rob Hainer/Shutterstock.com,
©iStockphoto.com/Sean Pavone, Mike Moors/stock.xchng, David Hart/stock.xchng,
Sandra Cunningham/stock.xchng

Cover design and page layout by Jennifer Bitler: www.doxologydesign.com

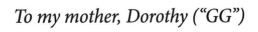

To my mother, Dorothy ("GG")

CONTENTS

PART 1

HE RESTORETH MY SOUL

T he wispy grayness of the Ohio winter sky was filtering between the groping, naked arms of the overarching trees.

I stopped my stereotypical white Chevy conversion van at the light, and couldn't help but notice the endless, rolling cemetery off to my left. The graveyard's low wall jutted right up against the recently widened street, so I could easily see monuments of countless shapes and sizes. Some of the surnames were vaguely familiar, while others made me wonder.

The light changed, but as I began moving forward, an enormous tombstone rose into view. I braked abruptly and stared. It wasn't the stone figure perched on top—a soldier leading a gallant charge and beckoning others to follow—that caught my attention; it was the *names*.

The car behind me laid on its horn, justly. But those names! Stephen Storeson, Father; Sara Storeson, Mother; Scott Storeson, Son. It wasn't the unusual surname, but the *given* names that arrested me: Stephen ... Sara ... Scott.

I'm beginning with that event because as I look back, the grouping of those three names seems far too coincidental. Since I don't believe in coincidence, I can only wonder, was this some kind of sign, or perhaps an omen?

My name is Scott Turner, and I'm a radically different person today than I was when I skirted past that graveyard nearly a year ago. Certainly, to some extent, we all can say this. Every cell in our bodies replaces itself every seven years—so physically we're different people today than we were even last week, and I daresay a few of us, including me, missed the improvement lane.

More importantly, though, unanticipated spiritual, emotional, and relational upheavals overhaul each of us persistently. None of us remains the same. If we think so, we're just blind stupid. A river looks the same every day, but the water passing by has never passed us before.

I'm not telling my story because I believe I'm special—far from it. Rather, I'm telling it because I believe that what I discovered, by the mercy of God, is important. Important enough to sacrifice nearly everything else in my life.

I'm writing this in a quiet upper room of our modern yet rustic cabin in southeast Maine, overlooking a river not far from Kennebunkport. Before me on my desk is a picture called *Christ Pantocrator,* traditionally considered the earliest existing icon of our Lord Jesus. Next to this is an early picture of my family: my wife, Diane, and our four children, Susanna, Elisa, Deborah, and Eddy. That was a happier time. Today, I feel very much alone, but I'm getting ahead of myself.

This journey began, I suppose, many years ago, long before my heart had any inkling it was on a journey. It picked up speed and came to a climax, however, over the course of one week that began the day I passed that cemetery.

The first thing I recall of that momentous week was the hot, delicious fragrance rising from two homemade cherry cobbler pies. My wife's mother, Dorothy, was placing them before a circle of hungry eyes. When she stood back smiling, the faces must have appeared contorted through the waffling, sumptuous air. Our youngest, Eddy, strained with impatience as he waited to be served. Diane had trained him well.

I remember all of this vividly because I was not enjoying those precious treasures, for I was preparing to leave my family for a one-week, personal excursion back East.

From the living room, where Diane and I were watching our family gorge themselves, she asked, her mischievous smile aimed temptingly up into my eyes, "Scott, honey, do you really have to go?"

Before answering, I gave her a lingering kiss. "It's not a 'have to,' darling. We've discussed this. But it's something that I need; to reconnect. I'm feeling . . . detached."

There were other reasons, but I didn't think she'd understand those.

"I know," she said, kissing my cheek. "I want you to go."

"Thanks. You're the greatest." I enveloped her in my arms, as passionately as was permitted within the sight of grandparents and children. I suppose you might say she was nearly engulfed by my bulk. (Though recently forty-five, I'm fairly vigilant about staying fit. To be honest, though, I may look like I could step back in time and take my place on the defensive line, but it's been nearly sixteen years since I turned in my professional gear and playbook. I would fall like tissue paper before the new breed of young bucks.)

"Awthum pie!" Eddy exclaimed through a mouth ringed with cherry filling.

Diane and I backed away to hide our laughter.

"I'll drive careful and check in with you around nine or so."

"All right, dear. Say hi to everyone I know."

With that we returned to the dining room for my departing speech.

"I hate to leave," I explained, shamefaced as I hurried around the table, shaking hands, kissing, or patting backs, whichever was appropriate. First Diane's parents, Dorothy and Homer; then our oldest daughter Susanna and her husband Stu; our middle daughter, Elisa, home from state college; Deborah, our youngest daughter, a freshman at Rowsville High; and of course Eddy. I avoided the cherry stains by ruffling his curly blond hair. I'd save my taste of cobbler for the road.

"Love you all," I said one last time and, grabbing a thermos of coffee and a brown bag of snacks, I dashed out the front door.

Within minutes, I had traversed the gravel country roads and was driving due north along a recently paved, four-lane highway. In a half hour, I would reach the turnpike, the official starting-point of my journey from the flat farmlands of northwest Ohio back to the mountains of New England, to the region Diane and I had called home for over fifteen years, and specifically to the peaceful and memorable mountaintop retreat called the Widow's Mite.

When I began that journey, I was serving as the new pastor of Rowsville Congregational Church, Rowsville, Ohio, named, I presume, for the only thing you see in any direction. Being a minister was certainly not my childhood dream. From the Pop Warner days of my youth, my dream, night and day, had been to play professional football. Unlike the thousands of other boys across America who had similar but unfulfilled dreams, I had the undeserved privilege of actualizing mine. God had blessed me with a modicum of natural ability and mass. Driven by good coaching and an infinite ego, I had won accolades as a high-school wrestling champion, a state champion weightlifter, and the beloved hometown football hero of Sumac Lake, Michigan. With grades that begged the question, my athletic prowess, nonetheless, led to a full four-year scholarship to play defensive end for Southern Michigan Tech.

Moving from the small pond of Sumac Lake to the midsize college of Southern Tech, however, was an unexpected challenge. I worked strenuously first to win a position against the reigning upperclassmen and then hold it against the annual influx of equally determined freshmen. In the end, I earned my stripes and went straight into the pros. I wasn't selected in the first draft or even the second or third, but when selected by the Massachusetts Colonials, I wept, which looked mighty strange for a 240-lb defensive end. I had attained my dream.

Twenty-three years later, as I drove north on that Sunday afternoon, a middle-aged, slightly paunchy preacher, I reminisced with reserved joy at the seven seasons I once spent in the trenches.

JUST the thought of racing through and out of the tunnel onto the field before seventy-five thousand screaming fans—some for and many against us—brought on the exhilarating adrenaline rush. I missed the camaraderie and the team spirit. I'd pass on the grueling weeks of August training camp, though, or the constant pressure to pop pills to numb the pain or pump the muscles, or the humiliating backstabbing of the pencil-necked news media. I didn't miss the daily physical and mental grind much either. The mere thought of experiencing another "stinger" was enough to erase any envy of those now playing the game. I still can't bend over without some pain from that disc-shattering blow from Bubba "No Prisoners" Tooly.

The money, though, had been great—I had made more in seven years than most people see in a lifetime. With the help of some trustworthy financial advisors, I stashed away a respectable portion of this fortune I'd made punishing my bones. To an embarrassing extent, however, I've kept my wife ignorant of the full extent of our net worth. Anyone who did know would certainly realize that I didn't become a minister "for the money." When I retired, I didn't need to work another day of my life, but what I've stockpiled is there for my family, my children, and their future, minus, of course, a generous tithe to the Church. I became a minister for the love of Jesus Christ. Thankfully, Diane and I have always been on the same page when it came to subsisting on a pastor's salary.

With all the downsides to pro ball, however, I will always wonder whether the money had been worth it. With shame I remember the days—and nights—of unrestrained debauchery, when I naively thought I was accountable to no one. I was a *professional*, a *hero*, a modern *gladiator*! My name appeared with praise almost weekly in the local sports sections. I was mobbed whenever I returned to Sumac Lake or the campus of Southern Tech, but the Scriptures would one day nail me to the wall: "Claiming to be wise, they became fools."[1]

One particular midwinter Sunday afternoon in Minnesota comes to mind. Steamy breath hovering about us as the opposing force listened to the barking commands of their quarterback, muscles taut and ready to spring, my team was holding a scant two-point advantage. This particular image remains in my memory because it was the last play of my last professional game.

NOW, I was only thankful, as I drove between the white fields, that all this was behind me. "But for the grace of God ..." and Diane.

Up until this stage in my trip, the four-lane highway north had been surrounded by farmland waiting for the snow to leave and uncover the good dark fertile soil. At about this point in my reflections, the fields, originally labeled the Black Swamp, morphed into suburbs and then into that graveyard I mentioned earlier.

Even with the people behind me blowing their horns, it still took a few moments for me to break away from that marble soldier, rallying his troops. *Stephen ... Sara ...* and *Scott*. These names will frame and define this story. And I suppose I should add Raeph and a few others, but again that's getting ahead of myself.

As I finally pulled away from the cemetery, before me was a partially frozen river valley. Beneath the frozen ice floe, frigid water eventually emptied north into a lake named after a decimated tribe of Indians. I could have taken the interstate around and then onto the turnpike, but I was curious. I wanted to see what was left of "the bridge," so I bore left.

Prattsburg and Meander. Two, small, nearly seamless Ohio communities divided only by the wide but shallow Meander River but connected by a new four-lane bridge. I glanced to my left as I traversed the river, and, just as I had been told, the evidence was now gone. Apparently, the engineers had presumed the crumbling, hundred-year-old concrete span would fall easily. Citizens from both sides of the river, otherwise brutal football rivals, had gathered to watch the detonation. The newspaper said everyone felt the ground shake as the scientifically placed charges ignited, but when the dust settled into the winding dirty stream, the bridge stood defiant. It appeared unscathed and laughing. Eventually, further thinking, planning, arguments, apologies, sweat, and explosives were needed to rid the two cities of an old friend from which neither wanted to part. Many a white bass and walleye had been taken there, on lines and lures cast into the northbound current passing serenely a hundred feet below. But it had taken a mite more dynamite to erase this tradition.

A mite more dynamite. A humorously poetic phrase, but an acute one. I loved the Widow's Mite, but I never dreamed, as I pressed on toward it, that my imminent encounter there would have such a dynamic impact on my life.

THE Widow's Mite is a renovated hunting lodge high up in the White Mountains of New Hampshire, owned and operated by a retired French Canadian couple. For thirteen years now, during some mutually agreeable week in February, the Mite has been the gathering place for a small cadre of Evangelically minded Congregationalist pastors actively "fighting the good fight" amidst the growing liberalism of our denomination.

I was a "charter member." In fact, it may have been my suggestion to Ron Stang that started us converging on this centrally located, New Hampshire mountain lodge. When I was in seminary, one of my theology professors had taken our class for a weekend study retreat out to the Mite and so began my infatuation. It instilled in me a dream to one day have just such a mountain getaway for my own family.

I fondly remembered my first visit to the Mite. Back then I drove an all-wheel-drive SUV, which helped me ascend the steep gravel entrance, from which the lodge had come into view atop the wooded knoll. Surrounded by tall fir and spruce trees, it overlooked a spring-fed pond, with a panoramic view of Mounts Lafayette and Washington. Opening the massive wooden front door, I walked into a spacious, real-wood-paneled living room. To the left was the fieldstone fireplace that filled one wall and served as the focal point for the entire structure. To either side of the fireplace were ceiling-high picture windows. Leather lounge chairs, brass lamps, and card tables were distributed around the room, arranged to encourage either clusters of conversation-seekers or individuals coveting a corner in which to hide with a book. Above three-quarters of the room was a second-floor landing, much like the balconies in large New England churches. Here were the second-floor bedrooms, some doubles, some singles.

Now during my long trek to the Mite again, with my family and church responsibilities receding farther behind with every mile I drove, it was to one of these bedrooms that I was most particularly drawn. Rarely in my life—except during my annual escapes to the Mite—have I had a room to myself. As a boy, I shared a bedroom with one or two of my brothers. With the death of my alcoholic father when I was two, my mother fought a constant battle to keep our large family—three sons and two daughters—together and fed. I was the only sibling who achieved any financial success, so eventually I was able to repay my mother for her love and determination. And all through college, I had roommates. During my pro football years, we certainly were paid well enough to have single hotel rooms, but I got married before my second season, and ever since I've shared a bedroom and bed with Diane. Don't get me wrong, I'm not complaining about this latter arrangement. Over the years, though, I've come to cherish the quiet, private solitude of an individual room at the Mite. Nowhere else in my world do I feel the same freedom from the pressures and responsibilities of being a full-time husband, father, and pastoral leader and model. At the Mite, I can close the door—in a room with only a bed, nightstand, lamp, closet, padded chair, small window, and bathroom, but no phone, television, or radio. There in this simplicity I can relax, alone before God.

AS I approached the entrance to the turnpike, I thought of that single room at the end of my journey and smiled. I took the toll ticket and glanced at my watch. "Twelve fifteen. Much better than expected," I said to the bobble-headed doll of myself on the dash—a self-deprecating memento of my last year in the pros.

My plan was to drive as far as possible into the night, then pull off at a rest stop and sleep briefly on the foldout bed in the van. I hoped I could make the Mite at least by lunch the next day. Setting the cruise at sixty-eight, I prayed for a safe journey.

I also prayed, however, about the true reasons I needed to get away, one of which was to come to terms with the many surprises of my new church. Already, one unexpected crisis after another was raising an ugly head—in ways that I was unwilling to admit to Diane. So far, she seemed unaware of these challenges, basking in the congregation's welcome, which in many ways had not ceased. I knew better, though—both from what I had gleaned from casual gossip as well as from what I had detected in the eyes and interactions of the rumored parties. I knew better than to expect Rowsville Congregational to be perfect. The cordial friendliness of the first few months had charmed us, but now I felt I had been hustled.

You'd think a small country church—only 185 official members, seven last names representing more than half, and two-thirds farmers—would overflow with peace and harmony. But bloodlines run deep and century-old offenses die hard. So far, I'd barely gotten a peek at the baggage that lay hidden beneath the countless day-by-day, mysterious, and usually truncated comments I either received or overheard.

The traffic was busy for a Sunday afternoon. I observed the vehicles in front, behind, and those streaming past, semis shadowing minis like rhinos pushing sloths. Strangely enough, it all reminded me of Rowsville Congregational. Rhinos, hyenas, giraffes, gators, gazelles, orangutans, maybe a few snakes, and of course sloths, mostly sloths. My church had them all, and I was to be king, the lion—or was that the lamb prepared for the slaughter?

A Congregational church is the ultimate microcosm of democracy. Each individual church has the freedom to decide for itself whatever it wants to believe or do or be, all by congregational vote. Generally, of course, most Congregational churches appear much like any of their neighboring churches, believing generally what other Christians believe. In particular, however, each individual Congregational church has its own unique blend of ideas and ideals. It isn't necessarily the easiest polity to work under—there were many days when I wished I had a bishop to tell me and my people exactly what we ought to do (or that I were that bishop!)—but it was a polity with which I had grown accustomed. At least until the year before, when my friend Stephen LaPointe had thrown the proverbial wrench into the usually smooth workings of the annual Widow's Mite retreat. He'd been the designated discussion leader for the three days, and what he'd said still stuck in my craw, but no one else knew that—especially my wife. This *Stephen* was the first name of the triumvirate on that gravestone, which led me to my next subject of reflection.

As I passed along the south shore of Lake Erie, I became fixated on the question: *What had become of Stephen?* I could not shake the guilt of feeling that I had failed him, that I had not tried harder to contact him, especially after the bizarre attempt on his life. But with the move and getting settled in at Rowsville—.

On my first trip across country to visit with Rowsville's pastoral search committee, I called Stephen in the hospital from my cell phone. After the usual niceties, the mystery only became more disturbing. At the time, I did not understand what Stephen meant, and to be honest I really didn't want to know. My cell phone then went out of range and I lost him. Two days later, I called the hospital back only to be told that Stephen had been released. Several months passed before I remembered to call again, but the secretary at Stephen's church abruptly reported Stephen's resignation and refused to give any forwarding information. I called his house, but the phone had been disconnected. None of our mutual friends knew anything. Stephen became a mystery.

AND this mystery was at the core of why I was driving along that straight, boring Ohio turnpike, why I was really driving halfway across the country.

One o'clock. It was almost time for the Cavs and Celtics and an excuse to get my mind off the heavies. Growing up in Michigan, I had always been a fan of the Detroit professional teams: the Tigers, Lions, Pistons, and Redwings. Even when I played football for Massachusetts, I'd always kept an ear open for how the Lions were trying to survive. The previous night the Pistons had broken a losing streak, beating the Cavs in overtime. I was still feeling the rush of victory. Today the Pistons were off, but Cleveland was playing my second favorite team, the Boston Celtics. So why not listen in as the Celtics put the crush on Cleveland?

I tuned the radio to the pre-game and, with the cruise control set, stretched as much as my bulk would allow to veg mindlessly for the next two hours and 130-plus miles.

2

As Scott Turner drove past that cemetery in northwest Ohio, someone then unknown to him was paying a visit to a sister cemetery in southeast Vermont.

There it was, finally. It wasn't the gnarly edged shovel but the toe of his right boot that had stumbled across it. With sweat-soaked knit gloves, leather palms peeling away, Raeph Timmons proceeded to brush the snow from the raised brass letters. It was a losing battle, though, with the wind swirling snowflakes back, as if the grave was resisting out of vanity. Once again, he cursed this modern, pristine, headstone-less cemetery. It was nigh on impossible to locate anyone in the midst of winter.

Some graves, more frequently visited, were decorated with toppled wreath-stands, birdseed rings, or gaudy artificial flowers, which stuck out of the barren whiteness like trash awaiting pickup. No one, however, had visited Walter's resting place in months, maybe since Raeph's own previous visit in September, on Walter's birthday.

He rested, leaning hard against the shovel, and read the epitaph aloud, prayerfully, as if delivering a eulogy to a crowd of mourners: "Walter T. Horscht. Born September 15, 1955. Died February 21, 2000." The stark text, absent any extraneous words of dedication, was offset to the left. The name of Walter's widow, Helen, was to the right, with only her birthdate. Raeph wondered with scorn whether she would ever allow her corpse to lie beside Walter's.

Raeph zipped his blue parka against the cutting wind. Glancing back to his clean and classic, candy-red Camaro, he noticed how haphazardly his search had crisscrossed the snowy ground. Once he had located the marker for Styford Grunge, a name he could never forget nor imagine anyone living with, he knew Walter's was but a few steps further to the northeast.

He wrestled open the rusty lawn chair he had brought along, placing it directly before the gravestone. The tarnished bullet-shaped head on one of the chair's grommets flashed a memory of that shocking night a year ago—the nightmare that led directly to his being here today.

Huddled against the blistering cold, he spoke to the marker before him: "Wasn't I the one who convinced you of these things? And so, aren't I to blame for what you did?"

He looked up to glare at the stark brass epitaph. Walter's name appeared exactly as he had requested in his will: WALTER T. HORSCHT.

"You always obsessed over the hidden meaning of everything. If two events occurred with even the slightest connection, you saw them as the handprint of God," Raeph said aloud, remembering the incident that had led to Walter's unique epitaph. Once, not long after his conversion, Walter had pulled him aside, overwhelmed by a new discovery: "Raeph, have you ever looked at my name?"

"Your name?"

"Yeah. There, hidden within the name that my unsuspecting parents gave me, are three crosses, just like those on the hill where

Jesus was crucified! In the middle of Walter, a T, then my middle initial, T, and at the end of my last name, another T! Right there in the midst of my very name is the crucifixion! It's a sign! A confirmation, that God has called me to do something special."

Now Raeph studied the nameplate in the snow before him. It reminded him of the numerous trios of large wooden crosses planted across the country by some well-meaning Christian philanthropist to draw travelers' minds to Jesus. This, too, had been Walter's hope—that his minimalist tombstone would have at least some evangelistic effect. Raeph wondered now with a smirk how Walter might read the significance of the dried bird-dropping that was masking the date of his birth.

"Walter," Raeph said to his friend out there somewhere in the Great Beyond, presumably in the presence of Jesus. "I'm sorry I didn't listen, that I didn't guide you better."

Raeph shifted in the chair's deteriorating plastic webbing and spoke to the grave marker. "I shoulda been more honest with you about where I was—and about where I saw you going. I'm sorry, old friend."

But could I have stopped him? Raeph demanded of himself.

FOR nearly twenty-five years, he and Walter had been the best of friends—since meeting in a VA hospital, two wounded warriors from a generally unaccepted war, recuperating in adjacent beds from nearly identical shrapnel wounds. From the moment they met, Raeph prayed that somehow his Christian witness and kindness would cut through Walter's deep-seated bitterness. At first, Walter had showed no interest whatsoever, but Raeph assumed it was probably his own bodybuilder physique that over time gave credibility to what Walter would otherwise have considered a sissy's religion.

Though shorter than most men, Raeph was generally far stronger. He had always been muscles from head to foot and loved to work out. Some likened him to the short, muscle-bound acrobat in that old guy's flick *The Devil's Brigade*. He was a hand shorter than most, but that hand never lost to anyone at arm wrestling, and Walter had been impressed. One evening, Walter had reluctantly accepted Raeph's invitation to attend an evangelistic crusade. Before the night was over, by the grace of God, Walter had surrendered, head over heels, to Jesus.

Over the years, there seemed to be no limit to the intensity of Walter's faith or his love for the Scriptures—especially whenever they discussed issues like the evils of popery, or the Rapture of the faithful and the imminent, catastrophic end-of-the-world-as-we-now-know-it. These topics had not only dominated their discussions, but frankly, as Raeph later realized, had become the lynchpins of his own faith. His own obsession about the coming Rapture in particular made it harder and harder to think seriously about planning for the future.

"Why should we?" he would answer his beloved wife, Patty, whenever she questioned his lackadaisical efforts toward putting money away for their retirement. "If we love Jesus, we won't be here to enjoy it. Might as well spend it now!"

But Walter was even more consumed than Raeph with these obsessions, especially when it came to suspicions about Catholic infiltrators who had secretly wormed their way into Christian churches. He believed that these secret "papists" were everywhere, hidden, feigning to be faithful Christians, akin to the old sci-fi *Invasion of the Body Snatchers*, scheming to pull innocent believers into the ranks of the damned. A portion of every phone call between them would involve the weighing of evidence concerning some new suspect. All this came to a head for both of them as the end of the twentieth century approached.

RAEPH and Walter were among those convinced that all of their apocalyptic speculations would merge on the eve of Y2K. During the final weeks of 1999, some of their friends were hoarding food, water, batteries, and other resources in anticipation of power outages and the impending economic crisis. But not Walter or Raeph. No, they were so convinced that the Rapture would occur at the stroke of midnight, that each of them spent nearly every waking moment in prayer, Scripture reading, or, especially, warning every friend or family member to be prepared.

Then that long-awaited night arrived. Frequently checking in with each other by phone—living more than fifty mile apart—they stayed up all night New Year's Eve, their hearts sinking deeper and deeper in disbelief tinged with embarrassment, watching the television news media mockingly broadcast the new dawn of each time zone. The expected crash of the computer and electrical grids never came— *at least as far as they knew*—and, unless he and Walter themselves were among the "left behind," the worldwide invisible church of true believers was still here.

Immediately Raeph ended all contact with Walter. Not just to avoid conversation, but primarily because he refused to tell anyone that the Y2K nonevent had rocked the foundations of his faith. He had so attached his entire Christian life to the imminent Rapture, that when it didn't come, he wondered whether he could trust anything anymore.

On the morning of January 1, 2000, his hands shaking with the realization of his mistake, he pulled from a drawer a folded piece of paper. Months before, a faithful friend had tried to warn him about his misplaced apocalyptic obsessions, but Raeph had refused to listen. That morning, however, he retrieved the paper, which contained a long list of previous apocalyptic predictions that had all proven wrong.

> In the 1830s, Joseph Smith had convinced his followers that they were of the final generation. He was wrong.
>
> In the 1840s, William Miller had convinced his followers that Jesus would return by March 21, 1844. When this didn't happen, he extended the deadline until October 22, 1844. But again he was wrong.
>
> The leaders of the Jehovah's Witnesses had predicted that Jesus would return in 1874. When this didn't happen they stretched it to 1914, then 1918, 1920, 1925, 1941, 1975, and finally 1994, each time justifying their miscalculations, and pointing ahead to another imminent date. But they'd been wrong every time.
>
> A best-selling book on the Rapture predicted that Jesus would return before the end of the 1980s. Once again the author was wrong.
>
> And then in 1988, a pamphlet entitled *88 Reasons Why the Rapture Will be in 1988* had predicted that Christ would return that September, but when the author was wrong, he

released a second pamphlet entitled *89 Reasons Why the Rapture Will be in 1989!* He made lots of money, but still he was wrong.

Before that first morning of the new millennium, none of this information had affected Raeph, but with the embarrassment of Y2K, especially standing speechless before his otherwise trusting wife, he felt so empty, so deadened, that it was as if all the faith he had ever had was leaking through the seams of his broken soul.

But he kept it hidden. To those around him, including his wife, family, and friends, he posed a stolid front. He avoided Walter, however, because he knew that he stood guilty of convincing his old friend of all this.

The few times Walter called and left messages, Raeph merely ignored, except for one time, five days before that crucial, awful night.

THE phone rang, and Raeph answered before checking the caller ID. It was Walter, and, without any hint that the failure of Y2K had made a dent in his conspiratorial suspicions, Walter launched in on his most recent Catholic infiltrator suspect, his own local pastor, Reverend Stephen LaPointe.

In that brief conversation, Walter, with a hint of reservation, asked Raeph whether he truly believed that Catholic priests had infiltrated their churches.

This was the perfect opportunity, in that grace-filled moment, for Raeph to come clean and bring Walter back on track, but he didn't. Instead, he parroted their old routine, even defending how Christians had always been justified in squelching Catholic infiltrators.

It was then that Walter had asked the question that Raeph now knew made himself guilty for Walter's actions and ultimately his death: "But would these actions be justified today?"

When Raeph answered, his mind was focused instead on surfing through the TV channels to see what basketball games were showing that evening. "That's a hard question, but in drastic times, sometimes the faithful need to take drastic measures."

And that is exactly what Walter had done. Blinded by his fanaticism, the flames of which had been stoked by the unguarded zeal of Raeph and others, he had done the unthinkable.

"WALTER," Raeph said now, nearly a year later, looking from the headstone to the sky and then to either side, "sure, I still believe that the Roman Catholic Church is the enemy, that the pope's the Antichrist, but Walter," he said with shame, "I never thought you'd take this so seriously. I never in my wildest dreams thought you'd actually try to kill him!"

The noise of a truck from behind so startled Raeph that he almost overturned his chair. It was the caretaker in a snowplow coming to clear the grid of graveyard passageways. Raeph waved, and, receiving back a wave and a smile, he returned to the grave of his friend.

"Dozens of times I thought about driving up to visit you in the hospital. Walter, it was really a miracle that you even survived that crash. For three days they told me you were in a coma, but then when you awoke, well, I wasn't sure you would even want to see me, after what I'd said."

Raeph reached down once again to brush away the thin coat of snow that had accumulated.

"When you called me that night to tell me you did it, I thought you had flipped out. That all our apocalyptic talk had gone to your head. I even admit," he said, looking up into the gray winter sky, "that I became embarrassed to be with you." Then with a slow look back to the grave, he said, "Later, I was even a bit glad that you were gone."

A shadow's sharp edge passed across the grave like a curtain closing on a failed play. If Walter could have seen his old friend, he would not have recognized him. Bound tightly against the winter cold, he would have appeared to Walter like that transgressing shadow. Dark receding hair spotted with gray, ten pounds lighter, Raeph had changed with the far too many changes in his life. The Old Testament Ezekiel had always been his model for courageously standing for truth, for shirking any attack and absorbing any ridicule for the sake of Christ. Now he felt more like Job.

"Walter, you probably know more now about how things work in this crazy world, but sometimes I wonder whether God and the devil made a wager for my life." With a note of sarcasm, he continued: "Did God boast, 'Look at my good servant Raeph Timmons, at his faith and his zeal, even in the face of ridicule and unbelief!' And did Satan answer, 'Yeah, but stretch out your hand and destroy his life and he will surely curse you!' Walter, you tell me, did God surrender me into Satan's hands?

"A day doesn't pass when, in the depths of my sorrow, I don't demand from God an explanation. This past year's been a living hell, and somehow it all seems connected with your death. A week after they laid you here in this ground, almost to the minute, my darling Patty suffered a massive stroke. She never recovered. A week later, again almost to the minute, she was buried.

"A month later, my oldest son, Tom, died a meaningless death. I was so proud of him. He was an honor student at that seminary out East and an outspoken, fearless evangelist. Then one Sunday night while walking home from a prayer meeting, someone came up from behind and smashed his skull with a wine bottle for a measly sixteen dollars and change. The swine was never found.

"And Ted. You remember Ted?" He dropped his face into his gloved hands. "Not long after we moved away from Red Creek, he ran away with some crazy, druggy friends, and I've never heard from him. He didn't come to either his mother's or his brother's funeral, so, as far as I know, he's probably dead somewhere in a pauper's grave."

Raeph noticed that the caretaker, who had started his plowing at the far end of the cemetery, was getting closer to his parked Camaro.

"On top of all this, in November I was fired! A woman named Eileen in the Parts Department accused me of sexual harassment, which was a bunch of bull. Nothing I said mattered, only what was 'good for the company.' I still remember that b_____'s smirk as I emptied my desk. She was given my job!

"Walter, old friend. If you are up there with Patty and Tom, and Ted, please tell them I love them."

His eyes washed over and, far from the likelihood of listening ears, he began to wail with sorrow. "They were all I had. And God allowed that lying harlot at work to destroy my reputation just to take my job."

The shadow lifted from Walter's grave. Raeph leaned forward, shivering. Then in a quieter tone, he turned his attention to the three crosses of the epitaph.

"You know me. I've never struggled with depression. I've always been the one to bring others out of the doldrums, but now I just can't seem to break the funk. I … I don't know. So much has happened. I feel responsible for what happened to you, and maybe all this is happening as some kind of punishment. And I'm starting to wonder whether you were right all along."

Raeph glanced around. The caretaker and his plow were getting closer, but no one else was there. Only one other set of footprints had broken the crusted snow, leading to a memorial yards away. No one had visited any of the other graves, at least since the recent snowfall. Raeph was nervous, though, about what he was about to say.

"You don't know, Walter—well, at least I don't think you know—I guess I really don't know how much you do know—being where you are and all. But, you see, I'm now all alone. There's no one left. I can't find a job, and, well, I think maybe God is testing me. I think He's trying to see what my faith is really made of."

Off in the distance Raeph heard a siren. He bounded from the disintegrating weave of his lawn chair, but as he focused his hearing, he recognized it as a call for volunteer firemen. He relaxed, sat down, and began again.

"So much has happened, and it all keeps bringing me back to a few things you said—things you believed that, well, yes, I know, that once we both believed.

"But Walter, something else has happened to top all this off," he said, scooting his chair closer, his feet almost on the marker. Glancing around uneasily, he continued: "Remember Reverend Harmond, that ex-priest who wrote all those books against the Catholic Church, who ran that ministry to rescue Catholics? Well, you will not believe this. This very morning—and I heard this from five different people— Harmond returned to the Catholic Church! Before I left for worship, the phone rang. They said he lay prostrate before a Catholic altar, renouncing all he'd said or done since he'd left the papist church."

Raeph leaned back and into the darkening of the swirling winter sky he repeated, "Walter, I wish you were here to talk to—I have no one else. I try to pray, but God seems to be hiding, holding back His love from me, as if He's been trying to reach me all along, maybe through you, but I was too blind and stubborn."

Flurries began to fall again, at first lightly, then with increasing intensity.

Raeph reached to touch the cross in the middle of Walter's name.

"As soon as I heard about Harmond's betrayal, I rushed up here to be with you. I drove all morning. You see, there's something else I've thought of. Do you remember how every year Reverend LaPointe used to sneak away for a few days to meet with other ministers some where up in the mountains? Well, it turns out that it's a place not far from here, a lodge called the Widow's Mite. I don't know whether he'll be there, but I think God's calling me to go and find out. I guess I owe you at least that much—to confront him directly, and then, well, I don't know."

Raeph stood up slowly, remembering that Catholics make a big to-do out of martyrs, people who died defending their faith, even if their Catholic faith was wrong.

"But Christians have their martyrs, too," he said aloud, as the gusting snow won the battle over the headstone. "Like the millions of men and women murdered in the Inquisition or the thousands murdered by Bloody Mary."

He folded the chair under one arm and started to turn away. Pausing, he glanced back again at the three crosses in Walter's name.

"I guess you're as much of a martyr as any of them. No one understood what you were trying to do, but I do, now, and I believe God's calling me to bring closure to what you started."

He turned away, trudging slowly toward his beloved red Camaro, his only real remaining object of value. Returning the chair to the trunk, he stopped. "Why?" he wondered aloud and threw it into a pile of dirty snow.

Pausing at the door, he glanced back again. "Please God, in the name of Jesus and for the sake of my friend and your servant, Walter, guide me."

3

The focus of her aging yet still attractive green eyes alternated between the reflection of her own image in the oceanfront window and the breaking waves beyond it.

A storm must be raging somewhere far out at sea, she concluded.

The spray dashed from the rough, moss-laden rocks that lined her own private seashore, a coastline to which her bare feet had become quite familiar. It reminded her of a favorite painting—her husband's favorite—that had once been the focal point of their living room. No longer, though; it was no longer *their* living room.

Next Sara LaPointe studied the dim reflection of herself. She wasn't pleased with what she saw because she wasn't pleased with the person she had become.

The glass showed much more than herself. To her left, a table lamp was replicated, under which her sons, William and Daniel, were playing chess, a game they had learned from their father. To her right was the reflection of another lamp, illuminating a La-Z-Boy rocker. The man sitting there, reading some mystery novel, wasn't her husband, though he had been once long ago, before she had met and married Stephen.

She returned her focus to the waves. The most recent onslaught was receding now to calm. The noise stilled, but then returned. Spray cascaded everywhere. The lighthouse horn on Straitsmouth Island moaned. The beam returned, outlined in the mist. Distant running lights bobbing in and out of sight gave proof of some fishing boat straining for the harbor.

Sara dropped her eyes and backed away from the window. She was at a loss how to restore life to what was once a great gift.

"Sarie, you all right?" said the man in the chair.

"Yes, fine, Frank.

"Mom, any more soda?" asked her soon-to-be fifteen-year-old, Daniel, waiting while his older brother pondered how to save face.

"I'll check." She crossed into the kitchen of her oceanside apartment and went through the motions—opening the refrigerator, removing bottles, retrieving ice—but her mind was elsewhere, to a different place, a different lifestyle, a different *world*, and a different man—her true husband, though she had no idea what he now thought of her. She had lost track of him, where he was living. Each day as she went to her graduate history classes or tried to make their new home seem like one, Sara couldn't shake the memories, or the guilt. Their vows had said "the two shall become one." She couldn't stop feeling like a half.

Especially when William, her oldest son, now a freshman in college, came home for the weekends. He lacked tact when it came to avoiding the past. Just the sound of his voice, more like Stephen's every day, was salt on a festering wound. She assumed that the only reason he was with her rather than his father was because her place was closer to his campus. And besides, he didn't know where Stephen was either. *At least that's what he claimed.* She knew that for a while the two had stayed in touch by email, but once Stephen had left his Jamesfield apartment sometime around Christmas, all communication ceased. Either Stephen had no phone, no interest, or no desire.

Sara knew this wasn't like him; he had always been a caring, considerate father: never forgot a birthday or anniversary, never let a church appointment keep him from at least making an appearance at an important sporting event or recital. But then again, Stephen had certainly changed, and Sara was far from understanding and even farther from sympathy.

Yet she ached for his love.

The drinks on the tray were becoming more precarious, the more she let her thoughts drift. With resolve, she reentered the present, into a room that everywhere was Frank. The painting above the living room couch was a gift from Frank. The brass lamp beside the chair illuminating his book, a gift from Frank. The chess set being enjoyed by the boys, ibid. Slowly, like an infection, she had let him creep back into her life. Not that his presence was necessarily a negative; he was certainly a different man than the one she had once married, and divorced, so long ago, back when she herself was also a much different person.

But they had ended their relationship mutually, had gone their separate ways. She had remarried, had become a pastor's wife—of *all* things—and had two wonderful sons. Yet this whole part of her life had ended in disaster.

What is he doing here, though? And why was she encouraging it?

"Actually, Sarie," Frank said, getting to his feet, book closed, "I need to get back. I've a deskload of papers to grade by morning."

William immediately glanced up at Frank, then enthusiastically eyeballed his mother.

Sara responded, avoiding her son's gaze, "I understand. Thanks for stopping by."

"Sure," Frank said. "See you boys."

"See ya," William said, becoming engrossed again with the chessboard.

"Yeah, see you, Frank," Daniel said, rising respectfully. "Are we still on for fishing next Saturday?"

"Of course," Frank responded, thumbs up.

Once the door had closed, Sara said to her older son, voice under control, "That was inappropriate."

"What do you expect? And why do you invite him over anyway? Is *that* appropriate?"

"William—" she started to say with far too much energy, her hand lifting to strike. Instead she fell back into the recliner in tears.

"Mom, I'm sorry," William said, crossing to her.

A used paper napkin was all she could find within reach. It had been Frank's. She changed her mind, and flung it away.

"That's all right, William," she said, leaving the room for her bedroom.

Once composed, she returned. "You're right. I shouldn't invite him. It's just that, well, things have gotten way too complicated."

Daniel, now a high-school freshman, was certainly of the age to understand all the issues involved in his parents' separation and his mother's renewed friendship with her first husband, but to her relieved puzzlement he usually seemed oblivious. This time he turned his focus from the chess pieces to the magazine he had been reading between moves.

Sara and her eldest moved, arm in arm, to the window.

"Remember your father's favorite picture?"

"Looks just like it." His cheeks gathered into a smile.

"Remember that tear in the bottom right corner?"

"Yeah," he said, tilting his head down toward the mother he had long since surpassed in height. "I never knew how …"

"I did it," she admitted, with a melancholy smile. "It's a long story, but I once threw a book that hit a lamp that felled that picture, and in the end," she said, once again fighting back a tear, "we're here, and I don't know where he is."

"Mom—" he started, but stopped. He wanted to console, but there were so many conflicting issues, the details of which he was only partially aware. *Wasn't it her decision that had separated them? Hadn't she overreacted when his father quit the ministry?* His father's decision was a great thing as far as William was concerned. He was fed up trying to fill everyone's expectations, tired of being the preacher's kid, of being pressured to one day fill his father's shoes. Now he was free to be whatever he wanted to be, which at least for now meant becoming a doctor.

He wanted to reassure her that one day they would all get back together. But was this what she wanted? Wasn't she the one who had returned to graduate school, who had taken Daniel and left Dad behind to sell their house and find an apartment, for himself, alone? Wasn't she the one who had said that as long as he continued thinking about becoming a Catholic, she would have nothing to do with him? Hadn't his father in fact delayed any idea of converting because of her?

William turned instead to stare at the raging sea. Some neighbors were doing something down near the docks, hurried and frantic, probably trying to secure a boat that had broken its tether.

He refused to let on, but William missed his father desperately. The whole Catholic mess was beyond him and certainly made no difference. So what? He was his father. William loved him—especially after the shooting.

"Mom," he said, hugging her tighter, "I do love you. Things will be all right."

She replied softly, her head resting on his strong chest, looking out to sea, "I hope so, dear. I hope so."

4

Scott Turner's Narrative

Halftime, and it didn't look good for Cleveland, which was just fine for me. When I wasn't countering my teammates' brags and bets, I was rooting the Celtics on in private. But they weren't the basketball team they once were with Bird, Parrish, and McHale.

The announcers were ranting on, making excuses for their mistaken pre-game projections. My sore spot for the "media dweebs" hadn't faded with the years distancing me from personal scrapes with them. Week after week, the pencil necks, who hadn't played a down of pro ball in their lives, would lounge in their air-conditioned, plush media boxes to evaluate and analyze, criticize and pontificate on how every play, good or bad, could and should have been done better. They always knew more than the coaches and graded each missed tackle, block, or rout as if the player hadn't already been playing hard-out for over an hour.

My hands tightened around the wheel, one particular sportscaster's neck in mind, but then relaxed. "Thank You, Jesus, for rescuing me."

And thank you, Diane. A sip of soda through a smile and I remembered our first "date."

"DIANE, meet my friend, Scott."

Bruce had preceded me on the team by two years and quickly befriended me. Together we presented a formidable left wall on the defensive line.

"Well, hi, ah," I had stammered. It's a myth that professional football players are smooth talkers and chick magnets. Sure there are the few standout hustlers like O.J., Montana, or Namath, but the rest of us were worse off than the average Joe. Women with less than Sunday-school morals were always around for the taking, but the kind of woman an upstanding jock dreamed about couldn't be bribed to be seen with him.

This was true of Diane. The sister of an All-American jock, she knew. But having been a competitor herself—in track and gymnastics—she also knew that there in the mix she might find that hidden gem.

It was a wedding reception. Diane looked ravishing in her royal blue bridesmaid's dress, setting off her shoulder-length blond hair. Bruce had pointed her out earlier, and I, with jaw on floor, had begged him for an introduction. Bruce warned me, but I badgered him until he gave in. Bruce waited until her back was turned, as she poured a glass of punch, to spring this 240-pound behemoth on his petite, 116-pound sister.

She turned while sipping, looked up, glanced at her brother, smirked, and walked away.

"Gee, Scott, I'm sor—" Bruce started to say, but I took his air away with the back of my hand to the stomach.

"It's okay, buddy. Remember that old war movie from the '40s? 'Damn the torpedoes'—save my seat."

I was not about to let this beauty slip away.

"Excuse me," I said, once I'd caught up with her, turning her gently around. "I thought I knew you well, from your brother's description, that is. But he was wrong. Your eyes aren't like a frog's," I said, staring, mesmerized, "they're as blue as a sapphire."

"I really—"

"Please, just a moment for a pompous, overrated jock from a two-bit town in Michigan? I just want to see if it's true."

"What's true?"

"That ...," but I'd become far too lost in her eyes to make sense. "I guess I've forgotten, but can we just talk a bit?"

Later Diane told some of our friends that though this had been by far the worst line she had ever received, the oxymoron of my soft, trembling voice and my looming hulk were intriguing. She says she fell in love with me on that first evening, and I have never looked at another woman. *Really.* Six months later, we were married, and then ten months after that, Susanna was born.

This didn't mean, though, that our relationship never had complications. Diane was what people called in the early '70s a "Jesus freak" and, by the time I met her, a "charismaniac." Hardly a day went by when she wasn't attending some prayer meeting or Bible study, or serving at some food kitchen or crisis pregnancy clinic. Since we met on a Saturday, the second day of our relationship posed a problem: whereas Diane never missed worship on Sundays, I never went. My normal weekend routine was to get stinking, staggering drunk on Saturday night, and then sleep in as long as possible on game day. Our first weekend together, however, changed my life. I refused to attend church—in fact, I didn't enter a church until our wedding day—but I agreed to curtail my drinking to be in her company. Throughout our six-month courtship, I pressed her constantly to give in to my sexual advances, but to no avail. I had had to wait until our honeymoon night.

I went along with her there, but I was pretty much a lost cause otherwise. We never argued, but no matter how hard Diane tried to coax me into church, I just refused. For nearly five years, we went our separate ways. Until the game when I was blindsided by Bubba Tooly. The resulting spinal fracture immobilized me for a month, but it would be the month that changed my life. Thank God for Diane and the Gospel of John.

WHILE I was musing on these significant issues from my early days with Diane, the back-and-forth broadcast of what I knew would be an inevitable win for the Celtics grew boring. I popped in one of my favorite tapes, Jim Croce, reflecting on what a sad loss it was to lose someone so gifted. The sign ahead said I was leaving the Keystone State, Pennsylvania, and entering New York State. I was making good time and even started to feel like I could continue driving all night and surprise them at breakfast.

That led me again to wonder: *Whatever happened to Stephen?* My eyes glazed over as I admitted, *He wasn't just pulling our legs last year.*

OF all our annual retreats at the Mite, the previous year's had been the most controversial, all because Stephen had foolishly believed he could trust us guys enough to spill his guts. Of those on retreat, Jim Sarver, Cliff Wilson, and I were his closest friends, alumni from the same seminary. We had been generally more aware of Stephen's plight than the rest and tried to be sympathetic. We gave him more of our time, but even after the blowup was past, the retreat was not the same. Everyone seemed caught up in his own personal concerns.

And besides, Stephen had slipped away from the retreat sometime in the night—without explanation—and that was the last time I'd seen him. Stephen had become a haunting mystery.

What had happened to him? Stephen had supposedly been very, very lucky. Two pistol shots at close range from an ex–Vietnam vet crazed with apocalyptic zeal, yet just a few days later the hospital sent him home with *only* chest bruises and a glancing wound on his neck. During our last brief phone conversation, I asked him in disbelief how this could have happened. Avoiding the apparent miracle, he instead told me something equally bizarre: the nut who had shot him—a man named Walter who I had actually met once briefly, but that's another story—was convinced that Stephen was some kind of Roman Catholic spy. All of this was bunk, of course, but then Stephen said something that bothered me: "But if Walter really knew what I was considering—"

At the time, I didn't understood what he meant by this—what he was "considering"—and to be honest, I didn't really want to know.

It was during our second gathering session, back a year ago at the Mite, that Stephen "let the cat out of the bag", explaining why he felt he had no choice but to resign from the pastoral ministry. His explanation, which consisted of a tedious verse-by-verse commentary of First Timothy, lasted over an hour. To the average Joe on the street, this might not seem like such a big deal, but to us, who also had followed God's call to abandon the world and dedicate our lives to preaching the Word, nothing could be more catastrophic. Much of what Stephen said made sense and surely riled some of our more staunch Congregationalist friends. Of all the things Stephen admitted, though, it was his very first comment that left an indelible mark on my memory.

"Paul, an apostle of Christ Jesus by command of God our Savior and of Christ Jesus our hope." Stephen had begun with chapter 1, verse 1, and then his commentary. He posed the question: By whose authority was he (and consequently all of us in the room) ordained a pastor? He recalled how twenty-some years before he had sensed a call from God to serve Jesus full-time; how a local minister and some friends had confirmed that call; how he had then gone to seminary, got good grades, graduated; and finally how a group of ministers and lay leaders confirmed his call through the laying on of hands.

I remembered Stephen's comic theatrics, his hands extending, beginning palms down in the posture of a blessing and then morphing into claws. All of us at the retreat understood his parody. He then explained how those well-meaning, sincere believers had ordained him, calling down the Holy Spirit to empower him—just exactly as it had been done to me.

RECALLING my own ordination rite of passage as from the celestial eyes of an angel, I saw myself sitting alone in the front pew of old East Congregational in downtown Boston. Only faintly had any alterations been made to that sanctuary since it was renovated in 1822. Many a committee had pressed for changes, but the lack of a majority had always squelched the "progressives." The Reverend James Calvin Krenshaw, my senior pastor, beckoned me forward, and I knelt—something I must admit I rarely did. A cadre of pastors, elders, and lay leaders from nearby Congregational churches as well as those on the staff of Old East circled me, while Krenshaw posed like Moses of old. Then at Krenshaw's request, their hands rested on my shoulders and head, weighing me down. Some were more considerate than others, merely touching, but several took me for a leaning post. I fought to stay erect, my knees—though conscientiously seasoned by decades of preventative exercise and weight-training—aching from lack of kneeling. And Krenshaw's prayer, summoning down the power and presence of the Holy Spirit, droned on and on. Was the pastor concerned that in my case the Holy Spirit needed some prolonged coaxing or was he grandstanding for the unusually large crowd? At the final *Amen*, the score of palms lifted like the parting of the Red Sea, leaving my hair and suit wet with sweat. With the oppressive weight of this cloud of witnesses lifted, I rose light as a feather and nearly fainted.

But I was ordained and empowered to carry out faithfully the command of Scripture: "Do not neglect the gift you have, which was given you by prophetic utterance when the council of elders laid their hands upon you."

To this day, I'm still not certain what *my* unique gift is. There had been no audible prophetic utterance—which was hardly to be expected from that gruff, staid, anti-emotional, constricted gathering of New England Congregationalists. I loved preaching and teaching the Scriptures, and at my previous church I had become amazingly effective in facilitating congregational and committee meetings— zing, bang, gone, the people were usually in and out and happy for it. Admittedly, however, the rest of my pastoral responsibilities— especially hospital and nursing home visitation, pastoral counseling, and funerals—were usually performed with moderate reluctance. I wanted to be helpful, to be consoling and wise, but I always operated under a cloud of inadequacy. Yet I believed this was what Jesus had called me to do, like Demetrius in the sequel to *The Robe:* to leave behind the glory of the gladiatorial arena for the glory of the Gospel. "I can do all things through him who strengthens me" has always been my clarion call.

But what is my unique ministerial gift, and who has the authority to tell me? This never-ending concern brought my thoughts back to the point of Stephen's prod, his words still calling my whole life into question.

IN the cramped meeting room at the Mite, Stephen LaPointe had posed the question whether any of the people who had ordained him (and similarly us) had the same authority that Paul had when he ordained Timothy? The apostles, whom Jesus had chosen and ordained, had confirmed Paul's revelatory calling, who in turn had ordained Timothy: Jesus to the Twelve to Paul to Timothy. By what line of authority were we ordained? What right did those men, who laid their hands on us, have to declare that we were specifically set apart by God to declare His truth?

Stephen was relating all this to his own ordination, but I was hearing him loud and clear. He even seemed to be looking at me when he questioned whether any one of us had the authority to ordain anyone, especially given the grossly divergent opinions about what ordination means, what it requires, who can be ordained, or even what ordination does.

The voices of several who had come to the Mite seeking a peaceful retreat erupted then in protest. I remained quiet, however, withdrawing from the scene like the focus of a lens zooming out to take in a far bigger picture, for I was hearing the booming reverberations of a hammer hitting a nail squarely on the head. *By what authority—by what right?*

I was reflecting on how the dreaded voices of inadequacy always attacked me whenever I was summoned—as pastor and representative of Jesus Christ—into the midst of a family grieving over the loss of a loved one: *Who am I to be consoling these people? Who am I to be telling these people not to worry about the state of their grandfather's soul? Who am I to say why God would take away a five-year-old child? Who am I to exhort anyone about the immorality of abortion or divorce or euthanasia?* In these circumstances, I'd prop myself up by remembering that I had been ordained and authorized. I was in that awkward yet responsible position through the laying on of hands, but why did those ordaining pastors, deacons, elders, and laymen have any more authority to ordain me than a greeter at WalMart?

Something unanticipated and inexplicable had happened to me at that retreat. I think I was successful at hiding it, but for the next year, whenever that voice of inadequacy started murmuring, I'd press on, but without the confidence of my ordination. I had left the Mite convinced that I was a pastor, not because of anything any man had done to me through the laying on of hands, but solely because I believed in my heart that Jesus had called me. This in itself, of course, is a gallant call—to follow Jesus wherever and whenever—yet, how could I know *for certain* that this and not some other course was my calling? Because once long ago on a cold, rainy afternoon, while lying crushed and aching under a pile of sweaty, smelly linemen, I sensed a call to the ministry? Because my lowly pastor and well-meaning wife confirmed this? Because I squeaked through seminary, and then some church hired and ordained me? Because I felt good about my work? Because my merciful, always supportive wife told me I preached good sermons? Because someone said my counseling helped? Because no one pulled me aside to counsel me that I ought to be doing something else? How could I know for certain that on that future day when I stood before Jesus, I would hear the words, "Well done, good and faithful servant," as opposed to, "Excuse me, but who gave you permission to pose as a pastor?"

After throwing that first bombshell, Stephen had plowed on with his awkward presentation. I had tried to remain attentive—even once coming to his defense when his arguments ruffled too many feathers. But I couldn't shake off the implications of Stephen's first point. I wanted to stand, cross my hands, yell "Time out," and focus the discussion solely on the question of the authority behind our ordinations, but it didn't help that every time my mind drifted back, Stephen was confronting us with yet another issue I couldn't ignore.

In one such moment, Stephen hit upon a second issue that ever since has upset my pastoral applecart. With a seemingly innocuous query, he asked us to recall how in seminary we had been trained to prepare our sermons. After some humorous banter which eased the mounting tension, he reminded us how we had been warned never to resort too quickly to biblical commentaries. In other words, we were first to thoroughly study a Scripture text on our own, coming to our own unaided conclusions, before we checked them with the opinions of biblical scholars and theologians. None of us had a problem with this. Our commitment to *sola Scriptura* meant that we believed the Holy Spirit would "guide us into all truth" whenever we studied His Word with an open and sincere heart.

But then Stephen inadvertently revived the tension by admitting something that he had discovered only recently. All the biblical commentaries on his shelves that he ever consulted had been personally selected because they reflected his own Evangelical convictions. Rarely did these scholarly opinions ever challenge or change his own conclusions. At first none of us got his drift, until he made his point, that from week to week he was essentially only checking himself against himself, and that the interpretations he was delivering from his pulpit to his people were never being challenged for their truthfulness. Was it ever possible that he and his carefully chosen commentators were blindly wrong on some important point of Scripture?

As I listened, my mind flashed to an image of my own library. It was surely more expansive than any owned by the other pastors in attendance because of the bounty of my football legacy. Whenever a seminary professor mentioned a book he liked, I bought it. Whenever a book met my fancy while browsing a Christian bookstore, one I felt I just might need someday, I bought it. Still, Stephen was right. Sure my glut of biblical commentaries contained the full range

33

from hypercritical liberal to hyper-literal Fundamentalist, but just as Stephen said, in the twelve years since I'd left seminary, I'd rarely opened any commentary that wasn't written by a favorite author or which didn't confirm or merely fine-tune my preset, conservative-Evangelical interpretation.

Stephen backed up his argument by pointing to the many conflicting interpretations of baptism. From their seemingly certain interpretation of Scripture, some pastors baptize only believing adults, while others baptize infants; some teach that baptism is merely a sign of an adult's faith or a symbol of salvation by grace, while others teach some form of baptismal regeneration. All read the same Bible, yet come up with different conclusions, and in the end, most check their conclusions only against biblical commentators with whom they already agree. And their congregations trust that what they are hearing is eternally true.

Several in our otherwise peaceful retreat had lifted their voices in an uproar, but my mind had frozen. *How can we be sure?* After that day, I was not able to prepare a sermon or Bible study without the taint of this challenge. My sermon prep protocol changed immediately. I began opening those other commentaries, comparing the wide range of opinions. In the end, this did not alter my staunch Evangelicalism, but for the next twelve months, it certainly confirmed the dilemma leading to Stephen's resigning the ministry.

Later in his presentation, discouraged yet undaunted by the lack of sympathy of his presumed friends, Stephen had only dug himself in deeper. He hit upon what would prove to be a third upheaval in my own sense of calling. In reviewing the apostle Paul's instructions concerning the office of bishop, he asked us why there was no office of bishop in the Congregational Church? Had we, through our myopic interpretation of Scripture, jettisoned what other Christian traditions had continued with their bishops, deacons, and even priests? Did it make no eternal difference how a church was structured, or was it possible that our tradition had merely opted out for institutionalized individualism, rejecting a more ancient and scriptural hierarchical system?

This nearly drove a few of the retreatants to start throwing things, but I remember feeling confused, torn. Since seminary, like most of those there, I'd accepted the conviction that our Congregational polity was the most ancient and authentic. We had concluded from our study of Scripture and the early Church, as one elderly pastor at the retreat protested, that "it was the Roman Catholic Church, enamored with the power of the Roman emperors like Constantine, that had imposed an authoritarian hierarchy on the once free churches and persecuted those who refused to bow down to papal dictatorship!" The motto of us independent Congregationalists had always been the Scripture, "For where two or three are gathered in my name, there am I in the midst of them,"[2] and, therefore, we had the freedom to gather in His name, to worship Him, to love Him, and to proclaim His truth, "without the imposition of popes, bishops, or other tyrants," as the good, elderly pastor put it.

Yet, with this, Stephen highlighted in red a thought that had been bugging me ever since seminary. Our highly respected, Evangelical seminary was interdenominational and, though many students began without any denominational affiliation, we were expected to attach ourselves to something by the end of our second year. Being even then a bit put off by the wide array of conflicting opinions between the nearly fifty denominations represented at our school, I was still undecided by my third and final year. Under pressure from the registrar, I "signed" with the Conservative Congregationalists. The primary thing that united this loosely associated group of about four hundred churches nationwide was their refusal to join in a merger of several thousand other Congregational churches that had imposed a more Presbyterian type of church polity. To the more conservative, "traditional," mostly New England Congregationalists, this seemed an unconscionable scourge on their God-given freedoms. "Look to Plymouth Rock" became their motto, "and never to Geneva," the founding center of John Calvin's Presbyterianism.

I chose the Association because I liked the feel of New England Congregationalism and its history. Thus I had no lifelong loyalty to Congregationalism *per se*, though I had grown to like and defend it. But when push came to shove (as was happening as Stephen's point sunk in), was I ready to claim that only Congregationalism had the true interpretation of Scripture?

No. *So where did that put me?*

I was startled from my reverie by a highway patrol car shooting up behind me, sirens blaring, red and blue lighting the van's interior like a carnival ride.

My adrenaline soared immediately. I checked the speedometer. No, it wasn't me. The car flew by. Another patrol car sped past and up over the horizon.

Through my reminiscing, I hardly had noticed that snow was beginning to flake against the windshield. I turned on the wipers, which whacked and squeaked in response, and wondered whether this might be the portent of a delayed journey.

Soon more sirens and a patrol car from the other direction crossed the grass median and spun around ahead of me. Passing over the rise, I had to slam my brakes to keep from ramming into a logjam of cars. Ahead about a hundred yards, the patrol cars were parked at sharp angles, flares positioned like an airport runway.

And there was the terrifying mess. Three, maybe four, cars gnarled together, one bumper poised five feet higher than normal. A fourteen-wheeler was jackknifed onto its side.

I hate to admit it, but the first thought that went through my mind was *Shoot! There goes my schedule.*

For a while I sat, content to wait, content that I hadn't been the culprit, but then I confronted myself: *Hey. Are you even the least bit concerned that someone might be hurt? Might need you?*

People were leaving their cars to gawk, but none appeared to be ministers.

Guess so.

I reached into the glove compartment and removed my white tab collar. Few Congregationalist ministers wear clerical shirts and collars; it's an optional discipline, left usually for the more high-churchy types in affluent downtown edifices. I, however, had decided to wear one at this new church with the hope that it would help me feel more like the minister I supposedly was ordained to be. It also helped that the last three ministers at Rowsville had worn one, so, essentially, I just fell into the tradition to which these Congregationalists had grown accustomed.

Generally whenever I traveled, I wore a colored clerical shirt, this trip a light gray, with the collar open. To most it just looked like some new fashion, maybe even a retro version of the old Nehru shirt. In the glove compartment, however, I always kept a white tab just in case. And this was just such a case.

Once in uniform, and with the single motive of being of service, I left the sanctuary of the van and hurried forward, forcing aside any self-centered, now defunct, schedule for the good of others, throwing my insecurities to the wind, and skirting more than a dozen idling cars and trucks. Faces glared out at me, but I presumed my clerical collar spoke for itself. The flashing, revolving, red-and-blue lights of three patrol cars illuminated the exhaust clouds, making me feel like I was in a scene from *Close Encounters of the Third Kind*.

Reaching the wreck, my knees and stomach quavered at the sight. More than cars and a fourteen-wheeler were entangled in the drifting snow. From beneath the pressed carriages of the disfigured vehicles protruded the limbs of several occupants. One of the legs had torn jeans and a small tennis shoe with a blinking red light in the sole. In several places, blood mingled with the slush on the pavement.

Against my intensifying emotions, I forced myself forward. A bevy of officers contained the scene in yellow warning tape. Initially I halted and attempted to identify which officer was in charge, but they all ignored me, focused instead on bringing order to the carnage.

Immediately before me, not three feet away, I saw a face move behind the window of an overturned Volvo. Quickly I raised the yellow tape and passed beneath. Kneeling beside the shattered glass, I motioned to a person I now recognized as an elderly woman, her body suspended upside down, her neck bent more than ninety degrees.

I asked the ridiculous, "Are you all right?"

Her eyes entreated me in terror while her mouth opened and closed like a largemouth bass out of water. Then her mouth stopped in mid-sentence, and her eyes glazed over. Stillness.

"I'll get some help …," I shouted, bounding up.

Then from behind me I heard, "Hey, Fathah."

I turned to see an approaching patrolman yelling at me in his strong New England accent.

"Oh, I'm not a priest."

"Then why the collah?" The patrolman was now standing directly and sternly erect before me. The image of my innocent yet distorted face glared back at me from the officer's silvered lenses. Though larger in size, I immediately felt small and insignificant.

"I'm a Congregationalist minister, and I just wanted—"

"Listen, sir, what these people need is a priest not some imitation. There is nothing you can do, so please return to your vehicle."

"But—"

"Return to your vehicle now," the bug-eyed officer demanded, pointing.

I backed away, speechless and mortified, and impotently plodded back to the van. Ignoring the belittling, sneering stares, I did my best to appear confident.

Once back in the warmth, I shouted, "Lord Jesus, I just wanted to help!" But the engines merely idled on, the wipers flapped, and the exhaust fumes billowed, symbolically replicating the drivers' tempers. So instead I faintly asked, "And who was I to presume anything on my ordination?"

5

From the first instant he had seen that candy-red Camaro, as a pimply sixteen-year-old several months away from driving and with five hundred dollars in the bank, Raeph had wanted it. It probably wasn't the first he'd ever seen, but it was the first he was aware of, and in that moment it won his heart. The neighbor who owned it had been drafted early to Vietnam, but he wouldn't be coming home. The family wanted it gone, so Raeph got it cheap.

The car he was driving now through this blinding, late-winter snow squall was that original Camaro, now a true classic, but a bear when the roads were slippery. Everything else in his life had gone down the tubes, but this thirty-five-year-old baby still hummed like new, actually better than new with the improvements he'd made over the years.

The retreat house called the Widow's Mite was about fifty miles to the north of Walter's cemetery.

The thought came once again: *Why am I doing this? Aren't there a thousand other things I'd rather be doing than driving headlong into this blinding, uphill nightmare?*

He shook his head to clear this temptation away and focused more intently on the road ahead. Every so often the near-balding tires of his rear-wheel-drive Camaro would lose traction, so he couldn't afford to drift mentally. Yet, he couldn't help thinking, *This crazy excursion into this snowy nightmare was all because of our fanatical convictions about the Rapture, Catholics, and Catholic infiltrators.*

And he remembered how this all had begun.

ONE storming evening years ago, clustered together in the basement of Red Creek Congregational Church, old Pastor Smith had read to them from the book of Matthew, where he believed Jesus clearly taught about the Rapture: "Then shall two be in the field; the one shall be taken, and the other left. Two women shall be grinding at the mill; the one shall be taken, and the other left. Watch therefore: for ye know not what hour your Lord doth come."[3] Pastor Smith explained that this verse warned that before the Great Tribulation all true believers in Jesus Christ would be "raptured" or translated into heaven, leaving unbelievers behind. Until this happened, the faithful would undergo persecution and the undermining of their faith by false teachers.

Walter had then asked a question that Raeph now realized led directly to his death: he had asked who those false teachers were. Pastor Smith responded by again reading from Scripture, Paul's First Letter to Timothy: "Now the Spirit speaketh expressly, that in the latter times some shall depart from the faith, giving heed to seducing spirits, and doctrines of devils; speaking lies in hypocrisy; having their conscience seared with a hot iron; forbidding to marry, [and commanding] to abstain from meats, which God hath created to be received with thanksgiving of them which believe and know the truth."[4]

Then Pastor Smith asked, "Okay, my friends, which religion forbids the marriage of its clergy and nuns, forces its members to abstain from meat on Fridays, and gives heed to 'seducing spirits' and 'doctrines of devils' by praying to the dead?"

Through gritted teeth, as if scales had fallen from his eyes, Walter exclaimed, "I knew it!"

And Pastor Smith confirmed his suspicions: "Yes, Walter, the Roman Catholic Church. Our forefathers left Europe for this continent to escape the clutches of the pope—the Antichrist—and his horde of demonic teachers, but they followed us here and have infested every community, every institution with their heresies, even our own churches with their lies, perilling millions to hell!"

As Raeph remembered Walter's next question, he wished he could reach back into time to silence him, for Walter had asked, "What do you mean, infiltrating our churches?"

Pastor Smith had responded with seemingly impeachable authority: "Ever since the Reformation, Catholic priests and laymen have secretly come amongst the faithful, posing as sincere believers, polluting and watering down the true Gospel, sometimes with legalistic rules that enslave men's hearts, other times with liberal ideas that lead to complacency and sloth."

From that night on, Walter's life, as well as his own, had become subsumed with the belief in Catholic infiltrators and the coming Rapture.

THOUGH Raeph's pace was slower now, for he was trapped behind a salt truck, his traction was greatly improved, so he could relax, slightly. Staring out through the fogged-up windshield, he relived that unbelievable shocking night almost exactly one year ago, as if it was an indictment against his own guilt.

PATTY and he had just finished the dinner dishes and were heading up to bed. With their oldest son, Tom, away at seminary, and their other son, Ted, well, missing, the two married adults were anticipating the conception of a third, maybe this time a girl.

But Murphy's Law kicked in, and the telephone rang.

Raeph remembered his beloved Patty, now gone, pining with a smile, "Why not let it ring?"

With hindsight, Raeph wished he had complied, but instead he had said, "No, honey, I better not. Might be Bill." There had been overruns and downed assembly lines all week, and everyone in the shop, including Bill the night supervisor, presumed only "Handyman Raeph" could fix things. *Even that b____ Eileen had praised him! Always the company man, I was! What a fool.*

Once again, without checking caller ID, he'd picked up the receiver, but the faint, gruff voice on the other end was not Bill's. It was Walter.

Raeph remembered smacking his forehead and giving his Patty a hopeless glance. He responded as genuinely as possible to this unwelcome voice: "Well, hey, Walter. How goes it? And why are you whispering?" Raeph had leaned on the kitchen counter, motioning Patty to head on up, he'd join her in a minute.

Walter said simply in a hushed tone, "I did it."

Expecting nothing more than the report of yet another breakthrough in Walter's thinking, Raeph answered, "Did what?"

"I ... I eliminated the papist."

Still not hearing Walter's seriousness, Raeph said, "What are you talking about?"

And then, no longer whispering but with escalating zeal, Walter declared, "The minister at our church, whom I told you about—the one I was positive was a Catholic infiltrator—he was trying to steal my daughter—so I shot him."

Raeph couldn't recall how he had responded to this, but he did remember exactly how Walter had replied: "But the other day, you said!"

When the police had converged on Walter, he had lost control of his car, sending it spinning bumper over bonnet into a fifteen-foot-high blazing inferno. In the morning, Raeph heard all about it on the news. It was then that he learned that the minister Walter had believed was a Catholic infiltrator and had tried to kill was Reverend Stephen LaPointe, their old pastor from Red Creek.

Two days later, Walter was gone, but somehow, miraculously, Reverend LaPointe had survived. Though shot twice at close range, neither bullet met its mark. The first bullet was stopped by a paperback book and some kind of religious medal tucked in his blazer pocket. The second bullet had merely grazed his neck, and after a few days he had been released.

NOW driving north into snowy Vermont, Raeph confessed aloud, "Walter, you were right. I had indeed said, '*In drastic times, sometimes the faithful need to take drastic measures*.'"

"And Walter," Raeph said, tapping his parka to make sure the package was still there in the inside pocket, "Reverend LaPointe resigned from the pastorate—just like you said in your cassette recording."

Raeph didn't know all the details, but a phone call to First Congregational Church in Witzel's Notch, LaPointe's last pastorate, revealed that he had resigned, sold his home, and moved away with no forwarding address.

It was now pushing five o'clock. The retreat wasn't scheduled to start until the next morning, so Raeph had time to kill. The basic details he'd gathered about the retreat he had first gleaned from LaPointe himself nearly ten years before. One Sunday from the pulpit, LaPointe had informed the congregation about his upcoming retreat. After the sermon and before the final prayer LaPointe had the audacity to attempt to justify being absent from the office from Monday through Thursday. He claimed their Congregational Association "strongly encouraged" all clergy to take two weeks away each year for continuing education or some such form of personal pastoral enrichment. He then summarized the history of his retreat at a lodge up in the White Mountains. LaPointe said he had attended every year, except the year before, when something had arisen to change his plans.

LaPointe didn't need to go into detail. The previous year's "something" was still an open sore. Someone had vandalized the cemetery next to the church, breaking and defacing a dozen tombstones. But not randomly. The old sandstone slabs had marked the ancestral graves of the church's pillar families, so the incident grew to a size-twenty headache for LaPointe and the church board. Things only cooled down when it was determined that the culprit was the high-school son of the church's most venerated pillar family.

Reverend LaPointe had concluded his infomercial by stressing his need to get away and fellowship with a few of his closest friends from seminary.

Closest friends. Fighting to see through the blowing snow and to keep his Camaro on the road, Raeph's mind again drifted.

42

He too had old friends that he missed. Lots of them. Some of the best he had made during his brief tour of duty. He had enlisted when he was only seventeen. His mom had badgered his dad against letting him go, but in the end, his dad had won. After nine months' training, he flew over and landed smack in the middle of the Vietcong's major spring offensive of '72. Hanoi apparently hoped to throw our successes back in our faces to turn the antiwar sentiment even more against Nixon in the election year. Raeph couldn't remember all that had happened, except that on his second day out, a Soviet-made grenade landed twenty feet from where he was hiding. The tree saved his life, but both arms were riddled with burning shrapnel. Never had anything been so painful. He spent the next year recuperating in a VA hospital—where he met Walter.

But those friends from 'Nam, guys from all over the country with whom he had trained and flown in, were the best of his life. Especially Keely. It was Keely who had carried him back to camp after he was wounded, even though wounded himself; it was Keely who had stayed beside him for two days while he agonized without any form of painkiller—their supplies destroyed; and it was Keely who had flown back with him stateside. Most importantly, though, it was Keely who, on one of those late, agonizing nights in the brush with gunfire all around and his arms burning like they were buried in live coals, had told him about his love for Jesus Christ.

Raeph had never given one thought to religion. His parents had shown no interest whatsoever. He had never entered a church, even for a wedding or a funeral. But Keely's eyes would light up whenever he spoke about the loving mercy of Jesus.

At first, Raeph's hackles would rise in protest, but Keely's friendship melted his ignorant, stubborn heart. By the time Raeph arrived back in the States, he was a "born-again" Christian, spending every waking moment reading the Bible or some Christian book that Keely had recommended. The baton had been passed on to him to reach others who didn't believe—and it was then that he had met Walter.

Besides their faith, however, there was another way in which Raeph and Walter were alike. They had their squirreled away collections of Vietnam memorabilia—swords, uniforms, miscellaneous gear, and other souvenirs—but most treasured were their Soviet-made revolvers. Of what was left from the auction, Raeph's revolver was, next to his Camaro, his most valued possession.

RAEPH reached back to probe beneath the remainder of his wardrobe hanging on a rod extending from door to door. There it was, the revolver that was identical to the one Walter had used in his pursuit of LaPointe. Back in the VA hospital, they had impressed each other with the things they had scalped away, but it was the coincidence of their identical revolvers that had jelled their friendship. To Walter, there of course had to be some divine plan behind it all, some specific purpose for which God had called them together.

Walter had given his life trying to complete the mission to which he believed God had called him; now Raeph was convinced that the baton had been passed back to him. Within twenty-four hours, he believed he would know exactly what part he was to play in the infinite and righteous plan of God.

The icy, skeletal branches of the trees swaying on either side of the road seemed to mock him in his aloneness.

With the little information he could recall and some patient searching on the Internet, Raeph had located a reference to the retreat center in another man's online newsletter, a pastor named Tom Sylvan. *At least he would know the name of one other person who might be there.* Raeph then called the Widow's Mite for more details, using a fictitious name. The pastors usually start showing up around eight-thirty Monday morning. Their first official gathering would be after breakfast around ten. Raeph wasn't sure yet what he planned to do— he hoped this would come to him in prayer—but he expected to show up by that first meeting.

The wipers fought the snowy onslaught as through a swarm of locusts, but only the passenger side was winning.

"Gotta replace that blade!" Raeph scolded himself once again.

Exhaust billowed into the early evening air as the Camaro pulled into the parking lot of Rogers Park, downtown Red Creek. He had an entire night to kill, so at a fork in the interstate Raeph had taken the exit toward his old stomping grounds.

Every familiar street corner or unchanging home, even the patterns of the age-old trees lining the narrow streets of this out-of-the way village in backwoods Vermont, brought on memories that set Raeph back into tears. It was here that he had met Patty standing in line over there at old Burt's Ice Cream Bowl. And it was there across the common that they were married in the white sanctuary of Red Creek Congregational Church, families arranged row by row, filling both sides, parents beaming, his brother, still in disbelief, the best man. A smile broke through the despair. Sam had been right. She was far more than he ever deserved.

But the despair returned with a vengeance, for it was there that his two sons, Tom and Ted, were baptized; where, though Ted always resisted, Tom truly surrendered to Jesus; where one Sunday, after a missionary from Nairobi had finished his spiel for more prayers and more money, Tom had tapped him on the forearm.

"Dad?"

"Shh, we're praying."

"But Dad, I think … I want to be a minister."

Raeph remembered that at that moment he had felt like a completed father. What more could Jesus have expected of him? Well, it seemed Jesus had expected more. Both Tom and Ted were gone, and now like King David mourning the death of his firstborn and Mary the loss of hers, he must strain to go on.

He switched off the ignition and sat in silence. As usual, few people were out and about this wintry Sunday afternoon. The sky was flaking away against the darkening vertical face of the village businesses. First Security Bank had not changed, living up to the image of its imitation granite façade. Adam's Dry Goods was now a part of the True Value hardware chain. The Good Morning Café now advertised cappuccino and other yuppie favorites, and Angie's Macramé and Boutique was now a used paperback bookstore.

Most everything, though, was the same. Only he had changed. Far too much.

Red Creek Congregational. *Should I stop by?* They probably still locked it after morning worship. *Wonder who's pastor now?* He hadn't heard one way or the other whether Pastor Gilson, who had followed LaPointe, was still there. He had liked Pastor Gilson, learned a lot from him, especially about how Jesus had systematically trained His twelve disciples to carry on after He was gone.

There next to the church was the church-owned manse. He could stop by and talk to Pastor Gilson—or whoever was pastor now. Maybe the pastor could help him make sure he was hearing God correctly. He had certainly been wrong before.

Was he now misreading God? The failure of their apocalyptic expectations on Y2K had taken all the wind out of his spiritual sails, leaving him adrift. He hadn't lost faith in Jesus but never had he felt so far from Him. And with all that had been taken from him, the only thing left that made any sense was to confront and either confirm or disprove what Walter had suspected.

He stared across the park, buried in snow, where no child whirled on the merry-go-round or flew up and out of the swings. There was the church where for nearly twelve years he, Patty, and later Tom—and, yes, even Ted—had been fed spiritually. *Were there answers there? Or would he feel awkward if ol' Gilson was still here?*

Across the street was Faith United Methodist. Tom, and for awhile Ted, had been active in the youth group there. In fact, it had been their youth minister that had convinced Tom to attend the conservative Evangelical seminary north of Boston rather than the more liberal Congregational seminary—and Raeph had emphatically agreed. *Might the pastor there help?*

Hardly. Few of the Methodists he knew would listen sympathetically to what Walter had done or why, or to his own convoluted quest. They would only glare moonfaced and laugh.

Ben Ware.

Raeph sat up straight.

It's been years, but, I wonder if Ben is still here?

The more liberal members of their church, who ridiculed their "apocalyptic conspiracy theories," had derided Ben, Walter, and Raeph as the "Three Musketeers." Raeph had not seen Ben since Walter's funeral and even then had avoided him.

Backing out and then spinning his radials on the icy pavement, he shot down Main to Fifth. On the corner was Ben's home and business, Ware's Plumbing: "*No leak or clog too big a Job.*" There was no denying it. Ben was the spitting image of the mailman character on *Cheers*, only Ben's world rotated around pipes and drains, low-hanging, too-tight jeans, and all.

At times, he and Walter had wished Ben would find some other fanatics to hang around, but at the core, Ben had always been a good friend. Raeph laughed as he decided that a better analogy for Ben's persona might be a combination of Gomer, Goober, and Ernest T. Bass from the eternally playing *Andy Griffith Show*.

After he knocked, he noticed out of the corner of his eye the rustling of curtains, and then almost instantly the door burst open.

"Raeph, old buddy, what in the bejesus are you doing here? Come on in out of the cold. Hey, Sylvia, look who's here. Raeph Timmons. Can you believe it?"

As Ben paraded him hurriedly into the kitchen, past a table being set for dinner, Raeph knew this had been a bad idea.

6

Sara knew, of course, that the phone itself could not make the call. Nonetheless, she sat staring.

The only sounds in the stillness of her lonely bedroom were the waves crashing periodically outside against the ice-covered rocks, answered only by the screeching whine of freezing gulls. The only light was a pale beam bleeding through the crack beneath the door from her private bath.

Sara intended to make the call, and a voice within her brain screamed for her to move, but her hand refused to respond. Instead, she waffled between guilt, fear, and panic.

Her hand moved, but only to wipe away a tear. She stirred, and, with a resolution to call tomorrow, she retired into her closet to dress for bed. Once attired, she turned on her nightstand light and cuddled down beneath a thick quilt to escape back into a mystery by P. D. James about a murder at an English monastery.

Through discount-drugstore reading glasses, she picked up the story again where a woman had been discovered dead in her rocking chair, knitting in hand.

But who?

She backtracked to the beginning of the chapter, but after rereading two pages, she still couldn't recall a thing.

I must find out tonight where he is!

This time her hand went directly to the receiver and, repeating the number, she dialed.

After several rings, a tired, female voice answered, "Hello?"

More than a year had passed since Sara had heard Ginny McBride's soft, irritatingly innocent voice, but it immediately brought on a surge of dark memories laced with bitterness, even jealousy. They had met almost ten years before in a church playground. Stephen had just been installed as the pastor of Respite Congregational Church, the third church at which they served together as pastor and pastor's wife. Ginny and her husband, Adrian, seemed the ideal Evangelical couple. Stephen had often prophesied at the dinner table how this staunch, on-fire couple would one day be the lay leaders in the healing and renewal that the congregation so desperately needed.

Then, with no explanation, Ginny began bowing out of the church activities and commitments she normally would have led. The rumor mill suspected marital problems, even an affair, but the truth was even more shocking.

Sara recalled that awkward confrontation in a bookstore where she finally realized what it was that had stolen Ginny's heart. The latter had given her a book to read, hoping it would help the pastor's wife understand why, but it had only made the thought of Ginny's "discovery" more revolting.

And then that evening several weeks later when Adrian and Ginny had come over. Adrian had hoped Stephen could convince Ginny to return to the faith upon which they had built their marriage, but the night had ended in a puzzling stalemate.

A very puzzling stalemate, and to this day, Sara credited that evening as the onset of Stephen's disenchantment with the pastorate and the eventual demise of their own marriage.

She remembered evenings when Stephen remained out late on supposed visitation calls, which caused her weaker nature to suspect that he was having an affair with, of all people, Ginny. Although Sara was certain this was never true, still the reasoning of that inner accusatory voice could be so convincing.

"Hello, Ginny, this is Sara LaPointe."

A brief pause and then a less dreary response, "Mrs. LaPointe, what an unexpected pleasure. Is everything all right?"

"Yes, everything's fine, and please, call me Sara."

Hadn't she told Ginny this more than a thousand times over the years? But old habits die hard. Or was Ginny turning the knife on their difference in age? It was awkward enough being addressed so formally merely because she was the pastor's wife, but now even more so since she no longer was one.

"I'm sorry to call you so late—"

"Oh, please, Mrs.... Sara, that is no problem, none at all."

"I just couldn't sleep, and wondered if you or maybe Adrian might know how to get in touch with Stephen?" Sara fully realized how strange this request must sound, given their long history and presumed convictions, without any preliminary explanation, but she had no desire to provide this. She just wanted information.

"Actually, we've—"

"I realize that he may have asked you not to tell me."

"No, it isn't that, not that at all. It's just that we've lost track of him ourselves. At first, after Stephen's resignation, Adrian and Stephen used to talk all the time, maybe once a week. As you know—well, at least I presume you know—Stephen was awfully depressed about what he should do after leaving the pastorate. He ..."

There followed an awkward pause, but Sara refused to fill the void.

Ginny continued, "He talked often about you and the boys. Adrian said Stephen would fight back tears whenever he realized what a mess he had made of things. It was rough when he finally had to leave the house in Witzel's Notch. But then this past Christmas he disappeared altogether. Since then no one has heard from him. If you don't mind my asking, Sara, haven't you heard from him at all?"

"Not since he sold our home in June." Sara was tempted to add that they had been in agreement about the sale, that it was the best for all concerned, but resisted. "After that I lost track of him. I became extremely busy in the fall with my graduate studies, and then the holidays."

"You mean you didn't hear from him even over Christmas?"

"No. He probably tried to call us, but of all things our phone recorder has been on the fritz. And I didn't know where to find him. He left no forwarding address."

"Well," Ginny said, "after he left Witzel's Notch, he moved to Jamesfield, New Hampshire. He first stayed for a short time in the rectory at St. Francis de Sales Parish, and then in an apartment above a hardware store where he worked part-time. Do you remember Father William Bourque?"

"Yes, of course." Sara certainly remembered the priest, a sweet-and-sour memory. It was this priest who had talked Stephen into leaving the ministry. It was also this priest, though, who had so helped Stephen recover emotionally from the attack that had nearly taken his life. Sara knew she should be grateful, but over the past year she had come to blame that priest almost as much as she blamed Stephen for the turmoil of their lives.

"Well," Ginny continued, "after Stephen moved to Jamesfield, Father Bourque was counseling him and helping him decide what to pursue as a career. He was on a seeming downward spiral into depression. For a few weeks, Stephen taught an adult Bible study at the parish, but then, without warning or explanation, he disappeared. I suspect, however, that Father Bourque might know where he is."

"Why is that?" Sara demanded.

"Well, Adrian pressed him on it once, but Father would only say that he presumed Stephen had left to make up his mind about his future. Adrian, though, felt that he was holding something back."

There before Sara on her nightstand was their last family portrait. All were smiling but, as the mother, she knew as no one else the complications that lay beneath each expression. Stephen had been in the midst of his struggles but, as always, concealed it well. William was falling head over heels for the daughter of the very man who would try to murder his father. Daniel was still oblivious to life in the big picture, filling his free time with the cyber battles of computer games. And there she was, putting on the best face she could amid these troubles, unaware of the crisis that was yet to come.

"What you're saying, then, is that to find Stephen I have to see your priest?"

"He's not our priest; he's just a friend, but he probably is the only person who might know where Stephen is."

This was certainly the last thing Sara wanted to do, but what else was there? Reluctantly she asked, "Do you have his number?"

Ginny gave Sara all the necessary contact information, but then added, "You do realize what week this is?"

"What do you mean?"

"I think this is the week when Stephen and his other pastor friends will be gathering for their annual retreat at the Widow's Mite Lodge up in the mountains north of Jamesfield. Stephen told us that it was at this retreat last year that he first made public his concerns. Just tonight, in fact, Adrian was wondering whether Stephen would show up this year. Even though his minister friends may not have understood or agreed with his decision, they were still his best friends. Adrian suspects that Stephen might just covet their friendship in the midst of his isolation."

"You're right, Ginny," Sara said, her mind racing. "He just might do that. Would Reverend Bourque know about this?"

"I don't know. You could ask."

"Ginny, thanks. You've been a great help."

"Oh, I'm glad to help. How are things for you and the boys and, well," and then, with stark boldness, Ginny asked, "Frank? I heard you may have returned—"

"The boys are doing fine," but Sara refused to address the rest. "Listen Ginny, say hello to Adrian, and if by any chance you hear from Stephen, please tell him that I'm trying to reach him. I need to go; thanks for your help. God bless."

"Sure, Sara—"

But Sara had already hung up.

She lay with the lights out, the quilt up to her chin, and as the sound of the breakers beneath her window suffused her thoughts, she considered her options. The simplest would be to call the priest first thing in the morning. But the more she contemplated just how her husband might act, given this annual gathering of old friends, the more she vacillated over what to do.

Then she decided. At first light, she would make all the necessary arrangements for her classes and Daniel, pack a small suitcase, and start driving west.

7

Scott Turner's Narrative

It seemed like hours before I could inch past the accident, in the narrow, congested emergency lane; I then pressed on into the growing darkness, my van cutting a vanishing path through the increasing storm. Snow caked the windshield, leaving a continuous residue of smeared grime. Oncoming headlights blurred into passing goblins. My only recompense was that I was still driving on a divided highway, which I would soon lose after I passed Albany.

Several hours later, through the mindless chatter of some local talk radio station, I snarled aloud to myself, "The idiot!" And with this, I became aware of my tense, prowling posture, my fists white upon the wheel. I forced myself to relax back into the seat, easing my death grip. A glance at the speedometer startled me. Even with the reduced visibility, the van had been blindly plunging ahead over seventy miles per hour.

Good Lord what am I doing? I glanced at the digital clock: 9:38.

Passing my hand across my face, as if to dismiss the past and move on, I refocused on the road ahead while mentally admonishing myself for how I had handled myself—or should I say mishandled myself—back at the wreck.

"What these people need is a priest, not an imitation." An imitation! I'm an ordained Congregationalist minister! But yet, did that small-minded patrolman—or should I perhaps more respectfully say, highly stressed patrolman—have a point? If those ministers and laymen had no more authority to ordain me than a used-car salesman, then why should I have had any more right to go forward than anyone else sitting steaming mad in their cars? Couldn't any one of them have merely proclaimed himself a minister of his own self-made religion

and crashed forward through the tape into the gnarled wreckage of steel and bodies with the notion of helping in the name of Jesus?

I noticed that my cell phone had a good signal, so I figured it was time to check in as promised.

Two rings and she was there.

"Hello, honey," she said, with alluring undertones.

"How'd you know?"

"Well, for one, you said you'd call."

"Yes, but I might have been one of your other lovers," I said with a smile, the wipers flapping while a BMW passed at high speed without a care in the world.

"That's true, but caller ID gave you away."

"I could never spy on you."

"Right again. So where are you?"

I brought her up to date on my travels, every turn, change in weather, or road delay, even the heated details of my at-the-accident rejection. She responded as a traveling, weatherworn husband might expect a wife to do, comfortably cuddled at home in the warmth of our bed, sipping decaf cappuccino. Yet, there was an inexplicable edge to her answers.

"Diane, what's wrong?"

At first, silence. Then hesitantly, "Nothing really," then again silence.

"What is it?" Now the troubled road ahead took on a different meaning. It stood for separation and miscommunication.

"I didn't want to say anything, because I didn't want you to worry."

"But?"

"Well, Mary called."

"Mary? So what's her latest gossip?"

"Now Scott, she means well, but this time, well, she apparently heard that Farmer Oakley was terribly offended by this morning's sermon."

I strained to see through the fogged-up windows and keep the van straight in its lane, while at the same time mulling over Old Farmer Oakley. Milford Oakley was a fifth-generation pig farmer with whom you did not want to be trapped in a small, confined space. He always mumbled, seemingly to himself, and then angrily expected you to have heard and understood everything. Whatever I did was wrongheaded, and any improvement I proposed had already been tried and failed.

"So what was it this time?"

"Now don't get huffy. Mary says that he was offended—at least Mary said that he said that he was offended—that you were aiming your sermon directly at him; that you specifically chose your Scripture," and this Diane said in a lower, gruff voice, "'to lambaste me just 'cause I don't agree with'm.'"

Should I tell her I was? Or at least him among many? Instead, I demanded, "But I didn't choose that Scripture! I've explained over and over why and how I end up with the Scripture selections for each Sunday!" I wasn't sure precisely who I was yelling at. My focus was out through the slushy windshield, wipers smacking, failing their job, leaving the tempered glass worse than they'd found it. In the stark blackness of the night, a highway sign flittered past: "UTICA: 32 MILES."

"Diane, you heard my sermon. Was there anything vindictive about it?"

She hesitated.

"Well?" I demanded, self-consciously.

"To be honest, darling, I was a little uncomfortable with your tone at times, but, honey, I also know some of the complaints and resistance you've received from this new congregation. So if you had a few specific members in mind, including Old Farmer Oakley, I don't blame you."

What ran immediately through my mind as I was driving off into the night was how blessed I was to have such a supportive wife.

"So, Diane, what's the damage?"

"Like I said, this only came from Mary, but she seems to think that Farmer Oakley is not going to let this rest. He apparently was so offended that he's trying to call an emergency meeting of the church board."

"But he can't do that while I'm gone!"

"Hey, babe, I'm on your side."

"Sorry, but what are they planning to do?"

"I don't know. Maybe nothing whatsoever. Maybe Farmer Oakley is not as influential as we think. It may just blow over."

"Can you let me know what happens?" I said, feeling the weight of yet another stressor. "I feel like once again just when I try to get away, the demons strike."

"Honey, I'm sorry. I didn't mean to make you fret. Please just forget about it. I'm sure nothing will come of it, and if things do start to escalate, I'll make sure—through my own channels of influence—that nothing happens until after you get home."

"Thanks, darling. I really need to set the stresses of Rowsville behind me for this retreat. I need the chance to recharge my batteries."

"I know, dear, and I want this for you. Just don't worry. The important thing is I love you."

"I love you, too. Listen, I'm coming up to an exit and need to get off. How 'bout I call you in the morning?"

"Okay, honey; drive safely."

"Will do. Love you."

"Me too."

This familiar benediction brought satisfactory closure to unwanted news. The eruption at home was too much on target.

The exit was a pleasant sight for many reasons. The van took its place beside a slough of other Sunday drivers, while I walked stiffly in. The restroom was grossly neglected, but passable. A chicken joint had the shortest line, so I "super-sized" and walked back, balancing spicy chicken, fries, and a gargantuan diet soda.

Once back, melded into the flow of turnpike traffic, I laughed aloud for a moment at the irony of the mess I had stepped into at Rowsville, for it connected directly to the reason I was pressing east through that snowstorm. As a result of what Stephen had said at the last retreat, I had begun questioning the validity of my ordination, of my own myopic interpretation of Scripture, and of our entire Congregational system. I had always been a bit insecure about my preaching—ex–football player to minister and all that—but this had left me feeling especially sheepish.

Consequently, when I took on this new church, I decided to do something that I had previously resisted but to which many of my minister friends had already succumbed. Rather than freely choosing my own selection of Scriptures and, therefore, planning, as I saw fit, my own preaching schedule—like most Evangelicals do—I decided to start using the Common Lectionary. This resource, used by most high-church, mainline Protestants, Episcopalians, and Catholics, provides the readings for Sunday services, essentially covering the Bible in three years, and grouping the readings—Old Testament, Psalm, Epistle, Gospel—according to the liturgical seasons, starting with Advent. This way I wasn't limiting my congregation's diet only to those texts I liked or with which I felt comfortable (or for which I already had sermon notes). Also, since ministers from across denominational lines were preaching on the same texts, there would be lots of current resources for me to peruse, to ensure that what I was preaching was checked by other perspectives.

Since it just so happened that I was starting in the fall at a new church, I informed them—during my interview process, mind you—of my intentions, starting with the First Sunday of Advent. There were no complaints or questions—to my surprise, it seemed a previous minister, whom most of them liked, had done the same.

So I began following the "playbook," as I called it, accepting these texts as the Word of God for us on any particular Sunday. All went well through Advent, Christmas, and Epiphany—all liturgical seasons to which we Congregationalists often gave nothing more than lip service, but yet to which over the centuries we had become acclimated. What was particularly good was that I was being forced to study and preach on texts I normally would have avoided.

Many of the texts for the Advent season dealt with the Second Coming of Christ, for example, but given my newness with this congregation and my presumptions about what the previous pastors had spoon-fed them, I skirted the issue, emphasizing instead whatever else I could glean from the texts. Often the Common Lectionary also chose readings from books that weren't in my Protestant Bible, like Baruch and Sirach, so you can be sure I avoided these!

What I could not avoid, however, was the continuing progressive emphasis on the necessity of growing in holiness for one's salvation. In fact, for the First Sunday of Advent we had: "May the Lord make you increase and abound in love to one another and to all men, as we do to you, *so that he may establish your hearts unblamable in holiness before our God and Father, at the coming of our Lord Jesus with all his saints.*"[5] This congregation, marinated on the social gospel, was quite comfortable with the call to love one another, but not so much with the goal of growing in holiness in preparation for their future judgment. And I heard about it, from Farmer Oakley as a matter of fact.

Then came the Second Sunday of Advent: "It is my prayer that your love may abound more and more … so that you … *may be pure and blameless for the day of Christ*."[6] This time I heard rumblings that I was preaching a form of "works righteousness," an accusation which for the life of me I couldn't figure out.

The verses kept coming week after week, mostly drawing us into seasonal themes, until the Fifth Sunday of, what the Common Lectionary called, "Ordinary Time," or February 4 of this year: "Now I would remind you, brethren, in what terms I preached to you *the gospel*, which you received, in which you stand, *by which you are saved, if you hold it fast—unless you believed in vain*."[7] This may seem innocuous enough, and I probably should have skirted by this without a stitch. But frankly, I was starting to get perturbed by the constant undercurrent in the congregation of what I considered hypocrisy.

I hadn't planned it, but in the midst of my sermon I got caught in the *Big Mo*. All preachers know the *Big Mo*, and I must admit I love the feeling, the rush, when the Scriptures capture all of one's emotions and the words just flow, words that I could never have preplanned, words that directly bridge the gap—at least that's what I presume— between my heart and the hearts of my congregation, drawing them up to the edge of the wave, the wave of faith and conviction and surrender. Whenever this happened, I sensed that I'd finally achieved at least some modicum of that for which I had left everything behind to become a minister: to help my lackluster, "name on the rolls," "my ancestors go back five generations," "I was born in this church", Christian members experience the born-again, spiritual explosion into true Christianity!

In fact, in the midst of that Sunday's powerful current of the *Big Mo*, I even said a few things I'd really never said before: that a person must believe, stand, and hold fast to the Gospel, or they might lose their salvation! Now not only do a boatload of Christians believe, following Luther and Calvin, "once saved–always saved," but certainly no one in this congregation believed anyone was in danger of damnation, since, to them, the Gospel and evangelization were all and only about telling people how much God already loved them regardless of how they lived.

The level of congregational rumblings rose significantly.

Then on the next Sunday, the Sixth Sunday of Ordinary Time, the text was Luke's version of the Beatitudes. Generally these work well with those who preach social gospel sermons. But there was something in those verses I had never seen before: "Blessed are you when men hate you, and when they exclude you and revile you, and cast out your name as evil, on account of the Son of man! Rejoice in that day, and leap for joy, for behold, *your reward is great in heaven*; for so their fathers did to the prophets."[8]

Your reward is great in heaven. I'm sure I'd read dozens of verses before that talked about receiving rewards in heaven. I always presumed these "rewards" referred to our salvation in Christ, but during the week I studied for this sermon, checking commentary after commentary, I encountered a breadth of new ways to understand our eternal rewards—ways that were far from usual for Congregationalists.

I treaded softly around this in my Sunday sermon, but afterward, in the short receiving line, Sara Guinness demanded, in as resounding a voice as she could muster, "So, pastor, what *did* Jesus mean about rewards in heaven?" Sara Guinness was the primary spokesperson for her particular infestation of Guinnesses. She reminded me of the Ma Kettle of black-and-white movie fame. "My great-grand pappy told me once—" was the foundation upon which she held anything to be true. Her usual quip was "If it was good enough for the Pilgrims, why mess it up?" It was of no avail to inform her that little of what we Congregationalists do now resembles anything the Pilgrims did then. I looked at her, seeing Old Farmer Oakley peering over her shoulder, and answered, "I guess it's my prayer, Mrs. Guinness, that someday you just might find out," and passed her along with a smile.

Then came my sermon on the morning I left, the one that seemingly hit the fan. On that Eighth Sunday in Ordinary Time, the Lectionary slammed me with two barrels. First, "Therefore, my beloved brethren, *be steadfast, immovable, always abounding in the work of the Lord, knowing that in the Lord your labor is not in vain.*"[9] Again, essentially, in the wider context, especially in the cumulative effect of the Lectionary, we must remain steadfast "in the gospel," or we could lose it all in the final judgment!

But the second barrel was the doozy: "Why do you see the speck that is in your brother's eye, but do not notice the log that is in your own eye? ... You hypocrite, *first take the log out of your own eye, and then you will see clearly to take out the speck that is in your brother's eye.*"[10]

To me these verses were pretty straightforward. Hey, don't judge lest ye be judged. Again, however, the *Big Mo* kicked in, grabbing me by the lapels, lifting me, transfixed, above my cowering congregation, and I began preaching about our need to clean up our own lives instead of pointing out all the flaws in the lives of everyone else. And I admit, I caught myself doing a fair amount of pointing, though as a gesture of emphasis not accusation. But, yes, I do remember finding myself eye-to-eye with good Old Farmer Oakley at the conclusion of one of my heated harangues.

I'd like to claim that what Old Farmer Oakley reacted to was nothing more than the clear unadulterated, uninterpreted words of Scripture. But I knew, and apparently he knew, that at that moment I was preaching past the log in my own eye to point out what I considered the logjam in his. But had I been preaching the clear unadulterated, uninterpreted words of Scripture, or merely my own opinion? There had been many biblical commentators who disagreed with my slant.

So what was I to do? To say?

Driving along, I once again drew back to the true reason I needed this trip out East. Sure it would be good to see old friends, as I had told Diane, but beneath my façade, I was being eaten alive. I'd never told Diane the details of Stephen's explanation, but for the past year those details had refused to leave me alone. Maybe it was the confession of Stephen's own guilt-ridden awkwardness in the pulpit that had caused me to feel likewise. I was *presuming* Diane didn't know—but then again, I remembered how it seemed she could always guess my thoughts and moods.

Under everything I had done that past year, the foundations upon which my entire ministry depended were crumbling. My real motive was to see Stephen and force him to admit the deeper implications of what he had only alluded to last year.

But would Stephen be there? And if not, then where was he?

I hoped to drive another hundred miles yet into the night, maybe into the darkness of eastern Vermont. In some rest stop, I hoped to spend a peaceful night, wrapped in my 20°-certified, L.L. Bean sleeping bag, on the rear, foldout bed in my conversion van, ready to make the final trek to reach the Widow's Mite, maybe by lunch.

But would he be there?

I stared off into the night, my sight interrupted by the back-and-forth swish of the wipers still losing their battle against the heavy snow. The road disappeared ahead into infinity, and the solution to my life and ministry seemed equally as obscure.

8

"Ben, I appreciate you and Sylvia inviting me to stay the night; this was a godsend." Raeph glanced impatiently at his watch.

"Aw, don't mention it."

There again was that dumb, "gaw-ly" Gomer smile.

"And don't you two worry about me in the morning. I need to scoot real early, long before you and Sylvia need to bother."

"Are you sure? Sylvia can whip up a batch of her famous French toast …"

"Oh yeah, I'll be fine." Raeph started backing into the bedroom trying to force the door on their conversation.

"But we could continue our discussion about—"

All that remained in view of Ben was his right ear. "Another time, but thanks. I'll call you when I get home."

He closed the door politely but firmly in the middle of one final plea. Ben's footsteps began to fade away down the hall, then paused.

"Please, God, give me a break," Raeph pleaded upward. In time, the steps resumed and faded away into silence, and Raeph collapsed into the room's only "chair": an orange vinyl beanbag held together with duct tape. Countless Styrofoam mini-balls poophed into the air.

FIFTEEN minutes into dinner had been sufficient to remind him why he had let the Wares slip out of his life. Ben was still a strange bird—certainly not on the same page as himself or Walter ... or the rest of humanity. For two hours, over a dinner of Sylvia's "famous" tuna casserole, Raeph had been unable to squeeze a word in between Ben and Sylvia's volleys of "I will never forget when—." It would have been at least palatable if they were reminiscing about events in which he had participated, but not one of the people they were describing, through glares of excitement and private guffaws, was familiar. At one point, they became so engrossed in fine-tuning a detail about which car they had driven in 1973 to Moosehead Lake that Raeph could have thrust back his chair and left unnoticed.

More than once he had screamed silently, *Lord Jesus, why did You bring me here? Or did you!*

Any question as to Raeph's purpose for coming back into the area had been conveniently ignored until after dinner. After Sylvia excused herself—*thank God*—Ben led him down to the basement for a friendly game of pool.

"So Raeph," Ben said upon executing a well practiced break, "you still into all that Rapture and 'left-behind' crap? I'll never forget how you, Walter—good old Walter—and I used to stay up nights wrangling over when it was all going to happen and why, and then what catastrophes would result, and which of our friends and family would be left behind to clean up the mess." With three random balls downed in the break, Ben chose solids. He then began circling the table, showboating his prowess.

Raeph, however, could not remember ever staying up nights with Ben.

"Well, actually—" he started, *but really, was the effort worth it?*

"You see, Raeph," Ben continued, cue elevated after a taunting follow-through, "I've come a long way from those days, thanks to Pastor Gilson. You know, the pastor that followed LaPointe?"

Raeph certainly did. Together the three had hoped Gilson would be more in line with their way of thinking than LaPointe. Instead, Gilson had been even less, making it a point to finish what they presumed LaPointe had started—to "rid Red Creek of the apocalyptic fanaticism that Pastor Smith had left behind," to use the phrase Gilson had made so popular. Then Raeph had moved away.

"After you left, Walter and I—well, mainly Walter—confronted Gilson. In time, Reverend Gilson's arguments—from Scripture, mind you—began making a lot of sense. And besides," Ben said, as he sank his last solid, leaving the cue ball to slide nicely into position to down the eight before Raeph had even taken a shot, "hadn't we been wrong about Y2K and the end of the millennium?"

Raeph considered venturing into this discussion, maybe even probing Ben's insight, but, with a laugh, quickly decided against it.

"What was that?" Ben asked.

"Oh, nothing."

"Were you thinking of one of our good ol' times?" Ben said, as he racked up for another game. "Why, I'll never forget the time when—" and Raeph spaced out.

It hadn't been until Ben insisted that Raeph spend the night in their daughter Tippy's vacated room that Raeph had regained consciousness, realizing with a start why Jesus, in His humorous mercy, had led him here.

NOW as he sat nearly to the ground in beans, he glanced around him. *So this is what the room of a modern teenaged cosmetology student looks like.* Its weirdness disturbed him. Magazine cutouts of modern hairdos covered every inch of the walls and ceiling. The cacophony of hair lengths, colors, dyes, spikes, curls, mixed with mesmerized glares and prune-scrunched smiles gave Raeph the willies.

He wrestled to free himself from the beanbag's clutches to prepare for bed, but a thought distracted him. From the inside pocket of his parka, he extracted the rubber-band-encircled packet. Glancing around the room, he saw on Tippy's cluttered desk, beneath a disheveled stack of beauty magazines and discarded candy wrappers, a combination clock/radio/cassette player. Clearing away the trash, he positioned the unit front and center. The small, rusted shade of an aging, high-intensity lamp poked up through the litter. He switched it on and laid the envelope on the desk in the center of its beam.

Two days after Walter's death, this envelope had arrived in the mail, doubly sealed with fiberglass tape. In shaky, nearly incoherent script, Walter had scribbled Raeph's address and across the bottom in bold strokes: "TO BE OPENED BY NO ONE ELSE!!!" The envelope contained an unlabeled cassette tape that Walter had recorded the day before he tried to kill Reverend LaPointe. Apparently, Walter had spent several cold afternoons in his car down the street from LaPointe's house, waiting for just the right moment to make his move. Walter was becoming increasingly concerned that people would misunderstand his act and label him a murderer instead of a brave and faithful defender of the faith. So, on what turned out to be his last day waiting and watching, he had recorded what was essentially his last testament.

Raeph ceremoniously opened the packet. One rubber band snapped and flew across the room. With slow, deliberate, robotic motions, he extricated the cassette, inserted it into the player, and stood silently to listen once more to Walter's final words of self-justification.

"Raeph—"

Walter's words immediately died away before the sound of a passing car. Once clear, he started again.

"Raeph. It's Walter. By the time you hear this, I will have, by God's grace, already completed my mission. Though you and I never actually discussed it—I knew that Jesus wanted me to keep it secret—we talked many times about what we would do if we ever discovered a papist infiltrator. Well, I found one, and you won't believe who it is, though you know him, and once I tell you, you may even see it for yourself. It's Reverend Stephen LaPointe. Yes! I've suspected it for a long time, but only recently have I become absolutely certain. For over a year I've confronted him by email—I let him know that I've seen through his disguise—but like the Jesuit he probably is, he never admitted it. And now that they are trying to lure my daughter Stacy away, I must act."

Raeph paused the cassette and thought: *The spark that led to Walter's escapade and death was nothing more than a misunderstanding. He had learned later that Stacy, fed up with her father's overbearing control and crazy ideas, had manipulated Stephen's son William into helping her run away from home. She returned with a contrite heart, but too late to prevent his fanatical death. He died in her arms, reconciled.*

Restarting the cassette, Raeph heard silence as Walter waited for a few more cars to pass. Then the voice continued in a whisper. "You know as well as I do that few will understand—most just don't get what's going on in our world or our churches. Even our families and friends can't hear us, or don't want to hear. They've become blind and complacent, like stupid sheep. So when you get this, it may be because I need your help. I may need you to explain why I had to do this, because I may no longer be alive to explain it myself.

"First. Please tell them how much I loved Jesus, that I did this because I loved Jesus with all my heart and would do anything—even at the cost of my life—to defend Him against the works of the devil and his horde."

Raeph paused the recording once again, to pray aloud: "Lord Jesus, Walter really did love You. He did what he did, no matter how opposite it seems to Your command to love your neighbor, because he was willing to do anything, even die, in obedience to You. So please, forgive him, even if what he did was wrong."

Raeph listened for sounds in the house, but hearing none, he restarted the player. The tone of Walter's voice had risen in intensity, his words running together from excitement and fear.

"Second. Tell them that I did this because I trust the Scriptures that tell us to expect this kind of infiltration in the End Times."

Wriggling himself into the lumpy beanbag, not unlike a cat circling until it found just the right position, Raeph listened as Walter recounted how old Pastor Smith, verse by verse, had convinced them that Catholic infiltrators were behind every evil in their churches. Raeph could feel his own ire rise with each text and each resounding innuendo.

Pausing the cassette once again, Raeph sat quietly, thinking. His mind had gone back and forth so many times on these issues, but his anger at himself was growing for not sharing his doubts with Walter, for all the things he'd said or neglected to say that led to Walter's act and death. And, thus, this was the reason he was intent on confronting LaPointe: to prove to himself whether or not Walter's suspicions were wrong, and therefore whether he was truly guilty of Walter's unfounded self-sacrifice.

He restarted the player. Another long period of silence. The sound of several passing cars could be heard in the background along with what sounded like Walter hunching down out of view. Then Walter began again, this time in a spy's whisper.

"And why LaPointe? I suspected him ever since those first Bible studies, when you, Ben, and I discovered that he was set against the truth of the End Times and the Rapture. And remember, he gave every indication that he believed in the authority of the Bible, but if you think about it, he was always open to other views. Just when you'd think he was going to give what you and I knew was the only true meaning of Scripture, he'd water it down by adding some alternative explanation. He was always making a big deal out of the fact that what we believed as Congregationalists was different from how other Christians interpreted the same Bible texts.

"But I saw through him. He sometimes seemed unsure of himself—but I suspect he was just trying to make us doubt our faith. I knew this when he began preaching the Roman Catholic line on pro-life issues, particularly against abortion and contraception. Sure, lots of Christians are against abortion, but what other Christian ministers do you know who preach against contraception? There were other things, though, that convinced me of LaPointe's guilt, like the fact that his name is French Canadian, which we all know must be Catholic.

"Now don't lose heart, Raeph. You know everything that we learned from Pastor Smith and Reverend Harmond. Remember when Smith said, 'Count my words, brothers: there will come a time in your lives, each one of you, when you may have to take a bold step to defend your faith and your family against the pervasive infestation of the Red Dragon of Babylon!' Well, I firmly believe my time has come. And Raeph, count my words, someday that time may come for you."

With this, Walter's voice ceased. The sounds of a passing truck mixed briefly with the familiar hiss of the cassette and then dead silence.

Raeph paused the player and walked to the window shrouded in black curtains. Pushing them aside, he leaned his weariness against the sill, unconcerned that his tousled hair was absorbing the condensation.

"Lord Jesus ..."

Few lights reached him through the trees. A passing car was the only sign of life. A far-off hound barked and set off a relay of neighborhood sentinels.

"... do You really want me to go through with this?"

But what is left of my life? Without my wife and family, without a job, and without even a permanent place to lay my head—like Jesus—what more noble cause can I follow than to bring closure to that which Walter had been willing to give his life?

"No greater love …"

Some mournful bell in some distant church tolled midnight. As the last toll faded, he returned to the desk, to give Walter the last say. With but the push of a button, he set the cassette rolling and Walter's voice returned from the grave, no longer with words of anger or panic justifying what he was about to do, but rather with soft and tender words of friendship and farewell.

When the recording lapsed into silence, Raeph removed it, rewrapped it, and stuffed it into his parka.

Dousing the lights, he laid on the bed fully dressed, staring into the darkness.

He pondered many things: *What if Walter had known the truth about his daughter Stacy, or that Reverend Harmond would abandon the faith? What if I had told Walter about my own doubts, would he have gone through with it? Yes, I suppose he would have; he probably would have presumed we'd all been duped. He would have stayed true to his cause, even if he were the last faithful Christian on earth. Nothing could have altered his course.*

But how about mine?

 9

Flames within the open hearth provided the only light and heat for the Spartan one-room cabin. Some coals were spent black, others white with ash though hot, still others glowed crimson.

Sometime in the mid-1800s a Franciscan hermit assembled the cabin out of hand-hewn logs. For years the hermit and his cabin enjoyed peace and solitude, but after the neighborhood encroached upon him, a series of new owners refurbished and remodeled it, but always preserved its hermitic simplicity.

The hearthstone was rough and gray, round and mortised, black in places from years of neglect. Spanning outward from the slate threshold, oak planks, smooth from a century of foot travel, stretched from wall to wall. A threadbare rug locally woven of Sussex wool lay before the flames.

The lone bed, like the rest of the sparse furniture made from tongue-and-groove logs, sat in the far shadows. The mattress and linens were neat and tidy, showing no evidence of recent use.

Another log cracked in the fire, breaking the stillness. Stephen LaPointe sat on the floor at the rug's edge opposite the hearth, knees pulled up tight to his chest, his eyes staring deeply into the flames.

A year ago this night he had slept restlessly, contemplating what he would reveal the next morning to his friends at the Widow's Mite. He and Sara had shared what turned out to be their last intimate evening together. The thought of her drove the pain even deeper.

"Sara—" he said aloud.

So much had happened, so drastic an aftermath. Never in a million years could he have imagined the resultant trajectory of his decisions. *If I had known, though, would I have done anything differently?* This question often hounded him as the demons attacked his inner peace.

Once again, he recited the advice of an ancient mystic writer named Evagrios the Solitary: "You should wish for your affairs to turn out, not as you think best, but according to God's will. Then you will be undisturbed and thankful in your prayer."[11] He had certainly remained mostly undisturbed in this isolated retreat, and thankfully so, but inwardly the peace he sought had remained fleeting.

Extending a stalk of straw, he extracted a fraction of the fire to light a beeswax votive candle, which served as the centerpiece for his self-constructed shrine. Beside the candle, lay a paperback book—a catechism. A small hole penetrated its center, blocked by an imbedded bullet. Upon the book lay a silver Celtic cross and an oval, concave religious medal. Propped against the book lay a revolver, with which a very confused man had once tried to assassinate him. He touched the scar along the side of his neck, and once again offered a prayer that God would forgive him for the mess he had made of his life, and his marriage.

The tiny flame danced in the cabin's draft, casting an ominous silhouette against the primitive log walls—the silhouette of a revolver.

Silently, motionlessly, he recited a psalm, contemplating its prophetic imagery of the Church, and asked himself, staring now into the fire, "Will they even hear or understand me?"

He glanced down at the revolver, and an inner voice taunted him with another solution.

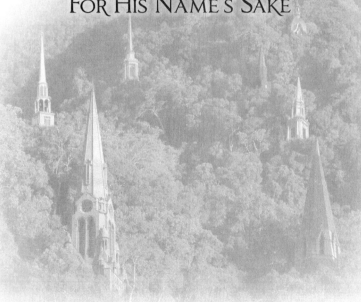

PART 2

FOR HIS NAME'S SAKE

10

Scott Turner's Narrative

The Viking ship, wide and shallow, weathered wood from stem to stern, terminated in the faded effigy of a blond, strapping maiden. It had lost its rudder and was drifting, impotent against the raging storm. Norse sailors, clad in animal skins, raced back and forth across the slick deck in a vain attempt to wrest control from the demon wind, for they knew: this was but the curse of their quest. They had ventured too near the edge, and this was nothing more than fulfilled prophecy. Had not the age-old stories warned them? Had they not surrendered to the greed of their quest for the great Horn Resounding?

But could I not help them? I was their captive, intended for barter with the gods, tied mercilessly to the main spar. For days I had stood, spent against the ropes, stripped of clothing, neglected, starving, doomed to die. Yet couldn't I somehow break free?

I wrestled against the knots of the wet leather tongs. A wave crashed, sending the ship upwards, drenching me in near-freezing, North Sea water. My struggling only tightened the bonds. As the bow crashed back into the sea descending below the writhing horizon, I noticed a light. At first dimly, but, yes, there through the mist, a brilliant round beam. It shone first to my left and then across to my right until it found me and pierced directly into my eyes, blinding me. What could this be? Some northern star or maybe a Valkyrie's lamp seeking any who dared venture so far west? But then again, it looked like the saving beam of some north shore lighthouse! How could this be? There were no lighthouses in Viking days! The beam, however, would not let up. It flooded out everything until nothing else could be seen.

I slowly opened my eyes, raising my hand instinctively against the inquisitive light. At first I could not place where I was, until ... ah, yes, my L.L. Bean sleeping bag on the reclined bed in my conversion van.

The light continued to invade my privacy. My nerves tensed as I realized how vulnerable I was. Miles from the nearest house in the predawn darkness, and unlike some of the young farmers in my church who kept shotguns in their pickups, I owned no weapons. My cell phone was six feet away, plugged into the dash. It would require a clumsy lunge over an open suitcase, a bag of half-eaten snacks, and a briefcase full of books—most of which came uselessly along for the ride. And besides, I was probably way outside the range of any cell tower.

The light dropped slightly, and someone knocked on the window.

"Hey," a male voice demanded from outside, "you all right in there?"

"Just a minute," I replied quickly. Dropping my legs from the sleeping bag I pulled on my wrinkled khakis. I peeked carefully through the blinds that covered the side window panel. Outside were two men, and they were not patrolmen, as I was hoping. Parked ten feet away was an idling pickup with New York plates.

"What do you want?" I asked.

"We were just passing by on the way home from night shift, saw your van, and thought we'd make sure nothing was wrong."

My hand moved toward the door handle, but then it stopped. As a few memorable scenes from the movie *Deliverance* surfaced in my consciousness, I inched my way forward to gain the driver's seat.

"I got tired last night driving through," I shouted with a confident air, "so I just pulled over to catch a few winks. I do appreciate your wake-up call, though. Couldn't have arranged a better time. I need to be getting back on the road again."

In the rearview mirror, I saw the two standing close, one reaching out to try the door.

They said nothing more.

When I turned the key, the engine thankfully started right up. In the mirror, I saw one man grab the door latch. Fortunately, I had parked the van so I could easily lunge forward onto the road east. The men backed off and ran to their vehicle, but I was around the first bend of the two-lane, Vermont, mountain highway before I could see what they were up to. I accelerated quickly up to and then beyond the speed limit. Once I reached a straightaway, I looked back until I saw their lights, far behind, but they were not gaining. I sped forward until their lights became lost in the past.

This was certainly not how I had planned to start the day. I had looked forward to waking with the sunrise, blessing it with a psalm and a cup of coffee brewed on the new 12-volt coffeemaker my Diane had given me for my birthday.

Instead, my main concern now was to calm my nerves and purge myself of the strange, slimy feeling that I may have encountered the enemy.

Most likely, those two men were just innocent locals checking out a strange, unidentified vehicle. Yet I couldn't shake the suspicion that there had been mischief afoot. Regardless, it looked like I had left them in the dust.

The red digital display blinked 5:15.

This was earlier than I had intended to awaken, but then again, maybe God had sent two angels! If there were no road tie-ups, I might make the Mite by breakfast.

I looked back with an improved attitude, but the headlights were gone.

Besides missing my coffee, I mostly regretted losing the chance to spend a few moments reflecting on the Scriptures for the coming Sunday. For the life of me, I couldn't recall what the "playbook" had allocated for the First Sunday of Lent, but, recalling the confusion caused by my last sermon, I wondered what headaches I would bring down upon myself this week.

I became lost in thought then, wondering what might be happening at the church in my absence. After quite a while though, I realized how useless worrying was, shook myself out of it, and decided to use my time more productively. Watching the otherwise empty but precariously curving road ahead—still bathed in predawn stillness, the dark pavement illumined by the van's searching headlamps and surrounded by grayish banks of dirty snow—I reached back to retrieve my large, black-leather, preacher's Bible. Inside the front cover I'd taped a list of the readings for the upcoming Lenten season. Switching on the interior light, I glanced back and forth from the road to the list and then into my Bible. The First Reading was from Deuteronomy.

Skimming the text revealed a terse summary of how God had saved Israel from Egypt. Nothing controversial there.

A car passed in the opposite direction, the first since I'd started my morning off with a lunge. The clock read: 5:45. No sign yet of the winter sun. Just the misty, snowbanked roadbed.

Flipping to what came next in the Bible, I turned then to the Gospel reading from Luke, the account of Jesus' temptation by Satan in the desert. This brought me a taste of "preacher's relief," for I'd preached on this passage at my last church, within the past year, so my prep work was mostly done. All I needed this time was a review of my notes, a quick glance at a few new commentators (per my awakened conscience), a new and improved sermon outline, and, zoom, I would be ready to go!

I focused ahead through the misty morning with a smile. God surely must have preordained this text so that I could enjoy the coming week without this additional anxiety.

Knowing this was hardly true, since this would mean that God had skewed the preaching schedules of thousands of ministers around the world merely to grant me an easy week, I glanced over to see, out of curiosity, what the Epistle Reading might be.

Another car passed, then another, and the horizon brightened as the congestion of an approaching small town increased.

I read the listing, Romans 10:8–13. I certainly should have known those verses by memory, but my mind was moving as slowly as the rising sun, so I rustled through my Bible, until I found the familiar passage. Then, with one hand holding the Word aloft, I read the text aloud: "'But what does it say? The word is near you, on your lips and in your heart (that is, the word of faith which we preach); because, if you confess with your lips that Jesus is Lord and believe in your heart that God raised him from the dead, you will be saved. For man believes with his heart and so is justified, and he confesses with his lips and so is saved. The scripture says, "No one who believes in him will be put to shame."'"

I closed the Bible and laid it upon the passenger seat, returned both hands to the wheel, stared ahead, thinking about the storm brewing from the last sermon, and said, "Good Lord, why me!"

YOU see, for many years I've recognized that there are basically three kinds of Bible verses: *clear*, *cloudy*, and *stormy*. The clear verses are those that are understood easily, whether literally or figuratively. For example, is there anything in the words "thou shall not kill" or "thou shall not commit adultery" that isn't clear, even though many in our modern world have found lots of wiggle room in both laws? Even the worst offenders know in their hearts what these verses say and mean.

Or, take that text I'd just looked up from Romans. Seems clear enough: "Confess with your lips that Jesus is Lord and believe in your heart that God raised him from the dead" and what happens? "You will be saved," period. Clear enough, and consequently most Evangelical ministers revert to those verses often.

Then there are *cloudy* verses, those that aren't quite so obvious, that need further explanation to prevent misunderstanding and especially misapplication. A good example is those verses where Jesus says to cut off your hand or pluck out your eye if it causes you to sin. We quickly need to understand that He was using hyperbole to stress how drastic we must cut sin and the occasion for sin out of our lives. When a preacher does his homework, he usually figures out the intended meaning of cloudy verses.

Some verses, though, like that Romans passage, can seem clear and cloudy at the same time. Many take that verse to teach "once saved, always saved." If you once came down front for an altar call and "accepted Jesus as your Lord and Savior," confessing "with your lips" the sinner's prayer, then "you were saved"; you'd arrived. Yet, the conundrum is that every Evangelical pastor knows someone who did just that, but at some later date drifted away into doubt, into sin, or even completely away from Christ. So was this verse not true? In such a case, a *clear* verse becomes *cloudy*, and needs further clarification: "Well, the person may have 'confessed with their lips' but they must not have truly 'believed in their heart.'" The perfect "out-clause."

Then there are those *stormy* verses—verses whose clear meaning contradicts either other verses or important doctrines. Generally, these are the verses that cause divisions between Christians, leading to schism, hatred, persecution, bigotry, even war. It's not that preachers can't come up with some explanation, it's just that the obvious meaning runs so contrary to what they believe and usually preach that most preachers just avoid them. Like good generals, they pick their battles carefully.

There were no stormy verses in this reading from Romans. There was something worse: *"a verse I never saw."* This is what I'd come to call the new, fourth category of texts I'd discovered over the past year. Let me explain. As a Bible-believing Evangelical, I always had my nose buried in the Good Book. If I wasn't preparing for some looming sermon or Bible study, I was foraging through some text in my private devotions. Since entering seminary, I'd read through the Bible twice, cover to cover, and on top of this, I was an avid proponent of Scripture memorization. If we're expected to fend off the daily onslaught of the devil the way Jesus did in the wilderness, then we'd better have our scriptural weapons primed and ready at all times—not merely in the pages of a book holding down a coffee table, but fresh in the front of our minds.

So I figured I knew the Bible as well as anyone, maybe better. Nonetheless, beginning with Stephen LaPointe's harangue at the last retreat, I'd begun discovering verses I'd never noticed before. It was as if someone was using some magical addendum wand to insert eye-popping verses that progressively began overturning my theological foundations. My only explanation was that previously I had so blindly read Scripture with my preconceived Evangelical Calvinist assumptions, that I'd merely read over and past many contradictory verses.

One such verse was the one that followed the upcoming Roman passage from the "playbook." Just four months before, I'd preached on: "How are men to call upon him in whom they have not believed? And how are they to believe in him of whom they have never heard? And how are they to hear without a preacher?" This had always been the text in which I'd found justification for my call to preach.

But then, in the process of my sermon prep, I *really* read the passage, maybe for the first time, and saw that St. Paul's statement continued on into the important next verse: "And how can men preach *unless they are sent*?"

Sent. This is no insignificant word. The word *apostle* is the Greek term for "one who is sent." In other words, St. Paul was already warning against the inauthentic preaching of self-appointed independent preachers—preachers who didn't have the right to preach in the name of Jesus. And St. Paul's first-century warning was making this twenty-first-century preacher squirm. Who now, twenty centuries later, had sent this preacher? Who had given him the authority to stand in front of a congregation and pontificate?

Certainly, as I drove along early on that quiet morning, I realized I could easily just ignore those additional verses—since the "playbook" stopped short of them. But that wasn't the point, for they brought me right back in spades to the very reason I was driving east: to hopefully talk with Stephen LaPointe.

The new snow crackled and squeaked as the Camaro's tires cautiously ascended the gravel mountain road. It was one of those crisp, bright, midwinter days when every breath, like the inhale after a strong mint, hurt a little coming in and formed a vapor trail going out. Everything about the morning reminded Raeph of the wonderful times when his father would take him up north hunting. He surveyed the leafless trunks around him, as his father had taught him, looking for horizontal lines which, besides fallen trees, might be a passing buck or wild turkey. This was but a passing diversion, for quickly he pulled his attention back to the road ahead.

Eventually, around a slow corner, a rustic wooden sign with hunter green letters loomed to the right: "THE WIDOW'S MITE LODGE: 1/2 MILE." He sped up slightly, anxious as he ascended the serpentine driveway, but then slowed back down to remain vigilant. The strobe effect of the patches of brilliant morning sun intermingled with sharp shadows played havoc with his nerves. He closed his eyes briefly to regain control, and upon opening them saw the parked cars. He jammed the brakes hard, and the Camaro started to fishtail. He let up but not before he bumped dead against a three-foot drift. A dozen or so cars were parked in an orderly way around the front of the lodge, but there was no sign of movement. Smoke rose from the stone chimney. He waited, watched. Apparently, no one had noticed him.

He gave the Camaro gas and after a brief spin, it pulled away. Raeph took a space between two new, high-end SUVs, and again paused, surveying his surroundings. Through the partially clouded lodge window he saw vague figures. His peripheral vision caught movement on the driveway. Another car. He killed the engine and hunkered down, waiting, watching. A man in a red ski jacket left his car briskly, dragging a duffle bag and briefcase, and entered the lodge. Raeph continued to linger, on the alert.

When he had found Tom Sylvan's online newsletter mentioning the Widow's Mite, it featured a link to a website dedicated to this annual retreat. There he found past photos of the groups, as well as activities such as basketball games and card tournaments, annual reports, and all kinds of miscellaneous information, including references to LaPointe. Raeph discovered that the usual group of thirty or so ministers consisted of either old seminary friends or new friends made in the heat of battles within their Congregationalist Association. Occasionally, new attendees joined, sometimes from Evangelical churches outside of Congregationalism, but generally by invitation only, and a few by word of mouth.

As he read, a bold idea had developed. *Why not merely drive up and walk right in, pretending to be a minister who had learned about the retreat from the Internet?*

Certainly he had been involved in church leadership long enough, on boards and committees, working beside enough ministers, logging sufficient sermon and Bible study ideas, sharing enough hospital and home visitations, to fake it. He probably could pull it off better than some ministers he knew!

Consequently, for the past twenty-four hours he had been pondering all the details, from every angle, concocting a new identity from some fictitious town in western Massachusetts. But again the voice of doubt harangued him: *What if they figure me out? What then? What if there's a minister from that part of Massachusetts? What if they bombard me with questions?*

In response to this potential onslaught, he decided that if caught he would merely say he was going through a time of great stress; that he had concocted his fiction as an admittedly foolish way of avoiding queries about a situation he did not want to discuss. He had come merely to listen, to pray, and be strengthened by their camaraderie. He was quite sure they would not be suspicious and delve deeper.

After several more minutes and no more arrivals, he decided it was time. Wearing his best dress shirt, tie, and navy blue blazer, he steeled his nerves, left the comfort of Ol' Red behind, and went in.

12

Gradually as if being reborn, the world along the bleak, snowbound south shore of the lower St. Lawrence River emerged on cue with the rising winter sun. Sea birds strafed the ice floes for carrion, piping their mournful calls, landing with reckless abandon, prancing about, heads cocked heavenward as if taunting the Creator. The icebreaker *Corge* out of Québec City inched its slow morning pass down the center of the channel toward the Gaspé. The cracking of the overnight freeze echoed through the morning silence.

Stephen LaPointe tore a v-shaped hole in the plastic lid of his coffee, releasing the soothing, familiar vapor, steaming up the windows of his parked car. The aroma was like a home away from home—*but then again he no longer had a home.*

A discarded copy of a Canadian newspaper on the counter of Marguerite's Diner had tempted him. The headlines that belittled the U.S.-British enforcement of the no-fly zone over Iraq were a distraction, however, that he wished to avoid.

What's the use? And what does some insanity way over there have to do with the hell in my own life right here?

Stephen was normally not so callous about the plight of people suffering in other parts of the world. He had always consciously stayed current, leading his congregations from the pulpit to pray earnestly for world peace and mercy. Now, however, after a year of second-guessing every decision and conclusion that had so disrupted his life, his depression had gotten the better of him. And it wasn't so much that he had become self-focused. He just wasn't focused at all. He questioned every goal, every direction, every purpose—and the voices within were becoming far too destructive.

He studied the birds, swooping, squawking, prancing, fighting over a lone, black remnant of fish protruding crushed from between shards of ice. A part of him had always envied the simplistic existence of God's lower creatures. Though their God-given instincts drove them to seek food, shelter, and safety, each specie nurturing offspring in its own way, still their cognition was free of the guilt and anxieties that so plagued the human heart. To them, the past never existed, the future was beyond conception, and the present was driven solely by the need to satisfy whatever momentary urge ranked highest in their sensory organs. If this meant yanking a morsel of rancid meat from the beak of a neighbor, they felt no guilt or remorse, and the deprived merely squawked without understanding and moved on.

And moved on. Such a different world. Such a free world.

Having a preacher's mind, a verse passed before his mental eye like a marquee: "If you continue in my word, you are truly my disciples, and you will know the truth, and the truth will make you free."[12] Hadn't he always trusted in this promise? Hadn't he believed that as a sincere disciple of Jesus Christ, as a pastor committed to following and proclaiming His Word, he was safe and secure to follow God's truth no matter where it led?

Well, what he had reaped was indeed freedom, but a freedom he would never have wished on an enemy. Freedom from his beloved job and vocation as a minister of Christ. Freedom from any meaningful employment. Freedom from mortgage, bills, responsibilities, and seemingly any kind of future. And most critically, freedom from his marriage and sons. He knew that some might call all this freedom, but for him it meant despair. And this outlook was compounded by the feeling that God had abandoned him, that God had played a nasty trick on him.

Stephen sipped his coffee. Two months ago, a glint of lingering hope plied his heart that things eventually would turn around. Sure, his career and vocation were admittedly derailed, but he lunged at every glimmer of light at the end of every tunnel. At forty-seven, his ministerial career was not necessarily over. Many trustworthy confidants had assured him that if he did make the jump, there would be lots of possibilities. He would just need more training, hierarchical approval, lots of patience, and of course a special dispensation, but it was possible. And his debt-free/mortgage-free existence was a blessing. He could move right in and then on through whatever vocational doors God might open.

Mostly, though, he had been certain that it would only take time and understanding to restore his marriage and his family. Surely the love he'd shared with Sara for nearly twenty years had been real; it couldn't truly end so abruptly over his change in religious convictions.

Then this seemingly hopeful tunnel of love caved in upon him.

With accelerating excitement, he had anticipated his first Christmas out of the pulpit, the first such since he was ordained twenty years before. He had not only accepted this but was looking forward to the blessed relief of being out of the limelight, free to relax in the back pew—his new, inconspicuous location of choice. As a pastor, he had always chided people to move forward, but now as the local "clergyman on the journey," he found it easier to pray without the constant gaze of the curious.

Ever since his farewell Easter sermon nearly a year before at Witzel's Notch, Stephen had not entered a Protestant church nor missed a Sunday Mass at St. Francis de Sales Parish in Jamesfield. All he had read and heard regarding the biblical symbolisms of the Mass, a "weekly rapture," so to speak, into the very worship of heaven, had proven true and more. He felt embarrassed as he recalled the hollow bareness of his own typical Evangelical Sunday "entertainment package." At the time, he had assumed he was falling in line with the latest trends advocated by the respected Protestant church growth experts: "Return to the simplicity of Acts chapter two, while at the same time doing everything to meet their felt needs." Now as he understood the centuries-old wisdom behind every line and action of the liturgy, he felt humbled and ashamed.

"So, my friend," Stephen remembered Father Bourque asking in jest as the priest robed in preparation for the Christmas Vigil Mass. "How are you handling your exile from the pulpit?"

"Exile? Actually, for once I can focus on what this evening is all about. Normally, my staff and I would be wringing our hands over whether we might disappoint those who for the first time in a year had graced us with their presence. Every year, we believed that

Christmas Eve, and Easter for that matter, had to be more moving, more inspirational, more musically impressive than the last. Honestly, I dreaded the after-worship receiving lines, which forced people to give exalted accolades—whether they meant it or not—as if I were the director of an off-Broadway play. We'd do all we could to make sure the worship service was like Jesus in the Transfiguration, but the receiving line was like Jesus in the desert, being tempted by Satan to glory in the praise."

"To some extent," the priest responded, fiddling with his buttons, "we Catholic priests experience the opposite. Sure, we have pews full of C&E Catholics, but the liturgy of the Vigil Mass changes little from year to year. Nominal Catholics doing their annual duty expect to find the same, and can get pretty huffy if they get anything different. They essentially want to come and do their duty without any unexpected, creative, choreographed challenges to their lives."

"That's funny. Protestants castigate Catholics for their slavish obligation to fulfill the Church's rules about attending Mass, yet especially at Christmas and Easter, nominal Protestants come out of the woodwork in slavish obedience to their own self-imposed rules. If the prodigal husband refused to accompany the family to Christmas Eve, there would usually be hell to pay."

A misguided altar boy caught the priest's attention. Stephen remained in the sacristy, out of the way, watching silently as the priest finished his liturgical preparations. Over his clerical blacks, the priest, with whispered words of ritual, donned his robes and surplice, each action clearly carrying symbolic meaning. Stephen recalled his own "ritual." He'd wear his best dark suit to the church. Then as the time for worship approached, he'd remove his suit coat, don his black, flowing, preaching robe, two golden stripes circling each sleeve, indicating the level he had reached in his theological studies. Over his shoulders, he'd position a seasonally colored stole. At the time, he was unaware that he was following ancient Catholic custom. Rather he was following the evolving practice of modern Protestant liturgists, whose influence had won over the local Christian bookstore. Finally, he would place around his neck the large, silver, Celtic cross his parents had given him upon ordination.

Nothing of this had been done with any sense of ritual, just habit. Yet often he would pause to pray, asking God to bless his words and leadership and to open the hearts of his congregation to the good news of the Gospel.

The meaning of the priest's behind-the-scenes rituals was a mystery to Stephen, and at that a guarded mystery. Stephen had expected Father Bourque to let him in on the secrets—one clergy convert to another still on the journey—but the priest had remained reserved. Looking back, he wondered, *Was it this unintentional slight that sealed my decision to leave?*

Once Father Bourque, with a brotherly wink to Stephen, left the sacristy behind the altar servers for the front of the church, Stephen followed, hanging back to avoid any appearance of hedging into the procession. Slipping in from the vestibule, he veered into the back pew, first genuflecting self-consciously.

Kneeling, he forced his mind to focus in prayer, but surrendered to the temptation to peer around at the full house, at the backs of hundreds of heads, some with lace coverings, many bald, most gray, and all a level more reverent than ever seen in his Protestant churches.

The music began: the organist was mediocre and the lead soprano a warbler, but Stephen didn't notice. His eyes kept drifting across and around the congregation, feeding his loneliness for the past, for his family, for his wife, for some intimate companionship. It was then that he knew he must leave. The conflicted crosscurrents of his melancholic past, his lonely present, and his directionless future drove him to panic. The altar boys had processed forward, the first hoisting a large crucifix, the others following two by two, with one lone older boy lingering behind, holding high the Book of the Gospels, his face stolid with a sense of importance. Finally came the priest, who as he passed gave Stephen a brotherly nod. But it was when the priest kissed the altar and crossed to his chair behind the pulpit that Stephen realized to what extent he had lied to Father Bourque, for he did indeed miss being in that pulpit, preaching, and leading the congregation in worship.

He could not wait one more moment. Either he made a positive step toward his future, or he surrendered dead away to the inner voices of discouragement that reveled in the mess he had made of his life.

He crossed himself and rose.

In the aisle, he genuflected toward Jesus, supposedly present, Body, Blood, Soul, and Divinity, in the tabernacle. While the priest began Mass with the Sign of the Cross, Stephen left—and not just the Christmas Eve Vigil Mass, but Jamesfield. Hurriedly, he had walked to his apartment above the hardware store, had thrown what clothes and things he had left into his car, and had headed north.

ROUSING himself from his memories of that fateful night, Stephen now glanced at his watch: 7:43. Plenty of time, but he couldn't dawdle. Ever since arriving in this northern land of his ancestry he had wanted to make this special trek, and now his window of opportunity was about to close. An hour and a half out, maybe an hour there, then an hour and a half back. Should be no problem. The question was, would this special trip be all that he had long anticipated? Or would it be nothing but a waste of time?

An aromatic steam rose from a tall stack of blueberry pancakes. A white porcelain pitcher of hot, pure, Vermont maple syrup waited nearby. Within the vicinity sat plates of scrambled eggs, buttered toast, sliced melon, and a pitcher of chilled orange juice.

"Whoa!" Daniel exclaimed, as he entered the kitchen. "Did I forget my birthday or what?"

"*Your* birthday?" William said, following close behind. "Blueberry cakes are my favorite."

"It's no one's birthday," Sara said, adding a plate of hot bacon to the feast.

"So what's the occasion?" Daniel asked.

"Well, if you'll join me in prayer first, I'll tell you." Before bowing their heads, the two brothers shared a quizzical glance. Certainly this had been their longstanding family tradition before the separation, but ever since, they had followed their mother's lead and let it slide.

"Dear God," she began, but then restarted: "Dear Father, we thank You for this food and the many ways You have blessed our lives. I … I ask You to forgive me for the problems I have brought onto our family—"

"Mom?" William interrupted.

Sara raised her hand gently to silence him. "—the problems I have brought to our family, and ask that You watch over my sons as I try to find their father and my husband." She started to tear up but struggled to keep her composure. "This we ask in Your name, Jesus, amen."

William quickly demanded, "Mom, what is going on?"

Taking her seat and unfolding her napkin upon her lap, she said, "Last night I made a decision that I should have made months ago. I'll be gone for a few days, so Daniel, I'm leaving you here alone—"

"Whoa!" Daniel beamed at the possibilities of unsupervised freedom.

"—but I expect you to check in with Mrs. Ayers next door every night. And William, it would help if you could break away from the dorm a little more often to check in on your brother. I'm going in search of your father."

The two boys looked at each other and then back to their mother.

"William, are you sure you haven't heard from him? That you don't know where he is or how I can contact him?"

"Yes, Mom. I haven't heard from him since just before Christmas, and even then he didn't say where he was. I've tried his email many times, but it just bounces back. And my friends back in Witzel's Notch know only what we do, that he's left the area."

"Mom," Daniel asked, pushing a piece of blueberry pancake around in a puddle of syrup, "I'm sorry, but I still don't get what happened with you and Da—"

William cut him short with a jab to the ribs.

"That's all right, William," Sara said, setting down her coffee. "There is a lot more about our separation that you two ought to know, to help you understand that this is certainly not all your father's fault. You see, before your father and I met, it was never my wish to be a pastor's wife. I was what your dad called a flaming liberal feminist with a grudge against marriage and family. My plans were to get a PhD in history and focus on the plight of women in America."

"You're kidding," William asked, feigning a heart attack.

Sara answered over a bite of bacon, "No, I'm not, and you better watch it," accenting her words with jabs of her fork, "I can still resurrect those feelings of subjection and servitude!"

They saw through her, though, for she was now even more a critic of "Marxist feminism" than their father.

"I was teaching high school history when I met our 'dear friend' Frank. We fell in love, got married, and tried to make it work."

She stared blankly into her plate wondering whether to 'fess all, but knew she couldn't. She had never even told Stephen the primary reason for the demise of her first marriage—the one most regrettable, unchangeable, unforgivable mistake of her life.

"I'll spare you the details, but suffice it to say that our marriage had been wrong from day one. We quickly divorced, and as a rebound I threw myself back into my studies, determined even more to pursue my career. Then I met your father. He was a seminarian and contagiously enthusiastic about his Christian faith. In time, we fell in love, against all my inner warnings—I realized what marriage to your father would mean: pastor's wife! But I loved him—and still do, very much!"

William went to her with a hug of support. Daniel ate more pancake.

"Thank you, William," hugging him back. She kissed him on the cheek as he returned to his breakfast. "In time, I got used to being a pastor's wife. I became pregnant, then again, but I suppose most significantly through all this my heart truly changed. It wasn't just an act, I really did fall in love with Jesus. I even got to like our pastoral life. I began teaching Sunday school and doing all the stuff pastors' wives do, until step by step I let my personal dreams drift away, accepting this as God's will for my—for our lives."

"But what changed?" Daniel asked, working his food systematically around his plate.

"Well, sometime during those eighteen years and three churches, your father began to question his call to ministry. There were numerous reasons, and not a few my own fault." She was tempted to scold the boys for being so rudely inattentive with the clanging of their silverware, but thought it best to ignore.

"What bothered your father most, though, was the radical difference between what he taught from what other pastors taught, all supposedly teaching from the same Bible. At night after you boys were in bed, he would tell me about it. At first, it was just in little things, but eventually he saw that in every aspect of pastoral work there was confusion and contradiction between otherwise faithful Christians. He didn't want to upset you boys, so he saved it all up for me."

"I knew," William admitted, slicing a piece of bacon.

"You did?"

"My room adjoined yours, remember. I pretty much knew all about Dad's struggles, and frankly I was cheering him on. I was glad of the prospect of no longer being a 'PK.'"

"How much else did you hear?"

Smiling as he ate his bacon, "Those walls were mighty thin."

"Well, anyway, Daniel," feigning displeasure in her older son's direction, "initially your father assumed that he was the problem, that he was not interpreting the Bible correctly. In time, though, after discussing his concerns with his pastor friends, he began questioning his Protestant faith, which as you know," a quick glare at William, "began causing tension at home. This is what led to our first separation just before he was shot."

She paused to study her sons. Daniel was listening intently, smiling supportively, but William was avoiding her eyes.

"You see, when your father concluded that he had no alternative but to quit being a pastor, I felt I had been hoodwinked, cheated out of my own dreams, out of my life. So, I decided that if he was going to abandon his calling, I was free to pick up where I'd left off. I truly didn't want us to separate, but, well, with his increasing interest in the Catholic Church, I could not follow him"—*and she was not about to be forced to tell him or her children why*. "We agreed that our separation would only be temporary, but difficulties and disagreements and miscommunications only escalated until here we are, completely out of touch."

"But what about Frank?" William demanded, placing his napkin in his lap.

She rose to refill her coffee. "Over time I guess you could say we accidentally reestablished our friendship. He had changed a lot since we divorced. He too had experienced a Christian conversion but, believe me, our relationship has never progressed beyond friendship. Honestly. Yes, since your father's and my separation, Frank has been pressing more, as you both can tell with his frequent visits, but I have remained chaste and faithful to your father."

William's troubled expression relaxed as he dug into his stack of pancakes again.

"Admittedly, there have been times when I felt lonely and rejected, when I wondered whether it was truly over between your father and me, but I have refused to give in or to give up. I know your father loves me, and still loves you. I'm sure he's alone somewhere, just trying to figure everything out."

Sara hoped she was sounding convincing. Yes, she still loved her husband and hoped beyond hope that they could get back together. But yet, did she really know Stephen anymore? It was not like him to abandon them, to hide away. At times, she was even tempted to question his mental state.

"It was Christmas that brought it all back for me. I apologize for allowing us to drift away from church. Once I was free from the pressure of being on display, always under someone's judgment, I began making excuses, and you boys weren't complaining any, though you, Daniel, seemed more committed."

"Like I said," William added, "I, too, was glad to be out of the limelight."

She continued. "But as Christmas approached, I remembered how much my life of faith with Stephen meant to me, how much I missed him and even our life together in the ministry. There are parts of being a pastor's wife that I miss—it wasn't all complaints. I miss the fellowship of prayer, the Bible studies, and the good people who sincerely love God and try to love each other. I miss the intimacy we often felt together, your father and me and Jesus." She quickly intercepted an escaping tear.

"Boys, I'm not promising anything. I might be gone for just a few days or maybe a week, but I need to do whatever I can to at least find your father and see what it will take to get us back together."

"Where are you going?" Daniel asked.

"I'm not exactly sure, but I'm going to start by going back to New Hampshire."

"Aw, Mom, can't I go with you? There are so many old friends—" Daniel pleaded.

"Not this time, Daniel. I need to do this alone. You may not remember this, but it was exactly a year ago when your father went to his annual retreat up in the mountains. It was then that most of our problems began. I may begin my search there because—who knows?—maybe he'll return there to be with his old friends. I'll keep in touch, though."

They cleaned up the kitchen, said their good-byes, and with a few final mandates, she threw her stuffed luggage into the back of the minivan she had "inherited" from their conflicted marriage, and headed west.

13

Scott Turner's Narrative

It's hard to describe the joy that rushed through my being as I ascended the gravel road to the Mite. I'd made that ascent dozens of times, but every time it seemed like a fresh opportunity to start over, to forget the past—the "old man"—and put on the new.

Ahead of me, inside those rustic wooden doors were friends who had walked the same walk, who knew the struggles and frustrations of the pastorate. Each one of us had left everything else behind, in differing degrees of course, to dedicate our lives in service to our Lord as ministers of the Gospel, and had entered seminary with idealistic expectations of the pastorate: proclaiming the Gospel full bore from the pulpit or line-by-line in a standing-room-only Bible study, leading fallen-away members remorsefully back to Christ after a pointed funeral eulogy, or inspiring teenagers to follow Christ with abandon at a weekend retreat. These had been our elevated expectations, but we gathered here every year because, to a man, few of these expectations had proven true. From week to week, our—well, my—sermons mostly just bounced off stony faces immunized to the Gospel after years of watered-down Christianity. If a dozen showed up for my Bible study, I was lucky. Funeral eulogies rarely brought anything except waxy smiles and fish handshakes. And teenagers. How can you get teenagers to take their faith seriously when their parents don't?

We all came to the Mite to cry on each other's shoulders, to share words of encouragement, to build each other up, and hopefully to return to our charges refreshed, inspired, and equipped for the true battle against the invisible Evil One—the Deceiver, the Prince of Liars—who was out to do everything possible to undercut our every effort.

As I reached the upper tier of the parking lot, I found it surprisingly empty. Every year since the retreat's inception, a minimum of two dozen or so pastors had broken from their heavy schedules, but that particular morning I could only count maybe a dozen cars. Two, maybe three, of them I could identify as regulars—especially Ron Stang's rusty, old Volvo wagon. Ron was the man whose bright idea had started this retreat.

But where was everyone? I checked my watch. Eleven forty. They should all have arrived by now.

The reason was obvious, though, and disconcerting. Stephen's tirade the previous year had spooked the regulars. I looked closely, but none of the vehicles looked like his. I parked, grabbed my bags, and headed in.

The great room was empty, meaning that the group was still huddled in the meeting room for the first presentation. I couldn't remember who was on the docket as this year's discussion leader. *Hope it wasn't me—?* I posited with a laugh, knowing that this once had happened. Four years before, Cliff had arrived ready to take it all in, only to discover that he had been scheduled to give it all out. Eventually, everyone rallied to cover his behind, and by grace it was one of our best retreats.

Not knowing to which bedroom I had been assigned, I set my bags down at the foot of the wide central stairs and made for the conference room.

"Scott Turner! Well, God love you," cried a female voice from the kitchen. "I prayed God you would come. What would it be without you?"

"Mrs. Cousineau," I exclaimed with enthusiasm. "How could I survive a year without your cooking?"

"Let me tell you something, Reverend Turner. Every year you and your friends rave over my cooking, but then in private, you joke about your need for antacids."

"*Moi!?*"

"Now just you hush," she said with a smile. "I finally realized that our French Canadian cuisine was probably a bit rich for your weak American stomachs, so this year I'm toning it all down."

"But … but … what about your cinnamon rolls? Our contract!"

"Now don't give yourself an ulcer. The rolls are here. There, look."

I glanced and saw that my long journey was not in vain. Suzette Cousineau's cinnamon rolls were worth driving halfway across America for.

"But wouldn't you agree that your stomachs might be thankful for the lack of poutines?"

I certainly was not about to expose my relief, for her homemade poutines—French fries and cheese curds smothered in gravy—always seemed to linger for days in our stomachs like bowling balls.

"I suppose, but what will Tom Sylvan do? It was always his job to supply the group with antacids." I wished I hadn't said that, and looked closely to make sure I hadn't offended her. She only smiled.

"This will just leave him more time to eat, which, between you and me, is usually quite a lot." She winked and turned away, but before retreating to the kitchen she set a plate of her famous cinnamon rolls before me. What was I to do?

As I munched away, I pondered who might have come and heard from the meeting room the voice of Ron Stang. That was strange in itself. Ron was the organizer who always delegated discussion leadership to some other regular member. *Why was he teaching?* I listened longer, to identify any other voices, but the room was strangely quiet.

I cautiously opened the door, poked my head in, and half the room erupted.

"Scott!" Ron exclaimed, and other familiar faces rose to greet me. A half-dozen new faces merely turned, looking blankly from their seats.

"Sorry I'm late. I drove all night and actually got here earlier than expected."

"Great to see you," said Terry Darcy, shaking my hand. Terry was a regular who normally remained quietly on the fringe, but with the more outgoing regulars absent, he had ascended in the pecking order as a representative of tradition.

Besides Terry and Ron, there were only four other familiar faces: Larry Wycliffe, an ex-Marine whose life-changing conversion to Jesus in a Korean P.O.W. camp still fed his pastoral ministry with limitless enthusiasm; Birch Herbert, a fine pastor whose role at these retreats was usually one of comic relief; Tom Sylvan, known most for his wide girth but by far the best preacher of the bunch; and Kyle Reuther, an extraordinarily gifted, confident, yet gentle pastor whose recent pastoral assignment had gained the reputation here as the definitive "congregation from hell." My heart sank as I reconciled myself to the absence of the three I'd most hoped to see.

"Please, Ron, don't let me break the flow of things," I said, taking a seat in the back.

"Actually, this is a good excuse to conclude the first session and break for lunch."

"Sounds good to me," Birch quipped, dropping into a sprinter's stance. The regulars laughed as expected. The new members showed reserve.

Ron closed with prayer, and the room emptied for the lunch counter. I greeted with affection my friends as well as the newcomers, but one stood out as different from the rest: a short, muscle-bound man, about my age, the only one wearing a sport coat. He looked like guys I knew in high school with good weight-room work habits and big dreams: if they only had a few more inches in height, they'd qualify for the front line of any football team in America. Besides his suit fitting awkwardly, which is not uncommon with strong men, he looked a little bedraggled, but like myself he may have driven all night.

I extended my hand, greeted him, and he responded with a guarded smile and a strong but brief handshake.

I ended up last in line, but since the fare was as extensive as ever, I had no problem filling my plate. I started for a table, but from behind, Ron grabbed my elbow. "Let's talk." He motioned me to a table set apart, across the room.

"So, Ron, need I ask the obvious?"

He started to answer, but then noticed Terry gesturing for permission to join us. Ron waved him off, and Terry relented benignly. I wondered whether Ron had an agenda.

"No need to, and it's more than the lowest attendance so far that troubles me. Even the regulars who made it seem cautious about being here."

"Again the obvious: because of Stephen?"

"And Jim and maybe even Cliff."

"Cliff?"

"Seems he's contaminated with the same discontent. He hadn't registered, as usual, so I called his office. When I asked for the pastor, someone new said Cliff had resigned unexpectedly in November. He refused to explain further. Like all of us, Cliff had skeletons in his closet, but nothing that would necessitate resignation, so I presume he's succumbed to his friend's arguments."

I had not anticipated this. Not at all. I feigned disinterest.

"What about the new folk? All friends?"

"Mostly. Four came with friends, two by word of mouth, but that other one, there." He nodded slightly toward the man in the sport coat, sitting alone, devouring an overflowing plate of Mrs. Cousineau's spaghetti. "He's who we need to talk about."

"Never seen him."

"Me neither. Walters. Says his name's the Reverend Raeph Walters from the First Congregational Church of some small town called Samstead in western Massachusetts."

"Never heard of it."

"Well, Scott, now that's the problem. He said he read about the retreat on our website."

"I told you it would help entice new members."

"Soon after he arrived, I ran a web search. There was no particular reason to be suspicious, but I was checking my emails anyway and was curious. There is no Reverend Raeph Walters anywhere, and there is no First Congregational in Samstead. In fact, there is no Samstead, Massachusetts."

"So why the charade?"

"I don't know," Ron said, a distracting piece of spaghetti dangling from his mouth. "But he's not right, somehow. He's evasive, hangs back, his eyes keep flitting around. All through breakfast and our first meeting, he kept staring at the front door, watching, as if waiting for someone."

I glanced over, and sure enough, he was seated facing the front door. It was clear that he wanted to see without being seen by someone entering. But who?

"So, Ron, is this some spy from Association headquarters checking up on us conservative subversives?"

"Don't I wish. The liberals in Minnesota could care less about what a few fanatics are saying or doing out here in New England. No, there's something else going on, and I suppose we ought to find out sooner than later. The one thing we don't need this year is another surprise."

"Okay, so what'cha gonna do?"

Ron smiled.

"Me? Why me?" I asked.

"He knows I'm the retreat leader. If I cull him out, he'll know something's up. But if you invite him, say, to hang back for a bit before the next discussion, say, over there in the great room by the fire, you might be able to figure him out."

"I could repeat, 'why me?', but who else, right?"

He smiled and sipped his coffee.

"Hey, what can I say? I owe you far too much, old pal," I said, leaving unsaid the debt I owed this fine Christian brother who'd always been there by email or phone to answer any pastoral question.

He patted my shoulder as he got up with his half-eaten lunch and, grinning, said, "Let me know what you discover."

For a few minutes, I studied my quarry. He had two focal points: his food and the front door. Occasionally he peered around to see if anyone was watching him—I quickly turned away to focus on something else inane. In time he emptied his plate and, following everyone else's lead, deposited his tray in the kitchen. He thanked Mrs. Cousineau with sincerity and started milling about amongst the small crowd. Time to move.

"Excuse me," I said, divesting myself of my tray, "first time here?"

"That's right," he answered. His attention turned to a convenient table of magazines. The first one he picked up, though, he dropped as if it were infected with anthrax. He turned to face me, a look of horror on his face. Guess he didn't know the Cousineaus the way we regulars did. They were good Christian folk who ran a great retreat lodge. They were, however, lifelong Catholics, and though they never pressed their faith overtly, they left Catholic magazines, books, and other literature lying about just in case a roving eye might find them intriguing. Apparently, Reverend Walters did not.

"My name's Scott Turner," I said, extending my hand. As he took it, hesitantly, I studied him for any reaction. Guess it's my self-centeredness surfacing, always wondering whether anyone remembers. But no reaction. "How'd you find out about us?" I motioned him to two seats in front of the fire. Ron was corralling everyone else to the opposite side of the room.

"The Internet, and from an old pastor friend."

"Really, who was that, if I may ask?"

"Well, actually an old friend I haven't seen in a while." Surveying the room as he spoke, he continued. "I was hoping to surprise him, but he doesn't seem to have come. Reverend Stephen LaPointe. Are you expecting him?"

I fumbled with my coffee, spilling some on my pants.

"Here's a napkin," he said, studying my distress.

"Thanks. Stephen LaPointe, you say. To be honest, I was hoping to see him myself. He and I go back a long way. Were the two of you coworkers or did you meet through the Association?"

The stranger got to his feet, observing, "Hey, it looks like the next session is starting."

"Reverend Walters or whoever you are," I pressed, "why are you here?"

"What do you mean?"

"We checked the Internet. There were no hits for a Reverend Raeph Walters, or First Congregational Samstead, or even for a town called Samstead. So why the charade?"

His eyes stayed away. "Okay, you caught me, but it's not what you might think."

"What might I be thinking?"

He loosened his seldom worn tie. "This past year has been hell. I needed to get away, and, on the way here, I decided to be someone else for a few days, as if that way I could leave it all behind."

"Sorry to hear of your bout with hell, but you've come to the right place. There's always a few of the guys every year on the verge of cashing it all in. Merciless church boards or high-handed pillar families or radical feminist coworkers or unforgiving front-pew fanatics, we've all faced them and have helped each other through 'em."

But as I studied him, his explanation still didn't quite fit, so I asked, rising to regain a common playing field. "But all that aside, I still don't understand what else I might have been thinking? Why else might someone like yourself be lying his way into a private retreat of Evangelical Congregationalist ministers?"

"Uh," he hesitated. His face went as blank as a computer monitor in a thunderstorm, and then he suddenly made for the front door. I moved to block his escape. He was a solid water plug of a guy, but I was a half-foot taller and buried him in my shadow.

For some reason the thought struck me: "And what does your being here have to do with finding Stephen LaPointe?"

At that he bolted. He tried a fake, a right-left-right job I'd seen a thousand times from amateur halfbacks, so he didn't get far. One of us slipped or something because, before I knew it, we were wrestling all over the floor. I quickly ate my previous thought, for he was more than a handful. By then everyone had caught wind of the skirmish and formed a perimeter.

Eventually Ron commanded, "That's enough, Reverend Walters, or whatever your name is."

At first he refused to quit, but one glare from the shocked Mrs. Cousineau and he relented.

"What do you think you're doing in my house! Get up both of you! You're acting like a couple of teenagers."

"Yes, Mrs. Cousineau," I said meekly. I wanted to shout, "He started it," but that would have only confirmed her point.

"Sorry, ma'am," my opponent said sheepishly.

I felt like the two vanquished heroes groveling at the dinner table before Maureen O'Hara in *The Quiet Man*. "We meant no harm."

We picked up the table and chairs we'd overturned, while Ron motioned the rest of the group to give us space.

"So what's it gonna be?" I asked the stranger.

Shaking his head, he replied, "I'm sorry, Reverend Turner ... Reverend Stang."

"Come on, let's talk ... privately," Ron said, indicating the back hallway. As the three of us proceeded single file, the stranger turned, flexing stiffness out of a shoulder, and asked, "Geez, you play football or something?"

We entered what the Cousineaus called their study, a small oak-paneled room, lined wall to wall, ceiling to floor with books. In the early days of our retreats, we would explore this private library with reserved awe as to how and why this otherwise down-to-earth, blue-collar couple accumulated such an extensive collection of not only popular novels and lay religious self-help books but scholarly reference works as well. We learned in time that they had many friends—priests, deacons, and laity—who like us loved this mountain retreat and had donated this cache of religious treasures.

In time, however, we retreatants avoided the library because to our dismay we discovered that nearly all the books were of the Catholic persuasion, some even containing apologetic challenges to our Protestant faith. Every once in a while, someone would bring out a book exclaiming, "Hey, guys, listen to this," which would usually lead to a round of demeaning laughs or sometimes to lively, even heated theological discussions and a few ruffled feathers. So we quit using the library, and because of that, it seemed now the most secluded place to interrogate our deceptive visitor.

The three of us took seats facing inward. The stranger squinted as light from the only window cast a brilliant beam across his face. I imagined a cell in some old spy movie. Ron noticed too and pulled the curtains.

"Scott, how about bringing us some coffees? Want anything in yours?" Ron asked the stranger.

"No, thank you. Just black."

"Sure," I said, leaving reluctantly. Assuming Ron was taking advantage of our unanticipated "good cop/bad cop" arrangement, I hurried to the counter to afford a quick return, which in this group was impossible.

"Hey, Scott," Larry Wycliffe asked, pulling me aside with a nod. "What's up?"

Larry was not only a regular but a respected leader in the group, so his inquiry was valid.

Focusing my attention on the coffees, I asked, "Have you ever seen that man? All the information he gave us, his name, town, and church, is fictitious. Ron's in there starting the third degree."

"Never. I did notice him, though, when he first arrived. He was obviously a newcomer, feeling his way around the place. Birch greeted him, but the man was standoffish. What's the problem?"

"Don't know. Here, help me transport these, and I'll let you know what we find out."

We began our trek across the expansive great room.

"You sure have a way of welcoming strangers!" Tom Sylvan called, crossing from the conference room. "Actually, you might have something there. Every year we have our three-on-three basketball championships, but maybe it would be good to add other sports like Greco-Roman wrestling."

"Very funny, Tom, or maybe sumo wrestling?"

"Yeah, right," he responded with a smirk. As he turned his wide girth away, wider every year, I wished I could reclaim my words.

We pushed onward. At the door, I took all three drinks. "Thanks, Larry. I'll let you know," and backed into a lull in the discussion. Ron was standing with his back to me, staring out the window.

The stranger took the coffee with kind appreciation, and drank quietly. Ron accepted his and said, "Raeph, why don't you start from the beginning for Scott. He's a longtime friend of Stephen, and will find what you've said quite interesting."

"Well, my real name's Raeph Timmons." By then he had removed his tie. "I'm not a pastor, though I am a committed, active member of my church back home. Why am I here? Well, to be honest, I'm not completely sure. You see, more than ten years ago, Reverend LaPointe was my pastor back in Red Creek, Vermont."

He then recounted his past relationship with Stephen and a man named Walter Horscht, who had become concerned about Stephen and some of his views. Pacing the room, Raeph froze for a second in front of a shelf of books. His head jerked back as if shocked, he glanced back at us questioningly, and then resumed pacing.

"Let's just say, to simplify everything, that Walter was obsessed with conspiracy theories and became disturbed by LaPointe's Catholic leanings. He was so convinced that Reverend LaPointe was a papist that he shot him."

"Your friend was the man that did that?" I demanded, looking over at Ron, who stood there, white-faced.

"Yes, but thankfully, Reverend LaPointe survived."

"But how could he—" Ron began.

"Listen, if you were convinced that an evil man, an enemy of Christ, was stealing your daughter's soul away, what would you do? That's why he did what he did, and he died for it."

Needing to get into the meeting, Ron demanded, "So why are *you* here and why are *you* looking for Stephen?"

Beginning to pace again, Raeph continued, "What I said earlier was true, this past year's been hell. I feel exactly like Job: I've lost everything in my life, my wife, my sons, and my job, but on top of this I fully realize now that I'm to blame for my best friend Walter's death."

"You?" I demanded. "What did you have to do with Stephen's shooting?"

He turned to face me with no sign of fear. "Because I'm the one that fed Walter's conspiracy theories. Because he thought I agreed with everything he believed and did."

"Did you?" Ron asked.

He continued to study me for a moment before he turned to answer Ron. "Yes, at one time, but I'm not so sure what I believe anymore."

"But again," I retorted, "why are you here, looking for Stephen?"

He turned back to me straight on: "To determine whether Walter's sacrifice was justified or a groundless waste of a good man's life. All the things Walter believed were based on real observations of what Reverend LaPointe preached and taught."

"Like what?"

"Well, that the Bible cannot be trusted as the foundation of our faith; that the Church, not the Bible, is the foundation of truth; that contraception is a sin, which only Catholics believe."

Now I knew how Stephen's concerns were being received and interpreted by at least two of his members.

"So, Raeph," I asked, "do you agree with your friend's conclusions?"

"I don't agree with what he did, but with nothing left in my life, I believe that God's calling me to confront Reverend LaPointe, to either confirm or disavow Walter's suspicions—to erase the question mark that sits at the end of Walter's life."

"Are you doing this for God, or for Walter, or for yourself?" I asked.

"I guess it's hard to say." He dropped his focus, sipped his coffee, and when he looked back up, our eyes met, and, in a way I cannot explain, my heart changed. Maybe it was my pastoral heart, but somehow in that moment I knew this man to be a brother. Everything about him screamed sincerity. Here was a man, a good man, who desperately needed a friend. From within the convoluted implosion of his world, one could see why this man of God would seek a Job-like explanation behind everything, a hidden, purposeful meaning, a calling and a task to be completed. Apart from this he might give up on tomorrow. For all these reasons, he needed a God-fearing friend from outside the disintegration of his life, to help him hear more accurately the leading of his Savior.

"Ron," I said, "why don't you go ahead and check on the meeting?"

Our eyes met for a moment, then he said, "Oh, sure," and left.

"Raeph," I said, motioning him to sit, "we have a lot more in common than you might think. I've certainly not experienced the tragedies you have, but right now I, too, am trying to find direction, though no one in my life knows this—neither my wife nor my children nor any of these close friends here at the Widow's Mite. And like you, I believe the answer to my quest for meaning and direction somehow involves finding Stephen LaPointe. It was his words at this retreat last year that initiated a crisis in my thinking, in my pastoral work, and in my understanding of who I am."

"What was it he said?" Raeph asked.

"Maybe I'll tell you later, but suffice it to say, Stephen himself was on a spiritual journey that eventually forced him to resign from his pastorate. Then I lost track of him, which was partially my fault. No one here knows what happened to him. I hoped he might show up, but given what happened last year, I now know that's just not possible. I told my wife I was coming to get recharged with these old friends, but really, the primary reason I came was to find Stephen."

"So you have no idea where he is?"

"No, but how would you like to help me find him?"

A grin replaced the sadness on his face. "What else have I to do?"

I extended my hand, and we clasped in friendship.

"Your grip is not like any pastor's I've felt before," he admitted, jokingly.

"Just a residual from my days in football."

"Football? You aren't *the* Scott Turner that played for Massachusetts?"

I nodded, surprised that it had taken him so long.

"I remember you! Even remember that game you got hurt, when you got blindsided—"

There was a knock on the door, then Ron poked his head in. "Everything all right?"

"Yes, just fine," I answered, glad to change the subject. "Come in a second." Waiting until he'd closed the door behind him, I continued, "Looks like Raeph and I may not be sticking around for the rest of the retreat," and with that I explained our departure.

❧ 14 ❧

Several hours earlier, three hundred miles to the frozen north, Stephen stood for one last time, bundled against the cold, staring out over the partially frozen expanse of the St. Lawrence River. There was little but snow between the southern shoreline and the ground where he stood in the primitive graveyard near the town of Rivière Ouest, Québec. The river itself was broken into channels. Along both the near and distant shores, nearly five miles across, were massive piles of brackish ice floes, some reaching into the air as high as thirty feet. Down the middle, the water flowed freely out to the sea, the channel having been kept open by icebreakers as well as the constant passing of freighter traffic. Today the wind swept the passing gray water into white breakers. Beyond the river and the tidal plains, the Laurentian Mountains rose blue and mysterious, forming a surreal portrait of this northern land opening wide to the sea.

Americans tend to think of Cape Cod, New York harbor, Chesapeake Bay, or even the Mississippi River as the primary access to the sea and the world beyond. But in truth it was through the mouth of this tremendous northern river—which starts in its headwater somewhere up in the north woods beyond Wisconsin, flowing through the Great Lakes, over Niagara Falls, northeast past Montreal, Trois-Rivières, and Québec, out around the Gaspé Peninsula—that the first explorers of the northern New World found entrance. It was only due to our American arrogance that this truth was softened, denigrated, and ignored.

This was one of many things Stephen had learned to appreciate on his quest north. Now, however, he must return.

He shifted his gaze away from the magnificent river, back to the bleak cemetery expanding before him, reflecting brilliantly the morning sun. It made him think of how New York City might appear if it were buried in fifty feet of ice and snow. Unidentifiable stones and statues of random height and shape jutted up before him like the frozen figures crowding the palace of the White Witch in his sons' treasured Narnian world.

He glanced at his watch. 9:17. He had nearly four hours before he was expected for his shift at the shrine.

SINCE early January, Stephen had been volunteering part-time at a national shrine dedicated to St. Anne. He'd gotten this job on a very serendipitous invitation. A few days after arriving in Québec, after deciding he wasn't ready to return to the confusion of his life back in the States, Stephen stopped by the shrine on a whim. Father Bourque had once mentioned an old priest friend serving there as a chaplain to pilgrims. When he inquired, however, he discovered that the priest was away on sabbatical.

In disappointment, Stephen started to turn away, but the religious brother who had greeted him began probing gently into his situation. Before he knew it, Stephen was invited to work part-time as a guide. The shrine was shorthanded during the off-season, but needed help with crowd control due to an unexpected increase of pilgrims. For his service, he was offered the use of the cabin, owned by one of the shrine's faithful benefactors.

Stephen admitted he knew next to nothing about Catholic shrines in general and this one in particular. (He didn't let on, however, that he still was not too keen on praying to St. Anne, the grandmother of Jesus.) But the brother assured him he was only to assist with the many busloads of pilgrims, helping them get oriented to the shrine, find the restrooms, and answer any questions he could; others, including a Sister Ursula, would take over from there.

In the weeks that followed, Stephen learned a lot about the practice of popular Catholic devotions. He observed thousands of Catholics—lay, priests, and religious—arriving in bus caravans from all over the northeastern USA and Canada, as they knelt before the statues, pictures, and tabernacles, fingering their beads and mumbling their prayers. Sadly, he found little free time to have any lengthy, thoughtful discussions with the religious brothers, sisters, or priests. This, however, was partially his fault, because usually he escaped from the shrine once his shift was over at five, either to drive into Québec City to enjoy the pseudo-European ambiance, or to return to the solitude of his cabin for a simple dinner and to read, pray, and relax.

He had hoped becoming ensconced in the work of the shrine would nudge him along in his intellectual and spiritual journey, but the confusing dialectic between what Catholic books say Catholics believe and what he saw Catholics doing in their devotions only pushed him deeper into the mire of uncertainty.

One afternoon, for example, he heard loud voices coming from the otherwise reverent atmosphere of the enormous upper gallery. He walked forward to see whether there was something he could do to help and saw two elderly women kneeling side by side in the front pew, their heads covered with white lace mantillas. As he moved closer, he overheard their argument, coming in backwoods Maine English:

"You went to the 'Glory be' too soon! There's still two more 'Aves.'"

"There are not. You just can't follow the beads anymore with those arthritic fingers of yours!"

"My arthritic fingers? For over eighty years I've prayed the rosary and who are you—"

Stephen had backed away and out of the shrine, realizing this was way out of his league.

NOW he stood, gazing across the expanse of an old, French Canadian cemetery. "Idiot!" he said aloud, berating himself for thinking that he could merely stroll into the cemetery and, *voila*, there it would be. He opened a rusty iron gate constructed of interlaced fleurs-de-lys and entered into the maze of masked graves.

Glancing from side to side as he shuffled haphazardly forward, he noticed another entrance at the opposite end of the cemetery grounds and the back of what appeared to be a large sign. He hurried toward this through the drifted snow, and on the reverse side, he discovered the cemetery directory.

The glass covering was cracked and encrusted with ice. After several minutes of scraping with an expired credit card, he was able to see that the cemetery at some point far in the past had been divided into regions named after French saints. Only a few actual graves were named, but fortunately the directory indicated that what he was looking for was in a region off to his left dedicated to St. Eutropius. Excited, he blew into his frigid hands and plunged forward, until finally he found that for which he had traveled nearly three hundred miles.

It had taken Stephen weeks to discover the existence of this memorial, and then only by accident. He had been perusing a website run by amateur genealogists focusing on his LaPointe family tree, when he stumbled upon a chat-room thread from a distant, unknown LaPointe relative describing how much he'd enjoyed a recent pilgrimage to the family shrine. The dialogue revealed the location, and now this morning, possibly his last morning in Canada, he was standing before a memorial to the first of his ancestors to enter the New World.

When he reached what seemed to be the correct site, he noticed that the grave marker before him was certainly not the original. At first glance, it stood as nothing more than a nameless gray monolith. Recognizing that his expired credit card was unequal to the task, he began searching for something else to clear away the caked ice and snow.

As a child, Stephen had been told nothing about his ancestry or the origin of his name, LaPointe. He presumed his parents had not intended to keep this from him, but that they themselves just didn't know. His father's family was small, with few aunts and uncles and none who lived near enough to visit. Stephen's grandparents had both died before he was born, so as far as he knew, his ancestral history followed them to the grave. In time, he had discovered that his surname was French, but it wasn't until a few years ago that he had begun uncovering clues about his family's history, and this hadn't been difficult. Thanks to the Mormons and modern technology, the data was merely sitting there, waiting to be plucked.

Back when he was the pastor of Witzel's Notch, while perusing the Internet, he had stumbled across the first information that eventually enabled him to trace his family tree, ancestor by ancestor, back to the first LaPointe that had crossed from France to what was then called New France in 1667. Jean Pierre LaPointe, a single man in his twenties, had sailed across from Brouage, France, as an indentured servant to the struggling wilderness settlement of Québec. After seven years of indentured service in this bleak wilderness, none of which is recorded except for the purchase of a cow and his marriage to Xainte Marie Dit Chatillon Mignault, he either purchased or was rewarded land on the southeast shore of the St. Lawrence River, near the present site of Rivière Ouest. Eventually his children and children's children expanded into other farms along the south shore, some migrating west to find more land and opportunities for work, until soon after the War of 1812, Charles LaPointe purchased land along the west shore of Lake Erie, south of Detroit, near a settlement aptly named Frenchtown. Five generations later, Stephen was born, but by then all of this history had been forgotten.

But why? What was the mystery? The answer was there in the data, but it wasn't until this past year that the riddle began making sense. All of this French Canadian family history came by way of baptismal, marriage, and burial records. All of these records were in French and, of course, Catholic. Initially, this made no more particular difference to Stephen than the fact that he was using Mormon databanks. Then, however, when he found himself unexpectedly exploring the Catholic faith, as if in a flash of awareness, he realized that his own heritage was French Catholic. Apparently, his great-grandfather was the first LaPointe of record to marry outside the Church, to a Congregationalist emigrant from Northumberland England. This led to a division in the family, but the real scandal ensued when this marriage ended in divorce. It seems his great-grandfather was a less than honorable man, abandoning his wife and one-year-old son, and eventually getting caught up in the bootlegging racket of "Roaring-Twenties" Chicago. As a result, Stephen's grandfather was raised a Congregationalist and a nominal one at best. By the time Stephen had come along, none of his close family was Catholic, and his parents had never referred to his Catholic ancestry.

"*Bonjour.*"

Stephen jumped and threw the last dregs of his cold coffee high into the air.

"*Pardonez moi, monsieur; je n'ai pas entendu vous effrayer!*" A tall, imposing young man in his midtwenties stepped back to avoid the deluge. He was encased like a cocoon in a one-piece, tan snowmobile suit. To Stephen, he looked comically like a Canadian storm trooper, holding out before him, like an armed bazooka, a large whiskbroom. His broad smile indicated he had enjoyed his dramatic entrance.

"Good morning," Stephen answered, brushing his pants dry.

"So sorry, mister. You from around here?" The young man said with a laugh in natural English.

"No, just visiting."

"So I suspected. Can I help you find something? A particular name on a headstone? I only assist the graves-keeper a few mornings a week, but I've come to know the place pretty well."

"I think I've found it," he said, pointing toward the memorial.

"Oh, you've come to see our family monument. What do you think of it?"

"Well, I don't know. Can't seem to make hide nor hair of it," Stephen said with a smirk.

"Oh, right." The stranger moved up to the stone and began brushing away the snow. In time, the inscription became clear:

JEAN PIERRE LAPOINTE

After brushing away a path back to Stephen, he continued: "I know it means nothing to the rest of the world, but all of us Canadian LaPointes owe our existence to the bravery of this man."

"You're a LaPointe?"

"*Oui.* A direct descendant of this very man. In fact, my grandfather lives on land that has been in the family for over three hundred years."

"You can't be serious. That's older than the US of A."

"You're telling me? We LaPointes were here before any of the ancestors of your country's Founding Fathers."

"Well, then, I guess I can share your boast. I may be from Michigan, but my name's Stephen LaPointe, so you and I must be distant cousins."

"Then welcome to LaPointe land. My name's Charlie. Charlie LaPointe," he said, extending his hand.

For a moment, they stood together considering silently the epitaph before them. Eventually, Stephen spoke up, "You mentioned 'bravery' when you described our mutual grand ancestor. Do you have more information about him than is posted on the Internet?"

Charlie now took the stance of the resident scholar, his arms crossed upon his upturned broom. "Not particularly, considering I'm probably the one that posted it. Most of the LaPointes who care anything about our past want nothing to do with the Internet; the rest don't care at all."

"How then did you get involved?" Stephen couldn't quite envision this large Nanook of the North crouching over a keyboard.

"My whole life, my grandfather Charles Pierre—for whom I was named—has told me stories about our ancestors, taking me on outings to places he claimed were sites where former LaPointes had lived or plowed fields or even fought battles against you rebel Americans from the south. I grew up thinking we were the most important family in Canada. 'Course I learned later that this was hardly true. LaPointes have always been the bottom rung of society. Farmers, soldiers, fishermen, trappers, and now just mostly salesmen, or like me, a bouncer. But when the older LaPointes pooled their money to build this shrine, it kind of got me thinking about my own life, how much I probably owe this man. I certainly wouldn't be here if it wasn't for him, but even more than that, nearly 350 years ago, long before any of the everyday technologies we depend upon and take for granted were even thought of, he left everything he knew—his family and friends in France—got on a boat to sail two thousand miles across an open sea to a nearly unexplored land, without any hope of returning. What information we have indicates that he came to these shores as a single man. Had he left to escape a broken heart, or possibly from the law, we don't know. But he came without any expectation of meeting a woman to marry. As grandfather would always say, Jean Pierre was not unlike Abraham, when he was called to leave everything familiar behind, to leave Ur for what he was told would be the promised land. Jean Pierre LaPointe left France for what he believed would be his future promised land. It turned out to be a very difficult land, but it has been a good land, for him and his descendants."

Again they stood together in silence. The sun was higher in the sky but still only a glowing disk behind the cold morning fog. The cries of seagulls gave an eerie tinge to the otherwise pensive silence. A passing truck broke their reverence.

"So, you came all the way from Michigan just to see this monument?" the young man said, removing the weight of his bulk from the spindly carcass of his broom.

"Not exactly," Stephen replied, stuffing his hands in his pockets.

"Then business or pleasure?"

"Neither, really. I guess you could say I'm here on retreat, trying to decide which direction to take with my life."

"So, d'you lose your job or something?" He lowered his lance and resumed sweeping.

"Or something." Stephen examined this long-lost cousin, and strangely sensed a kindred spirit. A voice within seemed to whisper, "Tell this young man; he was sent here to help."

"You see, until recently I was an ordained Protestant minister, but after a lot of study and prayer and soul-searching, I resigned."

"Lost your faith, I guess," Charlie said with a chuckle, looking up from his work.

"No, not that. I still love my Lord and loved my work as a minister. I just, well," he paused, but then presuming on the sympathies of this surely Catholic, French Canadian cousin, he continued, "I found myself unexpectedly drawn to the Catholic Church."

"Now why would you want to go off and do such a foolish thing?" He had to retrieve the handle of his broom which had slipped from his grip.

"What?"

"What could possess you to be drawn to the papist church?"

"I'm sorry, I presumed you French Canadian LaPointes would be Catholic?"

Charlie returned to sweeping the path. "The older ones still cling to their superstitions, but I'm beyond that. In all the years my parents dragged us kids to Mass, I never heard one thing that made any sense. Everything was a warning or an obligation, or some syrupy devotion before some ugly figurine goddess. My life has been a whole lot more pleasurable ever since I kissed that club good-bye."

"But this shrine? Your devotion to it?"

"It's a memorial. Get it? Memorial. Like that supposed magic they call the Eucharist. That's just a memorial to some Jew who may or may not have lived centuries ago, who may or may not have died on a cross, and who certainly did not rise from the dead. This memorial is in honor of our common ancestor who brought our family to this continent. It reminds us of his bravery, but also reminds us that he died. Period. It, therefore, reminds us that all we got is the short time we've got. Make the most of it. And that's what I intend to do." With that, he gave a final sweep of the broom and headed toward his pickup, parked nearby.

"But—"

"And good luck in your search, ex–Reverend LaPointe," Charlie quipped as he reached the door, "but you'll have no sympathies from me. You're just exchanging one myth for another." A quick start-up and he was gone.

Stephen returned his attention to the memorial. He reread the epitaph, doing the best he could to guess the French. Looking around, Stephen noticed behind him a stone bench beneath a tree. Brushing away the snow, he sat down, hands in his overcoat pockets. He wondered who was worse off: his lonely ancestor who had fought the bleakness of this uninhabited wilderness centuries before, or himself?

A year ago he had been a successful pastor with a large staff, a growing congregation, and a burgeoning budget. From the congregation's perspective, all was well. On the home front, life indeed could be testy, but God had blessed his family. William always excelled in his studies and sports, and though he would chafe from the pressures of being a "PK"—"pastor's kid"—he was a good, solid Christian young man, with no smudges on his public record. At times, Sara and Stephen had bemoaned their son Daniel's seeming addiction to his video-game world, but so far his grades were perfect, plus he had enough other interests, such as soccer, to keep them from worrying too much. Like all ministerial couples, operating under the relentless observation of their congregations, Sara and he had had their struggles. Nothing, however, that would have suggested that their marriage was in jeopardy. *If only he hadn't started the ball rolling last year at the Mite.*

But he really couldn't blame that weekend, for the trouble had begun brewing years before within his heart. The Mite was merely the occasion when he thought he could safely check his sanity with trusted friends. Certainly, he had been wrong before in his life, but never so wrong. Within three months, the repercussions of that retreat would leave him without a job, without a vocation, separated from his family, and essentially without the majority of his friends from the adult years of his life.

In this way, he felt a unique kinship with that long-lost ancestor—except that, as far as he knew, Jean Pierre LaPointe arrived on these shores with a job, at first an indentured servant, but in time an independent farmer, clearing a bleak, forested wilderness by hand with no electricity, petroleum-powered machinery, or True-Value Hardware stores. Stephen laughed at the absurdity of this comparison, driven by the self-centeredness of his depression.

This place was so beautiful, though; so meaningful to the past he had newly discovered. The temptation returned: *Couldn't I just stay up here and start over?* Few at home seemed to care anymore, and no one here knew of his past. He could literally live out St. Paul's confession: "Forgetting what lies behind and straining forward to what lies ahead, I press on toward the goal for the prize of the upward call of God in Christ Jesus."[13]

But this, of course, would mean turning his back on everything else St. Paul had taught, especially: "Husbands, love your wives, as Christ loved the church and gave himself up for her."[14] The answer was always the same: there were far too many loose ends in his life, far too many eternally important commitments from which he could not run away, the greatest, of course, being his marriage and family.

This was one commitment he refused to break, for he missed them all desperately.

But do they want me?

Stephen's decisions had so alienated the people he most loved in this world and so disrupted their lives that he was plagued by the constant apprehension that they would never forgive him or accept him back.

It had been nearly nine months since he had last heard Sara's voice. Their final phone conversation, about the sale of their home, had ended in an argument, with a receiver slammed in his ear. He had hoped his emails to William might bring healing, but William's responses had seemed to grow bitter and terse, short and sweet, and noncommittal. Then no answers at all.

For the thousandth time, he asked himself, *Did I make the right decision? Imagine how different our lives would be if I had just shelved all my doubts and concerns about the contradictions in my Protestant pastorate and faith, shoved them out of sight, and just kept on keeping on. I would now be a senior pastor, content as a bug in a rug, and Sara, William, Daniel, and I would be happy and together.*

His free fall into self-absorption was broken by the approach of an older couple who were processing solemnly through the cemetery. Seemingly unaware of his presence, they halted before a newer grave. The woman, as if on cue, crouched painfully to deposit a small wreath of flowers and a picture. They crossed themselves, stood for a moment in silence, re-crossed themselves, and then trod solemnly back to their car.

When the engine noise had receded into silence, Stephen stood up. At the grave, he saw that the wreath was a circle of cheap plastic flowers. Either it was all they could afford, or they felt it would stand up better to this northern winter. The picture was a maudlin painting of Mary, pointing with her right hand to a graphic rendition of her bleeding heart, pierced with many arrows. It was of the style of Catholic religious art Stephen had not yet learned to stomach.

The name on the stone was partially blocked by the old couple's gift of devotion, but the last letters indicated that buried before him was another LaPointe. He started to move on, but curiosity drew him back. Reaching down, he nudged the wreath, and was shaken to his core. The stone read: "Stephen LaPointe. Born March 2, 1954. Died February 27, 2000."

This was Stephen's own birthday, and this apparently unknown, deceased cousin, dubbed with the same moniker, had died only weeks after his own proverbial death at the Mite.

And he died only a week after I was shot! This thought sent a chill through him.

Replacing the wreath, he muttered, "Maybe coming to Canada was a bad idea." He turned toward the parking lot.

"Oh, shoot!" he said under his breath. A frantic glance at his watch sent him running to his car.

15

Tints of red, green, and blue illumined the face of the priest as he walked back to his ornately carved, wooden chair to the right of the sanctuary. The colored hues descended from the enormous leaded glass portrayal of the Birth of Jesus, high on the southern wall of St. Francis de Sales Church, Jamesfield, New Hampshire. Floating dust seemed to give living texture to the glory.

As the priest took his seat, the dozen or so communicants sat back from their kneelers and waited, as they had long grown accustomed to do. "What's your hurry?" he would often preach. "Sit, pray, meditate, contemplate your Lord and Savior."

And so Father William Bourque sat, his head bowed slightly, his receding black hair disheveled—it had been a rather hectic morning—and his palms together before his face. Nearly three minutes passed before he calmly rose, signaling his flock to stand with him.

"Let us pray," he chanted, with his slight French Canadian accent. The altar boy held the large lectionary open before him. The priest gave him a teasing scowl to remind him once more not to wear worn tennis shoes with soles that lit up.

"God of salvation, may this sacrament which strengthens us here on earth bring us to eternal life. We ask this in the name of Jesus the Lord, who lives and reigns with You and the Holy Spirit, one God, forever and ever. Amen."

With his gaze caressing his small flock and his hands blessing them, he said, "And may the Lord bless you, He who is Father, Son, and Holy Spirit. Amen. The Mass is ended, now go in peace to love and serve the Lord."

"Thanks be to God," the congregation intoned. In some congregations, this closing phrase carried a tone of relief, but under Reverend Bourque's pastoral care and preaching, they knew what it truly meant: everything is a gift; now their lives must be signs of gratitude.

Back in the sacristy, the priest completed the ritual of removing his holy garb, and then went out through the sanctuary toward the vestibule. Silently he pleaded for some respite that afternoon to read or at least rest, but he knew what was ahead of him. Two parish leaders were at death's door, one in the hospital, one at home. The first from a gruesome car crash in which three in the other vehicle were killed. He prayed the rumor was false—that his friend and chairman of the upcoming parish festival had been drunk. The second had been performing a work of mercy. An elderly friend was remodeling a house. While lending a hand in the construction of a second-story wall, he stepped back blindly into an unguarded stairwell, breaking his neck.

Both men were comatose; neither were expected to live through the week.

It wasn't so much the consoling of the loved ones and soon-to-be widows that made him dread the afternoon ahead. Or even the ministering and administering of the sacraments to the brain-dead. Rather, it was the awkward incongruities that existed between the private and public lives of both these men, the full extent of which only he knew, due to the confessional. For over a year, the first man had carried on a clandestine affair with the second man's wife. Though this had ceased long ago, it left many awkward facets as to how he would address the two families.

"Afternoon, Fada," said Philomena Snootz, the parish helper, mopping the floor around the vestibule book trees. "Good turnout?'

"Yes, Philomena, like usual."

"Good, Fada. That means you doing good job!"

"Yes, thank you."

She returned her attention to the floor. It would be impossible to guess where her mind might be headed. Philomena was a good and kind soul, but as the parishioners hinted, she wasn't all there. She had been a fixture at St. Francis Parish for over forty years, all because of the efforts of a kindhearted Dominican brother. At age fifteen, she had become pregnant through the attentions of any number of local boys. Her parents were only too glad to use this as an excuse to distance themselves from their less-than-perfect child and kicked her out. Brother Simon, now retired, got her a room with the sisters and gave her odd jobs around the church to let her feel like she was paying her way. The baby was born and cared for by Philomena and the sisters and is now married with a family living somewhere near Philadelphia. But Philomena remains, the most dedicated and selfless worker in the parish.

She stopped in mid-stroke to stare at the wall as if distracted by a bug, and then asked, "Is he back today?"

"I'm sorry, Philomena, my dear, is who back?"

"Mr. LaPointe. Today?"

"Why, Philomena, you do have a good memory, don't you?" He removed his coat from its peg. "So what did Sister fix me for lunch?"

"Is it today, Pastor?" she persisted.

"I really don't know, Philomena. He'll be back if and when God calls him back, but you just keep praying for him."

"I do. Every day. He nice, but sad." Her boots were being cleaned along with the floor.

"Yes, he was a nice man. And, Philomena, bless you for your service here."

She blushed. " 'S'a blessing to be here," and she returned to her work. The priest dismissed himself and retraced his steps back to the sacristy where he had left his hat.

Up until five minutes ago, as she pulled onto First Street after the long monotonous drive, Sara's excitement level had peaked. Just the possibility of seeing her husband casually walking along the streets of Jamesfield, maybe even entering or leaving St. Francis de Sales Parish, made her want to burst with anticipated joy.

THIRTY minutes earlier, she had reached a crucial crossroads. With the morning mist burned away and the sun trying to make it a pleasant day, she had sat in her minivan along the side of the highway, staring nervously at a decision: either drive straight ahead or turn off to the right.

Straight ahead north led towards the Widow's Mite. Though Stephen had gone almost every year, and though Mrs. Cousineau had nagged the ministers every year to bring their wives, they never had. Stephen's reports had always been glowing yet tinted with just enough discouraging elements to dissuade her from really pressing to go along. She presumed the other ministers had done likewise—they coveted the Mite for themselves, and she really didn't blame them. *If only there had been just such a retreat for clergy wives. Who knows: things might have gone differently!*

So, should she go where she really had never been welcome? *But would he be there, anyway? Would Stephen, after the ruckus he apparently had caused last year and with all that had resulted in his and our lives, throw himself into the mercy of those old friends who last year had not shown themselves to be quite so understanding?*

Her other option was to exit the highway to the right and drive into Jamesfield, to the Catholic priest who probably knew exactly how to find Stephen. This was not the option she wished to choose. *Would I be welcome there?* Even though Reverend Bourque had shown himself so helpful and unobtrusive at the hospital during Stephen's recovery, still Sara carried too much baggage to trust him. What she was most afraid of, though, was how she might react if she discovered that, yes, her husband had surrendered to the priest's influence.

For nearly ten minutes, she sat in the idling minivan, swinging from one option to the other, unable to decide. Finally, vanquished, she closed her eyes, and through frustrated tears prayed for guidance, for some kind of sign. Not that she believed as confidently anymore that God would really answer—she was even tempted to question whether God was out there—but with some lingering hope she opened her eyes with the prayer that something somehow would prove an obvious sign.

She didn't know if it was the miracle she had expected, but strangely enough a lone chickadee alighted onto the van's wobbly hood ornament. Of all the possible birds, this happened to be one of her husband's favorites. *Hadn't it once been just such a bird whose precisely aimed dropping, on the center of his forehead, had given him a "sign" that none of the options which he was considering was viable?* Instead he had decided to move on to a larger church.

Watching the frail bird gripping tightly against the force of the wind, she prayed that God would somehow speak through this bird. *Whichever way it flew,* she vowed, *I will follow: If to the left, I will stay on the highway toward the Mite; if to the right, I will drive into Jamesfield to see that priest.*

She sat quietly and waited, as the small bird chirped, released its grip, and hopped across the hood toward her. Then, with the next gust of wind, the bird took flight, and to her astonishment, it flew directly into the wind, perfectly over the exit toward Jamesfield and that Catholic priest, until its small figure disappeared out of sight.

She sat in awe. Should she follow through with her silly vow? The thought of walking into the priest's office gave her the willies.

But she had vowed.

With a glance of resignation upward and a smile, she geared into drive, eased back onto the road, and then following the chickadee's lead, off the exit to her right.

"I only ask, Lord, that somehow, this will bring us back together."

For miles she had rehearsed all the possible scenarios of what he might say and how she might respond. *Should I be bold and forward, or reticent, or even difficult? Should I wait for him to apologize or apologize first?* Lost in her musings, she almost missed the turn onto Main Street, Jamesfield.

BUT that was up until five minutes ago—up until she had slowed her car to a stop in front of St. Francis de Sales Catholic Church. Then everything within her changed. It all came back. All the experiences of her life, all her admitted prejudices, all her fears, all of it resting like an oppressive stone on her conscience, locking her into her seat.

Now she panicked that she might see Stephen, walking out of the church, confirming all her fears, confounding all her hopes. She studied the front façade of the stone fortress. The formidability of its three massive wooden doors surmounted by stained glass windows paralyzed her, for they reminded her of her last visit to a Catholic church.

IT was on a weekend away from their first church at Red Creek. She was attending a conference at her college alma mater, and during a break she had stepped into St. Edmund Campion Chapel, the campus chapel. It all came back to her: the foreign surreal pictures and fleshy sculptures; the rows upon rows of flickering candles, with a sign asking for $4 donations; the ornate, wooden, front altar beneath a gaudy, bloody, violent crucifix; the maudlin statue of Mary smiling down at her, extended stone arms exuding rays of red and white stone light; and the kneelers.

In that moment so long ago, she had knelt in prayer, something she had never done before, even as a child beside her bed. (There had been no praying in her family!) Kneeling there, she begged God to forgive her for the myriad sins and lies and failures of her life—especially that one most heinous thing, which she had never told Stephen. But then quickly she became distracted by her surroundings: a statue of a monk in a robe holding a skull, a portrait of Jesus pointing to an exposed heart, and a statue of a small blond-haired child clothed in flowing royal robes, holding a golden orb. Her urge to jump up and run was shoved into high gear when a hunched, dark-robed nun carrying a long, brass candlesnuffer crossed before the altar and bowed in worship. At that moment, she had sworn never to enter a Catholic church again.

And then Stephen, of all things, decided to resign from his pastorate, abandon their Protestant faith, and become Roman Catholic. At least, that's where he was headed when she left him last summer, and what she presumed he had done. *But could he have done this without my consent? Would he?*

NOW she stared across the street at another Catholic church, the very place where Stephen met that priest last year, became convinced in his doubts, and where supposedly he had been hanging out ever since, nurtured and confirmed in his Catholic leanings, and possibly his apparent contentment with their separation.

It was this thought that did it. She had come this far to reclaim her marriage, to reclaim the man she loved, and she wasn't going to let any Catholic priest or daunting Catholic fortress stand in her way.

She flung the van door open as she made her way out and onward across the street to the church. After a few bold steps, however, a decision stopped her, not unlike the decision she'd faced earlier at the exit from the highway. Should she go into the church itself or to the building next door, which was obviously the parish office building. She debated the question a moment, until a lingering echo of her memory from Campion's Chapel set her path.

Beside the locked office door was the typical intercom wall of protection. She buzzed.

A pleasant female voice responded, "Yes, may I help you?"

What should I say? "I'm here to see Reverend Bourque."

"Do you have an appointment? He's not here at the moment."

"Ah, no, thank you," and she turned away with a certain sense of relief. She had taken a mere three steps away when the locked door behind her opened.

"Please, excuse me. I didn't mean to turn you away. I was doing three things at once, and pressing the intercom with my elbow. Can I help you?"

Sara turned and was startled to see the most beautiful nun she could imagine, in full habit and beaming a joyful welcome.

"I—" she was truly taken aback.

"Father Bourque is not in but should be back shortly. Would you like to wait for him?"

Sara found her voice. "Yes, thank you," and she followed the nun into a waiting room.

"I'm Sister Agatha. May I get you some coffee or water?"

"Actually some coffee with cream would be nice. I've traveled a long way."

While the nun was gone, Sara gave the room a quick study: several Catholic magazines on the table beside her, a traditional crucifix on the wall facing her, and across the room a rack of books for sale. Most of the titles were unfamiliar, even indecipherable on topics that were probably familiar to Catholics—but then there it was, right in the middle, that very same book! The book by that cardinal, *The Faith of Our Fathers*, that Ginny McBride had given her, which Sara had flung angrily across the room. All she could remember about it was the author's brash claim that only in the Catholic Church could one be certain of salvation—that in any other church, especially their independent Congregational church, no one could be certain that what they believed was true. At the time, her fear that this was where her husband was leaning made her throw the book as if it was a burning coal from hell.

"Here you go," said the nice nun, as she handed Sara a coffee and two cookies and then sat across from her. "Have you been here before?"

"No, but I've met Reverend Bourque. He visited my husband when he was in the hospital."

"I'm sorry, I don't think I got your name."

"I didn't give it. I'm Mrs. Sara LaPointe."

"Then you're Stephen's wife," the nun said with a kind smile.

"Yes, we've been apart for awhile," she said, taking another sip, "as I assume you may know. I was hoping Reverend Bourque could tell me where I might find him. I know that once he stayed here, the week leading up to his accident. Is he by chance here now?"

"No, I'm sorry, Mrs. LaPointe, he's not."

"But he's still here in town?"

Sister Agatha paused to straighten the magazines on the side table. "Well, no. He was living down the street in an apartment, but then sometime Christmas Day, we discovered that he was gone. He hadn't removed his belongings from the apartment; he'd just disappeared."

"With no mention whatsoever as to why or where he was going?"

"He left a short note to the apartment owners, who are members of the parish, telling them not to worry, but I think that was all."

Sara finished her coffee and asked, "Were you friends with Stephen?" The layered implications of this question to this young beauty were obvious.

"Yes, Sara, but only at meals," she said, smiling. "I'm chief cook and bottle-washer around here. I overhear the conversations and often the debates, but rarely join in. I'm called to serve, not pry. Another coffee?"

"No, thank you. There is one thing I'd like to know. Did Stephen actually join the Catholic Church?"

"Well—" and with that the front door opened, accompanied by a loud pronouncement: "Sister Agatha! I'll need to make my late lunch a quick one!"

"In here, Father."

The priest entered, and he and Sara recognized each other immediately. "Mrs. LaPointe, what a pleasant surprise." He extended both his hands to take hers.

"You remember me?"

"Well, yes and no. I do recognize you, and it is good that you're here. I must admit, though, that I was forewarned that you might contact me. Ginny McBride called to tell me that you had called her. She asked me to tell you, if I saw you, that you were in her prayers."

"Yes, she thought you might know where Stephen is."

"Well, no, I don't, but I do believe we'll be seeing him again soon. He and I have a long-standing appointment scheduled for later this week, so I'm counting on his being here. I apologize, though, that I've hardly enough time to sit down. I'm nearly late for a funeral, and then I have an evening of meetings, but are you staying until tomorrow? I have all day free—this week's day off—so, God willing, I'll give you whatever time you want."

"I guess so; I hadn't really thought that far ahead."

Sister Agatha offered, "Do you have a place to stay? You can stay next door with me if you'd like. There's a guest room in the mostly deserted convent."

"Oh no, thank you," Sara replied, repressing a raft of repulsive emotions. "I'll stay at a local hotel."

"Right down through to the edge of town is our only hotel," the priest put in, hand extended and bobbing vaguely. "Then can I expect you, say, at nine tomorrow?"

"Yes, thank you. And thank you, Sister Agatha, for your hospitality."

ONCE out of the office, away from the nun and priest, free from the oppressive Catholic surroundings, safe once again within the familiarity of her van, she finally relaxed. For a moment she considered chucking the whole quest and heading back home, but this was but a fleeting temptation. She started the van and went looking for the only hotel in town.

16

The unseasonal flood of pilgrims just kept coming. Most were elderly, and the majority were in wheelchairs, pushed by slightly less incapacitated seniors. Buses, mostly from Maine and upstate New York, filled the parking lot, with one particularly well-equipped bus from Chambly, south of Montreal.

"This way, please," Stephen beckoned. "Let's gather here in front of the window depicting The Agony in the Garden. In about five minutes, Sister Ursula will lead you in the Sorrowful Mysteries."

The wheelchair caravan progressed slowly forward. For some reason, it made Stephen think of oozing molasses.

"Sorry I'm late, Stephen," said a nun, working her way as courteously as possible through the crowd. Her hair and therefore her age were completely hidden by the white-and-black wimple crowning her full habit. Over the weeks, Stephen had guessed her to be around his own age, but her officious and abrupt manner always made him feel her inferior.

"I hear this is your last day," the nun said out of the side of her mouth as she corralled the flock. "Please come in as close as you can!"

"Yes, it's time for me to return to reality."

"Well, we'll miss you, Stephen. I'll miss you," she said with an unexpected smile, while reaching over and giving his hand a squeeze. "I'll pray that God makes it all clear for you."

"Thank you." He backed away as she turned to take charge. Partially hidden behind one of the massive stone columns that held up the basilica, Stephen listened for one last time.

"Au nom du Père, et du Fils, et du Saint-Esprit. Amen. Je crois en Dieu, le Père tout-puissant, Créateur du ciel et de la terre ..."

Automatically out of newly acquired habit, Stephen began following the recitation with the appropriate hand motions, crossing himself, while he quietly backed away, leaving Sister Ursula to lead the crowd from Maine, New York, and Chambly in the Rosary.

Genuflecting first toward the altar, he turned, left the Shrine of St. Anne, and escaped quickly to enjoy a peaceful, hot cup of tea.

February was normally a slow month for the shrine. As a result, most of the gift shops and restaurants surrounding the extensive grounds of the enormous granite Romanesque shrine were closed. That day, though, the one open diner, to his disappointment, was brimming with pilgrims, yapping incessantly in their nuanced Canadian French. He recoiled, ready to retreat, but a calming inner voice urged him in. In this crowd of Québécois, whose conversations he was not expected to understand, might be just the right place to lose himself.

"Hey, Stephen," said the man behind the counter. "Heard you're leaving us today. It's been good knowing you," he said, extending his hand.

"Thanks, Jean. I'll miss your beef, chicken, and pork pasties."

"I'd say they're the best in town, but you and I know better. Where you going from here?"

"Back to the States, of course. Can't run away from responsibility forever."

"You'll be in my prayers, *mon ami*. Here's your tea, and grab a cookie or muffin, on the house; it's the least I can do."

"Thanks, Jean. Appreciate it."

Stephen took his snacks to the only unpopulated table, in the corner. The other chairs from his table had already been commandeered to meet the needs of a large group to his left, so he presumed he was safe from the duty of hospitality, at least for a time.

After devouring the cookie along with but three sips of tea, however, his solitude was shattered. A woman wheeled a young woman of maybe twenty into the space directly across from him. He could tell by the condition of her body that she was probably paralyzed. He tried not to stare as Jean brought her an extraordinarily large hot fudge sundae.

"*Vous y êtes, Brigitte. Bon appetit!*"

"*Merci beaucoup, monsieur.*"

For what seemed an eternity, she sat still, while Stephen focused on sipping his tea, until she broke the silence. "*Bonjour. Je m'appelle Brigitte,*" with the inflection of a question. In other words, was he open for a conversation? Her face was a screaming contradiction to her condition. She beamed straight into him with a most unpretentious smile.

"*Bonjour, Brigitte,*" he responded, "*m'appell* ... my name is Stephen LaPointe." The weight of his ignorance of French was becoming oppressive. Then he realized his own blindness as he discovered hers. Staring straight at him, smiling, exploring her tray for the spoon, then determining the location and perimeter of her bowl, she confidently began enjoying her ice cream. A sense of gratitude mixed with pity infected his heart.

"*Êtes-vous ici en pèlerinage?*" she asked.

What should I do? He had to admit his ignorance, though the height of his pride before this young woman was still quite an insurmountable summit. "*Pardonez moi. Je ne parle pas français*—I do not speak French, at least not very well."

"Oh, good, that is okay. I love practicing my English."

"Did you study it in school?"

"Well, yes, I suppose so. I was homeschooled. My mother taught me."

This took him aback. Not homeschooling per se, but the thought of homeschooling a blind, crippled child. He remembered the trials and tribulations of *The Miracle Worker.*

Her smile never flinched, even as she made significant progress with her sundae.

Where to now? he thought. "What did you ask me in French?"

"Are you here on pilgrimage?"

"Yes and no, I guess." *Why am I being so precise with this young blind girl, who will never know me, never see me, and whom I'll never see again?* Nevertheless, he continued: "I've been helping out here at the shrine, but I guess I did come here on pilgrimage."

"Why?"

Her eyes were light brown, and her hair, held back in two identical braids, was long and pitch black.

"What do you mean?"

"Why did you come on pilgrimage? Did you come for a healing, like the people who have left their crutches behind? A woman who came with us last year claims her cancer stopped as soon as she prayed for Father Pampalon's intercession. The doctors are examining her right now to determine whether there is a natural explanation. You know that one more authenticated miracle is needed for Father Pampalon's cause?"

"No, I didn't." Stephen only had a vague clue as to what she was referring. During the past weeks, he had certainly passed by the chapel dedicated to Venerable Father Alfred Pampalon in the lower floor of the shrine, and, yes, he knew about the hundreds of miraculous cures attributed to prayers to St. Anne that had supposedly been granted to pilgrims over the years. Two of the large granite columns of the upper church were covered with cast-off crutches and braces. There were so many that a separate storage room contained twice as many as were visible to the public.

Unlike so many of his contemporary clergymen, Stephen had always believed in the miraculous. While others forced their rationalistic qualifications on malleable, trusting congregations, he accepted without hesitation the miracles reported in Scripture. He trusted in the guileless sincerity of the biblical writers under the gentle guidance of the Holy Spirit. If the multiplication of the loaves had been merely a "miracle of sharing," it would not have made it into the Gospels nor would it have said anything about the divine authority and power of Jesus.

But when it came to miracles happening *now*, on this side of the New Testament, to real people living in this twenty-first-century world of science, rationalism, materialism, new-age mysticism, and self-centered narcissism, Stephen leaned on the New Testament prayer of the father who hoped Jesus could heal his son: "I believe, but help my unbelief."[15] Stephen *believed*, but in truth he doubted. He was always cynical when people claimed God's healing intervention.

"You did not come for a healing then?"

"Is that why you've come?" he probed, diverting her far too intimate probes. Immediately he worried that he'd been too forward—how on earth was he to know how sensitive he needed to be to a blind girl in a wheelchair?—but she only smiled, right through and into him, as if nothing he could say could faze her.

"Yes, but not for what you might think. Not for my sight or my legs, but rather for my anger."

"Your anger?"

"I still lose my temper too often with my little brother, Pierre. I hope that St. Anne will intercede for me and ask Jesus to cleanse my heart of my selfishness."

"Brigitte, I guess I don't understand," Stephen said, cautiously, hiding his cynicism. "If you truly believe that the prayers of St. Anne and Father Pampalon are so powerful, then why not pray for the healing of your eyes or legs?"

Her smile never broke, even as she gulped another bite of sundae. "You are not a Catholic are you, Mr. LaPointe?"

Stephen sat silent, unsure how to respond.

She continued: "I've talked to many non-Catholics who, though they believe in Jesus, do not really believe in the power of God. Non-Catholics say they believe in the Bible, but in truth they rely on themselves to decide what the Bible says. The Church, which Jesus built on St. Peter, gave us the Bible, not the other way around."

And all this from a crippled, young woman who was blind.

"Brigitte," he asked uncomfortably, yet with a sense that this was no chance encounter, "what led you to say all that?"

"Mr. LaPointe, why should I tell you if you do not really believe in miracles?"

"I didn't say that."

"Ah, but the tone of your voice. You belittled what thousands of people claim Jesus did for them here in this wonderful place."

Stephen sat speechless. Then he said, "I understand why Catholics pray to saints like St. Anne and that they're not worshipping statues or pictures, but Brigitte, I also know that people have faked miraculous healings, for personal gain or prestige or power or merely for attention."

"Are you done with your tea?"

"Yes, but—"

"Then can you please push me over to the shrine?" She turned herself and her wheelchair away in the direction of the exit, so he knew she was not taking no for an answer.

"But your sundae?"

"Oh, Jean will put it in the freezer for me."

Stephen turned and saw Jean coming toward him with a smile.

"C'est okay, ma fille. Je vais l'enregistrer pour vous."

Stephen smiled back and proceeded to push Brigitte outside, into the escalating snow squall, a precursor of the projected four new inches by morning. When they turned the corner onto the sidewalk, the intensity of the storm doubled.

"Brigitte, are you sure?" he said, over the howling wind.

"Yes, please," she said, pointing, intent on moving forward, so he pulled her shawl up around her neck and proceeded down the sidewalk, across the side street, and onto the shrine grounds.

His eyes squinting against the oncoming snow, he said, "Brigitte, the wheelchair ramp up to the main church is closed for the season."

"That is fine." She pointed to the left in the direction of a side door. "In there." She had obviously passed this way many times before.

Inside, he turned toward the elevators, but she pointed forward. "Please down the hall and then follow the ramp down into the crypt." He acquiesced willingly, down the serpentine ramp into the lower level of the church. No Protestant church he had ever known had such a basement: a vaulted ceiling decorated with murals and intricately painted blue designs. At the far end was an ornate altar with a statue of Mary—any visiting anti-Catholic would have sworn this hidden basement chapel was proof positive that Catholics worshipped Mary! Stephen knew better.

The crypt church was surprisingly half-full of pilgrims. Brigitte pointed forward to the other side of the room as they exited the wheelchair ramp, and then down the far side aisle. He had no idea where she was taking him. Then even more unexpectedly, she aimed him back out of the crypt into a hallway, and then into a side room, lit only by rows and rows of votive candles. The room was almost oppressive with the smell of burning beeswax. For some reason, Stephen had never ventured into this room. To their right, they passed an older statue of Mary holding the limp form of her crucified Son.

Brigitte directed him onward to the left. He turned the corner and there, illuminated by the natural light of three windows was a tall, ornate, hand-carved, wooden altar. In the center was a statue of St. Anne holding her daughter, Mary.

"Please, Mr. LaPointe, wheel me up in front of the altar." He did so and was about to take a seat beside her on the sole pew, but the stiff, thin arm of Brigitte was pointing horizontally toward the statue. Not hearing a response, she began wagging her finger impatiently.

"Yes, Brigitte, what is it?"

"There, near the base of the statue of St. Anne, do you see some photographs?"

"Yes, there are several."

"Do you see a photo of an automobile accident?"

He went forward and thumbed through the collection, and sure enough, he found a black-and-white photo of what must have been a horrifyingly bloody accident. He looked closer, angling the photo in the dim natural light to make out the details. There about thirty feet or so below a broken guardrail was a twisted, torn, universally mangled vehicle, maybe a convertible, maybe a compact, he couldn't tell. It lay upside-down in a foot of water with the passenger compartment completely submerged. Except by the grace of God, no one could have survived this terrifying accident.

"I was in there," she said, in almost a monotone.

"What?"

She rolled herself slowly up to the altar, beside where Stephen was standing, and sat in silence, her face raised slightly upward. Then she dropped her sightless gaze and spoke. "I had only been licensed to drive for a month, and my two closest friends and I were out on the town. We of course weren't supposed to, but we had been drinking wine with our boyfriends, who obviously had ulterior motives. But we laughed in their faces and left, priding ourselves for how moral we were for turning them down. We were speeding away, covering up our own frustrations with jokes about the boys' sad yet comical pleas, and all of a sudden we were airborne. In the dark, I had not seen the curve. It turns out that there were signs, several of them, but we were having too much fun. All I remember is screaming; everything else disappeared from my memory."

She rolled her chair back and motioned Stephen to sit.

"I woke up in the hospital days later in a complete body cast. I think more than half of my bones were broken. It was not until the bandages were removed from my face that I realized the worst of my injuries: the injury to my head had severed my optical nerves. I will never see again."

A glistening tear traveled along the perfection of her tender cheek. As he studied the stateliness of her composure, he now noticed the faint scars of what must have been massive reconstructive surgery. One almost invisible thin line ran from above her left eye across the bridge of her nose down to the nape of her neck.

"Brigitte, I'm so sorry."

"Do not feel sorry for me, Mr. LaPointe. I was lucky. My two friends died in the midst of their screams."

Stephen sat speechless beside her. When the silence became unbearable, he reached over and lightly touched her arm, "Brigitte, how … you seem so full of joy, so hopeful?"

"There are two answers to that," she replied softly, "one more rational, one mystical, the first more public, the second private, but for you, I will tell both." She turned her chair to face him more directly.

"After I left the hospital, I concluded that as a penalty for my self-centeredness that had killed two friends, I had been condemned to a dark, lonely life in this chair. What made it seem even more desperate, even more vengeful, was that due to the damage to my shoulders and tendons, I didn't even have enough strength to get myself in and out, up and down. I was totally dependent upon others for everything— and I mean everything," she said with a grimace. "Every day became a panic attack as I envisioned a life trapped in this impotent shell. My boyfriend stopped by to see me once. He tried to be kind, but we both knew we could never, ever share the kind of things other couples share. He never came back."

She scrambled for a moment through the pockets of her jacket to find a hanky. Dabbing her eyes lightly, she gripped it as if it were a friend, and continued.

"Then one day in June, four years ago, my mother planned a trip here to the shrine—my father still refused to speak to me. He was devastated by what I had done to my life and my two friends—and to his life, I suppose. But I would not go. I screamed when my mother tried to force me onto her tour bus. Defeated, she let me stay home with my aunt. I spent the day alone in my room, yelling and complaining out loud, berating everyone I could think of for my dead-end life, until 2:37 in the afternoon. I know the time exactly because when it happened I vaguely heard the announcer on the kitchen radio give the time and temperature."

Stephen was mesmerized by her peaceful countenance, for her sightless eyes seemed to see through him and beyond.

Echoing her words with her hands, she continued: "Now the 'it' that happened was a warm sensation that began somewhere in the middle of my chest and back and flowed outward to my shoulders and waist and then on into my neck, arms, and legs, until it reached every part of my body. The warmth felt kind of like the heated seats in my father's car. For a second, I mused whether my wheelchair had heated seats, but I knew it did not. Then I worried that there was a fire behind me, so I turned my head to look, and the significance of this act frightened me. I had moved my head," and she did so to illustrate. "I did it again, back and forth, up and down, and tears began pouring down my cheek—and I felt them!

"You see, Mr. LaPointe, up until that moment I could not turn my head, I could not feel a thing. I began weeping uncontrollably for joy, just to feel the warmth of beautiful tears on my face. I raised my hands to wipe my eyes, and was again ecstatic with joy just because I could do this. I yelled for my aunt, and when she saw what I could do, she grabbed me in a warm embrace. It felt so good, just to feel and move again. I quickly discovered, however, that I was not completely healed. I tried to move my legs and my feet, but there was nothing there. And I was still blind."

Again she dabbed her eyes and nose. Noise from several families with small children behind us lighting votive candles caught her attention, but she continued.

"That evening when my mother returned, my aunt met her at the front door with the news. Mama burst into my room, and we babbled at each other through our tears. Together we discovered the secret behind my healing. Exactly at 2:37—and she knew this because she had sensed the urge to look down at her watch—she was kneeling right where you are sitting, here before the statue of St. Anne, lighting a votive candle, and placing that photo there as an offering of thanksgiving."

"Thanksgiving?" Stephen asked, not meaning to interrupt, but the sentiment was unexpected.

"Yes, thanksgiving, and that is the key. My mother had been trying over and over to convince me to be thankful that God had spared my life, but I had refused to listen. She would repeat the verse from Philippians, 'Have no anxiety, but in every prayer and supplication *with thanksgiving* let your petitions be made known to God. And the peace of God which passes all understanding will keep your hearts and minds in Christ Jesus,'[16] but I would not listen. We now believe that through the intercession of St. Anne, Jesus healed me. I think it was as a gift for my mother's faithfulness."

The vision of that gruesome photo compared to the beaming creature before him was irreconcilable. There was much he wanted to ask, much of which was laced with skepticism, but in the end he blurted, shamefacedly, "But Brigitte, you ... weren't completely healed. You're still ..."

She smiled. "I know. That tends to be the most common critique, but somehow I thought you would understand."

She turned her chair back to face the altar.

"You see, Mr. LaPointe, the real healing that afternoon, at the instant of my mother's prayer, was not my body, but my heart. The warmth I felt was only secondarily in my body; it had exuded from within me, flowing out of the new heart Jesus had given me, like the fulfillment of Ezekiel's prophecy: 'A new heart I will give you, and a new spirit I will put within you.'[17] The miracle was that I was not discouraged by the incompleteness of my healing, but instead, saw that whatever physical healing I received was an extra blessing."

"Brigitte, you amaze me. Not just your attitude, but your surprising ability to articulate your faith."

"I guess I owe this to my spiritual director, Father Bourque."

"Father Bourque?" Stephen nearly yelled. His voiced reverberated out into the crypt, and the families lighting and praying beside the votive candles turned and glared. He started again, more softly. "Father William Bourque of Jamesfield, New Hampshire? You know Father Bourque?"

"Oh, yes. Not long after my healing, he led a mission at our parish in Chambly. On the first evening, my mother introduced me to him, and when he took my hand, I felt like I was touching Jesus. He took me aside, me alone, and we talked for over an hour. He did this every night for the rest of the mission, and ever since he has called me on the last Tuesday of every month at nine o'clock sharp—that is, if he hasn't been called away for an emergency. He has helped me, as he says, 'to understand the beauty of God's love and grace, and to seek holiness in the midst of my solitude.'"

"So you're St. Brigitte."

"Excuse me?"

Stephen hesitated to tell this stranger the details of his own spiritual journey. "Well, I, too, know Father Bourque, and his spiritual friendship has also changed my life. I was staying with him about this time last year, and right in the middle of one of our heated discussions, one Tuesday evening, he looked at his watch, said he needed to call St. Brigitte, and excused himself."

"St. Brigitte," she laughed. "He calls me that to jokingly remind me how merciful God has been."

"I can't believe we both know Father Bourque. I was a Congregationalist minister trying to get my life back together, trying to determine how I could know what was true. Father Bourque helped me discover for the first time the beauty and truth of the Catholic Church."

"Then, Reverend LaPointe, I know you. He did not mention your name, but he told me about a Protestant minister he was helping."

"Oh, he has helped many Protestant ministers along the path to Rome."

In her blindness, beaming with radiance, she extended her hand toward him. When he took it, she said, "I guess Jesus meant for us to meet. What is the healing that you need? What are you looking for?"

"I don't—" he went silent.

"I believe that Jesus wants me to remind you that all things are possible with Him; that whatever is holding you back, from doing what you know in your heart He is calling you to do, He wants you to remember, 'Be not afraid.'"

Stephen felt what could only be a tinge of the warmth Brigitte had described. It seemed to flow from her hand into and through his entire body. He glanced up, and the statue of the mother of Mary was smiling down directly at him. He pulled his hand away quickly.

"How did you know to say those words? Did Father Bourque tell you?" Then a new thought crossed his mind. "Did he tell you to find me here?"

"No, of course not, Reverend LaPointe. Do you not believe that Jesus has the ability to lead people together?"

He gently retook her hand. "Yes, of course, and I guess He could have placed those very words on your lips. When I was most lost, when I was near ready to give everything up, Jesus brought me back by haunting me with those words! Everywhere I turned, I ran into Him telling me, 'Be not afraid.'"

"Brigitte, there you are!" a frantic woman demanded in rough, Québécois English. "I've been looking everywhere, and don't give me that about I should have known you'd be about your Father's business." She smiled, "Sorry, sir, has she been preaching to you?"

"No, ma'am, she's been nothing short of a blessing."

"Well, the bus is waiting, Brigitte."

"Good-bye, Reverend LaPointe, you will be in my prayers," and with one final squeeze of his hand, she departed.

For a few moments, he sat in silence, looking up at the statue of St. Anne holding her daughter Mary, the Mother of his Savior and Lord. This was certainly not something to which he was fully comfortable, but he closed his eyes and asked for her intercession for him, his marriage, and his family, that God in His mercy might somehow bring them back together.

17

Scott Turner's Narrative

Sometime around three, Raeph and I drove away from the Widow's Mite together in my van, leaving Raeph's Camaro in the parking lot. Seeing the care this fellow had given his classic car elevated even more my appreciation for this sincere, though a bit misguided, brother in Christ. We figured the Mite's lot would be as easy as anywhere for us to stop on our return home. So he transferred a portion of what he claimed were the only clothes he had left, along with a small box for which he seemed particularly protective.

There were two ways to get from the Mite down into Jamesfield: back out to the highway and then south to the Jamesfield exit, or down through the woods on a less traveled, curvy, two-lane, New Hampshire back road. Both about the same distance, forty or so miles, though the highway route was probably quicker. But I wanted time for us to get better acquainted, so I chose the road less traveled.

After a few minutes of small talk, mostly about football, I turned our discussion to details about Raeph and his relationship with Stephen. He quickly deflected the conversation back, however, to my relationship with Stephen. Every time I shot a forehand, he sidestepped and returned with a backhand. Eventually, he knew all about how Stephen and I had become close friends—as a returning alumnus and representative of our Congregationalist Association, Stephen befriended me during my second year at seminary and ever since we and our families had continued our friendship despite distance by phone, email, and our annual rendezvous at the Widow's Mite. At first, given what I'd learned of Raeph's background, I was guarded, but his winsome smile and jovial demeanor fanned my desire to open up.

"So tell me," he asked, "what knocked you out of the NFL to Jesus? Were you always a born-again Christian?"

Having become sensitive to the "verses I never saw," I was already leery of the "born-again Christian" mentality, because any open-minded study of the related texts proved that being "born-again" originally meant receiving new life in Christ through baptism. However, when I experienced the life change he was alluding to, I was of his mind-set.

"It happened after that game you mentioned earlier, when I was blindsided by Bubba Tooly."

"Yeah, that was some hit," he said with a smile.

"Well, I guarantee it was a whole lot easier for you watching from the comfort of your living room than it was for me down on that field. All I can remember is watching their quarterback run around to my left. My next conscious thought was looking up into my wife's eyes from a hospital bed. A spinal fracture immobilized me for a month and benched me for half the next season.

"The first month I grumbled, bitter, vengeful. '*Tooly will pay*,' I'd say between my teeth. The second month I began to *hear* Diane. There was no other explanation. She had always shared her faith, both overtly and subtly, but for some reason—grace, of course—it finally began to break through. Taking patient advantage of her captive audience, she bombarded me from the kitchen with Christian television, radio, audiotapes, and videos until I relented and agreed to try reading the Bible."

"Whoa, watch out!" Raeph yelled, pointing to a car coming right at us.

The road down through the mountainous woods fortunately had been well cleared of snow and ice, but I had to keep my attention close to the wheel, because that was the second driver speeding up the mountain cutting corners that nearly forced us off the road to the right.

"Guess they're not used to strangers using their road."

I glanced over. He seemed to be genuinely interested in my story, so I continued.

"At first, I merely pretended to be reading, but a few verses would always get my attention: make me ponder, wonder. Then one night while she read her favorite book for the umpteenth time, *Sense and Sensibility* by Jane Austen, I 'pretended' to read the Gospel of John. My intent was to *appear* serious, studious, inspired for a time, and then once she had become distracted, I would shift to reading one of my favorite sports magazines. The problem is, somewhere around the third chapter, when Jesus talked about the need to be *born again*, I forgot all my pretensions. I had read on through the fifteenth chapter before I realized I had been changed.

"Faith is truly a gift. Somewhere in there, in the midst of those beautiful words of John's Gospel of love, I was changed within. I *heard* for the first time, and crossed the threshold from agnosticism to belief. Don't ask me to explain it. I can't. All I can say is that in that moment of change, the whole direction of my life and the desires of my heart also began to change: from then on I would dedicate my life to helping others experience this complete conversion of heart."

We turned a corner and the woods opened off to our left to reveal a pristine, fog-capped frozen, mountain lake. Out in the middle where the ice was open, Canadian geese had congregated. Raeph and I both admired the scenery until he broke the silence.

"What about leaving the pros to become a minister? I bet that blew your teammates away."

"That's an understatement. They had a hard enough time accepting the non-carousing, new 'born-again' me. After months of rehabilitation, I returned to active play leaner and stronger, bringing new speed to my position. Susanna had just turned five, our second daughter, Elisa, was three and a half, and as a family we couldn't be happier.

"But an inner voice was bombarding me. It was relentless. From somewhere deep within came a pleading I could no longer ignore. Unbeknownst to Diane, I tested the idea with our pastor, and sooner than I expected I received his confirmation. All that was left was to break the news to Diane. When I did, she was ecstatic because she had been led to the same conclusion. Truly united with her in love and our Christian convictions, I resigned from pro ball and entered the seminary, and now here I am just an old football player trying to keep from looking like a football."

His warm, genuine laughter suggested that some of his stiff, cold, suspicious tenseness was melting away.

"What about you," I asked, "what's your story?"

It was obvious his intent was to listen more than speak. After a few seconds of only road noise, I prodded again. "Were you one of those who just knew Jesus from diapers on up?"

"Hardly," he snorted. "There was no hint of religion in our home. I also found Jesus on a battlefield, but a different one: Vietnam. A brave soldier saved my life when I was wounded and saved my soul when I was lost."

He turned his attention back to the world outside.

"Raeph, I don't mean to pry, but it sounds like you've been dealt a rough deal this past year."

"Yeah, you certainly could say that," he said with a weak smile. "I still believe, though, that God's hand is in it somehow."

"You said you still have another son somewhere?"

He stared for a moment at the passing trees. "Yeah, that's right. Ted."

His tone and composure shouted how much he missed his son.

"Ever lose someone close to you?" he asked.

"No, I haven't, thank God."

"Yes, be thankful, very thankful. There's an empty ache in my heart that just won't go away. I miss my wife, and doubt if I'll ever be ready to love another woman."

"Well, grace can do amazing things."

"I know, Reverend Turner. I suppose honestly, right now though, I mostly miss Ted. I feel that of all the things I've ever done in my life, the one thing I failed in most was my relationship with him. I'm sure he left because of me. I don't know exactly what I did or said, or maybe didn't say, but, next to bringing closure to Walter's death, the one thing left that might bring hope and joy back into my life would be finding Ted."

A pickup passed in the opposite direction, spewing the van with slush. Thinking we had established some level of trust, I asked cautiously, "Raeph, earlier you said that your friend Walter was disturbed by what he concluded were Reverend LaPointe's Catholic leanings. What specifically?"

"Well, LaPointe preached against contraception."

"Stephen was fairly unique in this," I responded with a hint of sarcasm.

Raeph turned sharply and said, "But only Catholics believe that!"

"Yes, that's basically true, but, up until the 1930s, every Bible-believing Christian in the world agreed that contraception was a sin. That is, up until the Episcopalians knocked over the first contraceptive domino. Since then every Christian denomination—except the Catholic Church—has followed suit."

We drove on in silence for nearly a mile, the increase in traffic indicating that we were getting closer to town. Then I ventured in again, "But Raeph, even so, you said Walter shot him because he believed that Stephen was, as you said, a 'papist,' an evil man, and an enemy of Christ. I've known Stephen for many years, and he is none of these things."

Raeph answered, looking at the road ahead. "I'm not sure how to answer this, because I'm not sure where you stand on the Catholic

Church." He turned to study me. "That retreat house was infested with papist literature."

I smiled. "That's the Cousineaus. Raeph, I'm probably not as vehemently against the Catholic Church as you or Walter, but I am no fan either. I've brought many Catholics to faith and salvation in Jesus Christ. At my last position, some local Catholics dubbed me a sheep-stealer, but, hey, if they're not being fed the truth by their priest, then why shouldn't I offer it to them?"

"Well, you see," Raeph said cautiously, obviously testing the waters, "Walter was convinced that Catholic priests have secretly infiltrated our Christian churches."

"What?" I asked, nonplussed.

"You've never heard this? Neither had I before I was told this by the pastor we had at Red Creek before Reverend LaPointe. Since then, I've read a lot of books that make this claim."

He then gave me the rundown on how Walter became convinced that Stephen was a "papist infiltrator."

"Stephen?" I laughed, but then stopped, and, unfortunately, muttered aloud, "Although, given what he said last year, I can see how someone might think that."

"What's that?" Raeph demanded.

"Oh, nothing, just kidding. Stephen is no Catholic infiltrator, if there ever was such a thing. It's true that some of his sympathies were leaning in the Catholic direction, but, believe me, Stephen isn't that good of an actor. He's a solid Evangelical, though maybe a bit confused."

Raeph said with nervous intensity, "But why should I believe you? You're his friend. Maybe you're in this with him."

"I thought you said this was Walter's conspiratorial fantasy?"

He ran his hand through his hair and then admitted, "I don't know what I believe anymore."

We returned to silence for another mile or so. The appearance of a few outbuildings—one a crumbling, abandoned log cabin, possibly one of the oldest structures along the route—was a sure sign we were nearing Jamesfield.

"So, Raeph, what else led Walter to suspect Stephen of Catholic tendencies?"

"What really bothered Walter was that LaPointe denied things that are clearly taught in Scripture and insisted on things that aren't."

"Like what?"

"Like I said, he taught against contraception, which we all know is nowhere taught in the Bible, while at the same time he denigrated what the Bible clearly teaches about the Rapture of the Church."

"Raeph, my new friend," I said, slowing the van down as traffic became more congested, "I hope you believe me when I say I truly love Jesus—He is my Lord and Savior—and that I accept the inspiration of the Bible just as much as you do. I say this because I suspect you may not like my answer." The van ground to a halt behind a pickup hauling a trailer of firewood. "However, the truth is …," I fumbled a bit for the right words, "the Rapture is really not as clearly taught in the Bible as you might think."

I anticipated a quick rejoinder, but, to my surprise, got none. He was about to, but caught himself, his eyes widening as if he'd remembered something important.

I continued cautiously. "Every verse used to teach the Rapture far more clearly teaches the Second Coming of Christ. And although Stephen's convictions against contraception are not specifically mentioned in Scripture by name, the underlying concepts are there, much like our belief in the Trinity."

"What does this have to do with the Trinity?" he asked, with a irritated toss of his hand.

"Well, the word, *Trinity*, is not in Scripture, and neither is the doctrinal formula that we believe: one God in three Persons. Many throughout history have taken the biblical references to God the Father, to Jesus Christ our Lord, and to the Holy Spirit, and come up with a wide assortment of heretical conclusions. Some of these ideas are still held today by groups like the Unitarians, the Oneness Pentecostals, or even the Jehovah Witnesses or Mormons. These groups took the Bible as the inspired Word of God, but came up with alternate conclusions to our belief in the Trinity."

Raeph for a time just stared silently out the window. Then he asked, "So, is that what Reverend LaPointe said last year that upset his friends and led to his resignation?"

"Basically. Stephen was so troubled by the cacophony—to use his word—of contradictory biblical interpretations, that he lost faith in his own ability to know that what he was teaching was true. He no longer trusted the doctrine of *sola Scriptura*. He, therefore, did not feel he could stand with integrity before the people who trusted him, so he resigned."

Raeph glanced at me briefly, gave a slow nod, and then stared forward, speechless. I interpreted this as a sign of understanding. I was about to drop the same bomb on Raeph that Stephen dropped on us last year—*What is the pillar and bulwark of the truth?*—but Raeph interrupted me.

Thumbing toward a passing village limit sign, he read: "'JAMESFIELD. FOUNDED 1807. POPULATION 3,862.' Looks like we're here. So what are we looking for?"

"There's a small hotel on the other edge of town," I said, as I turned right onto Main Street, "not far from a nice restaurant-pub called Burson's Tavern. I'm sure we can find some rooms there."

"Like I said, Reverend Turner, I don't have any—"

"Don't worry, Raeph. I've got it. And please, call me Scott. We're in this together on the same quest. See that stone tower?" I pointed over a row of businesses to the left. "That's St. Francis de Sales Catholic Church. You want to go there now and get it over with?"

Raeph stared silently out over the buildings, then turning toward the front said, "No, I think I'd rather wait. How about in the morning?"

"Okay. First thing tomorrow, we'll confront that priest about Stephen."

"For now, if you don't mind, I'm just looking forward to a room and a bed. I didn't get much sleep last night."

"Me neither," I said with a laugh.

We checked in, and as I was signing for our separate rooms, he tapped me on the arm, said, "Thanks again, Scott. I'll meet you in the restaurant at eight for breakfast," and took off.

"How about dinner?" but he was gone.

Once ensconced in my hotel room, I plopped down on my bed, turned on the television for distraction, but could not shake the suspicion that my long-anticipated, relaxing retreat was as far from my grasp as a startled flock of sparrows.

Ever since Raeph had entered his room and bolted the door, he had been resting relieved in the room's comfy recliner, sipping a cola, staring out the window, reviewing with confused disbelief all that had occurred since he had "escaped" early that morning from Ben and Sylvia's. How differently everything had progressed from what he had expected. Never could he have anticipated the turn that his confrontation with Scott and Ron had taken, or that he would have left the retreat with Scott as his trusty scout in search of LaPointe.

Regardless, all this was bringing him closer to his quest. He watched enviously the silent falling snow, wafting here and there, pleasantly, without human cares or concerns. Back and forth his mind raced, reviewing and critiquing, sometimes reconsidering and often rejecting Scott's explanation of what LaPointe believed and why in the end he had resigned.

Raeph wanted to understand. He was even strangely sympathetic to LaPointe's—and Reverend Turner's—concern over the disturbing number of conflicting interpretations of Scripture. He didn't have a good answer for this, yet he knew how the Evil One works by planting seeds of doubt and confusion.

He needed a distraction, so with the remote, he turned on the usual one. Flicking mindlessly through the channels, he watched in unequal spurts of consciousness news channels, talk shows, soaps, a judge deciding ridiculous cases, a foreign soccer game, an infomercial about a weight-loss breakthrough that required no exercise, a black-and-white movie about a place called Shangri-La, until giving up, he switched the TV off and sat in silence again watching the snow falling outside.

As if by inspiration, he remembered, and from the inside pocket of his overcoat lying strewn across the bed he removed the rubber-band-encased bundle. Providentially—*certainly a sign from God*—the room's alarm radio was a high-tech, multi-functional system with a cassette player. Rewinding the recording to the beginning, he sat back full into the recliner.

"Okay, Walter," he said, almost like a prayer, "let me hear your explanation again, and I'll compare it with Reverend Turner's."

Fifteen minutes later his snores overtook the pleading tone of Walter's farewell.

18

S tephen sat in the stillness of his cabin, a cup of freshly brewed coffee in one hand and a telephone—the cabin's sole surrender to modern technology—in the other. It was to be his last night.

Before the line went uncomfortably silent, Stephen had received the frank greeting, "I'm sorry, sir, but Pastor Wilson is no longer with us."

Stephen answered, taken aback, "You mean he's—?"

"Oh no, no, I'm sorry, I didn't mean that. Pastor Cliff is no longer our pastor. Well, I guess I should also say, he's no longer anybody's pastor."

"Now what do you mean?"

"He's resigned from being a pastor altogether."

"Do you know how I can reach him?"

"Yeah, sure. Just a moment. Yes, here it is. He's living up near Worcester in some kind of retreat center or something. This number's for the front office. He said for anyone who wanted him to call and leave a message, and he'd call back."

"Thank you," Stephen said; he wrote down the number, touched the button to end that call, and then quickly started another.

His encounters of the morning, from opposite extremes of the Catholic religious spectrum and everything in between, had set him back into a lonely panic. Just when he thought he was convinced in one direction, the data gained from some new encounter would shout a contradiction. It wasn't actually his mind that was shifting positions, but his emotions. The result of his convictions had so isolated, even divided, him from everything he had loved—his calling, his friends, his family, his wife—that the constant wavering emotional onslaught had eaten away at his confidence like floodwaters against the foundation of a home. Just when he felt convinced enough to move forward, another voice would call him back, and now more than ever the voices were becoming more self-destructive, enticing him to consider otherwise unfathomable solutions to his dilemma. He desperately needed to talk to someone who might understand. So he called Cliff.

This time a gruff male voice answered, "Hello, St. Anselm's Friary."

Stephen sat speechless.

"Hello," the voice demanded, "is someone there? May I help you?"

"Yes, sorry. I'm calling for Cliff Wilson. Is he there?"

"As a matter of fact, he just walked by." Faintly, Stephen heard the gatekeeper call down the hall for Stephen's old friend. The voice returned to the receiver: "Who may I say is calling?"

"Stephen LaPointe."

Again he heard the voice convey the message, which was immediately followed by the sound of running, clomping steps down the hall, getting louder and louder, until an out-of-breath voice said, "Stephen, hey, is that really you?"

"Yes, Cliff, but don't have a heart attack on my account!"

"I just came in from shoveling the walks and haven't disrobed yet. You know me, I need twice the clothes as you Northern white folk."

They laughed together, old buddies reunited. Stephen smiled just to know he was connected once again to this tall black friend from seminary.

"Stephen, are you here in town? How'd you find me?"

"No, I'm actually calling from Canada. I've been up north for a few weeks getting my head together. For months I've had you on my list to call, though, and just decided I needed to hear that familiar, conflicted, Connecticut–South Carolinian–Haitian accent of yours."

"Well, massah, you's called de right place. Hold on for a minute; I'll pick this up on another line."

Cliff's voice morphed into the familiar soft Gregorian chant album that had so astonishingly soared to the top of the charts. Stephen concluded that this had become the standard monastic elevator music.

"All right, I'm back," Cliff said, still breathing hard. "So how've you been?"

"No, I'm the one who needs to be asking how you've been? Your secretary said you're no longer a pastor. What's going on?"

"I presume the same thing that's happened to you and Jim."

"But you just published your book—you just put your name on the line scolding us for leaving. Two-hundred and fifty pages arguing why a pastor must never leave his church, no matter how crazy the turkeys get at the front office. What was that you said? I wrote it down—" Stephen paused as he reached for his journal and turned to the appropriate page. "Here it is: 'Today's denominational confusion requires a new kind of martyrdom. Pastors need to honor their commitments for the long haul as an example to laity who feel drawn to jump ship after every less-than-perfect sermon or denominational vote.'"

"Kind of sounded like I was taking you and Jim to task."

"You can say that again."

"Kind of sounded like I was taking—"

"Cut the crap and explain yourself," he said, smiling to himself at their old routine.

"The simplest explanation is akin to Shakespeare's quote from *Hamlet*, 'The lady doth protest too much, methinks.' One should listen to oneself before writing and publishing a book. The week after the book came out, I attended the monthly ministerial luncheon. On one side of me sat a flashy, Pentecostal, health-and-wealth charlatan who is getting fat-and-sassy off his exploding congregation, and on the other side sat the local Episcopalian priest, who everyone knows is a flaming homosexual with a live-in lover. In both cases, my book just goaded their poor, duped, and victimized congregations to tough it out, to be martyrs to their hypocritical pastors for the good of their churches. When the light-in-the-loafers Episcopalian turned to me in his lispy whisper and said he'd read my book and couldn't agree more, I knew I'd had enough!"

"But of course!"

"He said that no matter how bigoted and behind-the-times some of his 'co-religionists' might be, he would stick it out to the end. However, the final straw came when the Pentecostal passed me the plate with the day's entrée, and every finger of his hand sported a diamond ring. I left."

"Don't blame you."

"What I had failed to appreciate throughout my book was that all martyrdoms ain't equal. Some are justified and honorable; others are just plain foolish, stubborn pride. When Jesus said 'Blessed are those who are persecuted for righteousness' sake,' He emphasized that all persecutions are not equal. I faced up to the bottom line: Is Congregationalism worth dying for? Was Jesus calling me to remain at the helm in an association of churches that has long since jettisoned its Christian roots and folded under the constant lure of modern liberalism and secularism?"

"If I may play the devil's advocate, what about the hundreds of faithful members still sitting in your old pews every week who need your leadership, who need you, as one trustworthy lighthouse in the blinding storm of compromise?"

"I guess that's what made me hold on so long, but in the end, I realized that this is based on a demonically false premise. This assumes that only what is important is an individual's personal relationship with Christ—that being a part of the Body of Christ, the Church, is unimportant, unnecessary; that churches are nothing more than man-made organizations, accidents in the history of Christianity, and a hindrance at that. But we both know that the Scriptures indicate that the hierarchical structure and organization of God's people was always His plan. As you said last year about that verse that gave you so much trouble, how can a disembodied, invisible 'Church,' which, therefore, is only visible to Jesus—that consists only of true, 'born-again' believers distributed across denominational boundaries—be any kind of helpful 'pillar and bulwark' of anything?"

"I wish you'd have spoken out in my defense last year."

"Sorry about that, but I wasn't then where I am now in my thinking. Like some of the others, I was blinded by my stubborn commitment to remain a Congregationalist pastor. But, Stephen, I began to see that the mere act of ascending into my pulpit was a loud statement against the necessity of the Church."

"What do you mean?" Stephen asked, sitting forward, listening intently.

"We both know that the essence of Congregationalism is that individuals need search no farther than their individual consciences to find truth, and that any two individuals who agree are essentially 'a church.' Now, although I preach that there are things that are ultimately and essentially true, as a Congregationalist—or should I say, as a Protestant—I have no more right in my conservative views than the money-hungry Pentecostal or the gay Episcopalian, or even those ritualistic Catholics across the street. Either there is a Church one can trust, through which Jesus Christ gives the grace we each need to grow in holiness and eternal life, or there are no churches that one can trust."

Stephen had risen from his chair to look out the window. The evening sky was clear, and the first stars were breaking forth.

"So what happened?" he asked. "Did you boldly proclaim this from the housetops?"

"I didn't get the chance."

"What?"

"I left that ministerial luncheon and went directly to my best friend, Carl, on the church board. I would have liked to have had someone in authority above me to go to—a bishop or district pastor—who could have guided me in my thinking, but, as you know, of course, we Congregationalist pastors are essentially on our own. I told Carl my dilemma, and together we decided it was better for me to resign, make a comforting, affirming farewell, and leave without dropping a bomb that no one in the congregation could or would understand. Fortunately, I had an assistant pastor who could step up and take over all aspects of the ministry until they hired a new senior pastor."

"Geez, Cliff, kind of drastic."

"Yes and no. We decided it was better for everyone. You see, there was another element that decided this for me. None of this was happening in a vacuum. Ever since your grand tirade last year at the Mite, I've been following your lead, reading the early Church Fathers."

"You were getting yourself into trouble."

"You can say that again."

"You were getting yourself—"

"Okay, you got me back. Besides the fact that the early Church was certainly no form of Protestant Christianity, there is no question that being a Christian has always meant being a baptized member of the Church. The idea of individual, independent Christians is a modern idea—a modern heresy, if you like. Third, all the early Christian writers, especially St. Augustine, stressed that there was no worse sin than schism, breaking from the unity and authority of the Church— and especially setting oneself up as an authority over the Church.

"So, for me," Cliff went on, with a self-deprecating laugh, "I was triply guilty. I was baptized and brought up a Catholic, by my good, faithful, Haitian, immigrant mother, who until recently mourned over the fact that her one son had not only left the Church but had become a renegade Protestant minister. Like St. Augustine's mother St. Monica, however, she had never ceased praying for my return. I guess, as the Bible says, the prayers of a righteous man—of two righteous parents— are always heard."

"So you're becoming Catholic?"

"Not only that: it looks like I will become a priest!"

"What?" Stephen said, grabbing his chair to steady himself. "How's that possible? I mean, so soon, with—"

"I know, but you see, God does 'work all things together for good,' as the Good Book says. You know most of the juicy details of the breakup of my marriage. When Cecilia left me, taking my children, to shack up with her old flame, I told even my closest friends that it was all because she cracked under the pressures of the ministry. Well, I discovered to my chagrin that there's a whole lot more dirt under the rug. Her old flame had been a constant bonfire behind my back. In fact, in the midst of the horrendous hell of the divorce—which as you know, I never wanted—she let it all out, that not only had she been seeing the jerk all along on the sly, but my daughter wasn't even my daughter."

"Good God, Cliff!"

"Stephen, you won't believe this. On the very night of my bachelor's party, when you and my other seminary friends took me out on the town, she was in bed with this idiot, conceiving our daughter."

"But Cecilia seemed so excited about the birth. I don't remember her showing any hesitation in her love for you or your child."

"And for nearly five years she had me fooled, too. I believed her, but when I came home early from a trip and caught her in bed with him, her shield fell. The only way I can describe this is that it was demonic. It wasn't merely repressed anger or bitterness. She had enjoyed her deception, feeding her twisted ego on seeing how successfully she could carry on two clandestine love affairs. In the end, what she hated most was her need to act holy as a pastor's wife. I don't believe she even has a conscience, for never once has she expressed one word of remorse."

"I'm so sorry, Cliff."

"Well, anyway, my bishop is quite confident that the tribunal will grant an annulment, and if so, then he will promote my vocation to the priesthood. We're just trying to discern whether I am called to the diocesan priesthood or to some religious order, like here with the Benedictines at St. Anselm's Friary."

"So when are you going to swim the Tiber and abandon us infidels?"

"What do you mean? I'm already Catholic."

"How's that possible?"

"Remember, I was originally a Catholic, baptized, catechized, and confirmed at St. Tatian's Haitian immigrant parish in New York. All I had to do was go back into the confessional after thirty years, purge myself of all the crud, receive absolution, say a mess of Our Fathers, and I was home again. And Stephen, all I can say is that it's great."

"Have you told all this to Jim Sarver? You know he finally became Catholic, last Easter?"

"Not only that, you won't believe all the others I'm finding out about. Jim was the only Protestant minister I'd ever heard of who'd become Catholic. I'd heard of Catholic priests, nuns, and laymen becoming Protestant. Jeez, I probably helped dozens to do so over the years. But since I've come in, I've heard of dozens of Protestant ministers who have either converted or are on the journey. Remember Julie Robinson, from seminary, the former Jew who was ordained an Evangelical Baptist? Well, she resigned her pastorate, entered the Church last Easter, and is on the speaking circuit."

"That's our Julie? I read something somewhere about a Julie Robinson taking on debates in defense of the Catholic Church, but I didn't know it was her."

"So, hey, that's enough about me," Cliff said, turning the tables. "How are you doing? I've heard a few things through the grapevine, but nothing definite."

Before he began, Stephen shifted the phone to his other hand. "Well, where to begin." He presumed neither he nor Cliff had the privilege of enough time for all the details, so he related only the talking points of the last year's journey.

Once he'd brought Cliff up to date, he admitted, "For nearly a year, therefore, I've become thoroughly convinced by the data of

Scripture, history, theology, and surprisingly even philosophy, of all the things you've said: that Jesus indeed established a Church in His chosen apostles, centered around Simon Peter; that He promised to give them the Holy Spirit to guide them into truth; and most significantly that this Church cannot be identified with any of my local Congregational congregations nor our Congregational Association of otherwise disconnected churches, nor for that matter any Protestant denomination."

"So then, Stephen, when are you entering the Church?"

"All of these convictions do not mean that my struggles are over. I'm still daily on an emotional roller coaster, because frankly I'm not dealing well with all the losses. Like you, I guess, I also am in discussion with my local priest—Father Bourque, you know him—about the possibility of priesthood, but I'm not sure it's possible because this journey not only led to my resignation but, as I mentioned, has broken up my marriage."

"It's really none of my business, of course, but, if I may ask, what happened?"

"To be honest, I'm not really sure. Certainly, there is a long list of potential causes—most center around me—but yet there's an elusive, irrational aspect to her decision to leave that has paralyzed me emotionally. I thought we were on the same page; I thought she understood all that I was going through and why; I even thought she agreed, but then when I finally followed through with my convictions, she reacted in shock, turned on me, and left. She said she felt betrayed and duped: she had given up her dreams to follow mine, and then I threw them all away to become Catholic. I haven't been able to speak with her since last June."

"Last June? Stephen, I'm … so sorry."

Stephen rose again to pace. "While I've got you on the phone, I've got an unrelated question."

"Go ahead, shoot."

"Ah, maybe skip that imagery," Stephen said in jest.

"Sorry."

"As I contemplate conversion, there's something that continues to bug me—about the seeming lack of objective proof that Catholic sacraments do what they claim. Catholics maintain that, due to the assurance of apostolic succession, they can know that their orders are valid and, therefore, that their sacraments deliver the graces needed for salvation. They also say that, though God in His mercy *can* convey grace through Protestant sacraments, no one can say with certainty that He does."

"That's what I've come to believe. So, what's the problem?"

"My problem is that I see no objective difference between the lives of Catholics and non-Catholics. I've yet to meet any Catholics who seem any more holy than the most faithful Evangelicals I've known. On top of that, Church history, even as told by Catholic historians, indicates that the people who have caused the most problems in the Church were the priests and bishops who had received the most sacraments: who had experienced the graces of baptism, confirmation, confession, ordination, and especially the Eucharist.

"So are the high-sounding theological and philosophical claims concerning Catholic sacraments as channels of divine life and grace no more than just that: high-sounding theological and philosophical claims?"

Stephen heard a gruff, muffled, background voice over the phone, then Cliff's anxious voice returned. "Geez, Stephen, I'm so sorry. You'll have to hold that thought. I almost forgot that I'm scheduled to lead Vespers, and the brothers are in the chapel waiting. I really have to run, but can I call you on your cell phone tomorrow?"

"Don't have a cell phone, and I'll be traveling."

"Then, please, call me back when you can. Gotta go. God bless."

And Stephen was left with a dial tone.

He returned to his coffee, which had long since gone cold, and sat in silence. Tomorrow he would head south, either to Jamesfield or on to confront his family in their new home out on Cape Ann. He had hoped Cliff would help him decide which destination. Instead, he would pray that either sometime in the night or during the long drive south he would be blessed with an inspiration.

With the remote in one hand, and her hotel room phone in the other, Sara reduced the television volume down so she could more adequately hear her son.

"Daniel, quit mumbling. Put whatever game your playing on pause, and speak to me."

"Oh, yeah, sure."

In the background, Sara heard the orchestrated triumphs of computerized war cease abruptly.

"Sorry, Mom. So, how was your trip? Have you found Dad?"

"No, not yet. So, I can assume he hasn't by chance called?"

"Don't think so, but then I've only been home for an hour or so. Had chess club after school. William might know."

"Is he there by chance?"

"No, either in his dorm, or, wait, he's probably at basketball practice."

"That's right, of course. Well, here's my number at the hotel if you need me or especially if your father calls."

She passed along her contact information, and said, "I'll let you go. Please tell your brother that I'll call again tomorrow night."

"Okay, love you."

"Love you, too. Good night." The phone went dead as her son returned with haste to resume his battle against the demons of darkness, so she could return her attention back to the movie on the television screen.

"How's Henry? I hadn't seen him for quite some time."

"Oh, he's fine, thank you. He's terribly tired and worried."

"I imagine he's having great difficulty raising money for the cathedral."

"Yes, it's slow work. How's your book coming?"

Sara was making the most of her lonely evening, and for this she couldn't have hoped for better. One of her favorite movies, a little past season, just happened to be the featured selection on the classic movie channel in her hotel's limited cable lineup. *The Bishop's Wife*, starring Cary Grant, David Niven, and Loretta Young, and every scene, regardless of any direct correlation, brought on a shower of nostalgic memories from her own life as a preacher's wife, which now seemed so long ago.

The tensions and stresses faced by the bishop were all too familiar. The movie—even with its strangely bent portrayal of what heaven might consider serious enough to correct by sending an angel—made her both miss the joys of being a pastor's wife and dread them.

> "There's something I'd like you to give Henry with my compliments for his Cathedral Fund. This has been my lucky piece, not that it's ever brought me any luck, except knowing you. It's an old Roman coin. I picked it up years ago in a junk shop. It has little value."
>
> "It's a wonderful contribution."
>
> "Nonsense. It might be called the Widow's Mite."

The Widow's Mite. *What a strange coincidence*, she thought. She sipped a diet soda, purchased from a vending machine down the hall. Cocooned in the hotel's generic paper-thin comforter, she cushioned herself against four pillows. Sara allowed herself to become lost in the comfortable familiarity of the movie. In time Cary Grant's angel character confronted the old professor:

> "I'm interested in Julia ... and Henry. What seems to be their trouble?"
>
> "I never see Henry any more. He has no time for riffraff like me. He now consults with the vulgar rich like Mrs. Hamilton."

God, however, had sent no angel into their marriage. No Cary Grant without wings had come to save it or to redirect Stephen's qualms about the pastorate. God had let him follow his doubts far out onto a precarious limb, and, without rescue, had allowed it to break, leaving them separated and Stephen unemployed.

Her thoughts left the movie, almost as if called away by a distant voice. *Where was he? Will I find him, or just end up returning home even more distant from him?*

"Please, Lord Jesus," she prayed, closing her eyes briefly from the distraction of this movie of hope, "whatever it takes, even an angel from heaven, please bring us back together. I have been wrong; I have put myself and my wants above what is best for my marriage and my family. I know that You called Stephen and me together, long ago, and I will gladly submit to his leadership, no matter where You are calling him—calling us."

"Look at that. Henry's old church, perishing from neglect."

"It's such a nice little church."

"Too little, I'm afraid. It can't stand up against the march of progress."

"Please, Lord," she prayed aloud, "I mean this. Just give me the grace to follow through."

PART 3
I Will Fear No Evil

19

So, you tell me. How can anyone know at the beginning of a day what's going to befall him by the end of that day? And if we did have any way of knowing, how many of us would choose to just stay in bed?

Dressed for the day, casual and warm rather than formal, for our anticipated encounter with the priest, I buzzed for the elevator. A glance to both ends of the hall revealed no one. Since checking in I'd seen nothing of Raeph. Down and out into the lobby, still no one.

"Two please, I think," I told the waitress, who led me through the vacant restaurant to a booth by the window. The decor was retro-1950s: stainless steel accented with red vinyl. Even the rip in the bench seat was patched with the same red plastic tape they would have used back then.

"Coffee?"

If I hadn't known better, I'd have sworn I was in a *Twilight Zone* episode. Everything about the woman shrieked the '50s—and it wasn't just a costume she put on every day; this was far too natural, frighteningly real. Either I'd been swooshed back or she (and this town?) had been locked in time. Maybe that was why no one else was here! I looked around for a stray newspaper to check. This was how time travelers always discovered the truth of their plight: the mind-shattering date.

"Coffee?" she again demanded, not unpleasantly, lifting the black-and-copper plastic carafe a little higher.

"Yes, please, I guess."

As she poured, I saw over her shoulder a connection to reality.

"Morning, Scott," Raeph said as he joined me. "I'll take some, too," he said to the waitress with a smile.

"Good sleep?" I asked after she'd left.

"Can't complain, and I do appreciate you taking care of all this."

"No problem, Raeph. God's been good."

He seemed to have changed his shirt but everything else was the same. I probed, "Sorry I didn't look you up last night, but—"

"No problem. After a bit of TV, I passed out; just needed some sleep."

"Well, you order whatever you like, and then we'll head down the road to the Catholic church."

A woman entered the restaurant, not from the street but from the hotel. At first, her features were blocked from view, but when she turned into her booth across the room, I recognized her.

"Raeph, I can't believe my eyes, but—yes it is." Leaving my napkin to drop to the floor, I approached, sure of my hunch. "Sara? Sara LaPointe?"

"Yes?" she said, looking up, then, "Scott! What are you doing here?" She left her booth, and we embraced. She grasped and held me far tighter than I might have expected. "It sure is good to see you, Scott," she added, reaching for her purse.

"Are you alone, or with Stephen?" I asked, glancing anxiously toward the entrance.

"Alone." She was using a hanky to dry her eyes.

"Then, please, come and join us." And then I realized the awkwardness of what I was bringing her into. "Ah, I think you may know the man I'm with. He was once one of your parishioners."

Raeph was sitting with his back to us as we drew near.

"His name's Raeph. Raeph Timmons."

She halted a few steps short of the booth. Raeph left his seat, turned, and with a flat smile said, "Hello, Mrs. LaPointe."

She responded almost in a whisper, "Raeph." With no easy exit line, she slipped across onto my side of the booth. I slid in beside her, blocking any escape—though without intent. "I don't understand—what are you doing here?"

As he slowly retook his seat, his eyes avoided hers. "Mrs. LaPointe, I hope you know I had nothing to do with what Walter did."

"Let's just say it hadn't crossed my mind that he had an accomplice. However, you two were always together on everything, like peas in a pod, especially everything that undercut Stephen's authority in the congregation."

"I know," he said, looking into his coffee. "I really am sorry, for everything. You need to understand, I hadn't seen Walter in years, ever since Patty and I'd moved away from Red Creek. When I found out what he did, it was too late." He went silent.

"What are the two of you doing here together anyway?" she demanded. "I didn't realize you were friends."

"Only since yesterday," I said, sorry that I had brought her into this, "but we're both here to find Stephen."

"Why?" she asked incredulously, glaring across at Raeph.

"Want some coffee?" I interjected. I hailed the waitress across the room. She returned with the carafe and filled our cups to overflowing.

"Raeph and I met yesterday at the Widow's Mite."

"What were you doing at the Widow's Mite?" she demanded across the table. "You're not a pastor?"

"I—" Raeph started, but I completed, "Sara, that's a long story."

"Mrs. LaPointe," Raeph continued, "I know I can't explain it very well, but I just want to talk with your husband, to pass along what Walter told me. It might help him understand what happened and why."

Sara was more focused on her coffee than Raeph's answer. Then with a look of revelation, she demanded, "So, he wasn't there?"

"Who, Stephen?" I answered. "No, he wasn't. I was assuming he was here with you. Will he be joining us for breakfast?"

Her response was long in coming. "No, Scott, he's not here with me."

She stopped as if finished, but then after a stern glance at Raeph and one to me of resignation, she began again, "Stephen and I have been separated for nearly nine months."

I had not heard this, which was amazing, given how fast the rumor mill usually works at the Mite.

"Sara, I'm so sorry," I said, reaching my hand over to grasp hers. "Nine months. I ... can't imagine ..."

"I'd rather not discuss it now," she said, with a unguarded nod in Raeph's direction.

Raeph looked at me, then slowly down into his coffee.

With caution, I asked, "Then I'm guessing you're here in Jamesfield for the same reason we are?"

"Which is?"

"To visit that priest, Reverend Bourque?"

"If you haven't been in touch with Stephen, then how did you know?"

"The Mite grapevine. Once Raeph and I realized we were on the same quest, we decided to blow off the retreat and drop in on the good priest this morning."

"Does he know you're coming?"

"No," I replied, glancing over at Raeph. "I just figured we'd drop in unannounced. We're not sure what to expect, but it might be better that he doesn't have time to prepare for us."

"Well, I met with him yesterday briefly."

"You did? Did he have any news about Stephen?"

"Not really, but we have a meeting scheduled at nine this morning."

"Oh," I said, then asked cautiously, "would you like us to come along for moral support?"

It was the first hint of a smile we'd seen since she'd joined us. "I'd appreciate it."

"Then let's order a nice big breakfast—it's on me—and then we'll go over together and press that priest to the wall!"

Sara's faint smile developed almost into a laugh, so I summoned the waitress.

At ten minutes to nine, we descended upon St. Francis de Sales Church from the north, easing the van quietly to the curb across the street. Our first approach had been from the south but finding no parking spaces, I circled the block and came the other way.

I quipped, "I'd say that was God's providence, for from this side of the street, we've got a much wider perspective." The three of us sat studying the confluence of church architecture, the traditional stone church next to the 1970s-design parish annex.

"Who's that?" Raeph demanded, pointing a nervous finger. A black shrouded figure passed between the church and the annex.

"That's Sister Agatha. I met her yesterday. She's very nice, and amazingly pretty," Sara said with an absent stare.

"Well, it's time," I said. "Are you sure you don't mind us horning in on your appointment?"

"Goodness no. I'm grateful you're here, because I'm certainly not ready to take on this priest alone."

"Let's go then," I said, exiting the van. The other two followed, Sara around the front, Raeph a bit more cautiously from the rear, and together we approached the church.

"We're to meet with him in his private study," she indicated, so we veered in the direction of the offices.

Upon reaching the front stoop, Raeph stopped and said, "Oh, shoot, I left my Bible in the back seat."

"You won't need it," I replied, ringing the buzzer.

"No, please, I want it. Is the van open?"

"Yes, but—"

"It'll only take a minute. You two go on in, and I'll join you." He turned and walked briskly away as the door opened.

"Oh, good morning, Mrs. LaPointe," the sister said, motioning us in, her eyes studying me closely. "Father Bourque will be with you presently. He's with a parishioner over at the church. Are you together?"

"Yes, Sister, this is Reverend Scott Turner, an old friend of ours. There's another gentleman with us, Raeph Timmons," she said, glancing back through the closed storm door, "who'll join us momentarily." Raeph, however, was nowhere in sight.

"I'll bring him to you when he comes. Please, this way." Sister Agatha led us down a hall decorated on both sides with black-and-white photos of men and women who I presumed were previous priests, nuns, and lay members of the parish. One ancient priest with a long beard but no mustache looked every bit like one of the Amish farmers that sometimes rode their rigs into the Rowsville farmer's market.

We were then escorted into a small study with walls covered with shelves and books, broken only by a lone window and the recently stoked wood-burning stove giving the room a crisp welcoming warmth. Before the fire were three rocking chairs, two facing the one that was obviously the priest's, for adjacent to it was a side table upon which were personal devotional items, a writer's journal, and a select collection of pipes and pertinent supplies.

"Would you like some tea or coffee?"

"Yes, please," Sara answered. "Coffee with cream."

I nodded, "Black."

Sister Agatha closed the door behind her, leaving us alone in the nervous anticipation of our meeting with the priest. Sara took the rocker nearest the fire, seemingly oblivious to the astounding wealth of knowledge and resources surrounding her.

I must admit, all pride aside, that I remained standing, mesmerized. I thought my personal library was something to brag about. Mine might be larger with sheer volume, but what defined Father Bourque's collection as exquisite was not quantity but quality. Perusing the shelves, my amazement escalated. Every single book, regardless of genre or topic, was a winner, and not just by Catholic writers but from the best of all traditions. There were a few books I was startled to find—rabid anti-Catholic tomes that even I would be ashamed to have displayed anywhere at my church or home—but in the context of his purposeful, highly informed collection, their presence made sense. What astounded me, however, was that it appeared this priest had read most every book. I opened a few at random—the collection was divided into topics: theology, dogmatics, history, philosophy, biblical commentaries, conversion stories, ecumenism, church documents— and every book contained underlining and handwritten notes in the margin. I suppose this is one of the blessings of being celibate: time to read without guilt.

The door opened and Sister Agatha reappeared. "Here you go, and if there's anything else you want, please don't hesitate to call. I'm just across the hall in the kitchen. Father should be here momentarily."

"Thank you, Sister," I said for the two of us.

After she left, I gave Sara a moment to sip her coffee before I asked, "So, how are you? I suppose it's been—" and I summarized the rest with a wave of a hand.

"Since you, Diane, and the girls were out at Thanksgiving—when was that, nearly five years ago?"

"Yes. Since then we've added Eddy to the menagerie. We're now living in Rowsville, Ohio, where I'm the new pastor of a tiny country church. But really, Sara, how are you and the boys?"

She gave me a quick, inquisitive glance from her warm, deep green eyes, but then returned her gaze to the fire. "Not so good, Scott. I don't know how much you know about what happened—"

"Actually very little."

"Well," she sipped her coffee, evaluating, I presumed, how much to reveal, "I really didn't want to separate from Stephen. I still love him dearly, as much as I ever have, and the boys miss him. They try to hide it, but their sadness is always there behind their words, behind their eyes. I suppose what I've done is unforgivable, but at the time I didn't know what else to do."

"Like I said, I know very little of what happened, at least since he was released from the hospital. That was the last time I spoke with him."

"You visited him?"

"No. We spoke by phone but only briefly."

A tear rolled down her cheek, reflecting the fire's glow. I started to go to her, but she raised her hand. "I'm all right, Scott." On the table next to the priest's chair was a box of tissues. I got this for her, and she took a fistful.

"It's just that I said so many mean things, I know he won't forgive me."

"Sara, you know Stephen and how much he loves you. I can't believe there is anything you can do that he wouldn't forgive."

She started to say something, but stopped, then said, with sadness tinged with anger, "Then why doesn't he call me? Where is he?"

"When did you last hear from him?"

"Last June, and I'm scared for him. This is not like him, to be so disconnected. He's gone, disappeared. He's abandoned us." Tears began to flow more freely. "I assumed that I'd just come and find him here with this priest, but I don't think he knows where Stephen is either. I was told that he had been here since August, I guess trying to decide whether to become Roman Catholic."

"Was he truly thinking of doing this?"

"Yes, against all of my ranting and raving, and the advice of his friends, except maybe Jim Sarver."

I decided to play dumb. "That's right. I'd heard that Jim had become Catholic. How's he doing?"

"Oh, I don't know, and I don't care." She set her empty cup down with force on the floor beside her. "I've lost track of him, too. He probably talks to Stephen all the time, probably encouraging him to become Catholic even if it means losing his family."

"I wonder what's keeping Raeph?" I said, getting up. "Excuse me, Sara. I'll check."

She nodded assent, so I left the room and went out onto the front porch. Raeph was nowhere. The van looked empty, and there were no familiar figures walking in sight. I reentered, and as I stomped the snow from my boots, a hurried male voice greeted me.

"Hello, you must be Mr. Raeph Timmons. Sister Agatha said you would be joining the others."

"No, actually, I'm the Reverend Scott Turner." I extended my hand to whom I assumed was Reverend Bourque, dressed from neck to floor in a priestly black robe interrupted only by a white tab at his throat, a white cincture around his waist, and flecks of dandruff on his shoulder. He looked to be in his sixties; his receding black hair was slightly awry, probably from a hat of some sort. His weathered face, sporting a day-old graying stubble, was tired-looking, but his smile was friendly and inviting.

"But Sister said—?"

"I came out to see what had become of Raeph, but he seems to have chickened out."

"Chickened out?" he queried with a smirk. "Well, maybe he'll find some courage and return. Come, let's join Mrs. LaPointe."

He motioned me down the hall, and we went toward the study, while the sister met us by the kitchen door.

"Here's your tea, Father, and a fresh plate of cookies." The priest dismissed her with a nod and took what we had guessed correctly to be his rocker.

"I'm sorry I'm late, Mrs. LaPointe. I was delayed by a needy parishioner, but I'm here now, and I trust Sister Agatha has supplied your every want and need?"

"Yes, of course," Sara answered quickly, betraying her anxious quest.

"And Reverend Turner, are you a friend of Stephen and Sara?"

"Yes, Fa—, uh, Reverend Bourque. We go back a long way." Calling the priest "Father" was still something I could not stomach. I had never called any man "father" other than my real father in Michigan (the now-dead drunk, God rest his soul). The words of Jesus' warning against this still rang too much in my ears, and to utter this word was the sign of a surrender I was not ready to make.

"Then I presume you are both here for the same reason?"

Sara blurted out, "You said last night that you thought we'd be seeing him again soon. When, and what aren't you telling me?"

Before he spoke, the priest carefully retrieved a hand-carved Meerschaum pipe from amongst the plainer ones in the rack, gazed down into its bowl, slapped it against his palm twice, looked again into its bowl, and placed it between his teeth. He rocked a moment, back and forth, studying the glowing hearth.

He finally answered. "Sara, and Scott, in case you didn't know, I am a convert to the Catholic faith. I was a Lutheran minister, and after my wife Lucy died," he paused to draw our attention to her picture on the table beside him, "I converted and, by God's grace, was ordained to the priesthood. I say this only to let you know that, at least to some extent, I know what you're going through. I also, therefore, realize that this may not make sense or seem fair to you, but I hesitate to reveal what things I may know because it's hard to discern which aspects of what Stephen has told me I can share. Since last August, he has been living nearby. We have talked many, many times, and . . . well, let me begin at the beginning. Do you mind?" he asked indicating his bin of pipe tobacco.

"Of course not," Sara answered, with an impatient little brush of her hand in the air.

The priest paused to study Sara, and then proceeded to fill his pipe and progress through the procedure of teasing it to a full, boisterous burn. A pleasant mixture of cinnamon and cherry with a touch of clove changed the room's ambiance. It seemed to cast a spell of relaxation upon us all.

"I know little of what transpired between the time he preached his final sermon last Easter, sold your home in June, and then ended up here in August. On the surface, at first, he appeared all together, confident, happy. When he arrived he looked great, a bit thinner than

I remembered, but dapper in his gray, herringbone, tweed jacket, blue Oxford cloth shirt, red-and-white striped tie, and khaki pants. He could have been a local bank executive or, of course, a successful, high-profile but low-church Protestant minister."

With this jaded quip, I found an ire mounting—though in another setting with different company I would have agreed heartily. Until then I hadn't realized how on edge I was. This priest was a pleasant enough man of God, more of a grandfather figure than the stealthy, Jesuitical brand of priest so often pictured by anti-Catholic controversialists. Yet, there was an anger inside of me. I felt anxious to jump on his words, to listen closely for hidden meanings, for misspoken hints of underlying agendas, for near-Christian illusions that were anything but. And I wondered, *was he playing Sara?* The mere thought of this shot my anger thermometer skyward. *Did he really know where Stephen was? Was he keeping them apart?* But I controlled myself.

The priest continued. "Once behind closed doors, however, here in my study, Stephen's façade fell quickly away. Sitting in the very chair in which you're sitting, Sara, he wept, face buried in his hands, trying to hide his grief. He was guarded, ashamed to tell me details. As his words spewed forth in uncontrollable sobs, I feared he was on the verge of an emotional breakdown. But then he regained his composure and apologized profusely. We talked long into the night, and," with a glance at Sara, "he told me most everything about your final weeks together."

Sara answered defensively, "You've got to understand I was angry; I felt betrayed. He threw everything away, everything he—everything we had accomplished. I felt like he was spitting in my face, making a mockery of my entire life."

"How is that, Sara?" Reverend Bourque asked, in a far bolder manner than I would have dared, but then again I tend to be far too sensitive, too reticent.

Sara rose to pace, speaking as much with her hands and arms as with her voice. "I never even wanted to be a pastor's wife. It never crossed the universe of my mind. I wasn't even religious, until I met Stephen. Then in my surrender of love to him and his goals I cast aside all my dreams. I became the loving wife, the mother of two sons, and the submissive, smiling, passive, pious pastor's wife."

"But Sara, was it all make-believe? Had you not discovered the beauty in being a mother and a wife, even a pastor's wife? Had you not come to fully believe?"

She turned sharply toward the priest, fists clenched, the muscles in her neck taut, eyes wide, but then all relaxed, and she fell into tears. Her rocker creaked as she sat down hard, face in hands.

The priest's hand extended toward her, communicating apology if necessary.

"I'm all right," she said, wiping away all evidence of vulnerability, "but, yes, you're right, of course. I loved it all; I loved our life together. I was so proud of him, up there leading us, and I liked the attention I received as his wife. I love my sons and I loved being a mother. I even loved being a homemaker, without the pressures and responsibilities that come with a career. I was teaching adult classes. It was great. It was all great. But then he threw it all away, and it was all because of you!"

The dam broke. She had come to find her husband, but maybe subconsciously she also had come to let loose her venom on the priest she believed had derailed their lives.

"Sara, dear, I think I understand—"

"Actually, Reverend Bourque," I interjected, "I don't. The last time I was with Stephen, sure, he was confused, but right in the middle, between there and the complete destruction of his family, is you. What happened when he stayed here with you?"

For a moment our eyes locked, but with a smile he turned away, and first, before he answered, he attended to the needs of his pipe. Then in a calm, controlled tone, he answered, "Reverend Turner, as I said, much of what Stephen and I discussed must remain private, of course, though I'm sure he'll tell you everything when you see him."

"But will we see him?"

"Yes, of course, I have no doubt of this. Later this week, in fact, we have a long-standing appointment together. It was made several months ago, and I doubt that he will miss it."

"What kind of appointment?" she demanded.

"Sara, again, I'm sorry. I don't feel that I'm free to tell you. It needs to come from him."

"Then he's done it. Without consulting me or the children, he's become a d_____ Roman Catholic." Oblivious to any response, she turned her face, a mixture of bewilderment and rage, to the fire.

The priest raised both his hands toward her beseechingly, his lips beginning to form an answer. Then he stopped, once again constrained by what he believed to be privileged information.

As Sara sobbed and the priest sat momentarily speechless, I watched silently, questioning whether this surprise reunion had been a good idea after all.

"Excuse me," she said, rising to leave the room. The priest and I also rose, but seeing that Sister Agatha was there in the hallway to assist her, I awkwardly reclaimed my seat. The priest relit his pipe, while I cradled my lukewarm coffee, and together we stared silently into the fire.

"Scott, I must be honest. I fear for her. She is not going to like what is happening to her husband."

"What is happening?"

A cloud must have passed before the sun, for cold darkness suddenly drenched the room. This is at least how I explain the chill that passed through my body.

"As I began explaining earlier, Stephen showed up on my doorstep sometime in August, alone and unemployed. I don't want to say homeless because that, of course, would give the wrong impression, but he was essentially without a place to call home. He stayed here in one of our guest rooms for a few days while together we tried to discern God's plan. He decided to find a temporary, non-ministry job here in Jamesfield. So, through the usual channels, I got him a job at the local hardware—the owner is a faithful parishioner—where Stephen was also able to live upstairs in a furnished apartment.

"Everything was going fine. We continued getting together to talk about his journey of faith and vocational issues, as well as his broken marriage, but then on Christmas Day he was gone. When he didn't show up to work or daily Mass we all became concerned. Then three days later I got a note from him—here, I think I've still got it."

The priest walked over to a rolltop desk tucked into the shelves of his library. From an inner compartment, he withdrew a folded letter.

"It doesn't give specific details," he said, as he returned to his rocker, "but tells us not to worry. Let me read what I can:

Dear Father Bourque,

I'm sorry if my sudden departure has caused you or Sister Agatha or any of my other friends any concern. I'm fine, but just need to get away. It was sitting in Christmas Eve Mass that broke this camel's back! It brought everything back. It reminded me of how much I miss being in the pulpit, how much I ache to be preaching and leading people in worship. And, of course, how much I miss my family. I just needed to get away by myself to think everything through. I know this is a bit much to ask, but please thank the Flarens for the job and apologize for my sudden departure. I'll make it up to them when I get back.

In Christ,
Stephen

"I haven't heard from him since," the priest said, refolding the letter.

"And you have no idea at all where he might have gone? It isn't like him to go this long without contacting anyone, especially his family."

"I suppose I could make a few guesses, but it doesn't really matter because there would be no way of locating him. Stephen is trapped in the dilemma of a decision that he knows he must make but is hesitant to carry out."

"What decision? I assumed that his resignation meant he was on the same road as Jim Sarver: that he was going to pope, if you excuse my grammar."

"Well, he hasn't yet. I guess you could say he's paralyzed in 'no man's land.' Because of what he has learned, he is convinced he can no longer remain Protestant, and though he says he's worked through all his qualms about Catholic beliefs and practices, he can't make the jump. I guess the final issues are his marriage, his family, and his vocation as a minister."

No man's land. I hadn't heard it put this way, but as the priest spoke, I knew he was also describing me. He was describing exactly how I'd felt that past year after being blindsided by the same things that had upended Stephen. I, too, could no longer remain the Protestant I'd been, and, though I hadn't faced up to this yet, I guess that meant that I, too, could not remain a minister. But unlike Stephen, I had never, even for a second, considered the Catholic Church as an option.

The priest continued, "Stephen is facing a problem that all married Protestant clergy face when they consider converting to a church that is committed to clerical celibacy. There are options, of course, but if he converts, he will have to accept the possibility that he may never preach from a pulpit again."

"But why does the Catholic Church insist on this archaic restriction for its priests? Look at the problems priestly celibacy has caused! It didn't stop priests from having affairs and has made the priesthood a magnet for men with sexual aberrations."

"Many even in the Catholic Church feel the same way you do, but there are strong biblical, theological, as well as historic reasons for the requirement of priestly celibacy and continence in the Latin Church. The problems in the clergy and the Church are not caused by celibacy. In fact, statistics prove that the problem of sexual misconduct is actually greater amongst Protestant clergy and public school educators than amongst Catholic clergy. This sad fact doesn't make the front pages of our newspapers, but the data clearly shows that allowing clergy to marry in the Protestant churches has never stopped immorality, whether heterosexual or homosexual. The flaw isn't with celibacy but with experiencing a true life-changing commitment to Jesus Christ.

"As for Stephen, I'm sure if he finally decides to enter the Church, and if he continues to sense a call to the priesthood, the local bishop, who confirmed my own call to the priesthood after I converted, will be open to considering him for a dispensation from celibacy. The primary issue, however, that stands in the way for Stephen, which I suspect is the reason for his absence, is Sara. He is unswervingly committed to Jesus and to following Him wherever He might call, even if it means into the Catholic Church. But equally, he loves Sara and his sons and does not want to do anything that would pose a permanent barrier to their getting back together."

"But Sara seems to think he's already crossed the divide. He allowed his questions about the faith and his interest in the Catholic Church to come between them."

"Yes and no. He didn't want it to separate them, but he was torn apart by the implications of what he believed he had to do. Through all that he'd learned, he had become convinced that the Catholic Church was the one true Church established by Jesus Christ in His apostles. Knowing this, Stephen could not go back or turn away, but yet, he could not leave his beloved Sara. Is it not true that he didn't leave her, but she left him?"

"I guess, but—" I really didn't know enough details to say any more.

"You see, Scott, since they've not been able to talk it out—for whatever reason—Stephen has no idea what's going through Sara's mind and heart. He was devastated when she left him. He said that he'd tried to call a number of times but unfortunately never got an answer. I'm afraid for him, because he has been sliding increasingly into despair. The destructive voices from within keep bombarding him with the lie that the devastation he brought upon his family, marriage, and career is beyond hope."

I studied this minister of a different persuasion, and considered that he must have once had the same awakening to faith and then call to ministry that I'd had. He too had been to seminary, experienced a laying on of hands, and though he had taken the bold, unfathomable leap into the Catholic priesthood, I could tell by the books on his shelf, as well as his demeanor, that his heart and faith had never changed.

"So tell me, what can we do?" I asked.

"You can help Sara understand how much Stephen still loves her, but for Stephen the most important thing we all must do—especially Sara—is pray. Only God knows where he is right now and what's going through his mind—what kind of spiritual battle he might be fighting. He needs God's grace and mercy, and His protection."

It was time for me to come clean.

"Reverend Bourque, Sara may come back any time, but there's something you need to know that Sara doesn't. Yes, I am here to find my old friend Stephen and help them get back together, but my being here with Sara was completely coincidental."

"There are no coincidences—"

"I know that;" I said with a laugh, "that's pretty obvious. But I had another reason for wanting to find Stephen. I drove all the way from northwestern Ohio to talk with him about the things he said last year at the retreat, the same things that led to his resignation and the mess in his life and marriage."

"Are you on the same journey?"

"Let's just say that I'm in a similar kind of 'no man's land.'"

"Would you like to talk with me about this later this evening? I'm free."

This was all happening way too fast. A voice within cried: *Do you really want to let yourself into the same dialogue with the same priest that has thrown such a wrench into your friends' lives? But, I argued back, If this priest's arguments were strong enough to convince two friends whose intellect and integrity I've never doubted, then why not hear for myself?*

"Okay, that sounds—"

The door opened and Sara's pretty face, now refreshed, appeared. "I'm sorry for running off."

"That's understandable, my dear," our host replied.

"Scott, can you take me back to the hotel?" she asked. "I guess I just need to wait and see if Stephen shows up in the next day or two," she directed these words to Reverend Bourque, "so I better make a few calls to let people know my plans and where I am."

"Sara, either Sister Agatha or I will contact you the minute we hear from him. In the meantime, if you want to get back together to talk some more, I'll gladly do so, between my usual appointments and Masses, of course."

"I may do that. For now, I think I'll just go back to my room and rest." She left the room for the front door.

I shook the priest's hand, and said, "If that offer's still open, when should I return?"

"How about tonight after dinner, say 7:30?"

"Thanks. I'll try and be here, assuming all goes well at the hotel. I still don't understand what happened to Raeph."

The priest escorted us to the door where we said our good-byes. Sara and I walked out to the van without a word, though I could tell that, like me, she was scanning the frosty neighborhood for Raeph.

Once seated inside with the engine running, I asked, "You all right?"

"Yes, Scott, fine, but please, just take me to the hotel. I'd rather not talk right now."

So we drove silently along the slushy main road of Jamesfield, leaving St. Francis de Sales behind us, *sans* Raeph, and not a smidgen closer to Stephen.

 **20**

When Raeph bowed out of meeting with the priest, he slipped safely out of view around to the other side of the van, turned, and crouched down, peering cautiously back around the edge of the bumper. He watched with one eye as the nun motioned Sara and Scott inside and then paused to look back in his direction. Quickly he pulled back, flattening himself against the van, his legs up to the calves in a snowdrift. A memory surfaced, bringing cold, clammy sweat to his brow: his first patrol in 'Nam, stalking, crouching low and last in a long line of new recruits, feeling their way through that strange, dank, southeast Asian vegetation, trying to locate base camp. Walking last, glancing frequently behind him, certain they themselves were being stalked, Raeph had been inundated with every fear he had ever known. Then a sharp whispered command came from up front, and the entire column dove into the bushes, leaving him standing momentarily alone, frozen in indecision. Scanning quickly around for movement, he saw a eucalyptus tree to his right, and dove for cover, and just in time. The air was rent with a shower of AK-47 fire passing only inches above his head. He pressed his back tight against the tree and waited long after the barrage had ceased.

Now as he pressed himself against the van he felt the same fears welling up. He glanced carefully around. The nun was gone, the door to the offices closed. He relaxed, wiping the sweat away with his sleeve.

"Wha'chu doin', mister?" a child's voice inquired from only a few feet away.

Raeph jumped. Losing his footing on some street ice, he fell full length into the drift.

The air rang with children's laughter. Regaining his footing, Raeph saw two small black boys escaping from view around one of the soot-blackened homes that lined the street opposite the church. Standing caked with snow, he saw their two little faces glance back around the house at him, like Buckwheat and Stymie of old.

"RAHH!" he yelled, lurching toward them, but their heads popped back out of sight. He laughed, brushing away the snow, sharing the joy of the moment from their perspective. The sight of his startled face, followed by his Keystone Cop's slosh into the drift would certainly have made their day, as it would have his if he had been in their shoes.

Clean but wet and cold, Raeph walked quickly away from the van, down the sidewalk toward town, keeping as much out of view as the row of parked vehicles allowed. He had no immediate plan, where he was going or what he should do. All he knew was that he was not entering that Catholic church. He had never set foot in one and had sworn he never would.

In his confrontation at the Mite, he had been drawn in by Scott's welcoming and winsome friendship. For a time, he truly believed they were on the same page. But then as Scott rambled on during their drive down the mountain, revealing his own struggles with Scripture and especially his doubts about the Rapture, Raeph began to panic. Scott was sounding far too much like Reverend LaPointe.

The busyness of a congested intersection loomed before him.

It wasn't that Raeph now suspected Scott of being one of old Pastor Smith's "Catholic infiltrators." Instead, as of last night, while listening once again to Walter's farewell, Raeph thought he finally understood what was happening. Just as had happened to LaPointe and probably the other minister they mentioned named Jim, it was apparently happening to Reverend Turner, and maybe even Mrs. LaPointe.

But it was not going to happen to him!

At the corner, he found what he was looking for. Turning to his right, he walked along a freshly shoveled sidewalk, between two waist-high ridges of snow. To his left, a familiar billboard proclaimed: "CH_ _CH: What's missing?" This had been posted with plastic characters from three separate alphabet sets with slightly different font, size, and shade. Below this creative invitation was a name—"Pastor Douglas V. Guilford"—plus a sermon title: "The Leaven of Modern Pharisees." Along the top of the sign in gold letters, Raeph read, "JAMESFIELD BIBLE FELLOWSHIP."

His mouth formed a wry grin. He had found his own respite in the storm.

The waiting area in the offices of the Jamesfield Bible Fellowship Church was a haphazard arrangement of used furniture and artificial plants, probably the non-refusable donations from church members clearing their own living spaces for new, more stylish furnishings. On his right, a sliding glass window separated the waiting area from the office, but to his left, was a sight that drew from him more than double take: a larger-than-life oil portrait of, presumably, the Reverend Douglas V. Guilford. The pastor was poised, ready to pounce, arrayed in a tan, three-piece suit, before the typical mottled blue-green backdrop used by most church directory manufacturers. An enormous, black-leather Bible spilled over from the edge of his left hand, an exhortative finger with pristine fingernails rose from his right hand, directed upward toward the Almighty, and a glare of challenge emanated from eyes that no one anywhere in the room could escape. His lips were pursed into a judgmental scowl, while the slight lilt on one side gave the appearance that he knew something no one else knew. His was an inside scoop.

Raeph forced himself away from the local icon to the sliding office window. Behind it, he heard the sporadic sound of hunt-'n'-peck typing. The gold nameplate read "Miss Maeda McLeary." Having encountered many a church secretary, his expectations were quite low. But regardless, he tapped, and after a pause, the window slid aside.

"I'm sorry, I didn't hear you enter. May I help you?"

He stood mesmerized. Before him was undoubtedly the most striking woman he had ever seen. Her gaudy, black, librarian-style reading glasses, worn low on the tip of her nose, were not in themselves attractive, but in his eyes they seemed an alluring decoy, a camouflage of sorts to convey the outward impression that she was far less attractive than in reality.

Gaining composure, he asked, pointing up to the wall behind him, "Uh, you don't look anything like the mural."

She smiled. "That was a bad hair day."

He laughed, and her mirth broke through his otherwise sad heart. "Can I speak to the pastor?"

"He's in prayer," she replied, with a mysterious smirk, "reflecting on this coming Sunday's sermon, and insists that no one disturb him. I'm trying to transcribe his first draft right now. I do expect him anytime, though, so as soon as he comes out, you can see him."

"Thanks. I guess I'll wait." He backed away, straining to keep his eyes off her, and found his place in the vacant waiting area.

The chairs were made from bent chrome tubes overlaid with weathered lime-green vinyl. As he sat and waited, he noted that his pants were likely to dry quickly in the overly warm room, but they chafed miserably whenever he moved. Miss Maeda McLeary had left the dividing window open, so Raeph occasionally watched her work. Wires draped from ear buds into a tape player from which she was frantically transcribing. Typing was obviously not her primary skill, for her tiring routine was to listen, push PAUSE, type a few words, correct, type, backspace, type, read through, correct, type, then push PLAY to restart the audio. Periodically, she would glance anxiously over her shoulder to the door into the pastor's private study. She was obviously under the gun of a deadline she was likely to miss.

As he peered over the pages of some miscellaneous waiting-room magazine, his returning glances were always to confirm any lingering doubt, and they always proved groundless. Even with the distraction of her studious glasses, Maeda was indeed beautiful, at least in his eyes. Raeph was mature and levelheaded enough to know that his looks were not of the kind that turned women's heads or made them weak in the knees. He also recognized that the women he considered gorgeous—the kind who made him dizzy, causing stars and hearts to circle his head in delirium, as so often portrayed in the cartoons of his youth—were not necessarily beautiful in the eyes of other men.

Besides, Raeph was not in any way out looking for another woman. His heart still mourned over the loss of his beloved Patty, and he missed her with a deep yearning. Yet, still, he couldn't keep from glancing back at Maeda. He liked how she wore her auburn, shoulder-length hair, with several strands gathered together from the front and fastened around back to form a sort of crown. It gave her a faintly American Indian look, almost like Donna Reed when she played the Indian squaw in that movie about Lewis and Clark. It seemed obvious to Raeph, though, that Maeda was pure Irish, because of her rich and wonderful, undiluted accent. He guessed that she was probably in her thirties. Her skin was amazingly silky smooth, nearly transparent, like a child's, and her green, plaid, loose-fitting sweater failed to hide that she was pleasingly fit and shapely. Her lips were just the right unobtrusive shade of pink—precisely within Raeph's categories of rightness.

When their eyes met for the third or fourth time, hers looking over her black frames, she asked innocently, "Is there perhaps something else I can help you with, Mr. Timmons?"

"Oh, no, no. I'll just wait."

"I really do need to get this done."

"I'm sorry." He buried his attention back into the magazine, which he noticed for the first time was a popular Christian magazine for children, which he was holding upside down. He sheepishly placed it back on the pile and selected an out-of-date auto magazine.

He glanced again at Maeda's nameplate, and, yes, it did say "Miss." He turned back to the magazine and struggled to focus but could only stare blankly at an article about the "Best Compact Cars of 1999." His reverie was broken when the pastor burst forth from his private sanctuary, barking orders and depositing a manuscript before Maeda.

"See what you can make of these scribbles. I'll need this typed to take with me Thursday morning."

The pastor went silent as he listened to Maeda's soft message, followed by a sharp glance toward Raeph. His first reaction was a frantic shaking of the head, accompanied by the raising of open palms, but she continued to speak softly. A reluctant nod communicated that her pleading had won Raeph an audience.

The pastor retreated into his office, and Maeda rose, gesturing toward the open office. "He can see you now, Mr. Timmons."

"Thank you, Miss McLeary." As Raeph passed, his eye caught the rest of her: a blue-and-green tartan skirt, touched off with cordovan pumps, and for a moment he nearly forgot why he had come.

"Please, come right on in, Mr.—?" the pastor called from behind an elephantine maple desk.

"Timmons. Raeph Timmons," he said as he entered, taking a seat on this side of the managerial divide.

"So how can I help you? Are you and your family new in town?"

The forward sentries of an approaching winter storm began pelting the study window with sleet as the two exchanged introductory pleasantries. The pastor reclined and swiveled restlessly in his plush, leather executive's chair, distracted.

Already low on patience spiked with the nervous concern that Scott and Sara might be missing him, even out looking for him, Raeph cut to the chase. "I need your help, or maybe just your advice. Your church was the first one I saw that I thought might understand. I came into town to meet with the priest over at the Catholic church across the street."

Raeph dangled this bait hoping to discern the pastor's sentiments and received a solid bite. Guilford's attention was arrested. He leaned forward, bringing his feet to the floor. "Now why in God's precious name would you want to do that?"

"It's a long story, but we were hoping the priest might help us find a friend, a Congregationalist minister, who may have converted to Roman Catholicism."

"Reverend LaPointe?"

Raeph sat straight up. "You know him?"

"Yes, and I'm afraid he's a goner."

"What do you mean?"

"I've known Reverend LaPointe for several years. Last year about this time, one of my deacons came to me in a panic. His wife is a member over at St. Francis. She's always trying to convert her husband, but he knows better. She told him about LaPointe, thinking this would soften his resistance, but the deacon brought the news to me. He had never heard of a Protestant minister becoming Catholic, but then LaPointe left town before we could do anything about it. Later I heard about LaPointe surviving that shooting, and lost track of him, until he showed up again around August, back across the street. While he was here, he accepted my invitation to chat privately. At first, I thought we were making headway, but then he got all huffy and refused to listen to reason. Sometime around Christmas, he disappeared, I assumed to reunite with his family and continue his search for a job."

"Neither his family nor any of his friends know where he is. You say he converted to the Catholic Church, or," Raeph hesitated, "could he have been a Catholic all along?"

Guilford's brows tightened. "Stephen LaPointe?"

"I know the man who shot LaPointe. And I know why. He was alarmed by LaPointe's Catholic leanings on many doctrines and became convinced that Reverend LaPointe was secretly a Catholic all along."

The pastor's brows rose in sync with the emergence of a knowing smile. He reached back into a bookshelf behind him and removed a well-worn paperback.

Raeph said immediately, "I know that book. In fact, I even know the author."

"Gary Harmond?"

"Yes. He was a Catholic priest who became a Baptist minister, but now, well, as of two days ago, he has converted back to Catholicism."

"You're kidding." The pastor glared down at the paperback in his hand as if it carried a disease.

"Why'd you get that book out?"

Pastor Guilford thumbed through about to the middle, then spread it out on his desk, and read: "'In both of his letters to his understudy, Timothy, Paul warned about what to expect in the later days. His detailed forecasts of how the Christian faith would become corrupted have all come true in Roman Catholicism, but there is one warning that has always been elusive to prove …'"

As the pastor read, Raeph moved around the desk so he could follow along with each word.

"I've heard that! Walter read that to me."

"And who's Walter?"

"Walter's the man who shot Reverend LaPointe. It was partially because of what Harmond wrote that he became convinced LaPointe was a Catholic infiltrator. However, I'm not quite so convinced anymore."

"Convinced anymore in what?"

"Catholic infiltrators."

The pastor got up to retrieve an old book from a top shelf. "Here, listen to this from Edward Beardsley's *History of the Episcopal Church in Connecticut.* I'm certainly not a fan of Episcopalians, but he mentions this issue as an historical reality in New England. Here let me read."

He turned to the index, then back to the middle. "Here, listen: 'In the spring of 1809, the Rev. John Kewley, M.D., of Maryland, formerly a Romish priest, became Rector of the parish at Middletown, and for nearly four years he was one of the most active and influential presbyters in the diocese.'

"Middletown's only two hundred miles south of here," he said pointing vaguely out the window. "Beardsley reports that Reverend Kewley

> ... was an eloquent and evangelical preacher, who gained a wide popularity and impressed his hearers in all places with a conviction of his entire earnestness.... During his residence in Connecticut, Dr. Kewley had been honored with the confidence of his brethren, had been chosen a member of the Standing Committee, and a delegate to the General Convention; and when he removed from the diocese, it was to assume the rectorship of Saint George's Church in the city of New York. Here he manifested the same zealous interest in the salvation of souls, and for three years filled the position. [18]

"Now here's where it gets interesting." Laying the book open on his desk, Pastor Guilford slid his index finger along beneath each word, directing Raeph's attention:

> But one morning, his arrangements for a leave of absence having been previously made, Bishop Hobart was startled by a note from him, written on board the vessel that was to bear him to the shores of Europe, in which he stated that he was returning to his mother, the Church of Rome, to whose service he should henceforth devote himself and all his energies. Many have believed that, while acting in our communion, he was but a Jesuit in the disguise of Protestantism. It is certain that while in Connecticut, he tampered with one or two of the theological students at the Episcopal Academy, and advocated the duty of celibacy in the clergy with all the zeal of a cloistered bachelor in the middle ages.[19]

"You see, Mr. Timmons, many believed he was 'but a Jesuit in the disguise of Protestantism,' and this has been a long-standing suspicion, particularly here in New England."

"Pastor Guilford," Raeph said, returning to his chair on the laymen's side of the pastor's desk, "I really don't know anymore about that long-standing suspicion. What I do know, though, is that right now LaPointe's wife, Sara, and another minister, named Scott Turner, are both there, across the street, talking with the priest."

"Scott Turner? I know him. He's one of those pastors who attend that retreat up at the Mite."

"You know about that?"

"I attended once a few years ago. Good men, but as Congregationalists, they're fighting different battles than I am. That was the first time I met Reverend LaPointe, but you say Scott and LaPointe's wife are across the way?"

"Yes, and frankly I think Reverend Turner's leaning too far in the same direction as LaPointe. He didn't exactly say so, but some of the things he said on our drive into town make me wonder whether he, too, might be susceptible to the wiles of that priest."

Pastor Guilford rose to gaze out his office window, onto an enclosed courtyard. The snow had increased to the extent that visibility reached zero only fifty feet beyond the frozen fountain.

Without turning, he said, "I'm glad you've come, Raeph. I guess I needed just one more reason, one more data point, to push me into action, and you've provided it. You see, I've had my run-ins with that priest," releasing a sigh. "Just last month he stole another of our members, who I thought was a strong believer, but apparently he was ripe for the picking. Bourque complains when one of his members comes over here and joins, but he has no qualms about stealing my sheep. And this morning, not long before you came in, I got a call from a woman whose husband was meeting with Bourque earlier this morning, apparently about 'returning to the Church of his birth.' It's high time I confronted him directly, once and for all, before another good Christian gets lured away."

Returning to his desk, the pastor continued, "Are you staying in town?"

"Yes, at the hotel down the street."

"Can you come back here tonight? I'm calling a meeting of a few leaders from the local community who also have a grave concern about Reverend Bourque and his proselytizing of our people. It's time for us to act, and I'd like you to be here to tell them what you told me."

Ten minutes later, Raeph was walking through the blowing, snowy nor'easter, in the opposite direction from St. Francis Parish toward the hotel. Maeda McLeary's desk, to his disappointment, had been empty when he'd come out, so he'd reluctantly left without a formal farewell.

At the first intersection, where three stone churches and a bank vied for supremacy, the thought crossed his mind to return and make a late appearance in the meeting with the priest, but this temptation passed quickly. He wasn't foolish. He would head for the hotel, check out, and move his things somewhere else for the night.

A crossing light changed: a red forward slash through the image of a walker began blinking at him, and in this Raeph saw a divine portent: *Why check out? Scott's footing the bill and where else am I to go? I can come up with some excuse why I didn't show, but actually, I need to stay: I need to find out what happened. What the priest had to say. And whether they found LaPointe.*

His pace increased, partially from the cold, but mostly from renewed excitement. *God is indeed leading me after all!*

21

Scott Turner's Narrative

People always talk about the lull before a storm. An inexpressible, unidentifiable premonition that something dreadful is about to happen. Usually though, at least for me, I don't identify this forewarning until after the fact, until after my life has taken a nosedive and I'm kicking myself for not reading the signs and implementing the necessary precautions. Such was the obliviousness of my world as I entered the haven of my hotel room.

The maids had done their duty, and everything was clean and tidy. The bed was smooth, neat, and inviting, with its modern beige spread tucked with a fine line beneath the two extra-large pillows, dimpled only by the two complimentary chocolates. A copy of the local paper lay ready for my perusal on the leather lounge chair, but most importantly, my lost cell phone lay beside it on the coffee table. You see, sometime the day before I had misplaced it, having unsuccessfully ransacked everything to find it. After making the same paranoiac search throughout the van, I figured I'd left it in the restaurant at dinner. But a quick check proved fruitless. All day, this loss had weighed heavily on the back of my mind. I felt disconnected, irresponsibly detached, not only from anyone at the church back home who might need me, but more importantly from Diane and the kids. My intent, upon my return from meeting with the priest, was to call home on the landline as soon as I entered the room, but then there it was, thank God!

From the dispensers down the hall, I obtained ice and a diet cola, all in anticipation of an extended period of retrieving and returning messages. When I checked my voice mail, there were indeed five. One was from Raeph, explaining that all was fine. He had merely panicked at the thought of entering a Catholic church, gone for a long walk, and was shamefacedly looking forward to catching up maybe later that night after some meeting he was attending. The rest were all from one person, my wife Diane, and it was obvious that something shockingly momentous had twisted her knickers.

I called.

"Hello?" It was that sweet, familiar, lifesaving sound from home.

"Hi, honey, I'm sorry—"

"Good God, Scott, where have you been! I've been trying all last night and today to get you."

"I misplaced my cell phone and—"

"Are you sitting down?"

"Of course, I'm sitting down, but what—"

"You've been fired! Canned! Put out to pasture!"

"What? Wha … what do you mean?" At this, I was no longer laid back but standing, my drink spilling freely from the dropped glass.

"Last night, at a secret emergency congregational meeting, those self-righteous, disgruntled farmers voted you out. Not everyone came and not everyone there apparently agreed, but there was a sufficient majority who had concluded that though we had only been here less than a year, you were not the one they wanted as pastor."

I was devastated, shocked, speechless, to say the least, and in that room four hundred miles away, I felt utterly impotent to do anything about it. All I could say was, "Why, wha … no one …"

"After the meeting, we received the news first from good Ol' Farmer Oakley. He made the obligatory stop by the house, greeted me, began with a brief apology for having to tell me while you were away, but then proceeded in stark coldness to relay the decision, that as of last night, you were no longer their pastor. They apparently had already contacted Reverend Stillway to fill in until they locate a permanent replacement. I guess that liberal Stillway was sympathetic to their concerns."

"But did Oakley say why?!" I was now sitting back limply in the chair.

"He didn't show us that courtesy, but minutes later, Marge Olsted called in tears. It took me a while to get her calmed down, but she gave me the skinny on what had happened. She and her husband were at the meeting and were two of the few dissenting voices. The main complaints focused on what they called your 'Fundamentalist fanaticism.' There was really nothing we hadn't heard complained about before, but I guess it finally hit the fan, and they decided to take advantage of your week away to drop the bomb. You are just too theologically conservative for them. They complained about your moralistic, biblically literalistic, and too evangelistic sermons. What they apparently wanted was what they had been fed by the last three pastors: the social gospel—feel-good, nonjudgmental, love-thy-neighbor, do-goodism. You were even too Jesus-focused for them!"

"And I worried when I came that I might be too liberal for them."

"Hardly. They felt you preached too much about sin, heaven, hell, and holiness. They wanted you to be with it: love, universalism, and social action. They wanted to hear you rant and rave about how the government was destroying the family farm. Marge said that even though a few came to your defense, eventually the pressure of groupthink won the day. When the vote was taken, a few thought the group was being too hasty, acting out of anger and frustration and without any sense of compassion and love. The board members, however, convinced the rest that this was best for everyone, to sever the relationship at once. Marge expressed her sorrow over and over,

Scott, but to be honest, I think she was mainly upset about how this all happened, and not so much in the verdict. I'm sorry, honey. So sorry this has happened to you. You deserve so much more."

"No, darling, I'm sorry for you," I said, with an unexpected sense of relief. "I'm sorry that you are there in that community alone to face all the gossip and head turning. I wish I could jump in the van and get there as soon as possible to confront each and every member of that board, of that congregation, to tell them how wrong, how unchristian their action was, but—"

Yet what could I really say? I had always known that this was the way Congregationalism worked. This threat had always been hanging over my head, as it does every Congregationalist pastor who lives at the whim of the power brokers who might decide at any time to react to anything said or done contrary to how they understand Christianity.

But there was something else, of course, going on inside that I couldn't tell my dear wife. Yes, this had come as an unanticipated shock, but I couldn't deny that it filled me with an unidentifiable sense of relief. As I sat there, I was now free. Wasn't this precisely why I had come all this way in search of Stephen?

I stood back up and strode to the window. Was this why God had brought me all this way to have these private meetings with this priest?

"Scott, are you all right? What are we going to do? What do you want me to do until you get here?"

"Honey, I'm not coming there. Ever again. Here's what I want you to do. First, don't you worry a lick about this. I'm perfectly all right. Honestly. I guess I've known that this might be coming, even though I've kept most of my concerns to myself. This action of the congregation only confirms this. In the big scheme of things, I have no doubt this was all a part of God's perfect plan, both for Rowsville Congregational Church and for you and me. We'll be just fine.

"Second, since they want us to be gone so quickly, then let's gladly cooperate, even more than they could wish. Hire the best moving company available. Spare no expense. Have them carefully pack up and move everything to our cottage in Maine. But don't you hang around for this. You pack a suitcase of clothes and things for you, Deborah, and Eddy. Go spend a few days with your parents, if you'd like, but then fly on to Boston where I'll meet you."

"But—"

"What else can we do? Sure, there are a few friends there, to whom I presume you'll express my kind good-byes, but you just tell the moving company to pack everything carefully, and then you get out. Like the Israelites leaving Egypt, it's time to kick the dust off our feet and move on. Okay?"

"Okay, darling," she said, I could tell, with a tearful smile. "Just another adventure."

"That's right, and I've no doubt it's Jesus who's leading us."

After a few more shared words of tender affection, we hung up.

Ignoring the mess on the floor, I fell back freely, unrestrainedly, onto the smooth, creaseless bed, and bounced, bounced, bounced, until I settled into stillness. I stared blankly upward and experienced, as Yogi Berra once quipped, a "deja vu all over again" experience. I was sprawled on the wet, muddy, playing field at Western Ohio College. We were down by twelve points, and a notoriously brutal offensive guard had just caught me gazing upward and sent me flying head over tush. The next thing I remembered was lying senseless on my back, the proverbial birdies tweeting, and clouds floating by peacefully. Then my serene, unhurried contemplation of nature was invaded by the distraught faces of my teammates, asking me if I was alive. At first I just lay there, stone still, but then I turned my gaze to Fuzzy, my best friend on the line, and said, "Yeah, but they won't be. Let's get 'em!" I jumped up, ran into the defensive huddle, and on the next play I wreaked vengeance on that guard from Western Ohio. We won the game.

This time, however, the content of my vision was only the textured white ceiling with no concerned faces. And my heart, too, was different than in those pre-conversion days of college. I wanted no revenge and fought off any feelings of bitterness toward those Rowsville farmers. Allowing myself to melt into the softness of the bed, I merely asked, "Okay, Jesus, what next?"

22

The stark beauty of the northern winter floodplain still astounded Stephen. Smooth, white, nearly flawless snow blanketed the fields to the right and left. Tall banks, probably higher and wider this year than most, on either side of the blacktopped, four-lane highway stretched off into and over the horizon. About a mile off to the left, a continuous range of tree-covered hills, followed along as if checking up on his progress. A mile off to the right, the half-frozen St. Lawrence, mirroring the Laurentian Mountains, the first mountain range he had ever seen that matched the description proudly proclaimed in "America the Beautiful."

He had always lived in the north, mostly in New England, so he was no stranger to snow and bone-chilling wind. Until this excursion into Canada, however, he had never ventured to this even snowier and colder region between the St. Lawrence River and the U.S. border. The entire journey had been like a dream, like what he imagined a visit to Europe would be, except without having to traverse the great puddle.

Especially the magical city of Québec. So much history and culture. He could think of nothing in any city he had ever visited that could compare, especially the breathtaking view out from the cliff overlooking the St. Lawrence River. Below was the lower town where Champlain established his first settlement, centered around the small baroque Catholic church, which was not only still standing but an active parish. Behind him were the tight avenues of shops and open-air cafés, every bit an image of how he envisioned Paris. To his right was the massive presence of the Château Frontenac, surely the most recognizable shape in the city's skyline. He loved to stand there gazing out, as he had done just an hour before, a coffee in hand from Maurice's Café, watching with longing the passing ships and souring birds, and, with lonely sorrow, the passing lovers, cuddled against the cold.

And of course, there was the constant reminder, on almost every corner, of this French Canadian Provence's religious heritage. There was the infamous, at least from a Protestant point of view, Hôtel-Dieu, where a woman calling herself Maria Monk once claimed she had been held captive by less than holy nuns—a story which has long since been proven a fraud, though anti-Catholic fearmongers keep stoking the embers of religious indignation over it. There were the numerous parish churches, overshadowed by their big sister, the Basilique-Cathédrale Notre-Dame de Québec, and of course there were the shrines, especially the one he would always remember for his blessed encounter with "St." Brigitte.

Still, amid all this, what remained most indelibly in Stephen's mind were the churches where his ancestors must have worshipped on the south side of the river. The original log structures had long since decayed and gone back to the earth. But in their place, some dating back to the late eighteenth century, stood St. Xavier and St. Elizabeth parishes, and then of course, St. Sebastian's, adjacent to that cemetery in Rivière Ouest. He could fit most of the Congregational churches he had pastored inside any one of these awesome edifices. Of course, if he hadn't come to understand the meaning and purpose of statues, icons, and other Catholic religious artwork, the other aspects of these churches' décor would have been even more disconcerting. Instead, it had all been amazingly inspiring, and humbling. Everything he had ever done as a pastor paled in comparison to the beauty and depth of this faith he grudgingly was growing to love.

The road ahead continued onward, to the southwest, toward the land of his birth, parting the mounds of whiteness like the hand of God parting the Red Sea before the fleeing Israelites. Thankfully, the early afternoon traffic was thin. He had hoped to start his return trek south earlier in the day, but his new attachments to this country of his ancestry held him back.

Staring ahead, Stephen drove as if on a mission. His mind was set. He could not go on questioning the decision he had made, though all the inner voices seemed to scream against him. The very convictions that had always undergirded his life left him no option. *Trust in the Lord with all your heart, and do not rely on your own insight. In all your ways acknowledge Him, and He will direct your paths.*[20] For twenty-five years, this beloved text from Proverbs had stood as the sole beacon that had guided and shaped his life. And even now it exhorted him not to look back and second-guess himself. He must forge ahead, trusting that God was still guiding his path, especially because at this moment, with his "pedal to the metal" and his white-knuckled hands steering his Wagoneer, he was pressing forward without clear conviction. This he would decide as he passed south through the mountains of Vermont and New Hampshire.

He supposed his options were endless, but there were really only two: a cowardly return to his more recent existence in Jamesfield, or, more boldly, the grand, potentially unwanted appearance of the prodigal father on the doorstep of his family on the eastern shore of Cape Ann. Stephen vowed he would decide when he was passing under the shadow of his beloved Mount Lafayette, with the ancient stone profile of the Old Man glaring over his shoulder—*unless the powers that be chose differently.*

TWO hours later, he found himself creeping along bumper to bumper with others in a blinding white-out. Never before had Stephen driven in such a vicious snowstorm. Cautiously, he pushed west along route 55, the major Autoroute Transquébécoise, named after a former Premier of Québec, Jean Lesage. The nor'easter pursuing him from the Bay of Fundy churned out snow mixed with ice, attacking horizontally from his right. Visibility was not much more than a few car lengths.

Up ahead near Drummondville was the interchange south onto the autoroute named after Joseph-Armand Bombardier, the inventor of the snowmobile. Lesage and Bombardier, both men with lasting historical impact on the lives of the Québécois. Bombardier had conquered the barrier of the Canadian winter, while Lesage, head of the Liberal Party from 1960 to 1964, had led what many praised, but most religious French Canadians condemned, as the "Quiet Revolution." Stephen's major disappointment in his excursion into Québec, the land of his Catholic heritage, had been discovering how little the Québécois, especially the youth and young adults, knew their faith. Their absence made the physical witness of the churches and shrines appear as museums. The blame fell on the Quiet Revolution, and the road ahead for the Catholics in Québec seemed bleak—just like the literal road ahead for him, on which he was fighting his way west and south with yet no determined destination.

There through the horizontal layers of the blizzard he spotted the sign. Slowing and signaling, he followed the cloverleaf. Though the gale necessitated caution, he made the maneuver with confidence in his well-maintained green Wagoneer. The exit was timely, though, for both he and his car needed a pit stop.

Safely ensconced on the route south, the storm's ferocity subsided, assisting him from behind. Near the second exit, he saw the symbol for a service station, so he turned, and felt "a peace that passeth all understanding" the moment he set the car in park and quelled the engine. He sat back, relaxing his arms into his lap and paused just a few moments before opening the door out into the storm.

By now, he had given up the mental gyrations of transposing liters of petrol into gallons of gas. Once the tank was full, he merely went inside to charge it. He'd figure it out later.

He bought a large coffee and concocted a far from healthy snack/ lunch to go: cornchips, beef jerky, cheese crackers, and a package of cupcakes. As he was leaving, however, he noticed the pay phone.

Was it time? Time to attempt contact with Sara and the boys? To decide which direction to head: either south and east directly to them, or back to Jamesfield and Father Bourque?

It wasn't that he hadn't tried to call them over the past few months, but during this journey north, searching for answers, he purposely had held off. There were so many ways he had let Sara and the boys down, he didn't feel he should talk with them until he had decided what he was going to do.

But now he was ready. Up until yesterday, he had been hesitant, cowardly undecided, but after his encounters with Brigitte and Cliff, he felt determined. But *how* would he tell them? From far too many past experiences, he knew that good intentions for a peaceful meeting of the minds had rarely kept him and Sara from heated misunderstandings and disagreements. If there was one thing he would extricate from his marriage—one thing he would almost sell his soul for, except that this would obviously and eternally be counterproductive—it would be their tendency to fight. Would he ever admit to Sara—to anyone— that too often the happiest days of his life were days alone, away from the family and the stresses of the church, away from the hotbeds of conflict, away from the nagging guilt that he was always wrong. He knew, however, that he was not called to live alone but called to be a loving husband to Sara, his wife, with whom he had become one in marriage. His own soul's longing for solitude he recognized as a virtue that had been twisted and used by the voices of "the world, the flesh, and the devil" in an attempt to destroy his marriage, his ministry, his reputation. Thank God he had learned from Father Bourque the theology of "offering it up!"

This he immediately did, standing, sipping his coffee, watching the snow blowing directly onto the glass before him. Silently he offered to God the suffering, the misunderstandings, and the pain of his marriage—all for which he was at least half guilty. It wasn't, however, with reluctance that he considered turning toward home, his marriage, and family. He loved them dearly, and knew now, from all that he'd discovered, that he would not take any steps toward the future without them.

Turning from the glass portal to the storm outside, he moved with guarded optimism toward the pay phone along the wall.

The upstairs shower was running full bore, steaming the mirror, just barely overpowering the bellowing of William's joyful crooning. Faintly in the background, the phone down in the kitchen and the extension in his mother's bedroom began ringing.

After several rings, a voice emerged from behind the closed door of the boy's shared bedroom down the hall, "Can't you get it?"

The shower, steam, crooning voice, and the ringing phones continued.

"Come on, William! I'm in the middle of a mission!"

All remained as before until, after a few more tries, the ringing stopped. In time, the shower also ceased, as did the crooning, and after dressing, William descended to the kitchen. He began transporting from the refrigerator to the counter all the necessary fixings for what his dad used to call a Dagwood sandwich: two types of bread, three of cold cuts, two cheeses, pickles, lettuce, a tomato, mustard, and mayo. The construction then commenced.

"So who was it?" Daniel asked, as he entered in response to the sound of food.

"What do you mean?"

"Who was on the phone?" He had begun shifting the fixings for his own convenience.

"Hey, c'mon," William said, pushing his brother aside. "With your classes canceled due to a wimpy snow day, you can make your lunch after I leave, but I need to get to campus." Spreading mustard and mayo, he remembered and said, "I didn't hear the phone."

With more stealth, Daniel recommenced his construction. "It was ringing, and I asked you to get it, 'cause I couldn't."

"I was in the shower. What do you mean *you* couldn't?"

"You know. I was finally beating a mission and that stupid program doesn't save."

"So what are you doing here now?"

"I lost. You gonna use that pickle?"

William slid the jar over. "I've got an afternoon class, then an evening one, and then study in the library, so you're on your own tonight. If Mom calls, tell her—shoot, I wonder if that was her calling?" He went to check the message machine. "Dang, it wasn't turned on."

"It still doesn't work. Thought you knew. I don't know whether my b-ball practice is canceled for tonight, but if it isn't, and she calls, I guess there's nothing we can do."

After a brief glaring match, they shrugged their shoulders, picked up their respective Dagwoods, and went their separate ways: Daniel back up to their bedroom to make the most of his snow day, and William out to his car to battle the snow to get to his first class.

A half hour later, the lock rattled briefly, then the front door opened.

"Anybody home?"

No response, so Frank entered and closed the door behind him. Turning on the lights, he crossed to the cramped kitchen. Placing his toolbox on the floor by the sink, he turned on the faucet and threw the switch for the disposal. Instead of the familiar grinding whine, it only moaned.

"Yup. Either a utensil caught or too many potato peels."

He turned everything back off, and left the kitchen for the breaker box down the hall.

The weather outside had not abated as Stephen stood nearly lifeless before the pay phone. Handwritten numbers and lewd comments inviting and beguiling only increased his sense of impotent loneliness.

Where are they?! Out on the town, enjoying themselves, moving on with life—without me?

A snowplow passed outside, casting an enormous white wave. Cowering close behind was a caravan of lesser vehicles.

There was no hurry. Steadying himself, he sat on a crate nearby.

Head in hands, he thought, "Trust in the Lord with all thine heart, and do not rely on your own insight." *Lord Jesus, for years I've tried to live by this verse; I'm here alone in this godforsaken "winter wonderland" precisely because I believed I was not leaning on my own insight but following Your will, trusting You. But how can I know for certain whether I'm following Your will or just following my own and signing Your name to it? And to what extent am I just being led along by the Evil One? How can I know when not to trust myself, my conscience?*

"In all your ways acknowledge him, and he will direct your paths." *How can I be certain that I'm acknowledging You in my choices and actions, and not merely following my own presumptions about You? I'm in this mess because I recognized the confusion that results from all the conflicting views held by people who otherwise believe the Bible is a trustworthy, infallible foundation for truth. So is my view of You and Your will "true" or just my personal opinion? And if just my personal opinion, then why should I assume that You are "guiding my path"? Am I just presuming that everything that happens to me is somehow Your plan? Or is it possible that I've become completely duped, misaligned, blinded, and, consequently, way off track from Your path?*

"Lord Jesus," he uttered softly, "how can I be certain that what I have done to my family, to my life—"

A man's voice startled him. "*Hé, monsieur, ça va?*"

Stephen lifted his head and stood up, saying to the cashier, "Yeah, ah, *oui, très bien.* The storm's just got me down."

In perfect English, to Stephen's relief, the cashier answered, "Well, the news says the worst is past, and if you're heading south, it gets even better."

"Good. Thanks." Stephen headed back out into the storm, to his car. He brushed away the accumulated snow from his windshield with his sleeve. The Wagoneer started up without fail, and he was back driving southward like a snowmobile down the Autoroute Bombardier.

"But where am I going?" *At least toward Jamesfield. Maybe I can try the call later.*

ANOTHER slow two hours down the highway, and it was clear that the service station cashier's report had been far from accurate. The wind and whirling snow had not abated, and snowplows were barely keeping up with the accumulation. The consistent message from the radio forecasters was that at least until tomorrow afternoon the nor'easter's onslaught was here to stay. And then the expected below-freezing temperatures would prevent any melting of the eighteen-inch accumulated snow cover.

Just short of the border into Vermont, Stephen decided to find a motel where he could hole up until it passed. He felt like Moses, stranded one step short of the Promised Land. Presumably in the morning he could safely cross into his home country.

Through the blizzard conditions, he took the first exit; past the lights of a service station and a small grocery, he saw the red neon lights of the Land's End Motel and Cottages. The VACANCY light flickered, but it was on, so he turned in. The assortment of one-room log structures that made up the Land's End Motel appeared like brown-and-green toy boxes strewn randomly amidst the silvery hills.

Only one cabin remained vacant, the more expensive of the grouping, but Stephen didn't care. He had no choice.

Once unloaded, he plopped into the cushy recliner to unwind. He hoped the food wouldn't be too bad in the motel's diner. Before him was a gas fireplace, which he lit. A card on the table beside him indicated that the full cable lineup guaranteed that if he got tired of reading or praying, he wouldn't be bored.

For now, his only schedule constriction was his upcoming Thursday afternoon appointment with Father Bourque, and being only three hours away, he had no fear of missing this. If worst came to worst, he would wait the evening out, enjoying a few college hoop matches with crucial implications for the looming March madness.

Should I try again? Surely by this time someone should be home.

He sat staring at the phone, and decided to first make himself a cup of relaxing tea. The piercing whistle of the kettle derailed his musings. With a Lady Gray tea bag brewing, he returned to stare at the telephone.

He placed the call, and the phone rang once, twice, three times. Half-disgusted, half-relieved, he was about to give up when the ring was interrupted.

"Hello?" The man's out-of-breath voice was unfamiliar.

"I'm sorry, I must have dialed the wrong number. Is this the home of Sara LaPointe?"

"Yes, it is, but she's not at home."

Strange. "May I ask who you are?"

"Just an old friend of Sarie's, Frank, here fixing the kitchen plumbing."

Stephen paused in silence, then hung up the receiver.

Stephen couldn't move. His mind raced, confused, bouncing between anger and frustration, rage and despair, like a blind man trapped in a room of taunting hoodlums.

He hurled his tin cup into the fireplace, its trajectory marked by a line of tea across the ceiling, and began to pace.

"What in God's name is Frank doing there? Lord Jesus, what are You doing! Why?"

His arms were gesturing his rants, and to anyone watching, he surely would have appeared a mad man.

"So what now, Lord!"

You've driven me into this dead end. I can't go back. Ministry is the only thing I know how to do, the only thing I've ever done, but that's gone. And now my marriage, Sara and the boys, it must be over, too.

"Lord God, what am I to do?"

His pacing had brought him back to the teakettle and, after a pause, he restarted it. But he needed to talk to someone. "Jim Sarver! He'll know what to do."

Stephen dialed the number, having to try thrice due to frantic carelessness, but there was no answer.

"D_____! What about Scott?"

But would he understand? And besides, he moved to some new church in Ohio somewhere, and I don't have his number.

"Cliff. I'll call him again. He'll certainly understand."

He dialed.

"Good evening, St. Anselm's Friary."

"Is Cliff Wilson available?"

"I'm sorry. The brothers are in Evening Prayer. Can I have him call you?"

"No thank you." Stephen hung up.

The kettle was whistling loudly by now, so he stopped and made himself a second attempt at Lady Gray.

So why, Lord, are You forcing me to face this all alone?

To arrest his conflicted mind, he reduced the room lighting and sat cradling the hot tea in the flickering light of the gas fire.

Then he remembered. It amazed him how he had forgotten—*Had he purposefully blocked it from his memory?*—that only a year ago, exactly, after he had left the retreat and before he returned home, he had locked himself away similarly in a hotel, away from family, friends, and the rest of the world.

As he looked around, it startled him how similar the arrangement of this room was to that room where he first confronted his anti-Catholic presumptions with the startling facts in his first textbook of Catholic apologetics.

He looked down into his tea and then over to the fire, watching the flames dance across the artificial logs, and remembered.

The Mite. Tonight was the last night of the annual retreat.

"What is wrong with me?" *There at least I might find some old friends, Scott and maybe Jim, who might provide a sympathetic shoulder.*

He was only three and a half hours away! He looked at his watch, then out the window. The storm was not letting up, but heading south, he should be able to keep ahead of its ferocity, and avoid being snowed in. All he had to do was repack, check out, and then get back on the road.

Anxious to see familiar faces, anxious for a smile, anxious for some light at the end of the tunnel, to pull his mind away from the nagging, persistent, destructive voices trying to convince him that now there was truly no reason to live—all of this outweighed any of the dangers of the storm.

He glanced up at the splattered tea. With a quick whisk of a bathroom towel, he was gone.

23

Scott Turner's Narrative

For nearly twenty minutes, I lay there motionless, spaced, my mind racing back and forth between conflicting guesses as to what in His precious name Jesus was trying to tell me. Then, I remembered: my evening appointment with Father Bourque. I suppose I could have, maybe should have knocked on Raeph's or even Sara's door, to see how they were doing, but I preferred not to see either.

I decided to postpone lunch and dedicate a few hours to punishing myself in the hotel fitness center, though admittedly I spent much of that time getting waterlogged in the Jacuzzi. After a shower and a clean set of clothes, I left the hotel in my van for a private, undisturbed dinner at Burson's Tavern next door, but I was really just biding time.

At 7:30, I knocked at the priest's front porch, and, as if he had been waiting patiently on the other side, he responded almost immediately.

"Reverend Turner," he said, greeting me with a warm smile, "welcome back. Come on in where it's warm."

Down the familiar hallway we went, turning right into his study, which now conveyed an even warmer, more intimate ambiance as the now-darkened window gave more prominence to the glow of the wrought-iron woodstove. Two softly lit floor lamps beside only two of the previously three leather-padded rockers indicated that the priest had carefully arranged the room for my visit. He had ensured that his schedule for the evening would be clear and undisturbed.

"Come, sit. What can I get you? Some coffee or a soda, or could I tempt you into joining me in a glass of red wine? My sister sent me a bottle for my birthday. I suppose I could save it for some future celebration, but the day has been such that I wouldn't mind a taste of the grape to help me unwind."

"I normally don't, as you probably presume, knowing where I'm coming from, but, with what's happened between our meeting this morning and now, I do think something a little more potent than diet cola may be necessary."

"Then please, just hold that thought, and I'll be right back. Sister Agatha is out this evening visiting one of our sick widows, so we're fending for ourselves."

Alone in the priest's priceless library of theological treasures, I normally would have jumped up to browse, to peruse titles and authors, topics, themes, and collections. But I didn't. I was too concerned with where and how I would begin and to what extent I should reveal the stages of my thinking.

Jim Sarver and Stephen had bared all to this priest. As a result, both rethought every aspect of their Protestant faith, and where had this led them? Resignation, unemployment, confusion, and strangely, coincidentally, in both cases, marital problems. I certainly didn't want this, but hey, I didn't have to worry about resignation—I had been fired! I was already unemployed, though not in any danger financially. Confused? Yeah, that was why I was there, waiting for this priest to return with two glasses of wine and a seemingly bottomless fund of pastoral wisdom.

Marital problems? Let's just say that, as I sat there, I assumed this was not something for which I had any worry. I merely smiled and felt calm flow through the veins of my worry. Diane had proven over and over, in the worst of times, in the best of times, to be the "through-thick-and-thin" type. But how would she take it if I returned with the kind of answers Stephen or Jim had brought home to their wives? And anyway, I mean, come on, was there really any chance of this happening to me?

"Here you go," the priest said as he reentered with a tray of crackers, meat, and cheese, and two stout glasses of Merlot.

"I will admit, Reverend Bourque, that I rarely treat my counselees to such a scrumptious spread."

"I'm not thinking of you as a counselee, Reverend Turner, but rather a compatriot, a coworker in Christ, a friend, and we're gathered before this warm fire to enjoy each other's company and talk about how good our Lord Jesus has been to us." With that, he handed me my glass, and with a clink of crystal, he offered, "For the greater glory of God."

"Amen!" and I let the wonderful warmth of the wine soothe me from within. "Please, Reverend Bourque, call me Scott. I'm not sure you should technically call me 'Reverend' right now, anyway, for I'm churchless, pulpit-less."

"What happened?"

"I was canned. Sacked. The threat that we Congregationalist pastors always live under came down on me last night. I found out several hours ago over the phone from my wife, Diane."

"Good gracious, Scott. I'm so sorry to hear that."

"I guess if I had connected the dots I should have guessed, but like most of us, I never for a moment believed that it would happen to me."

"Well, how about, before you tell me about that, you back up a bit and tell me about your walk with Christ? About when and how you heard the call from football into the pastorate."

"You know?"

"Of course, Scott. I may be more of a Canadian football fan, but I've always followed Massachusetts and remember your career well. You were an important part of the team and sorely missed, both during your rehabilitation and after you resigned. I guess I heard the rumor that you had gotten religion and went to seminary, but then I lost track of you. It was a truly unexpected joy when you showed up here with Sara this morning."

"I don't bring it up very often, not because I'm in any way ashamed of those years, but mainly because my mind and life are now in a different direction. I play on a different team, for a different coach, and for a whole different set of reasons and goals."

"Then we won't talk about football, but what did happen? How did you get religion and become a pastor?"

For the next half hour or so I related the details of my conversion and call to the ministry. We also chatted about some of the common struggles we'd had as pastors. In the midst of that discussion, I pumped him for details of his own journey from Lutheran pastor to Catholic priest.

"It's a long story, Scott, with far too many curves, cliffs, and dead ends to go through right now, and besides we're here tonight for you."

"I understand, but could you at least tell me what started your journey toward the Catholic Church? Had you always been leaning in that direction?"

"Hardly! Like Jim and Stephen, it was the last thing I'd ever considered. I'll just say that it was primarily through suffering that Jesus brought me home. My wife suffered through an extended bout with leukemia, and in the process, I discovered that I did not have an adequate understanding of the meaning of suffering. I'd appease the concerns of my parishioners by passing along the usual preprogrammed Lutheran or Protestant dose of theological comfort, but when my wife lay dying, I had no answers that comforted either of us.

"Scott, if I may ask, what do you teach about the meaning and necessity of suffering?"

I hesitated. In all my years of ministry, I sadly admit that I avoided the topic. This wasn't something I wanted to divulge to this priest, but, frankly, I did not know how to explain, especially to someone mourning a lost loved one, why God allows suffering when I also taught that He is all-sovereign, all-knowing, all-powerful, somehow hears our prayers, and yet predestined all things from the beginning of time.

So did I admit all this to this priest? No, I just said, "Not sure, but how did suffering make you a Catholic?"

"I came across a verse of Scripture seemingly for the first time, which led to several months of reflective reading and study, but in the end, I knew the inadequacy and incompleteness of my Lutheran faith."

After a small sip of wine, the priest sat in silence.

"May I ask what that particular verse was?"

"Oh, of course, Colossians 1:24. Do you recall it?"

I racked my brain trying to remember it, but couldn't. Certainly I'd preached and taught from Colossians, many times, but I just couldn't place that verse. "No, Reverend Bourque, I'm afraid I don't."

"Then, maybe that would be a good place for us to start." He pulled two Bibles from a shelf on his left, but before he handed one over, he said, "Now, at least before your present journey into 'no man's land,' you believed in *sola Scriptura*, which included the conviction that all we need is the Holy Spirit to understand the truth of Scripture?"

"That's correct."

"So why do Protestants use commentaries and study Bibles?"

I looked at the priest, to determine his angle, and answered, "I guess that begs the question, which is one of the reasons I'm now in 'no man's land.'"

He handed me the Bible. "Assuming what you used to believe about the perspicuity of Scripture, read Colossians 1:21-24 to yourself, and then tell me how you taught these verses."

After turning to the passage, I began reading, and immediately recognized these verses as true representatives of those "stormy verses" I used to skim over quickly because I could not explain them; they did not fit into my Evangelical Calvinistic theology. I felt like closing the Bible and casting it aside, because my inability to explain these verses made my "no man's land" seem even more bleak.

"So, tell me, how did you understand and preach these verses?" he asked.

"I didn't."

"You didn't?"

"I did not understand or preach on these verses, at least not verse 24."

"Then let's begin with verses 21 to 23, but as I read, think how you would explain it according to *sola Scriptura*."

As the priest read aloud, slowly, giving plenty of opportunity to digest each phrase, I listened, sitting back in my rocker. "'And you, who once were estranged and hostile in mind, doing evil deeds, he has now reconciled in his body of flesh by his death, in order to present you holy and blameless and irreproachable before him, provided that you continue in the faith, stable and steadfast, not shifting from the hope of the gospel which you heard, which has been preached to every creature under heaven, and of which I, Paul, became a minister.'"

I waited a few moments to collect my thoughts before answering. "The first half is pretty straightforward, describing the new life we have in Christ, but the second half is far more difficult, given my Calvinist background. Reminds me of some of the recent readings from the Common Lectionary."

"You're right," he said with a laugh. "St. Paul clearly warns how necessary it is for us to 'continue ... not shifting from the hope of the gospel,' implying it is possible for a Christian not to continue."

Taking his pipe from his lips, to stare into its bowl, the priest added, not in a tone of exhortation but one of presumed agreement, "And this emphasis on 'continuing' in the faith is a constant theme of Scripture. We are called to remain, to abide, to hold tight, to conquer, to stay faithful to what we have heard, received, and accepted. Maybe one of the most important things Jesus ever said was, 'If you continue in my word, you are truly my disciples, and you will know the truth, and the truth will make you free.'[21] So, Scott, as an unemployed Congregationalist minister, how can you be sure you are continuing or abiding in the Word of Christ?"

The warmth and glow of the fire were trying to expand my comfort level, but they weren't succeeding. "A year ago, I would have said through prayer, meditating on His Word, and through love of God and neighbor. Now, however, I'm not so sure, because these four things are far too generic, too open to contradictory opinions and abuse. Anyone can make these things mean anything they want."

"You're saying that, for this important question, *sola Scriptura* doesn't work?"

I confirmed this with a toast of my wine glass.

"Let's examine verse 24 through 26, then, the one that began my journey to the Church. Again, as I read, consider how you would explain this through *sola Scriptura*: 'Now I rejoice in my sufferings for your sake, and in my flesh I complete what is lacking in Christ's afflictions for the sake of his body, that is, the Church, of which I became a minister according to the divine office which was given to me for you, to make the word of God fully known, the mystery hidden for ages and generations but now made manifest to his saints.'"

After a few seconds of reflection, I responded, "I really do not know. The first phrase is easy: Paul accepts with joy his persecution as a preacher of the Gospel, as Jesus said, 'No greater love—' And the last part is also easy. In fact, I could use this as a confirmation of what I believed about my own call to the ministry. But I have no mental file folder for explaining how Paul completes in his flesh 'what is lacking in Christ's afflictions for the sake of his body, that is, the Church.' I've always understood Christ's sacrifice to be complete, lacking nothing, from the moment He said, 'It is finished.'"

"We Catholics would agree."

"I suppose if I were back in my library I could dig through a few commentaries, for I'm sure some Protestant scholar has some explanation."

"But that wouldn't be *sola Scriptura*, and besides, just because someone figures out how to fit that verse into their theology, or to explain it away, doesn't mean they've got it right."

"So how do you as a Catholic understand this verse?"

The priest reached over with a long-angle iron to rearrange some of the embers in the woodstove. "Obviously, the apostle Paul is not one of those 'health-and-wealth gospel' preachers, who claim that suffering is a sign of a lack of faith and spiritual depravity. Rather, 'continuing' in the faith involves accepting suffering as somehow part of God's sovereign plan for our justification and sanctification. In Romans 8, Paul clearly warned us that 'we are children of God ... fellow heirs with Christ ... provided we suffer with him.'[22]

"But what Paul teaches here is what Catholics call 'redemptive suffering,' or more commonly, the theology of 'offering it up.' For fear it may raise more questions than we can answer in one night, let me simply say that we believe that suffering, when willingly accepted and offered up in union with the Passion of Jesus, can remit the just punishment for our sins and the sins of another."

"That's like nothing I've ever heard."

"Understood, and that's why, rather than our delving into this tonight, I want to focus on the more important issue for now: that the Bible *alone* is not sufficient to lead us into all truth."

"Actually, I'd already arrived at that conclusion, but our discussion is making it even more clear that I haven't a clue how to determine what is true."

The priest was about to answer, but the phone rang. He looked at the caller ID, and said, "Scott, I need to take this, since Sister's still out. It looks like it's from St. Brigitte."

"St. Brigitte?"

"I'll explain later."

"It's probably a good time to break anyway. I need to visit the little boy's room."

"Of course, Scott, down the hall to the right."

"Thanks. I promise I won't run away."

He laughed empathetically as I left.

24

With her back to him, Maeda McLeary was locking her office door when Raeph returned to the palm-studded lobby of Jamesfield Bible Fellowship Church. It was almost as if Jesus were answering the prayer Raeph had refrained from praying. Bent over slightly, struggling with the lock, her attractive curves captured his imagination, but Raeph quickly reminded himself that he was here on a mission for Jesus; he must not allow the devil to poison his resolve, so he forced his glance away and coughed.

She straightened and turned, startled. "Oh! Mr. Timmons, I didn't hear you come in."

"Yes, Miss McLeary. I'm here for the meeting?"

"It's back in the Sunday School annex, last room on the left." She stood, smiling.

He nodded and proceeded on, but had a time pulling his eyes away from hers. *Were they suspicious or alluring? Were they scolding or inviting? Were they just being patronizingly kind, the daily mask of a conscientious church secretary, fulfilling her role of being the first Jesus most visitors see, or were they more?* Realizing with embarrassment that he was walking north with his head locked southwest, he, slowing, brought his attention back on course, stopping six inches short of a column, as some interesting unanticipated chills, what some might call vibes, raced across the back of his neck.

A serpentine array of hallways and classrooms—decorated with elementary class pictures, student art projects, and plaques honoring the meritorious service of various teachers and Sunday school administrators—led Raeph away from the main church sanctuary and offices. After one final turn, he saw an open door exuding light and the sound of boisterous chatter from the last classroom on his left. He turned in, cautiously, and was stopped cold by the setting of the arena before him. A tight cluster of mostly men were arranged facing him in a large half-circle. In the center, waiting he knew for him, was an empty chair poised in their direction. Standing slightly behind this and the protection of an ornate wooden podium was the Reverend Guilford.

Raeph made to back out, but the pastor raised his hand and came quickly toward him. "No, please, Mr. Timmons, come right in." They shook hands while the chitchat and crowd movement stilled. With a laugh, Reverend Guilford said, "I guess the setup is a bit daunting. Sorry about that. I just wanted to make sure these sympathetic friends could hear your story."

Turning toward his gathered audience with a pastoral smile, he continued, "Gentleman, and of course Reverend Denard and Mrs. Krisby," he paused to nod at the ladies, who returned the gesture, "I invited Mr. Ralph Timmons—"

"Raeph."

"I'm sorry, what was that?"

"Raeph. My name is Raeph Timmons."

"Oh, yes, of course. I'm sorry. Mr. Raeph Timmons to join us tonight to share his story and a bit of disturbing news I'm sure you will all want to hear. He stopped by my office today for help, and after I heard his story, I knew God was finally calling us to take some action. Mr. Timmons," he said as he positioned his guest in the evening's hot seat, "before you start, let me introduce you to your very sympathetic audience."

Raeph quickly surveyed from left to right the eclectic collection of characters gathered to hear his story and wondered with a panic into what kind of circus he had stumbled. One would have to work extremely hard to recruit a more diverse assembly of body shapes, personality types, and, he was soon to discover, denominational perplexity.

"Starting from left to right," Reverend Guilford began, "the Reverend Eddy Collins, pastor of the Zion Apostolic Temple on the south side of Jamesfield." Raeph and the lone black pastor of the group exchanged pleasant nods. Of the group, Reverend Collins wore the most formal and ornate clericals: a black sport coat covering a purple shirt and white clerical collar, and a six-inch pewter pectoral cross hanging from a chain around his neck. "Next we have the Reverend Irene Templeton-Denard, pastor of the Fifth Street, Four-Square Gospel Tabernacle." Though Raeph nodded with a smile, she remained stiff and straight, scowling over her reading glasses. She reminded Raeph of the skinny bank secretary on the old *Beverly Hillbillies* sitcom, dressed in a guardedly conservative, leisure-type, suit dress.

"Next, Pastor Buddy Tyree of the Free Will Baptist Church on the north side of town." Pastor Tyree was the most casually dressed of the group, with a corduroy coat, open collar, blue Oxford cloth shirt, and jeans.

"Now we have the Reverend Irving Prescott, pastor of Second Congregational Church." Raeph wondered whether this lanky clergyman perhaps had come directly from a dress rehearsal of the Headless Horseman, for he looked the very image of Ichabod Crane. Reverend Prescott sat easily a foot higher than, and must have weighed half as much as, either person beside him. And when he listened at length to anyone, his face would fall forward, but his eyes would remain focused on the speaker, growing larger proportionally. His full-circle, dingy, white clerical collar hung loosely from his thin neck. Raeph struggled to avoid his stare.

"In the center of our semi-circle, Dr. Lawrence T. Steinitz, pastor of St. James Lutheran." To Raeph's mind, Dr. Steinitz could not have more perfectly fit the professorial image and pose: fairly long, combed-back, gray hair with a matching Freudian beard, a brown tweed jacket with leather elbow patches over a green vest, and, of all things, a purple, paisley bowtie. He sat motionless, legs crossed at the knee, hands together in front on a black walking cane, chin slightly raised, straight mouthed, studying Raeph through small, John Lennon–style glasses.

"Next, Pastor Dick Thomas of the Church of Christ." Of the group, he was the only one to which Raeph felt the least bit drawn. Dick was obviously an active body builder, like Raeph himself, evidenced by his skintight and taut coat sleeves and arms that bowed slightly outward. His facial expression was always pleasant, always ready with a supporting nod or grin, and Raeph supposed this was because Dick, too, had noticed their common interests.

"I don't think I know the next two gentlemen," Pastor Guilford, said inquiringly, eyebrows lifted. The two men were fairly nondescript, dressed in clean work clothes.

"They're deacons from my church," Pastor Thomas answered. "Curt Jonas and Bortlan Cordley." They sat mostly silent, though obviously anxious to hear Raeph's tale.

"Finally, to my far right is good Mrs. Dwayne Krisby." Dressed as if in mourning, with kerchief in hand and a black felt hat with a veil drawn back, she gave Raeph a nod that seemed to thank him for his courage. He wondered whether this was for his courage to speak out or in front of this group?

Pastor Guilford then began. "Each of you here knows of my deep concern about the threat posed by the Catholic church across the street and especially their parish priest. Before he came, you might say we were winning the battle here in Jamesfield against the Whore of Babylon. As a result of our preaching and faithful Bible teaching, a steady stream of believers have been rescued from their doom and brought into our churches, into a saving relationship with Jesus Christ. And though, admittedly, we brothers in Christ, and sisters, of course," he said, bowing benignly toward the women, "from such divergent Christian backgrounds and creeds might otherwise not gather like this in such apparent unity—"

Reverend Collins gave a quick, confirming laugh; the Reverend Templeton-Denard raised her head a tad more with a "humph!"; Pastor Tyree yawned; the two deacons whispered to each other; and the professor gave a glance around that indicated he was having second thoughts about being seen with this room full of lesser lights.

"—yet we are drawn together now because we face a common enemy. Ever since the arrival of that priest, whom they call, against all biblical warrant, 'Father,' not only have we seen fewer Catholics rescued, but now we are seeing a steady stream of our own people lured away into that fold of the Antichrist. Is this not true, my brothers and sisters in Christ?"

The first response seemed so startling and out of character, that Raeph's brows went up in disbelief and glee as he bit the inside of his cheeks. While most in the group talked amongst themselves, raising a racket of affirmation, the professor lifted his right hand slowly, pointing first to Pastor Guilford and then around to the rest, bringing a hush to all, a sign, Raeph assumed, of his perceived authority and scholarship amongst the Jamesfield ministerial community. When he spoke, however, the voice that came forth was far higher pitched and tighter than Raeph could ever have imagined.

With an exaggerated foreign accent, he declared, "Indeet, Reverent Guilfort, you haf shtruck zee nail ont zee headt. Nearly fife hundert years ago, zee great Ludter, inschpired by Got, tsaw Rome unt zee pope for vat zey vere, unt varnedt us to alvays be vigilehnt, for as Zimon Peter vrote, 'Zee devil alvays prowleth aroundst seekink somevun to devour.' Vee may haf thought zat vee vere vinink zee battle, but vee hat become complacent! Unt now vee are payink for eit. Over zee past year, I haf lost six members into zee hants of dis messenger of Zatan, unt he must be schtopped!"

Raeph noticed that Reverend Collins was straining to contain his own laughter, and when their eyes met, Collins winked, with a shake of his head. Obviously, not everyone in town was equally impressed by the professor's persona. Raeph assumed that under different circumstances, Collins and the others would have quipped that there were far more obvious reasons why the Lutherans were leaving in droves for more churches than just St. Francis de Sales. But lest this could be blurted out loud, Reverend Guilford hastily regained the floor.

"Thank you, Dr. Steinitz, and that is exactly why I have asked you all here. At one time or another, we have all discussed this concern privately amongst ourselves, comparing notes and casualties, but because of two very imminent and disturbing events, I believe it is indeed time to act."

He turned to his right and bid Mrs. Krisby to stand. Dabbing her eyes dry with her handkerchief, she rose, fighting back tears. "They've got my husband, Dwayne. Everything was just fine, up until about a month ago. Dwayne was a faithful Christian, a good husband and father. We never missed Sunday worship together or a Wednesday-night Bible study, is that not so, Pastor?"

"Yes, Luella, that's right," Reverend Guilford confirmed to all. "Go ahead, if you can."

"As some of you know, Dwayne has always been active in the local prison ministry, ever since his brother Daryl was sent up. He goes two-three afternoons a week. He really wants to help them prisoners come back to God. Well, what I didn't know was that Dwayne met that priest on one of his visits, and they became friends." She stood pointing in the direction of St. Francis Parish down the street, fighting back tears. The two deacons next to her shared knowing scowls, and a few of the pastors started whispering.

Then as she dug into her purse for a fresh hanky, Reverend Guilford suggested, "Luella, why don't you sit for the rest of your story. We can hear all right."

"Thank you, Pastor." She dabbed herself dry and continued. "Dwayne began acting strange. He wouldn't tell me why, but then I noticed that he was leaving earlier in the morning for work. Then last week, Gwendolyn Dweavers pulled me aside after our Women of Lydia prayer meeting to tell me that she had seen Dwayne coming out of the Catholic church that morning. She said he was scurrying down the alley to his car, hiding his face beneath his overcoat as if he were trying not to be recognized, but she knew it was him. That night when he came home, I confronted him directly, and he told me all!"

She broke down again.

"Luella, if you can't go on—"

"No, I'll be fine, Pastor," she said regaining her composure. "I know how important this is. Dwayne said that about a month ago he and Father Bourque—he had the nerve to call him that—began having coffee together at the prison. Dwayne began asking questions about what Catholics believe, and that priest convinced him that we have been wrong about what Catholics believe. He now believes that Catholics are more faithful to Scripture than we are!"

This brought a raft of elevated whispers.

"Dwayne tried to give me some examples, but I refused to listen and ran to my room. Later I insisted that he quit seeing that priest, but he would not promise. Since then he has continued attending morning Mass. Then last night," the tears began once again, "he said that, though he was very sorry about everything, he believes that the Holy Spirit is calling him to become a Roman Catholic."

Pastor Thomas broke in "Luella, I'm so sorry!"

"Thank you, Pastor Dick. You've always been such a good friend to Dwayne." Turning back to address the group, "One of the reasons Dwayne gave for converting is because he says the Catholic Church is the only church that is committed to defending all of the pro-life issues."

This brought Pastor Tyree to attention. "Why, that's not true!" he shouted. "From the moment the Supreme Court folded on *Roe v. Wade*, my congregation and I have spoken with one voice against abortion, premarital sex, homosexuality, genetic engineering, and euthanasia. And we have usually outnumbered the papists at every local pro-life rally."

Raeph noticed the deacons becoming more intense in their private communications. One started to speak, but was pulled back by the other.

"Those are the obvious ones, Buddy," the Reverend Templeton-Denard charged back, with an intensity far greater than one would expect from someone otherwise so frail, "but what they avoid mentioning are the myriad other human rights issues they trample on, especially women's rights, and I should know. You here don't know this, since as Doug says, none of us in this room normally accept each others' fellowship, but I was brought up Roman Catholic, and even more than that—hold your seats—I was a nun!"

"Oh, come now, Irene, you're pullin' our legs!" said Reverend Collins with a laugh. Pastor Tyree became as contemplative as a stone.

With a scowl that would melt ice, she shot back, "No, I am not! Like the ever-obedient little Catholic girl, I jumped through all the expected hoops: baptism, parochial school, catechism, First Communion with the prissy little white dress, parochial high school, and, because I obviously wasn't destined to be the prom queen, my parents talked me into becoming a nun. So they dropped me off at the Convent of St. Thérèse of Lisieux, and for ten years I jumped through a whole new set of hoops as a novice, then a postulant, until I became, with the impartation of the veil, a full-fledged, down-on-your-knees-five-times-a-day, Catholic nun. Every day, I said my prayers and ironed my white habit, and said the Daily Office, but it wasn't until I was thirty-five years old that anyone ever talked to me about accepting Jesus Christ as my Lord and Savior. And that person also opened my eyes to the chauvinistic sins of that hierarchical synagogue of Satan, where women are not allowed to become priests but are given the great 'privilege' of wallowing on their knees to scrub floors for the high and mighty priests, bishops, cardinals, and the highest and mightiest of all, his royal Is-ness, the pope."

There are many things Raeph was thankful for, but one certainly was that God had not called him to marry this pathologically angry woman! As he glanced around, he thought he read the same relief on the face of every man in that room. Except, surprisingly, the thin and lank Reverend Prescott, who, nodding his head, reached over to pat her supportively, but received a quick slap on the hand in response. Raeph presumed there was a whole lot more going on in this strange pack of friends than he wished to know.

Pastor Tyree resumed his boredom, while the whispers from the deacons conveyed a level of suppressed humor.

Reverend Guilford reclaimed the floor, "Luella, thank you for sharing. We all know what you must be going through, and are very sympathetic." He shot a daggered glare at Reverend Templeton-Denard, but then reset his face into his usual, winsome, pastor's smile. "But the last straw—the flame that lit the bomb that forced me to ask you all here tonight—was the visit I received this morning from this fine Christian man sitting beside me, Mr. Raeph Timmons. Though he's not from around here, he's got quite a story to tell that affects us 'right here in River City,' as the old line goes. Please give Raeph your full attention, and save your questions until he's through."

Pastor Guilford left the podium and pulled a chair up next to mourning Mrs. Krisby to join the anxious, enigmatic audience. Raeph opened his mouth to speak, but as he glanced from face to face, a question shouted in his mind: *Walter, what have you gotten me into?!*

It certainly would have been customary for Raeph to condense his witness down to the primary peaks of interest, leaving aside the less significant valleys and dreary plains, and then quickly move on to the topic at hand, especially given the makeup of this particular audience. What concerned Raeph, however, and forced him to be even more concise than usual, was his growing unease with these people. Yes, they shared a common dislike, or at least distrust, of the Catholic Church, but there was something about seeing the vestiges of his own fanaticism mirrored so dramatically before him that gave him pause. He had hoped they might help him rescue two good and faithful Christian ministers from becoming lured away into Romanism. Instead, he was being used to fan the same flame of fanaticism that he thought he'd left behind.

"So, as I told Reverend Guilford this morning, I believe that Reverend LaPointe was a sincere Christian pastor, but then that priest across the street lured him away from his true Christian faith, which led to his resignation, the breakup of his marriage, unemployment, and now who knows where he is, lost in his confusion. And this morning, another good and faithful Protestant minister, Reverend Scott Turner, was over there meeting with that priest. On top of all this, Stephen LaPointe's wife, Sara, a good and faithful Christian woman, who because of her husband's journey could herself become susceptible, was also there meeting with that priest. So, you see, I want to stop these three from falling into the grasp of the pope. I need to do this, not only for their sakes, but to make up for how I misled Walter."

"I'm not zo sure you misledt yoor friendt Valter," Dr. Steinitz interjected, holding up one hand to gain the floor. "Grantedt, I do see yoor side of zings—zere are alvays many vays to explain zings, many angles, but iz it not also poszible zat you yourzelf haf been blindedt by zeir creatif ingenuity? Vee all here know how vinsome Vatter Bourque can be, ven vee meet him on zee street or in minischterial meetinks, vhy he can be possitifly saintly! But vee must nefer forget vhat zee great Ludter varnt us: vee must not trust anyvon who schtandts loyal to zee pope in Rome! Zey cannot be trustedt!"

"That's right," Pastor Tyree chimed in. "Maybe this other pastor is luring you here to win you over?"

Raeph started to answer, "Gentlemen, please, I—"

"I told you, Pastor Thomas!" shouted the deacon named Jonas, shooting to his feet. "I'm sorry. Pastor insisted that if I came I had to keep quiet, mainly because I tend to get a bit too rambunctious. I know, and I'm sorry, Pastor," nodding to his superior, "but the time for words is past. We need to act! I know I have no right to talk, and I know I'm certainly not without sin, but when my daughter was raped and got pregnant, I'm sure it was that priest and his mistress, that nun, who talked her out of aborting that seed of fornication. Now she lives alone with that devil's child, and that nun visits her every week, poisoning her mind. Then last week, I found out that a Catholic girl from St. Francis High School has stolen my eldest son's heart. I've warned him never to see her again, but I know that he goes behind my back. Just like the Mormons, I wouldn't doubt that Catholics encourage evangelistic dating, too, so we must do something. Now! And if you all don't, then I will!"

"Mr. Jonas, please, be seated," Pastor Guilford insisted.

"But don't you see, tomorrow night, the day they worship as Ash Wednesday, would be the perfect time to let them know—to let that priest know—what we think of their satanic church!"

"Please, we're not here to incite violence; we're here to determine what we need to do sanely to stop their influence in our town, in our families, in our schools. But to do this we must stay in control. We are called to 'speak the truth in love,' not let our anger become sinful."

"Gentlemen," Raeph said, getting to his feet, "I need to get back to my hotel. Reverend Turner is probably wondering—"

"You didn't tell him about our meeting, did you?" Reverend Prescott asked, leaning his tall, thin frame forward from his seat, looking much too much like a looming praying mantis.

"No, oh no. He doesn't know anything about my stopping by this morning or where I am tonight. But I'm sure by now he's getting concerned." Raeph started backing toward the door, "And I do hope what I've said has been a help, and thank you, Pastor Guilford, for all your help."

"But Mr. Timmons—"

It was too late. Raeph had exited, shut the door behind him, and his loud anxious footsteps could be heard moving swiftly down the halls and out safely from the church.

25

Scott Turner's Narrative

M ind you, a voice from within was screaming at me not to go back into that den: to bolt free and clear of this place! Make a swift getaway! But another voice held me back—my own desire to hear this priest out.

The door was ajar when I returned, and, glancing in, I saw the priest patiently waiting.

"So, may I ask what you meant by your 'St. Brigitte'?" I asked, retaking my rocker.

"Yes, of course. Brigitte is a friend from Chambly, Canada, a young woman to whom I offer spiritual direction. We talk the last Tuesday night of every month, if possible. Usually I make the call, but this week she called, with great excitement, to tell me she had met a mutual friend of ours, yours and mine."

"Ours? Who's that?" I said as I resumed my wine where I'd left off. "Stephen LaPointe."

I swallowed and carefully set down my second glass of wine, knowing my propensity to accentuate the positive. "Thank God, but does that mean he's up in Canada?"

"Well, she met him while on pilgrimage to a Catholic shrine near Québec City. She says he's been working there as a guide."

"Are you saying that Stephen left his family and ministry, to move to Canada to work as a guide in some Catholic shrine?" The collage of these ideas passed as bizarre before my mind.

"I don't think so, Scott. He had told me he wanted to visit Canada someday, to explore his family roots, but I didn't know that that was where he'd gone. All Brigitte said was that they had a nice conversation, and that in the process they discovered our mutual friendship."

"Is he coming back?"

"He apparently didn't say anything about his plans," he said, refilling his pipe.

"Well, should I tell his wife?" I retrieved my wine.

He lit his pipe before answering. "No, I don't think so. Not yet. I'm concerned that if Sara has left everything out East to come here, no telling what she might do if she's convinced he's living up in Québec. Let me tell her tomorrow. I have a friend who works at the shrine that I can call. And besides, she may not react well to the news. Oh, and another thing before we press on, I was wondering about this friend of yours, Raeph, who didn't show up with you this morning."

"I'm still wondering, myself."

"Another friend of Stephen's?"

"Well, kind of, but he's a bit of an enigma. He's one of Stephen's old parishioners, and frankly about as anti-Catholic as they get. He's been through a lot lately, and I suppose you could consider him a kind of modern Job."

"Why's that?"

"Within the past year, his best friend died in a car crash, he lost his job, his beloved wife died of a stroke, and his oldest son, a seminary student, was murdered. On top of all this, the one person left in his life, his younger son, Ted, has been missing for years. Raeph said Ted took off with a bunch of druggie friends and has never been heard from since. He assumes Ted must have died, but, honestly, I think the one lingering hope that keeps Raeph going is that Ted is still alive somewhere."

"Has he tried to find him?"

"Not sure. He has no money. He's more or less given Ted up to God."

"Maybe I can help," the priest said, as he turned to jot a note on a pad beside him. After a sip of wine, he queried, "So, would you like to continue our discussion?"

"Yes, if you're still up for it?"

"Thoroughly enjoying it, my friend."

"Then, if you will, here's the great black hole into which I've fallen: As a result of what I learned from Stephen, buttressed by my own studies, I recognize the problem of Protestantism and why there are thousands of competing and conflicting denominations all claiming to be the sole, true interpreters of Scripture. Though I still accept the Bible as the inspired, infallible Word of God, I realize that God never intended it to be used as we Protestants have done. The problem for me, however, is that this all is leading me in a different direction than that taken, I presume, by Stephen and Jim."

"And what is that, my friend?"

"Ever since my adult conversion, and especially during my days in seminary, I have become convinced that the Church—or should I say churches—are nothing more than man-made institutions that became both necessary and a hindrance."

"And given the cacophony of Christian denominations, that's easy to understand," the priest said, adding another log to the fire.

"That's one of Stephen's favorite words."

"Mine, too. I wonder which of us taught the other?"

I left him to ponder that.

"I came to believe that right from the beginning, during the time of the apostles, various independent Christian communities developed, centered around the unique teaching of each apostle, each following Christ's promise that 'wherever two or more are gathered in my name, there am I in the midst of you.' What each community believed was a combination of what they had learned from their missionary founder, checked by what they learned from the memoirs of the apostles, the precursors to the New Testament. Then sometime during the fourth-century reign of Constantine, these divergent, independent communities were forced together into one worldwide 'Church' under the suppressive hand of an episcopal government, all under the thumb of the bishop of Rome, mimicking the political structure of Rome and her desire to rule the world."

I paused to study the meaning of his blank expression. When he noticed, he smiled and said, "No, please go on, Scott. I fully understand where you're coming from."

"So, when I followed God's call to become an ordained minister, I understood this to mean my willingness to give of myself fully for Christ to whatever small or large gathering of Christians He called me, just as Paul said in that verse we read earlier, 'to make the word of God fully known.' And I generally looked down on those who made too much of their church or denominational structure, like the Episcopalians, Lutherans, or Presbyterians. To me, 'Church' is where you gather with other Christians to worship Jesus, even if in a trailer out in a vacant lot."

I took a sip of wine to give the priest another opportunity to interject a word or challenge if he wanted to. He merely nodded, smiled again, and motioned me to continue.

"Given my understanding of Church, it's not surprising that a congregation of believers like those in Rowsville could up and vote me out. We have no bishop to oversee us or any direct responsible connection with or to any other church. For us Congregationalists, it's just us and Jesus, or sadly, in the more liberal Congregational churches, just us and whoever or whatever the group votes to believe.

"But through all of this, I believed that the Bible *alone* was sufficient to ensure that what I believed and taught was truth—that we were abiding in the Word of Christ. I stood in my pulpit and preached what I believed the 'Bible said' and really didn't give much thought to what other ministers taught.

"And then Stephen dropped the bomb." That wine was tasting particularly good.

"Scott, everything you've said I can relate to, from my own journey of faith, but I was one of those Lutheran, high-church pastors you didn't appreciate—" he said with a friendly squint. "I, also, always wondered, though, whether the Church was truly necessary. Isn't my relationship with Jesus all that is truly important? And isn't the Church, or churches, sometimes nothing more than an unnecessary distraction?"

"Yes! Exactly!" I blurted out, for the priest had cut to the chase what I'd been pussyfooting around. "The only way I could follow the same path that Stephen and Jim—and, I guess, you—have taken, is if I can accept that Jesus intended that membership in a church, any church, is somehow necessary for salvation."

"You've opened a difficult conundrum, haven't you?"

"I just don't hear Jesus anywhere saying this. Yes, He speaks about building 'His Church' on the rock of Simon Peter, but nowhere else does He require anything other than a complete surrender of faith and obedience to Himself."

"Well, I don't mean to quibble with your argument, but that isn't exactly true. Remember later in Matthew when He gave instructions on dealing with conflicts between Christian brothers? Actually this may address your specific difficulty. Here let me read," he paged through the Bible next to him. "'If your brother sins against you, go and tell him his fault, between you and him alone. If he listens to you, you have gained your brother. But if he does not listen, take one or two others along with you, that every word may be confirmed by the evidence of two or three witnesses. If he refuses to listen to them, tell it to the Church; and if he refuses to listen even to the Church, let him be to you as a Gentile and a tax collector.'[23]

"Now, if all it takes is for two or three gathered in the name of Jesus to make a church, then why wasn't the problem solved when the two or three witnesses confronted the wayward brother?"

I just sipped my wine, looking at him and thinking.

"And what would prevent the wayward brother," he went on, "from finding one other person who agreed with him, so they could merely form their own church? The 'Church' Jesus started in His apostles must be something different, bigger, and of more authority than just any two or three Christians who agree."

"I never thought of that," I said. I wanted to pause everything and just think, for this undercut everything I had assumed about the nature of the Church, but he continued.

"Back to your question, let me ask you this, Scott: Was it essential for Jesus to say that His Church was necessary for salvation? Isn't it possible that in the Jewish context into which He chose to be born, carried out His ministry, and out of which He selected and formed His twelve Jewish apostles, that nothing more specific needed to be said?"

The muted sound of the front door opening and closing forced a pause to our discussion. I waited with mixed anxiety over just who among the few known and infinite unknown possibilities it might be coming down the hall, while the priest sat unconcerned, repacking his pipe.

Though the peak of the nor'easter had passed, the clouds and diminishing snowfall continued to block what would have been a nearly full moon. Some external illumination from two street lamps—one out front by the main thoroughfare the other from two blocks away—lent the window curtains the eerie stare of a winking goblin. A brilliant rainbow of colors exuded from a backlit, stained-glass portrait of some saint, shining forth from the parish church across the alley, where the choir could be heard practicing.

The patter of soft, delicate steps escalated toward us down the hall, then a tap-tap on the door.

"Father, is everything all right?"

"Yes, Sister. Please, come in."

The door opened slightly, enough for the tip of Sister Agatha's black-over-white hood to peek through. "Oh, hello, Reverend Turner, I forgot you were expected. Is there anything I can get you two?"

"No, thank you, Sister. I know it's hard to believe, but we grown men should be able to fend for ourselves the rest of the evening. You go get some rest."

"I don't know, Father. The lid to that cookie jar can get pretty heavy after a long day!"

"Sister, there is one thing more," Father Bourque said, in a voice directed more privately to her. "Could you call Keith Torrance, and tell him I need to speak with him preferably later tonight or first thing in the morning? I want to claim that favor he owes me."

"Yes, Father. Will I see you in the morning, Reverend Turner?"

I figured she was used to inquirers like Stephen, Jim, and now me stopping by for late-night discussions that often necessitated the use of the guest room. "Not directly, Sister. I'll be heading over to the hotel soon, but I'm sure I'll be back tomorrow."

"See you then. God bless." Sister left for the evening.

"A favor he owes you? So you Catholics do operate like the mafia?" I jabbed with a smirk.

"Keith Torrance is a local detective, and a member of our parish. The mafia shtick is a running joke between us. Yes, most of the mafia were Catholic emigrants, and this reputation has fed the appetites of many anti-Catholic propagandists. But any sane observer knows that these gangsters were poorly formed, unfaithful Catholics, and that faithful Catholics denounced these connections, as did the Church officially. Just one more tool the devil has used to undercut the witness of the Church."

"We Protestants certainly have our share of less-than-faithful members too. They just don't get the same media hype."

"Another difference, though, actually gets us back to our discussion. Let's begin this way: when that crazy guy with the multicolored wig holds up a sign at a sporting event marked 'JN 3:16,' what is he hoping will happen and why?"

Interesting dodge, I thought, at least because I was clueless as to where this was leading. "He's hoping that someone will see him, get curious about what John 3:16 is, look it up in their Bible, read maybe for the first time that 'God so loved the world that he gave his only begotten Son that whosoever would believe in him would not perish but have everlasting life,' get convicted by the Holy Spirit, drop to their knees, surrender to Jesus, and consequently be saved once and for all, forever and ever, amen!"

"Why the sarcasm? You don't believe Jesus can save people by merely reading His Holy Word?"

"Sure He can. Honestly, I don't know why the sarcasm. Maybe I'm not really a man of faith."

"No, I don't think that's it; I think it's because you know that there is a whole lot more to faith, salvation, and following Jesus than what one verse can communicate. This verse is the kernel of the Gospel message we read in evangelistic tracts and hear preached door-to-door, from park benches, from Evangelical pulpits, or from television preachers every day, yet it says nothing about the Trinity, baptism, sin, the Church, loving one's neighbor; it doesn't mention the name Jesus or even explain what it means that He is God's Son.

"For this reason, few Bible preachers leave this kernel alone. Each adds to it according to his own particular tradition or individual preference. For example, wouldn't you agree that most Evangelical Calvinist preachers feel that Romans 8:1 is an essential addendum: 'There is therefore now no condemnation for those who are in Christ Jesus'? In other words, emphasizing 'once saved—always saved'?"

"I certainly used to."

"But Methodists, Holiness, Wesleyans, Pentecostals, and many other Evangelicals see this as unnecessary, even heretical, each adding their own preferred addendum. My point is that even Protestants preach that salvation involves a whole lot more than merely accepting Jesus as Lord and Savior, but there's a disturbing disagreement as to what else is required—and for such an eternally important subject:

salvation!" The energy of this lifted the priest to his feet and got him pacing.

"You see," the priest continued, "what this all points to is an ignorance, if not a brash denial, of the continuity in God's plan of salvation, between how He dealt with His Old Testament chosen People of God on through the birth, ministry, death, and Resurrection of Jesus and then on to the New Testament People of God, Christ's Body, the Church. Those who truncate salvation to simply John 3:16, or even add on to it what they consider essential, ignore most of God's eternal plan of salvation.

"Before we go on, would you like another glass of wine? I see you pretty well enjoyed that one to the bottom."

"No thank you, but if it isn't too much to ask, I wouldn't mind a good stiff cup of black coffee." The Merlot had been good, quite good, but a chaser of caffeine might help to keep my faculties intact and offset the growing buzz.

"Knowing Sister Agatha, I'm sure she has anticipated you perfectly. I'll go get us some cups."

He left the room briefly; when he returned—the scent of fresh coffee restoreth my soul!

"Now, if you don't mind my picking up where I left off?"

"Of course, not. This coffee hits the spot!"

"Good. The reason so many today ignore or outright deny the continuity between the Old Testament People of God and the New Testament Church is precisely because the Protestant Reformers rejected the authority and authenticity of the Catholic Church. The Catholic Church had always assumed this direct continuity, so Protestants had to rethink the connection between the Old and the New Testaments, and more specifically the continuity between how God dealt with His people before and then after the death and Resurrection of His Son Jesus. And as you know, the conflicting views of this separate Protestants everywhere.

"If they only took the time to examine the earliest writers of the Church—especially the apostolic Fathers who received the faith directly from the apostles—they'd discover that these early writers saw no division, no break between the Old and the New Testaments, between the Old Testament People of God and the New Testament

Church. The New was not an end of the Old but a contiguous fulfillment of the Old in and through Christ."

After a quick sip of coffee, the priest resumed, "Scott, the key is that nowhere does Jesus teach that His Gospel of the Kingdom involved an abrupt break from the old understanding of salvation as an obedient member of the People of God to a new understanding where individuals—regardless of any connection to any institutional, hierarchical body of believers—receive salvation individually merely by believing in Him. In other words, nowhere does Jesus jettison Judaism and replace it with a 'He-and-me' individualism."

"But Reverend Bourque, yes, Jesus does not specify this radical shift, but nowhere in the New Testament does He give specific instructions on how His Church was to be built or structured. He seems to have left this up to His disciples, which is the crux of why there is so much divisive confusion amongst Christians."

"But isn't it at least possible that, given the religious environment into which Jesus came, and the convictions of the time, which He accepted and followed, that unless He specifically said otherwise, we should presume that He intended it all basically to continue?

"Here Scott, let me summarize, for I know it's getting late, and I'm sure it's been a long day for both of us."

He could say that again. I certainly wasn't getting tired or taxed by this discussion, but I felt that we were opening far too many cans of worms to close in one evening.

"Forgive me if I get a bit obtuse in my desire to be quick," he continued. "Every aspect of the Old Testament People of God—of which anyone wanting to be right with God had to be a member— was fulfilled in the Church that Jesus built on Simon Peter and the apostles. The Old Covenant became the New Covenant; the old sign of circumcision was replaced by the new covenantal sign of baptism; the commandments of the law were consolidated, summarized, and reemphasized in Christ's commandment to 'love one another as I have loved you'; the traditions of the Jewish people and their Scriptures were fulfilled, expanded, compiled, and passed down through the Church as Sacred Tradition and Sacred Scripture; the hierarchy of the Jewish people, who had guided them and told them how to live out their obedience, was fulfilled and carried on through Christ's hand-picked apostles, who in turn chose and appointed others, all the way down to our bishops today through apostolic succession; and the old rituals, as represented by the temple sacrifices, synagogue worship, and festivals were fulfilled and carried on through the Divine Liturgies and the sacrifice of the Mass, and especially the Eucharist.

"I realize fully that this is far too big a bite for one evening, but I just want you to see that there is a clear continuity in all aspects between the Old Testament People of God fulfilled in Christ, passed on in and through His apostles—as is witnessed plainly in the texts of the earliest Christian writers—and then carried on today in the teachings, practices, rituals, and hierarchy of the Catholic Church."

The priest paused, I suppose to see whether I had any questions, but I didn't know where to begin. I now just needed time to let this all percolate, ferment, and congeal into some fine-tuned, well-honed, pointed questions.

"I'm sorry, Scott. I fear I've given a truckload when only a forkful was requested."

I rose to help bring closure. "No apology needed. You've given me much to ponder. Would you have time tomorrow, if I condense this all down to a few pertinent questions?"

"Unfortunately, tomorrow will be an extraordinarily busy day. It's Ash Wednesday, the first day of Lent, so I'll have two Masses in which I anticipate a high turnout, plus a schedule full of appointments. Thursday morning's open, though." He began leading the way to the front door. "If you're free, why not stop by tomorrow at one of the Masses? Ever been to a Catholic Mass?"

"No, I haven't." Nor was I particularly anxious to do so. But then again, with all I'd been learning, how could I justify not at least seeing what Jim and Stephen and this ex-Lutheran-minister-convert-priest had found so appealing?

"Well, if you can, please stop by."

I was reaching for the knob when he interrupted, "Here, wait a second," and returned down the hall into his study. A minute later he returned and slipped a folded paper into my coat pocket. "Just a few notes to peruse if you have some free time tomorrow. We can talk about it on Thursday if you like."

I nodded my thanks and was reaching once again for the door when he suggested, "How about a word of prayer before you go?" I pulled back and, taking the typical Protestant pose—closed eyes, bowed head, clasped hands—I listened as he prayed a very Christ-centered prayer, ending with a blessing in the name of the Trinity.

I thanked him again and, with a few more inconsequential words of closure, he saw me off into the night.

26

When Raeph rushed from the church, he found what many would regard as a winter wonderland. Though the temperature was below freezing and the snow was floating lazily down in a myriad of huge artistic lacelets, the wind had ceased, making the outdoors quite comfortable.

He scooted quickly through the fresh snow down the long path by the ostentatiously lighted church billboard, and upon reaching the sidewalk, he forced himself to stop, take a deep breath, and calm down, wondering, *what am I running from? Why all in a panic?* He turned up the collar of his favorite, dark gray, wool overcoat and stood for a moment at the intersection of the walkways, examining the clouds from his breath wafting into the night air.

To his left a block away across the street was the edifice of St. Francis de Sales Parish, lit creatively by a series of choicely placed flood lamps. At the pinnacle of the three-story belltower and steeple, the clock read 8:48. He assumed, of course, that Scott and Sara would have long since concluded their interview with the priest, but with a glance he noticed something through the trees and parked cars directly before him. He stepped off the curb, through a pile of shoveled snow, out into the road for a better look. Yes, it was still there! In a different location—not across from but directly in front of the rectory—but yes, it looked like Scott's van. To get a full view, he had to trudge further down the street, and then he was sure. They were still there, with the priest.

Could they still be waiting for me? It had been hours since he'd abandoned them. *Why were they . . . had Reverend LaPointe returned?!*

He realized that with this thought he had unconsciously started off down the slushy street in the direction of the church. He stopped and propelled himself out of view between a dark blue Ford SUV and a rusting hand-painted yellow VW bus, covered from front to back with End of the World/Rapture bumper stickers, anti-Catholic slogans, and doom-and-gloom warnings. He backed away wondering which of those in that gathering of crazies drove this gaudy billboard.

Should I walk down to St. Francis to see what's happened? But what if LaPointe hasn't returned? What if Scott and Sara are trapped in the same kind of theological discussion that lured LaPointe away? Shouldn't I go intervene and counter whatever arguments this priest might be using? Could this be the very mission to which God is calling me, a more charitable fulfillment of Walter's convictions—to declare to Reverend LaPointe what Walter never could, and possibly, by the power of the Holy Spirit, turn his heart away from destruction and back toward home? And to help Catholics discover their ignorance and accept Jesus as their Lord and Savior?

Raeph kicked his shoes together, knocking away the accumulated slush, readjusted his coat collar, and watched several cars pass slowly between him and the Catholic church. *But who am I?* he demanded of himself. *Why do I think I can answer this priest more than Stephen and Scott? They went to seminary, and Sara was a pastor's wife for twenty years. I'm certainly not stupid, but I don't have any delusions about myself either.*

He gave one final, guilt-ridden look to the church and Scott's van, and a scowl at the yellow monstrosity, then slogged back across the drifts to the sidewalk, proceeding in the opposite direction, toward their hotel a mile away on the outskirts of town.

The previous realization of how perfect a night it was for a walk recaptured his mind. Passing by Reverend Guilford's church, he glanced toward the one glowing window far to the back of the Sunday-school wing. He wondered what schemes they were debating, bantering back and forth, and in the end what they would decide to do to stop that priest from luring away their families. But he didn't waste his time long on this. He returned his attention to his pleasant stroll through the tumbling flakes and stillness, putting that lunacy behind him.

Main street, downtown Jamesfield, consisted of three blocks of circa-1800 up through contemporary offices and storefronts. The street had been tastefully lined on both sides with imitation gaslight street lamps. He felt he had been transported to a more peaceful and relaxing Dickensian era. The town fathers had apparently agreed, whether freely or under duress, to follow the same plan for the future, to resurrect historic Jamesfield not only as a monument to nostalgia, but hopefully as a lucrative tourist attraction. Every business—whether travel agency, bookstore, confectionary, legal firm, Laundromat, shoe outlet, or chiropractor—had bought into the overall scheme, transforming their establishments into pleasant transports into the past.

All cynicism aside, Raeph liked it, taking it all in, pausing without hurry before each showroom window. *Am I doing this merely in memory of Patty?* Surely it was not like him to enjoy all this commercial hype. In the past, whenever he'd made this kind of trek with Patty, he would impatiently press forward, waiting at each corner to communicate how bored he was with her mindless window-shopping. But what he wouldn't give right now for one more chance, for even the precious gift of one moment to stand beside her, to make it all up to her. If he had it to do all over again, he would instead walk beside her, arm in arm, no hurry, letting her set the pace, no matter where she wanted to go, for hours if she wanted, if only to let her know, as he never let himself do before, how much he loved her, how much he missed her.

A deep loneliness welled up within him, a seemingly black tunnel of hopelessness.

Next came an exquisite Scottish import shop, featuring kilts, pipes, various paraphernalia, and, of course, the appropriate selection of clannish plaids. Timmons was English. In fact, everything he knew about his ancestors screamed, "Death to the Scots!" None of this, however, was in Raeph's blood. He found himself lingering far longer than his ancestors would have approved before a magnificent Black Watch kilt. He couldn't imagine any occasion when he would have let himself be seen in it, and the store was closed anyway, so he passed on, pausing respectively before an eclectic Christian bookstore, a backwoodsmen's outlet, a knitting emporium, a high-priced coffee shop, a secondhand clothing store, an all-night diner, and—

Raeph froze.

The diner was mostly empty. Two locals sat at the counter sipping coffee, lazily reading every last word of the daily paper. But at the only occupied table, graciously receiving a whipped cream–crowned slice of pumpkin pie, sat Maeda. She was alone, and her table was the second from the window. He could not have missed her.

Something like white fire shot through his heart. Here he had been wanting to show Patty a facet of his love that he'd missed the opportunity of doing before and what he saw through a window that finally riveted his attention was another woman. He was overcome with a shame that part of his mind recognized as unwarranted, but whose power he could not shake off. He loved Patty; he always would. *How can I even think of looking at anyone else? Isn't that somehow a betrayal to her memory?*

He stood as though nailed to the sidewalk. Then a gentle whisper passed through his mind, sounding remarkably like Patty's: "Don't worry, honey. I *want* you to be happy. It's okay."

The icy vise clenching his heart loosened its grip and gradually began melting away.

He had been staring at Maeda so long that she finally perceived it and looked up. Now there was no escaping her. After an initial startled glare, she smiled recognition.

He nodded back, but remained paralyzed, unsure whether to continue forward as if untouched by their unanticipated encounter or respond with the presumption that she was extending an invitation to come in and join her. The awkwardness was getting intense to the point that a decision in either direction would require an explanation, but then, with a beckoning gesture, she made it all quite easy.

"Hello, Maeda, I … well, the word was everywhere that this was your nightly hangout, but I didn't believe them," he said, boldly claiming the opposite seat, then signaled to the waitress for a duplicate of Maeda's order.

"It's hard to be subtle," she answered, with a welcome smile.

"So, what does bring you here? The entertainment is to die for, and the selection of companions is, well, interesting?"

"I schedule one night a week here just to put everywhere else into perspective," waving generally about the world outside.

The waitress deposited his order, with a flat, speechless smile then left. Raeph and Maeda looked at each other, and, as if old friends, had to constrain their laughter. He wondered with confused joy, *How did we become so friendly, so comfortable, in so short a time?*

"So tell me, how did a good Irish girl like you end up in this far-off-the-beaten-path, New Hampshire mountain town?"

Her facial expression went through a series of subtle shifts, all bordering on the brink of acceptable standards of pleasantries. Raeph, however, was oblivious to anything but the fathomless sincerity of her eyes. They drew him in, as if they were magnetically attracting his very soul to, through, and into those two doors to her own soul.

"That's a long story, Raeph, which I'd rather not discuss right now. Nothing I'm ashamed of, mind you; at least nothing outside the usual bounds of people havin' dreams that pull 'em away from their home only to be shattered unexpectedly on some distant shore. But I'll only say that I do like it here. Surely, I miss Ireland, but there are many good things here, too."

"Where in Ireland are you from?"

"From another far-off-the-beaten-path village, along the south west coast, on the Dingle Peninsula. What about you? Are you from around here?"

He was amazed how her smile communicated such genuine interest. This launched Raeph into a nostalgic but not too detailed description of his childhood and family life in rural Vermont. As soon as he could redirect, he asked, "What about your family?" Raeph's glance shifted awkwardly away to his now half-eaten pie.

"Mum and three sisters—one married to a fisherman, the other two still at home. I came alone, if you can believe it. Oh, they all said I was crazy, Mum especially, but she gave me her blessing, and here I am."

"And working for Pastor Guilford at Jamesfield Bible Fellowship," his mouth still busy with pie and fighting back sarcasm, he asked, "was this what you came looking for?"

She had to grab for her napkin to sop up a few drips of coffee that were expelled with her laughter. "Hardly! I'm surprised I've lasted this long. I'm hardly more than a two-fingered, hunt-'n'-peck typist, but I heard that his last secretary had left suddenly in a huff, and we were both desperate: he for help and me for food! I'm, well," her expression dropped slightly, her eyes guarded, "I'm a singer and an actress. I don't know anyone or how the system works here in the States, nor, mind you, am I nursing some overinflated, grandiose dream about some future on Broadway or in Hollywood, about becoming the next Maureen O'Hara," she said with a grin. "Singing and acting are just what I do best and what I've always enjoyed. When I was a little girl, they filmed a movie in our coastal town, starring Robert Mitchum, and many of the townsfolk were hired as bit actors. I stood in a street scene with my mother, all dressed up like we were living in 1916. I guess you could say that put the spark in my mind. I could easily have spent the rest of my life in that little town in County Kerry, married probably to a farmer, fisherman, or town clerk, with a dozen little'uns or so pullin' at my worn-out skirts, but before that happened, I at least wanted to try and see if there wasn't something else that God might have in store for me."

"Are you a member of the Bible Fellowship Church?" With his elbows positioned on the table, he brought his coffee up to his mouth with both hands, like a crane lifting a heavy load. He then studied her eyes through the hot, rising aroma.

"No, no, and Pastor Guilford didn't require it, though I'm sure he assumes that I'll join one day. But I don't expect to be here all that long. I have my dreams, you know. By the way," she then asked with guarded eyes, "I was wondering how the meeting went tonight."

"The meeting? Oh, yes, at the church. Fine, I guess, but—" and then he caught himself. He was about to come clean about how disconcerted he'd felt—how the anticipated oasis of common thinkers had turned out to be a mirage, a crowd of fanatics—but decided against it.

"You were saying?" she asked, her cup poised before her lips.

"It seems there are a fair number of people in this town concerned about the antics of that priest across the way."

"That's what I hear, too. Of course, I've only been here a short time. I heard the pastor mention that they were hoping to come to some plan of attack. Did they?" her cup again hovering in front of her face.

"Actually, I left before that. I spoke my piece, and when someone interrupted with something about tomorrow night, I excused myself and left."

"Tomorrow night?" Setting the cup down a bit hard, she splashed a little in his direction. "Oh, I'm terribly sorry," she said, handing him her napkin.

"No damage, no damage." While all was wiped up, the dialogue lapsed into silence.

"You said something about tomorrow night?"

"Oh, yes. A layman, from I think the Church of Christ, stood up with great conviction about how tomorrow night was the perfect opportunity for them to do something, but I left before I heard what he meant."

"Is there anything else I can get you two?" The waitress had appeared suddenly and apparently out of nowhere, just doing her job in the usual way.

"No, thank you," Maeda replied, reaching into her purse as she also made to stand. "I do need to get home, though."

"Please, Maeda, let me get it." He quickly snatched the check, then threw down a ten, which included a generous tip. Given his unemployment and limited reserves, this gesture was a step outside his usual conservative boundaries, but he couldn't help himself. He assisted Maeda with her coat, then walked silently behind her to the door. Outside, he asked, "How far do you have to drive?"

"Actually, I live across the street, above the bakery. It's a very beautiful apartment, though pricey. The building is quite old, but like everything else here in Jamesfield, it's been remodeled, updated, and priced accordingly."

"Well, may I at least walk you to your door?"

Taking her arm, which she freely gave, Raeph led her carefully through the snow and slush, pausing briefly for a few cars to pass, to her apartment. A set of stone steps to the left of the bakery led up to the apartments above. At their base, Raeph stopped and backed away, sinking both hands into his coat pockets.

"Thank you, Maeda, for letting me join you this evening. It was certainly an unexpected and pleasant surprise."

"Likewise for me." Up two steps, she turned back to face him.

He looked up at her, taken by this unanticipated turn of events, but even more taken by the move he was about to make. Up until meeting this lovely emigrant from Ireland, the thought of finding another companion had never entered his mind. But now lost in her eyes, he asked, "I was wondering if you might join me again, say, tomorrow for lunch, same place—or another if you prefer?"

She smiled. "I would like that, Raeph. At one?" She reached down, and when he responded, she squeezed his hand with genuine affection, then turned toward the door and went inside.

For about four storefronts, Raeph kept it under control, but then he lost it. A yell of joy escaped him as he accelerated almost to a run. Stopping briefly to assist a woman whom he'd startled retrieve her bags, he resumed his pace and didn't falter again until he passed through the lobby of his hotel and on into his room.

The day had certainly been long, with many a turn of events, but this last one might just be the one to bring some semblance of meaning, direction, and hope to his life.

 27

The nearly full moon was high in the night sky when Stephen pulled off the main road onto the slippery gravel driveway up the hill to the Mite. A pleasant rush filled his heart as he ascended to this favorite of all places. It had been so hard not to attend this year; except for his first year at Red Creek, he had not missed a retreat since they began. His life had changed so dramatically, though, and he wasn't sure he was welcome. It's one thing to have different views, even strongly divergent views on lots of things, but it's another to rock the foundation upon which these pastors had built their lives and careers.

The drive up was like a dark tunnel, trees of all sorts bending their limbs over a quiet passage forward and upward. The storm had stopped, but the soft residue on every limb glimmered under his headlights. In his rearview mirror, the white glimmer evolved into red, receding into nothing.

At the summit, he found the parking lot surprisingly bare. *Only twelve cars? Twelve where normally there would have been two dozen! What had happened? Was it all because of what I said last year?*

Other than the outside floodlamp above the walk leading from the lot to the house, no other lights were visible. He knew it was late, but how late? He looked at his watch, holding it to receive illumination from the floodlight: 12:17. All must be in bed, and not a creature stirring.

So now what? He parked his Wagoneer next to a snow-plastered red Camaro, turned off his engine, and got out. He glanced around at the vehicles. Only a few familiar. Most were new.

What should he do now? It was far too late to get a room in the nearest hotel, and it was too cold to sleep in the car. So, why not? He might as well find an open door, then an empty bed, and explain in the morning. He had no reservation, but he knew that, at least in the eyes of Mr. and Mrs. Cousineau, he was always welcome.

Grabbing his night bag, he walked the last fifty feet to the Mite, his entire countenance filling with the warmth of this welcoming friend. He tried the front door, and it was open. Why had he doubted? The Cousineaus never locked their house. They trusted God, believing that anyone desperate enough to make the long trek out of town and up the hill to the Mite, needed their help and the love of God more than a locked and barricaded rejection. There was always room at this inn.

As he closed the door behind him, a light came on in the kitchen. The Cousineaus' private living quarters were directly off the entrance hall, in the back.

"Hello?" Mrs. Cousineau said in her familiar, soft, but aging voice. "May I help—Reverend LaPointe! How good to see you, finally! I so prayed you'd come."

Stephen had barely dropped his night bag before he was embraced in a tight hug by the woman of the house. He responded, of course, with great affection. Mrs. Cousineau, as well as her husband Tom, were the purest, most unreserved examples of Christ's love he had ever known.

"Everyone's asleep, I take it?" Stephen asked as they took their usual positions, she in the kitchen and he on a stool this side of the large serving counter.

"Oh yes, in fact they all retired a little earlier than usual. You know, this was the day of their annual 'world championship basketball free-for-all.' It always wears you fellows out so, if not bringing on more aches and pains than you wanted! Tom always says, 'A bunch of out-of-shape desk jockeys pretending they're teenagers again. One of these years, someone's gonna break a neck or a back, and we'll have to close the Mite just to pay the hospital bills!'" she scolded with a comical wagging of a finger.

"Now you know I quit with all that foolishness years ago," though he hadn't, "mainly because after eating my share of your poutines and cinnamon rolls, I couldn't jump higher than a flea's knees anyway."

"You want one now? Not a poutine, of course. I wouldn't give one of those this late to an infidel! No, no, no, of course not. A cinnamon roll. There's a few left from this morning in the fridge."

"Well, in that case, need you ask?"

They both laughed as she reheated two rolls in the microwave and made a small pot of decaf.

"So, the number of cars seems smaller this year. A smaller group?

"Unfortunately, yes. Some of the same old faces, a few new ones. But everyone has been talking about you, even the new men, wondering how you're doing. How are you doing?" she asked as she placed the midnight snack before him. "Was it true what I heard about your being shot!"

"Yes, it's true, but by God's grace, I was spared and have no residual effects, except for a minor scar."

He pulled away his collar, and shaking her head, she uttered, "Tcsh, tcsh! You were spared!"

"Yes, by God's mercy."

"But there are other rumors, about you leaving the pastorate, and even about your considering the Catholic faith, and, well, I also heard something this morning about your marriage—" She was never one to pry. Stephen knew and appreciated this, but yet she was one who cared deeply about her "boys."

"Mrs. Cousineau, thanks for your concern, but it's complicated and requires more time than I can give at this late hour. Yes, I did resign, and as a result, Sara and I are experiencing, what should I say, a, hopefully, brief time of separation."

"We'll keep you in our prayers. You staying the night?"

"If you don't mind and if there's room?"

"Oh, there's room all right. The group is so small this year. I'm anxious to find out why, because I'd hate to see your fine annual retreat end. It always seems to be so helpful, so encouraging for you boys."

"And that it is, Mrs. Cousineau. I'm sure the attendance will pick up again next year."

"Anyway, I reserved your usual room for you, just in case, and sure enough here you are."

"Thanks, oh and here's something I need to return." Stephen reached into his night bag and removed a package wrapped in tissue paper the size of a large paperback book.

"Last year, Jim Sarver grabbed a book from your shelf and 'lent' it to me, assuming that you certainly wouldn't mind, once you knew why he was doing it. This book answered so many of my questions and opened my mind to the truth about your faith. So much of what I had believed about your Church was wrong, either through misinformation or probably out-and-out lies that I'd accepted without examination. I'm sorry, Suzette, if I've ever said anything disparaging about your Church and especially your pope, John Paul II."

"Oh, Stephen, you've never been anything but a gentleman. Sure, some of the boys can be insensitive, sometimes saying hurtful things that I'm sure they don't mean, but you've always treated our faith with respect."

"And you've always made us infidels feel at home."

"Infidels! I never."

"Anyway, I read and reread the copy Jim lent me so many times, underlining key passages, that I had to buy you a fresh one. So here, and thank you again."

"You certainly didn't have to do that, 'cause that's what all those books are there for anyway. Sure, we don't shove our Catholic faith down you boys' throats, but that don't mean we can't leave a few hints around the house for the Spirit to work with."

"And in my case, the Spirit certainly did."

"So tell me, Stephen," she asked, collecting the dirty dishes, "have you decided? Are you coming home?"

"'Coming home.' That's the way both Jim and Father Bourque describe it."

"Father Bourque?" she said, directing her attention to putting the dirty dishes in the dishwasher. "You know Father Bourque?"

"But of course! Jim sent me his way, figuring he'd straighten me out, too."

"He's a saint of a priest! Tom and I go down to St. Francis every time we can, especially when he gives midweek missions. But here I am talking your ear off. You must be tired. Go on up, and we'll see you in the morning."

Stephen kissed her on the cheek, and, collecting his bag, went upstairs to what was for so many years his home away from home. As he turned on the light in the sparsely furnished room, he wondered whether this was in fact the closest thing he had to a home.

He set his bag down and then himself onto the bed to look around the familiar room. On the desk, he noticed a book, lying apart from those between the bookends. He approached, cocking his head to read the title: *But the Two Had Become One: Healing a Broken Marriage*, by Father William Bourque.

He smiled, "She knows a whole lot more than she lets on."

It had been a long grueling day, but he could not ignore the serendipitous events of Providence. So, without changing his clothes, he merely lay back on the bed to read what his priestly friend, and the caring woman of this house, wanted him to hear that might mend his broken life.

PART 4

FOR THOU ART WITH ME

❧ 28 ❧

Scott Turner's Narrative

The night had been an unusually sleepless one, my mind distracted by disheartening images of failure and confusion, inadequacy and aimlessness. More than once, I'd tried to read myself to sleep with some mindless novel I'd purchased downstairs, but my mental hard drive wouldn't hibernate. Over and over, I reenacted confrontations with those who had decided I was unworthy to be their pastor, who had voted me out. Again and again, I rehearsed imminent conversations I would have with Stephen and Father Bourque, Raeph and Sara, and especially Diane—how would I explain clearly the confusion as well as the increasing convictions?

I also tried to fathom what Stephen was doing up in Québec. Had he moved there temporarily, or just given up on everything?

Finally around six, I threw back the less-than-adequate covers and gave up. I must have slept a little, for the light was on, the novel was splayed on the floor, and next to my face the pillow was soaked with slobber. I started the four-cup coffee maker and began the day as usual with what the ancients called *lectio divina*, a prayerful meditative reading of Scripture. Still plagued by distractions, however, I found this attempt at spiritual rejuvenation to be futile, so I dressed for a return workout in the hotel's meager fitness center. A two-mile run in place atop a swirling conveyor, a quick pass through the stations of a weight machine, and fifteen minutes in the Jacuzzi, which left me sweatier than before.

Off the hall between the fitness center and the elevators was the dining room, and as I passed, I saw Raeph sitting there, facing me, so there was no avoiding him. He nodded recognition, and with a clumsy combination of hand motions, I pantomimed getting different clothes and then returning. I hurriedly took a tepid but refreshing shower, my mind lost once again in rehearsed anticipated dialogues, vacillating between curiosity and anger, anxious to confront him on why he'd abandoned us.

"So what happened to you? Oh, and just give me the same as him," I said to the elderly, more than overweight waitress beside Raeph, pot in hand. They had gotten into some heated discussion that ceased when I arrived. With a final "Hrumph!" she poured me a coffee and left.

"What was that all about?"

"Actually I'm not sure," Raeph said, containing a belly laugh, his face beaming with inexplicable joy. "I just told her she looked particularly attractive this morning, and she read me the riot act. Must not have been what she needed to hear."

A shrill bark shot up through the order window: "Two over easy, bacon, cakes, home fries, and biscuits with honey." A handful of plastic dishes crashed into a holding bin.

Hidden from her view, Raeph communicated a look of terror to me. "Bet her husband's anxious for her to get off duty!"

"Some of us are just born lucky. So where you been anyway?" The humor of the moment had softened my tone.

His feigned terror relaxed into an expressionless stare. "Yeah, I did prove the coward, didn't I? Guess those stained-glass windows peering down at me got my goat. I just couldn't shake the willies, like I was being lured into the devil's web or something."

"I know the feeling."

"So," he probed, syrup dripping from a full mouth, "how'd the meeting go without me? Any news about Reverend LaPointe?"

"No substantial news."

"That must have been quite a long meeting."

"Why's that?" I asked, wondering where he was headed.

"I saw your van there late into the evening." His focus remained on his food.

I wanted to ask whether he had remained outside all day and evening, hiding in the bushes, but decided that would be unproductive. "No, Sara and I came back to the hotel late morning, but I returned alone to talk with Reverend Bourque last night."

The perky voice of a different, younger, more enthusiastic waitress said, "Here you go," as she conveyed my four-course breakfast. "Anything else?"

"Aw, what happened to ol' Tilly?" Raeph said, mock-quaveringly.

She winked. "Been a long night. 'Turning this into an all-night café wasn't my idea' is her regular whine. But she did just come off a long night streaming with low-tipping truckers, and whatever you said was the final tip to her scales. She's thrown in the towel and gone home to Harold."

"I'm sorry if—"

"No need to worry," she said as she bussed an emptied dish or two. "Her antics have been this café's tradition for nearly forty years. Everyone within fifty miles knows ol' Tilly—and they know from experience what not to say to her first thing in the morning." Tapping the side of her blond head, she left us with a smile.

"Have you seen Sara yet?" I asked.

He responded with a shake of his head, his mouth once again full of food.

"I'll call her room, see if she's going to join us."

I went to the front desk, where a tired, elderly, night receptionist sat reading the morning paper. I asked him if he would ring Sara's room.

"You Scott Turner?"

"Why, yes," I asked, assuming he must have recognized me.

"This is for you then," he said, sliding a note across to me. He then returned to his reading.

The folded note had my name as the recipient from Sara. Inside it read:

Scott,

Please, nothing personal, but I've decided to spend the day alone, mostly in my room, collecting my thoughts in anticipation of Stephen's return. If you'd like, I'll join you tonight for dinner.

Sincerely,
Sara

"Thanks," I said to the receptionist.

"Don't mention it."

"She coming down?" Raeph asked, as I slid into my side of the booth.

"No, she's decided to spend the day all to her lonesome, but she'll join us tonight for dinner." After a quick revisit to my cooling breakfast, I asked, "So tell me, after you ran away, tail between legs, what did you do with yourself all day? Harass old waitresses?"

He laughed, but then his smile again became guarded, his eyes flitting up and then away from mine. "I have a confession to make."

"You becoming a Catholic?"

"Catholic?! Good God, no." He studied me closely, but then smiled. "Oh, 'confession.' Hah. No, hardly," as he used his fork to move his remaining food around his plate into clearly defined regions. It was obvious he had something to share, but in the end I'm not sure whether what I got was the truth or a hedge.

"Actually, I did little but wile away the day. I walked around the town a bit, visited the Bible church across the street, and met the pastor—I suppose anything to stay away from that Catholic church." He took a few bites, then added, "Scott, even though that priest may seem like a nice guy, you do know that the Catholic Church is still the enemy of Christ?"

"Raeph, my friend, you say you 'know' these things to be true. How do you *know*?"

"You are getting lured away, aren't you? Just like Reverend LaPointe."

I wondered how much I should tell him; how candid should I be.

"It's not like you think, so don't paint me into a corner, but I'd like to talk about this—I need to. I once felt just like you and your friends. If challenged, I, too, would have sworn I knew these things to be true, until I learned the hard way the difference between knowing and believing. Raeph, you ever think you knew someone, really knew their character, only to discover later you were completely wrong?"

His lips moved quickly, deliberately, in a one-word response that was overpowered by the deafening roar of semi rigs, passing on their morning routes.

"What'd you say?" I asked.

"LaPointe. We first thought he was a godsend to our struggling little church, but then we became convinced that he couldn't be trusted."

"You were wrong about Stephen. He's always been faithful, even now. The problem is he's more honest about searching for and knowing the truth than we are. Most of us aren't ready for the upheaval this would bring into our lives. Raeph, would you agree that there are many things we claim to know are true when in fact we can only believe them to be true?"

"I don't follow," he said, pushing aside his empty dishes, and facing me straight on.

"Take, for example, the sound of those semitrucks passing a moment ago. How do we know they weren't two low-flying crop dusters or maybe two Tyrannosaurus Rexes?"

"Given the way some truckers drive, I'd say there's no difference."

"Good point! But seriously—"

"Seriously? You're kidding."

I held my hands up, begging for patience; he nodded assent.

"With our senses, we hear sounds we recognize from experience to be diesel trucks and then our eyes confirm this. Through our senses, we can more than believe, we can know that the sound was made by trucks. Now suppose you had been away visiting the little boys' room—"

"You're positively clairvoyant!" he said, sliding across the booth seat. "Hold that thought."

As he left with a wry, urgent grin, I turned to my neglected breakfast and wondered whether my attempt at logic was being lost on this otherwise good soul, but more likely it was the fault of my own obtuseness.

If I added up the time Raeph and I had spent together, it was little more than a few hours, but even so I felt strangely drawn to this human water plug. And it wasn't just because we were both jocks, or at least old jocks trying to keep from evolving into giant sea slugs—Raeph was a likable guy, unpretentious, or as Jesus described Nathaniel, a man without guile.

Making and keeping friends has never been one of my better traits. I presume the fault is mine, but I've been burned enough in life—believing one thing only to discover another—that I've far too often kept most people at a safe distance. Even Diane. She constantly needles me about my inability to show her the affection she needs, and wants—and deserves—but I guess the bottom line is I'm just afraid of getting burned. Like the comic strip image of Lucy promising Charlie Brown just one more time that he can trust her to hold the ball steady for him to kick. The last image always shows Charlie a trusting fool. But isn't that what friendship as well as marriage is all about? Giving of ourselves freely even after we've been burned?

"Boy, I needed that," he said, regaining his seat, which produced strange sounds as he scooted across the vinyl. "So any dinosaurs pass while I was away?"

"Would you believe me if I said yes?"

"Believe you? I hardly know you!"

"Funny. But just for the sake of argument, suppose when you came back you found me beside myself with excitement, swearing that two Rexes had passed while you were gone. Would you believe me?"

"I'd believe—no, I'd know you were either pulling my leg or just plain whacko."

"Why?"

"Because, duh, everybody knows that dinosaurs no longer exist. They died out in the flood."

Not wanting to get distracted by the literalistic creation vs. science debate, I pushed ahead. "How does everyone know dinosaurs no longer exist? How do you *know* this?"

"Because no one has ever seen one alive, only bones, footprints, and frozen carcasses of mammoths."

"But what about Nessy?"

"Scott, that hardly proves your point, 'cause everyone knows that that's just a hoax or the d.t.'s of inebriated Scots."

"Raeph, you say you *know* that dinosaurs no longer exist, but I suggest that you can only *believe* this to be true. You've never seen any, but this world is very large; there are still places humanity hasn't fully explored, especially in the depth of the seas. The majority of witnesses, alive and dead, agree with you, I agree with you—I do, trust me—but then there are those reports of sightings, all throughout history. So in the end, the best we can say is that we believe, we are convinced, our unwavering opinion is that dinosaurs no longer exist. But we cannot say we *know* this definitively to be true."

"Scott, lighten up," he said, turning sideways in his booth to lean against the wall. "What's the big difference anyway?"

"Plenty. Now hear me out, please. We can apply this to almost everything we believe. We believe that God exists, and that He sent His Son, Jesus, who lived, died, and resurrected for our sins. We believe these things to be true for many, many reasons, including the witness of the apostolic martyrs and the Scriptures, but in the end we cannot say that we *know* these things to be true. We *know* things through our senses, our personal, direct experience of things, and, the bottom line is, you and I were not there. Our Christian faith consists in accepting the witness of those who were there, and, as it says in Romans, 'If you confess with your lips that Jesus is Lord and believe in your heart that God raised him from the dead, you will be saved.'[24] We may claim to *know* these things to be true in our gut, but what we actually mean is that we truly *believe*. Does this make sense?"

With a shrug, he answered, "Sure, but where's this all going?"

"Simply this. Our lives are full of things that we swear we know to be gospel truth but in fact we've merely accepted them as true without examining our sources. Today we are surrounded by hundreds of alternative gospels upon which people build their lives—diets, muscle-building programs, get-rich-quick schemes, return-to-nature simplicity, global warming, save our mother earth or the spotted owl, you name it. And people get sucked into these things without taking the time to examine the claims of some inspiring, convincing, charismatic speaker or writer. But all we need to do is go into any large bookstore, look on any of the shelves containing the books of these alternative gospels, and we'll find hundreds of conflicting opinions.

"And in that same bookstore, in the religion section, you'd really see what I'm getting at—every conceivable opinion about who Jesus was and what it means to be a Christian, all claiming to speak authoritatively, but far too many preaching, not only contradictory things, but out-and-out heresy." With this, I tidied up and pushed my empty dishes aside.

"Now, here's my point, Raeph: far too much of what you and I have assumed we know about the Catholic Church has been based on misinformation, bad experiences, and sometimes out-and-out lies. For example, we believe that Catholics worship Mary, right?"

"I know they do."

"You believe they do."

"Whatever!" Raeph said, with a dismissive flourish of his hand. Then pointing at me and bringing his feet back under the table, he asserted, "I grew up next to a Catholic family. They had statues of Mary everywhere, even a life-sized one that the mother dressed up in long-flowing gowns. Many times as a young boy, I'd sneak a peek at her through the window. There by herself she was kneeling before her freshly clothed statue with a doily on her head, praying her beads to that statue. It was spooky!"

"Whoa, I guess you've pointed out one other way we pick up wrong ideas about Catholicism, from either poorly taught, or nominal, or, in your case, overboard, hyper-devotional Catholics. If that lady was worshipping Mary, especially if she somehow was worshipping that particular statue of Mary, then she was being disobedient to the teaching of the Catholic Church, which teaches that worshipping Mary and statues is a sin, a heresy. All Christians up until the Reformation believed that people who have gone before us into heaven can intercede for us in prayer to God. Now, whether you or I agree with this, the point is that this is what Catholics are doing when they pray to Mary or Joseph or any of the saints. They are asking for their prayers."

I could tell by the look on my new friend's face that, though I may have scored a few points, I needed to proceed with caution.

"Now Raeph, don't get me wrong. I'm not trying to convince you to accept any of this. I'm merely challenging you to do what I had to do: take a big step back mentally and consider that most of the things you and I hate about the Catholic Church and Catholics may not be true, that in fact Catholics may be—at least those who are faithfully practicing the Catholic faith—sincere believers in Jesus Christ and, because of this, saved by grace."

"That's hard for me to accept." He peered into his coffee cup to see if anything was left.

"I know, I know." I paused for a moment to consider my next move. "Raeph, let me ask you this: have you ever taken the time to read the *Catechism of the Catholic Church*?"

"You're kidding? Of course not."

"That's what I mean. We're willing to believe everything else we hear about the Catholic Church but not willing to listen directly to the Catholic Church itself."

"But what if the *Catechism* is lying? Like other secret societies that hold back the truth about what they believe and tell something else to the public?"

"Raeph, that's called paranoia. Why not believe this about every organization? How can you know this isn't true of the church you attend? That the pastor and his personally chosen friends aren't meeting secretly every week, using your donations to carry out their secret clandestine plans? Raeph, the Catholic Church is far too large and too public."

Raeph turned in his booth, stretching his legs out into the room. "Man, you've wore me out with all this. What's your plans for today?"

"Nothing really. Just waiting around the hotel for any news about Stephen."

"Well, last night on my way back from town, I noticed that there's a local branch of the Global Fitness Center. I think I've still got a few weeks left on my membership. Interested in a workout, throwing a few weights around, maybe some racquetball?"

He must not have caught the drift of my earlier pantomime, so I just said, "Excellent idea! Let's do it."

"Long as we're done by one. Got a luncheon appointment."

"Really? Did you run into someone you know or something?"

"Not exactly," he said as he exited the booth, "but I'll tell you on the way."

We separated to retrieve our exercise getups with plans to rejoin at the van in ten minutes. Actually, I was glad to break from my exhortation. It's surprising how self-convicting one can become when preaching to others.

29

The early dawn atmosphere around the three tables in the dining area of the Mite was a mixture of melancholic solitude and boisterous camaraderie. Mrs. Cousineau's rolls were especially good that morning, and for some undisclosed reason, she had doubled the batch. Eggs, bacon, sausages, buttermilk pancakes, juice, and coffee had made their rounds as the lively cackled and kidded, while the more contemplative ate and listened, hoping that maybe next year they might feel more like regular members.

"Good grief, Birch, how many times do we have to listen to this?" bewailed Larry Wycliffe in feigned despair. "You lost! Get over it. Move on." One hand over his heart and the other poised off to the distance, he dramatized, "'Forgetting what lies behind, I press onward' and get a life!"

Laughter rose from his table, causing those at the two others to stop and turn. Birch wiped syrup from his lip then replaced his napkin on his lap in awkward silence. Larry saw that his jest had struck deeper than intended.

"I will say though, and mark me," he said, widely addressing all those around, "I wish we had instant replay, 'cause the hang time between the moment Birch left the foul line and laid that ball up so gently with one hand was nothing short of divine levitation! I swore for a second we were seeing computer generation in real life." This fishing drew the smile from his friend.

"Levitation, my foot!" added Joe Lees, a first-timer who'd quickly won himself into the ranks of the regulars. "He wasn't touching the ground 'cause he was on top of me."

"And me, too!" Kyle Reuther added. Actually, Birch had knocked down four men in his enthusiastic, vintage Doctor J drive to the hoop, and it would have won the game for them, if it hadn't been such a blatant charge.

"If you guys hadn't been so dumbstruck at the sight of such heavenly grace, you would have gotten out of the way!" Birch answered.

"Heavenly grace?" mocked Terry Franks, another newcomer, "that was a depraved will that bowled me over."

"All right, guys," Ron interjected as he refilled his coffee, "it's too early to mix sports banter with theological metaphors. Keep the discussion inane."

The sound of some unaccounted-for person descending the main staircase turned a few heads. Mrs. Cousineau smiled at her well-kept secret.

"Stephen!" exclaimed Kyle. "When did you—?"

Larry, Birch, and Tom Sylvan all swarmed to greet him. Unrestrained greetings accompanied by clasped hands and bear hugs squelched any qualms Stephen may have had about returning. Ron rose slowly amongst the newcomers, glanced toward Mrs. Cousineau, and saw her pleasure. After using a napkin to dab his face, he threw it down and went to greet his prodigal friend.

"So, Stephen," he said, extending his hand and thus communicating much more than anyone else in the room could fathom, "when did you arrive? Here, come on over," directing Stephen to a seat at one of the tables left empty due to diminished attendance. "I'll buy!"

The seats around Stephen were quickly filled with regulars, friends who had known Stephen for as long as twenty years, leaving the newcomers to listen from afar or return to their food as they wished. Ron brought a tray of everything, including the famous rolls and coffee, and then claimed the one remaining chair, directly across from their illustrious guest.

"So when did you arrive?"

"Late last night, after you all were sleeping off your overexertion on the courts. Actually, on the radio coming in, I heard about some rumble happening up here. Apparently someone had the delusion he was a human bowling ball and took out four others he'd mistaken as pins."

"Yeah, right," Birch said. "You overheard us."

"But Stephen, how are you?" Ron asked. "We heard all the rumors, and, well, when you didn't return, I … we just didn't know what to think."

Stephen sat silent for a moment, contemplating how God could not have selected a more perfect subgroup of the usual retreatants for Stephen to relate the trials and tribulations of the past year to. Some of the regulars would have only received his tale with a critical, cynical ear; others would have interjected sarcasm or comic relief; and a few, like Jim, Cliff, and maybe even Scott Turner would have been too curious about certain details and leanings, and interrupted him with pointed queries. But Terry, Birch, Larry, Tom, Kyle, and even Ron—whom Stephen expected was the most personally wounded by the negative impact of last year's presentation—were friends, who, though anxious, were content to listen quietly.

So he recounted the past year, from the time he'd left the retreat without explanation. In time, Kyle had to ask: "The man shot you because he thought you were some kind of Catholic spy?"

Before answering, Stephen refilled his coffee, noticing that several of the newcomers were listening intently. "I'm sorry," he said in their direction, "how rude of me not to introduce myself." He greeted them all, finding out from which churches they had come to this mountain respite. Duties done, he returned to his seat to address the hanging question.

"I would say, 'Yes, isn't that strange or weird?' except that we all have in our churches those hyper, overly zealous conspiracy theorists who see some agent of Satan lurking behind every suspicious-sounding theological bush. In one of my previous churches, I was hounded by a tight clique of these fanatics, who were convinced that the end of the world was imminent and the Whore of Babylon in Rome had sent his minions everywhere to lure the faithful away into his grasp. Yes, at first those three and I were great friends. I had high hopes they would be my strongest supporters in the church. But in time, Walter, Ben, and Raeph—"

"Raeph?" Birch interrupted. "Why, he was here, looking for you."

"What?" Stephen demanded, his face ashen.

Ron said quickly, "Yes, Stephen, there's a few things I need to tell you, but later. Finish your story."

Stephen tried to read more from Ron's face, but the latter had turned away to his coffee. Looking instead to Larry and Birch, he got a shrug and a tilt of the head, so he continued, telling nearly everything, except anything to do specifically with his theological leanings and plans.

Eventually, Ron nodded toward Larry, who then rose from his seat. "Brothers in Christ," he said, addressing the group, "even with the return of our prodigal friend, we must try to stay on schedule. It's 8:45, so we're only fifteen minutes behind. If you would please, quickly bus your breakfast dishes, take care of any necessary pit stops, and then gather in the conference room by nine for devotions."

All obeyed without complaint, but as they went, Ron tapped Stephen's arm and with a quick tilt of his head, bid him to follow. They went together to the library. Ron held the door and, looking askance, silently motioned Stephen in.

As he reached the chair furthest in, Stephen said, turning as he sat, "Hey, Ron, I'm sorry to see such a poor turnout this year. I hope it's not because—"

"Put a clamp on it, LaPointe." Ron stood with his back to the closed door. "It's all because of you. And Jim and Cliff and who knows who else. Funny how things happen. All along I was on my guard against pollution from liberals, and then you three blindside me. I spoke with all the regulars who refused to return. They said they sacrificed time away from their families and busy schedules to come here to rest and recharge, not to question and defend everything their lives and ministries stood for."

"I didn't mean—"

"I know you didn't. You intended to do nothing more than air your personal frustrations, but your tone became far too pointed and accusatory. You put all of us on the defensive, even your closest friends, implying that your conclusions required not only your resignation but ours as well—as if any of us who refused to agree were blind, unfaithful guides." Ron's arms accented his words like he was shooing flies.

Stephen rose to meet his accuser face level. "I thought the reason for this secluded gathering was so pastors could vent freely about the otherwise unspeakable strains and stresses of ministry and marriage?"

"To share and listen to brotherly advice, not undermine and poison. Do you know what happened to Cliff because of your innocent speech?"

"My speech played only a minor role in his decision, and besides, he's happier now than he's been in years."

"So you think we all should just up and resign, proclaiming that everything we've stood for is nothing but a bunch of lies?" Ron moved in closer, fists clenched at his side.

Stephen held his ground; their eyes locked, both breathing nervously.

A crescendo of voices distracted them as a group of retreatants passed on their way to the conference room.

Ron's fists relaxed and, his eyes closing slowly, but still in tense tones, he murmured, "Stephen, I'm sorry."

"Me too, Ron. I shouldn't have come."

"No, that's not what I meant to communicate," Ron said, running a hand back through his hair. "This is exactly where you should be able to come."

"Well, anyway, I'll not be staying." He moved past Ron toward the door.

Without turning, Ron said, "You did hear that Scott Turner and some guy named Raeph are out looking for you?"

Stephen stopped, hand on the knob, head pivoting slowly around, "I don't understand how or why those two are together."

Ron began to relate the confrontation and ruckus of Monday morning, but a persistent knock interrupted him, along with a voice from the hall: "Hey, you guys going to join us?"

"Anyway, Raeph and Scott left here Monday together to find you. Again, I'm sorry, Stephen. I do need to go, though. You're welcome to stay, of course, but it might be best for you to go into Jamesfield and find your search party."

"Suppose you're right."

"We've been friends a long time, Stephen, but I just don't understand what's gotten into you, Jim, and Cliff, and frankly I'm not sure I want to. Later, after the retreat's over, maybe we can talk. Be seeing you." Ron extended himself, shook Stephen's hand, and left.

The Mite library, swimming in shadows, no longer exuded its once-inviting welcome, as Stephen stared out the empty doorway. To him, it had always been a warm, relaxing comfort, a refuge in which to take down a book, maybe at random, and then, far from the maddening, often thankless, demands of church and staff, congregation, and even family, read: truly and slowly and patiently read, and enjoy, not in preparation for some impending sermon or board presentation, but just read.

But no longer. His connection with the Mite had been severed. Oh, he would always be a welcome guest to the Cousineaus, whose French Canadian, Catholic heritage would make them sympathetic to the cut of his theological jib, but he knew, reading between the lines of Ron's words and actions, that to this annual gathering of ministry compatriots he was now excommunicate. The leadership was essentially casting him adrift for fear of any further contaminating influence.

He glanced one final time around. Of the hundreds of books squirreled away here, most out of print, more than half were of a theological slant that in previous years he merely had looked over, ignored, but now he hungered to read, ashamed at his historical, philosophical, theological, and mostly prideful ignorance. The caressingly warm leather chairs, the soft, indirect, natural light carrying in the natural, unadulterated quiet of the mountains, the likely private respite from random chatter. Stephen turned and left, head canted, pulling the door behind him.

In his room, he threw his clothes—and the half-read book he assumed was a gift from Mrs. Cousineau—into his overnight bag, anxious now to complete his departure and kick away the dust from his shoes. The door to the conference room was shut. Muffled voices from some indistinguishable discussion reached Stephen's ears but only accelerated his departure. Within but a few feet of the outside door, a male voice arrested his escape. "Stephen! *Bonjour!*"

Inexcusable shame rose up within him and made him turn. "Mr. Cousineau. So good to see you."

"I not expecting you this year, *mon ami,* but so glad you finally come." The familiar man of the house, one leg slightly shorter from birth, but a joyous character that knew no handicap, hobbled out from behind the counter, arms extended for a welcoming embrace.

From deep within the kitchen somewhere around the oversized freezer, Suzette called out, "*Pardonez moi, mon amour.* I forgot to tell you. He arrived late last night."

"How come you not tell me my good friend Reverend LaPointe has come!" he said, holding and studying Stephen at arm's length. "So what you been doing with yourself this long year? I hear many tings trough grapevine. You okay?"

"Yes, I'm just fine, Mr. Cousineau. God was very merciful."

"And your family? Your wife, what's her name … Sara, *oui*, Sara, and the boys?" He motioned Stephen toward a tall stool by the counter, presumably for an extended chat.

"Fine."

"Oh, that reminds me, *mon ami*! A woman called for you, when was it, sometime yesterday afternoon."

"What?" Stephen dropped his bag and turned full toward the old man.

Suzette emerged quickly from the back kitchen. "What? You didn't tell me this."

"Since we decided that Stephen wasn't coming, I felt there was no need to tell. You were gone, remember, over at Nicole's for your weekly gossip, and, well, I forgot."

"What did she say?" Stephen demanded.

"She just asked if you were here. She didn't say who she was or anyting. When I say no and that we weren't sure if you coming, she didn't say anyting more, at first."

"At first, you oaf?" Suzette said, wiping dough from her hands.

"Bridle it, woman!"

A towel flew through the serving window, enveloping Tom's gray pate. A string of indecipherable nasal invectives emerged as he tried to disengage his hair from unbaked batter. Suzette winked playfully at Stephen.

"So what did she say," she demanded, "what did she say!"

Freed from his facial shroud, Tom turned to Stephen, but a few lingering clumps of dough gave the impression that he had just walked beneath a pigeon colony.

"She told me to tell you, if you came, that she'd be in Jamesfield."

"Jamesfield?" Stephen responded, head and then body jerking away. "Jamesfield?" He went for his bag. "Tom and Suzette, I must go right away."

"But, Stephen, what does it mean?" Suzette asked.

"My wife, Sara, is waiting for me. I've got to go. I'll call you," and he was gone.

The snow had stopped sometime in the deep dark of the early morning, but the temperatures had continued to drop. With a quick swipe of his arms, he cleared the windshield, started the Wagoneer, and without the usual warm-up, shot back and then out of the Mite's partially shoveled lot. For three straight days the snow had fallen, but temperatures had fluctuated above and below freezing. An erect icing of snow edged every tree, limb, and twig along the descent down the mountain, giving the landscape the artificial appearance of an amateur painting, masking demonically the ice beneath.

Shooting down and around the steep, snow-covered gravel, Stephen's mind raced through every conceivable scenario, every possible motive that might have brought her to Jamesfield.

The gravel road snaked down the mountain. Through the fogged windows, Stephen noticed a lone set of footprints progressing toward him in the opposite direction, spaced neatly between the tread marks of Mr. Cousineau's morning plow, but thought nothing of them.

Aloud he wondered, "Is it possible she's waiting for me at—", but he didn't finish. Without caution, he had followed the plowed path down and toward the last sharp curve, and then saw Tom's stalled plow, parked in the center of the drive. He hit the brakes and turned his wheels, but the vehicle continued straight on course. Ten feet short of the tractor, at the point of the curve, his car shot off the embankment and over a fifteen-foot ledge, landing upright in the wedge between a pair of hundred-year-old oaks. Secured by his seat belt, Stephen weathered the flight, speechless, helpless, but upon impact, the Wagoneer careened down between the two legs of its captors. One strong limb crashed through the passenger window, jamming his head back against the headrest, knocking him unconscious and limp.

In time, the engine stalled. Other than the chirp of waking birds, the chatter of squirrels foraging for cached nuts, and the breathless whisper of the pines, the world returned to the silent stillness of a New Hampshire mountain morning. Stephen was left unconsciously, anonymously alone.

The pages of her murder mystery novel were turned slowly forward and sometimes back. Sara fought against an onslaught of diverse distractions, to enjoy this time alone, locked away, isolated, beyond the beck and call of her sons, her studies, her well-meaning but badgering friends, and especially Frank. Her eyes shot back to the printed page, her forefinger fighting the drift of intellect and memory, her will forcing her from one word to the next, much like the famous bouncing ball of old-time sing-a-longs. Eventually, she gave up, threw the book aside, and reached for the phone to place the call she'd been hesitant to make all morning.

A familiar female voice answered. "Good morning, St. Francis Rectory. Can I help you?"

Sara stood to pace and grabbed a fistful of Kleenex. "Sister Agatha, hello. Is Father Bourque in?"

"Hello, Mrs. LaPointe. Good to hear from you. No, Father is out and will probably be busy all day. It's Ash Wednesday, and the Lord has left no stone unturned to keep him extra busy."

"Then do you know whether—"

"Whether your husband has returned? No, not yet, but as Father said, we really do expect him soon and will call you the moment he arrives. Are you still at the hotel?"

"Yes, yes—" Outside the window, a young father passed, two boys in tow. By their overstuffed clothes and gear she guessed they were on their way to the nearest snow hill.

"Actually, this is amazing," the sister continued with enthusiasm. "I was just about to call you. One of my blessed tasks every Wednesday is to visit a young invalid in our parish. Because company does so much to raise this girl's spirits, I usually bring someone along, but the woman who normally comes can't get away from her secretarial job today. Sara, would you be willing to accompany me? Stephanie, that's the young girl's name, would so enjoy our visit. You and I can chat along the way, and then afterwards I'll buy you lunch."

The father and sons had passed from view, leaving only footsteps splayed larger than life like snowshoes in the blowing snow. Excuses began lining up in her mind awaiting inspection and deployment, but as if from orders higher up, none were selected.

"That would be nice."

"Wonderful! When could you be ready?"

"Anytime actually. I'm just sitting here reading, awaiting word—"

"Then I'll meet you out in front in, say, fifteen minutes?"

With the receiver's click, Sara rushed into a routine that normally demanded at least twice that time. "I guess that's the difference in being a nun," she said before the mirror studying her hair and makeup. "A skirt!" Quickly she changed out of her relaxing wardrobe—jeans and a cardigan sweater—and into a gray tweed, calf-length skirt that matched the cardigan. Then cordovan boots with matching gloves, full-length camel-hair coat, Shaw tartan scarf, a look around at the state of the room, and she was on her way.

RUNNING out the front entrance of the hotel, Sara halted in disbelief, mouth agape, eyes wide, speechless. The oxymoron of a black-and-white habited nun awaiting her in a shiny blue Miata sport coupe fit no preconceived categories.

"I know, I know," the sister said, pushing open the door.

"I'm sorry," Sara said, laughing as she worked herself down into the tight passenger cavity, "I guess I—"

"You never expected a nun to be driving anything except a rusty old Chevette or maybe the parish's institutional stretch van."

"I don't think I was thinking anything."

With a playful "vroom," the racy import left for the outskirts of town. "It was a birthday gift from my older brother, Satch, who I'm sure was motivated by the irony. But what can I say, I do love it. Father Bourque made a point of preparing the entire parish, at every Mass the Sunday after it arrived, that I hadn't wasted parish funds to fulfill some frivolous, worldly lust. Even so, there are still a few gray-haired ladies that raise their noses whenever I whoosh by, leaving them to chirp and cluck like hens. Probably the worst impact on the congregation, however, was the appearance of several other new sport coupes. I suppose there's a few angry wives blaming me for giving their husbands permission to succumb to their otherwise long-suppressed temptation. The teens love it, though. You should see them go crazy when I take Father Bourque for a ride."

"Father Bourque fits in here?"

"It's a bit tight, but between you and me, he has borrowed it several times for a spin up into the mountains, far from the eyes of the parish."

Sara studied the beautiful nun, her hand working smoothly with the Miata's standard shift, her focus half on the road, half on humorous, friendly small talk. A mile out of town, Sister Agatha pulled off into a small wayside park. The parking lot outside the bathroom and concession area was empty, the picnic tables upended for their winter rest.

"The trailer where Stephanie and her daughter Tina Marie live is just up around the corner, but I probably need to prepare you. I said this was one of my weekly blessed tasks, but I fibbed a little. I can only trust that she enjoys our visits and that they lift her spirit. You see, Stephanie Jonas is a bit of an enigma. On the surface—her protective shield—she is brutally angry, bitter, insisting that we leave her alone. I've never visited her when I wasn't cussed out and condemned as a messenger of the Whore of Babylon, when she hasn't thrown something at us to scare us away."

"Then need I ask: why do you go back? I realize you go in the name of Christ, but still, as a pastor's wife, I used to visit people all the time, but eventually, if I gathered that I wasn't wanted, I granted their wish and left them alone."

Sister Agatha lowered her face, paused silently, then responded. "Four years ago, two weeks after graduation from Jamesfield High School, Stephanie was raped, brutally beaten, and left to die along a deserted gravel mountain road. She was discovered the next morning by the paperboy, whose own life, let it be said, was shocked back on track. That's a whole other story—a moving conversion from a belligerent to a humbly obedient son. He saved her life, carrying her to the nearest farm. While she was recovering in the hospital, they discovered that she was pregnant by the rapist. Everyone in her life, the majority of Jamesfield and even her Fundamentalist Christian parents, encouraged her to abort the child, but she refused. She argued that it wasn't the baby's fault, so why should it be murdered for someone else's sin? Three years ago this month, Tina Marie, a sparkling, blond, blue-eyed princess, was born."

Sara diverted her eyes away to the world outside the Miata. Stephanie's story, a story far from her own, still had an important overlap, that uncomfortable, unforgettable intersection where Sara's past remained and where she believed her freedom to move on ended.

"Was the rapist—the father—ever caught?" she asked, more than curious.

"No. Stephanie insists she has no memory of who did it, but Father Bourque and I think she is protecting someone."

"Was she a member of your church?"

"Oh no, her family are members of a Fundamentalist church outside of town. It's terribly sad. After the rape, and especially when they discovered that she was pregnant, they began shunning her. When she refused to abort, they began whispering that the child was the seed of Satan and Stephanie the Beast of Revelations. Stephanie gave birth to Tina Marie in the middle of the night with only a nurse attending. In the morning, a cross, painted with dripping blood, was found on her hospital room door. In the three years since, as far as I know, she has never seen or heard from any of her family or former church friends." The nun's eyes closed briefly, head shaking.

"How did you and Father Bourque get involved?"

"The rest of the Christian community didn't abandon her. The Methodist and Presbyterian pastors visited her in the hospital, as well as Father Bourque and I. He and I alternated daily. When she and Tina Marie were ready to be released, she had no place to go, so our three churches went in together to help her with the rent for a mobile home and expenses, which kept escalating. The doctors have all concluded that, short of a miracle, Stephanie will never walk again."

"You would think she'd be grateful for all this attention and help, and especially your weekly visits."

The shadow of sadness spread across Sister Agatha's countenance, and with the release of a sigh she continued, "That's why we need to talk first before we go in. Stephanie is anything but friendly and grateful, at least on the surface. When she hears us coming, she'll start bombarding us with curses and insults, seemingly to drive us away. She'll dodge every question, subvert every comment, and denigrate every gift with sarcasm."

"Why?"

"The easy answer is that she's just bitter and self-indulgent, some even say—especially those who no longer pay her visits—that she's possessed by a demon of bitterness. But it's probably a little more complicated than that. She was a sincere, active, believing member of her very anti-Catholic church. Then she was raped, by someone we think she knew, and rejected by everyone dear to her, until the only ones left showing her any attention and love are a Catholic priest and nun."

"You mean all the other churches—?"

"They've all given up, and I really can't blame them. Stephanie's language can get pretty dicey. Other than a little help with expenses, Stephanie and Tina Marie are now solely our project. Father Bourque believes this has left her in a confusing and complicated dilemma. Her family's Fundamentalist church is known for their outspoken anti-Catholic agenda. We believe she is caught between believing them— that all that has fallen upon her is the work of Satan—and believing the love she has received from God through us. For this reason, we will never cease caring for her, no matter how difficult she becomes. We must help her discover that we do truly love her, that we will never abandon her, and that we and the Catholic Church are not messengers of Satan but of our Lord Jesus Christ."

Sara slowly extended a hand across the gearshift toward Sister Agatha, who received it warmly. "What then do you want me to do?"

"Just be my companion in carrying love to this lost soul, and most importantly, be my prayer support. You need not say a word, if you wish. Just pray that God will protect us, and Stephanie, with His angels as we enter into battle. Pray that my words remain tempered by His love and compassion and not surrender to the temptation to retaliate in kind.

"But two things to look for: first, notice how well Tina Marie is cared for. This tells us that when we're away, Stephanie showers her daughter with precious love. Regardless of whatever conflicted feelings she might have about God's love, she dearly loves Tina Marie. And second, listen carefully as we leave. After all the curses and epithets, after we've left her alone, as we're almost ready to slam the doors on her world, listen carefully, for you will hear her final soft message."

With that, the nun squeezed Sara's hand affectionately, then jerked the blue sports car into gear, backed away briefly, re-shifted, and then out of the park for their encounter with a lost mother and child. Sara watched the snowy landscape pass by in a blur, silent, the focus of her mind elsewhere.

As the sun moved slowly upward and westward on its daily journey, it finally reached the height in the midwinter sky, where its forward edge peeked through one of the Mite's six dining room skylights. Before these were added—"and at great expense!" rang Tom's caustic but prideful refrain—the room required constant fluorescent lighting. Afterward, the fluorescents were only needed in the evening and on days of dense overcast—"and at great savings!" rang Suzette's triumphant rejoinder.

As if taking her side in the ongoing argument, the first direct beam of this late-morning kiss struck Tom square. He squinted in annoyance, waking with a start from an unplanned nap. His dream had included an incomprehensible mixture of swamped fishing boats, mindless television talk-show hosts, an angry state trooper, and some overly attentive high-school sweetheart who lately seemed to return often to his dreams, though he could never afterward identify her—and besides, he had had no high-school sweetheart. Being the youngest son of an ever-growing brood of Catholic siblings, he had been his parents' gift to the diocese, so he had attended the all-boys pre-seminary. Try as he might, however, with every intention of being a very obedient son, he nevertheless fell far short of everyone's expectations. Graduation was a gift of grace, for all concerned. The afternoon of graduation, he dropped his books in the trash, and returned to his one love: fishing. He signed on as a hand with a deep-sea fishing fleet out of Québec, worked his way as far up the ladder as he could rise without being related to the owner, then bought his own thirty-four-foot cruiser and, with his wife of eight years, started Tom & Suzette's, a quaint fish-and-chips diner. For nearly ten years, they were amazingly happy, Tom and a helper catching the fish, Suzette and a helper cooking them. But when the fast-food chains began alluring their clientele, their banker and priest agreed they should sell while the selling was good, so with their eyes set on a quiet retreat from the craziness of the ever-escalating tourist trap, they moved to a run-down mountain hunting lodge in the shadow of Mount Lafayette that Suzette had inherited from her grandfather.

Initially, they had only wanted to hide away, to relax, fish, hunt, and enjoy a serene retirement in the woods. Then one day, she invited the local priest to use the lodge for a staff retreat, and their privacy became history. The nameless lodge became the Widow's Mite. Now for years hardly a month passes when some group, Catholic, Protestant, or even secular, isn't renting it for a weekend or weekday retreat.

At first, Tom had resented the constant intrusion, but in time, some of the groups began returning year after year, and they became family. Like the group of Evangelical pastors here this week: all good, faithful, God-fearing men. They might not share their Catholic faith, but who knows: an afternoon's reading of one of the carefully chosen books in their library, and with the Spirit's help, another one of these men just might be on the road home to the Church. Hadn't this happened with Jim? And now Stephen? Who would it be this year?

Tom noticed that the remains of his coffee had spilled on the floor. *"Mon Dieu!"* he exclaimed, shooting a prayer for mercy upward, knowing that Suzette would have his skin. From the kitchen, he retrieved a towel, wiped up his mess, and upon replacing the towel, remembered. He glanced at the clock: 11:15. The remains of one cinnamon roll, cut neatly in half, lay temptingly before him. He stuffed it in his mouth—for nourishment, mind you—re-doffed his winter wear, and went to the shed for a can of diesel.

What a brilliant, beautiful day. The sky was painfully clear, a stark, robin's egg blue, and though the temperature was still below zero, the bright sun was instigating a progressive drip to the ice- and snow-covered trees.

Descending before him, around and through the cavernous road down from the Mite, was the clean, crisp white results of his earlier plowing, spoilt only by the tracks of one exiting car. *Must be Reverend LaPointe's*, he thought. Though on the outside he was seventy-eight, he had always felt younger on the inside, much younger, and like an adolescent, he tried to descend one foot after the other inside one of the car tracks. His handicap made this an unusual challenge. First it led him down to the left and then around to the right and then down the long, steep straightaway. He glanced up and saw, a hundred yards below him, a glimpse of his stalled tractor, facing to the left, following the curve out.

260

His focus returned to the car track. The tread marks were distinctive, deeply grooved, angled backward. *Must be one of those newfangled anti-skid tires*, he surmised. He laughed at the memory of pushing his dad's Model-A pickup out of a deep muddy rut. His three brothers were all helping, but the car was so buried, well above both axles, that it seemed hopeless. Vaguely he remembered, when the family had taken a trip west to visit relatives, seeing a sign along the old Alaskan highway that read, "Choose your rut carefully, for the rut you choose you'll be in for two hundred miles!" He couldn't recall whether this had been an official sign, or one made by some sarcastic local, but it fit perfectly the memory of that buried Model-A. Eventually, a farmer had passed with a team of Percherons and, with more than the deserved round of verbal harassment, had extricated the truck.

The track below him continued onward, and he was impressed with how successful he was in keeping his steps within the tread path, especially given the imbalance of lugging the can of diesel. Immediately afterward, he stepped slightly outside, losing balance temporarily, and scolded himself for his cockiness. He focused more intently, wondering what Suzette might be doing. *What was it she said we were having for lunch? Some kind of corn chowder? Let's see, Thursday. What was her usual midweek menu? And what would she say if she were watching me walk one foot carefully in front of the other down the middle of a car path?* He smirked. *Who cares? And besides why move into the middle of an endless woods if one can't enjoy it like a child?*

He refocused more intently down into the seam of the car track, the now-familiar repetitive pattern of the tire's footprint. Some while back he had noticed a distinctive flaw in that pattern caused, he guessed, by a stone lodged in the tread. Every three feet or so, the flaw would reappear, a smudge where there should have been a clean ridge of raised snow. He had readjusted his stride so that the fall of his right foot coincided with the reappearance of the smudge.

And then suddenly he noticed something strange. His accurately placed right foot had landed in unplowed snow. He stopped and glanced to his left. The plowed drive indeed curved to the left, following the driveway out and down, but the car treads had continued forward. There was the tractor sitting idle, facing downhill, and an unidentifiable fear rose within him.

His face jerked forward. The car tracks continued straight forward, without variance, through the unplowed snow and on over the horizon of the bank toward the two familiar oaks, a combination that had always mentally marked this last turn before the driveway emptied out onto the highway below. Something else wasn't right. The V-arrangement of the slanting oaks seemed wider than he remembered. And the oak on the left. *Isn't that a new scrape or scar on the bark?*

He dropped the can of diesel and lunged forward, working his legs hard against the snowbank, and as the horizon expanded, the car below gradually came into view.

"Stephen!" he screamed, for he knew that green Wagoneer.

Plunging down feet-first over the bank, he slid buried to his shoulders, working his arms like a snow angel to keep free.

"Stephen!" he screamed again as he fought against snow and the buried accumulation of limbs and leaves. The Wagoneer was wedged upright between the oaks, the doors blocked and crushed inward.

He forced himself around to the front, snow well above his waist, his heart pounding with exertion and fear. Through the windshield, he saw with horror Stephen jammed against the driver door by a tree limb that entered the car through the passenger window. But no movement.

He slammed his fists hard on the crumpled hood and screamed again and again, *"Stephen, non! Mon Dieu, non!"*

30

The two worn-out, aging warriors descended the steps from the Global Fitness Center.

"Thanks again, Scott, for the workout. I frankly can't remember the last time I was with someone who could so challenge me."

"Same here, pal. You honestly could hold your own with some of those professionals I used to bump bodies with. And probably a whole lot better than I could today in my present slovenly state."

"Thanks anyway. I suppose we were both breathing a little harder than we did ten years ago. But if I can still move, maybe we can do it again tomorrow."

"Great. Want a ride to your rendezvous?"

"No, I'll walk. It's just over there," Raeph said, pointing down Main to the diner.

"Then see you tonight at dinner? Sara's planning to join us."

"Be there. Hey, how 'bout keeping my sweaty clothes till tonight? I'd rather not turn my luncheon appointment's stomach."

"You say her name's Maeda? That's a new one on me."

"Irish. That's where she's from.

"Well, you have a great time. See you tonight." With a handshake, they parted.

Raeph checked his watch: 12:50. Ten minutes to walk the three blocks.

The weather was cold but clear. Midday traffic seemed unusually busy. Raeph surmised that it was probably because skiers were either passing south from the mountains on their way home or north for the weekend.

"But it's Wednesday," he said aloud to himself. With a shrug, he pulled his coat closed and walked briskly down the cleanly shoveled walk. As he refocused on his anticipated rendezvous, the hint of a smile appeared and became contagious to the rest of his face.

"Let me help you with that, ma'am." An elderly woman was trying to load groceries into the back seat of her subcompact. Raeph noticed that across her forehead was a dark gray smudge, as if she had been foraging around in a dustbin. He started to ask, but let it go.

At the window of the diner, he paused to scope out the clientele. The counter was full of mostly men, buried in their papers, stuffing their faces with their free hands. Most of the tables were full, with the remaining interspatial passageways being crisscrossed by the few overworked waitresses and the patrons coming and going.

He scanned every face or silhouette, but she wasn't there. One ten. Had she stood him up, or was she just late like himself?

He looked down the sidewalk in the direction of Jamesfield Bible Fellowship, but no sign of her.

With one last look around, he left in the direction of the church. *Assuming she's just late, it's probably better for me to escort her anyway.*

His focus was downward as he walked, his mind considering every reason for her tardiness, when his peripheral vision caught a familiar but unwelcome sight. The gaudy yellow, traveling "billboard for Jesus" passed quickly, spraying him slightly with street slush. He turned to glare, but he saw no faces through the darkened windows. *Did they recognize me, and splash me on purpose?* He didn't think so, 'cause why would they anyway? *They wouldn't have any reason to question my loyalty to their cause.*

He turned his attention back to his quest, and as he neared the front walk of the church, he saw her, dressed against the weather, coming toward him.

"Raeph, I'm so sorry I'm late. I got away as soon as I could. Thank you for not giving up."

He gave her his arm. "Understand fully, and as far as giving up, this luncheon with you was the one thing I was looking forward to today."

"Then let's get some of Mabel's homemade corn chowder."

They walked in silence, both feeling a little awkward and projecting that onto the other. At the diner, Raeph took the lead: "Table for two, please."

"Take your choice," barked the elderly waitress.

"Let's take the one furthest back, Raeph," Maeda suggested. "Far less traffic."

"Okay." They threaded their way to a table in the back corner and sat beside each other against the wall.

After ordering, she broke the ice. "Did you have a good morning?"

"Yes, Scott and I worked out at the gym down the street. He's a retired pro football player who turned minister, and we spent the entire morning proving that we aren't kids anymore."

"You certainly seem in good shape to me," she said with a slight blush.

"Winter clothes cover years of sloth."

The chowder came, with chunks of homemade bread, and for Raeph a side order of cod and chips.

In the midst of his first bite of fish, Raeph's eyes wandered around the room, and Maeda noticed them widening. "What's wrong?" she asked.

"What's with this town? There's more of them, here in this room."

"More of what?"

"Look," he said, nodding slightly toward a man at the next table. "I keep running into people who look like they haven't washed their faces in weeks."

"You're kidding, aren't you?"

He returned only a blank stare and a shrug.

Maeda smiled. "It does look like that, I agree, but those gray smudges are what remains of crosses that were traced on their foreheads by a priest. It's Ash Wednesday. The palm fronds from last year's Palm Sunday celebration are burned, and the ashes are used to trace a cross on the forehead. All of those 'dirty' people are Catholics who went to noon Mass. You've never seen this?"

"Not that I can remember. How'd you come to know so much about it?"

"I'm from Ireland, remember. Only a few in my County wouldn't have dirty foreheads on Ash Wednesday." She turned to the passing waitress, "Can I have some fresh cream?"

Once they were alone again, Maeda changed the subject. "Raeph, I need to tell you that Reverend Guilford encouraged me to have lunch with you."

"What do you mean?"

"Well, he was asking that I work through lunch, to finish some typing I hadn't completed, but I told him of our luncheon date."

Raeph smiled, then concealed it with a bite of cod, washed down with coffee.

"When he heard that I was meeting you, he acted pleased. He said," here Maeda affected a gruff caricature of her boss, "'Then please, can you do something for me? Find out more about this stranger. He left us all wondering last night when he left in a hurry.' So you see, Raeph," she said with a mischievous expression, "I'm here to spy on you."

"Then let's make sure we give him a story to lose sleep over. By the way, did you hear anything about what they decided last night?"

"Actually, they had another meeting this morning."

"I thought I saw one of their vehicles. The ugly yellow van."

"Don't think I know it. Anyway, some of those who were there last night showed up and demanded to meet with the pastor. He reluctantly met with them briefly in private—I didn't hear anything of what they discussed—and then just a few minutes before I could break away, they left in a huff. One yelled back something like, 'If you're a coward, then I guess we'll have to do it by ourselves.'

"When I asked Reverend Guilford about it, he just said to ignore them, then gave me the orders to get the scoop on you. Maybe he thinks you're somehow in league with their plans."

"I never saw any of those folks before and have no idea what they might be planning, except that it may be something against the Catholic priest down the road. Do you know him?"

She took a spoon of her soup before she answered, "Yes, I know Father Bourque. Don't you have any idea what they might be planning? Where I come from, the Protestants and Catholics too often settle their differences with violence. I hope and pray that's not true here in upstate New Hampshire."

He was about to say, "Of course not," but then remembered: what Walter, Ben, and he had boasted they might do to punish papists and, more specifically, what his determined friend Walter had actually done. Instead, he merely returned, "Me, too."

For a while they ate in silence.

"More coffee, dearie?" asked a passing waitress.

"Yes, ma'am, thanks. So, Maeda, do you like sports?"

For the next half hour, they talked freely about everything and anything else but religion and the scheming of the local anti-Catholic militia. Anyone watching would have concluded that this was at least the rendezvous of two close friends, given the free expression of their laughter and their glances of affection.

"Oh, Raeph, I'm so sorry," Maeda said, glancing at her watch and rising quickly. "I'm already twenty minutes late."

"Then, you'd better go; I'll take care of the bill." But as she moved away through the crowd, he called out to her, "Can you by any chance meet me tonight after dinner?"

"I really can't tonight, Raeph." A waitress walked between them, but Maeda continued. "I'm busy tonight, but can you call me at work tomorrow?"

"Yes, of course," he answered, and she hurried off.

Given that his reserves were getting tight, he threw just enough on the table to cover the bill and a minimal tip, and then worked his way through the crowded diner. Once outside, he looked and saw her hurrying figure far down the street. He watched her, weaving through pedestrians, pausing at crossroads, and then hastening on, until she turned up the walk toward the church and out of sight.

Hands in pockets, he himself turned around and headed for the hotel.

It had been a good day. A far more enjoyable lunch than he could have imagined, especially when he considered how lonely he had felt just one day before.

But she said she was busy tonight. With someone else? Someone special?

He walked on, absorbed in thought, anxious over a concern that just a day before he would never have dreamed of having.

31

As the two angels of mercy walked slowly back to the Miata, Sara's stomach was tight with anger and disgust.

"You d____ b____es!" A high-pitched woman's voice emerged from the trailer at the tail end of a long harangue. "I don't understand why you keep bothering me. Can't you see I want to be left alone?" The rest trailed off beyond recognition.

Sara wrenched the passenger door open, slipping slightly in the deep snow. She sat down hard and was about to slam the door, when she was stopped by her companion's hand. With a finger to her lips, Sister Agatha appealed for patient silence. For nearly thirty seconds, the world was still, except for the casual conversations of birds and two bickering chipmunks.

Then a still, small, trembling voice floated from the trailer: "Thank you … Sister Agatha … Mrs. LaPointe … bless you."

A tear wended its way down Sister's soft, beautiful cheek, with a gentle nod; they closed the doors softly and drove away.

Upon the Miata's leaving the snow-swathed gravel drive and accelerating up to speed on the paved highway, Sara could no longer contain herself. She broke into uncontrollable sobs, her face buried in the folds of her coat.

"Sara, what is it?" But Sara only cried, shaking her head back and forth. When they reached the car park, the sister pulled in.

"Sara, please, what is it? Can I help?" Still no answer, just sobs. "I'm sorry about the way things were with Stephanie and Tina Marie. Actually, she was more toned down than usual, a bit less aggressive, and I'm sure that full diaper she hit you with was meant for me. I'll take care of getting your coat clean; I'm sure it will be all right."

"Oh, that's not it, Sister," Sara replied, her sobs interrupted by a momentary smile, but then she fell back into it fully. Assuming now that Sara would talk once she could, the nun just sat quietly. In time, Sara pulled a fistful of Kleenex from her coat pocket and attempted to regain composure.

She said, looking not at Sister Agatha but out at the picnic tables stacked like elephants parading in a circus, "I'm not crying about Stephanie, exactly, though her situation certainly deserves it. I'm crying selfishly for myself and the mess I've caused in my own life."

"Sara, I'm sure once Stephen gets back and you two have a chance to talk that everything will be just fine."

"You don't understand. There's a whole lot more about me that you don't know, that even Stephen doesn't know, that makes it impossible for us to ever get back together, not with what he's decided to do with his life."

"I don't understand. Please tell me, so I can help. I'm sure nothing can be that bad."

Sara surrendered to sobs again briefly, but regaining herself, she turned to Sister, "Yes, it can. You see, before I met Stephen, I was married briefly, which ended in divorce. The guy named Frank was a fallen-away Catholic, and we were married by a radical priest in a write-your-own ceremony in our apartment."

"But that doesn't pose an insurmountable problem. Given those circumstances, your first marriage probably wasn't sacramental in the eyes of God, so getting an annulment shouldn't be a problem."

"Oh, that's not the issue, Sister," Sara said, as her fists, clenching the wadded Kleenex, slammed down on her knees. Silence turned to more tears, then, "I'm so sorry. I'm just so ashamed of the mess I've made. The primary reason Frank and I got married was because I had gotten pregnant while we were dating."

"Then is one of your two sons from that first marriage? Just because a previous marriage is declared invalid and nullified doesn't imply anything about the children from that marriage. It doesn't mean they're illegitimate or anything."

Sara looked over at her companion, studying her eyes, eyes that seemed genuinely compassionate, warm, and welcoming, trustworthy. Painfully, Sara told this habited Catholic nun what she hadn't revealed to another person in twenty years, something she hadn't even uttered since the day it happened.

"So you see," her face contorting as she held back the tears, "Stephanie is a far better mother, a far better person than I will ever be."

Silently, Sister Agatha placed her arm around Sara's shoulder, and though she was young enough to be that child Sara never had, she drew her in like a mother comforting a child. Sara responded freely, crying into the folds of the nun's black habit. After a moment, she pulled away, turning toward the passenger door.

"Sara, I won't belittle what you've done with trite words, nor say that I know how you feel, though actually, in this case, I might." She glanced out the window briefly in the direction of Stephanie's now-distant trailer, and then continued. "But know this, Sara: what you have done is not the unforgivable sin. There is nothing that we can do, ever, that God won't forgive, if we are contrite and ask for His forgiveness. What you did years ago, likely at a time when you were mixed up, confused about what you were actually doing, will not stand in the way of reuniting you with your husband or prevent you from walking with him in his journey of faith."

"But I've known Catholics who because of what I've done were excommunicated, were separated from the sacraments and worship, were ostracized from church fellowship, and felt rejected by their church and eventually joined our congregation where they were received and loved!"

"What you've seen is sadly how imperfect Catholics can treat other imperfect Catholics, but not what the Church teaches or how Catholics ought to act toward each other. It's a bit complicated to discuss now, but I see nothing that should stand between you and Stephen or the Church."

"But, Sister, I've never told Stephen about this. When he was recovering in the hospital, after we had learned that he would quickly and totally recover, I almost told him. If he was going to completely redefine our lives, then he needed to know everything, but I couldn't. There was never the right moment, we were never quite alone, and then I grew afraid that my sons, William and Daniel, might find out. I'm ashamed to tell you what happened next, but several weeks after Stephen had returned home and was almost completely recovered, I took the boys and left."

"And have you found it to be what you expected?"

Sara's tears had dried up now, for through this unanticipated, cathartic, nonsacramental "confession" to this willing nun, Sara was sensing that life was flowing back into her like color flowing into a black-and-white world. "No, Sister, I know I was wrong. I miss him desperately, and so do the boys, although they don't talk about it. I think they keep quiet because they're afraid I'll get angry, and given my past, I don't blame them. I'm here because I will not go on without him, but how can I tell him? I'm afraid he'll be so shocked that I've lied to him all these years, he'll reject me."

"Your sons are afraid to tell you they miss their father because you'll get angry, and you're afraid to tell your husband the truth because you think he'll reject you. Please, no offense, Sara, but you're describing a family that's either kind of dysfunctional or doesn't know each other very well. Is this true?"

Sister Agatha's eyes looked a deeper, richer shade of blue as Sara stared into them with no sense of discomfort. Here was a true friend in Christ. "No, that isn't true." She pulled back, looking away, now in shame. "With me, yes, the boys have reason to fear my anger. I lose it far too often. I wish I didn't, but I just do, God forgive me. But with

Stephen, no. I really don't know why I'm afraid to tell him, because I know he will forgive me. He always has. He always will."

"So the problem is in you: you can't forgive yourself."

Sara nodded slowly as the tears returned.

"Then let me tell you something about myself. Something that few people know, not even Father Bourque. I was a rich debutante in Boston society, the most popular girl in school—at least among the boys—and was voted the most likely to marry "up." In other words, I was known for my worldliness. I bounced back and forth between the quarterbacks and other team captains, student leaders, but never got serious. Until my senior year. I pushed too hard to be seen with the captain of the football team, and paid the price. We left the senior prom early, so we could steal some time alone and still get home before curfew. For the first time in my life, I went too far and a month later discovered I was pregnant. Without a second thought and without telling anyone, I made arrangements and had an abortion."

"You?!"

"Yes, and as far as I know, my parents never found out. At first, I had no regrets whatsoever. I moved on with life as if I had just gotten over a cold. Until my first year in college, when I experienced a powerful conversion of faith. There in a philosophy class, taught by a teacher I dearly loved, I not only converted to Catholicism, but heard a clear, undeniable call to the religious life. Under the graces of the sacraments, the kind guidance of several good priests, and the mother superior of my order, I faced up to the guilt and selfishness of my past. I experienced the beauty of becoming a new creation in Christ, and since then I've never looked back. My life now is overflowing with joy in service to my Savior and to His people.

"Sara, there are three certain things that I know to be true. First, I know that in Jesus Christ we are both equally forgiven and loved by God.

"Second, I have no doubt that Stephen will also forgive you, and love you, and understand why you have waited so long. Father and I have come to know Stephen well over the past year, and I think I know his heart. He loves you far too much and knows his responsibility to love you as Christ loves the Church. I don't believe there is anything that could turn away his love for you.

"And third, I think what you really need, Sara, is the grace of the sacraments, especially confession. I know you said that you adopted your husband's faith, but have you not been an active, believing Christian all these years?"

Without hesitation, Sara said, "Yes, of course. Stephen's faith became my faith long ago, and though I might rant and rave, I do love Jesus."

"And haven't you asked Jesus over and over again for forgiveness?" Before giving her a chance to respond, Sister Agatha continued, "Yes, of course you have. If you're like me, a day didn't go by when I didn't relive the horror of what I had done. I would have given anything to wipe that day away from the history of my life. But I was never able to let go of my guilt until I experienced the grace of the sacraments, especially the grace of confession.

"After I was received into the Church, the first sins I confessed were my fornication and abortion, and after the priest gave me the gift of Christ's forgiveness, I left the confessional and knelt in the front pew to say my penance. As I did, I literally felt the renewing process of the old going and the new coming in. The problem is, Sara, that on your own you can't forgive yourself. In the same way that apart from Him we can do nothing, apart from the power of the grace He gives through the sacraments, we cannot fully forgive or love or follow Him. You see, Jesus gave us the Church, and as we read in the Gospel of John, He gave His priests the power to forgive sins—"

With a smile and a nod, Sara interrupted, "I know, Sister Agatha, I know."

"You do?"

"You see, I've certainly never admitted this to Stephen, but from the moment he began his spiritual journey, I began one of my own. It began with a book written by a Catholic cardinal, a book I so hated that I threw it across the room, breaking one of Stephen's favorite pictures—something else I've never told him. Then I read a book of conversion stories of nuns who had left the Catholic Church to become Protestant. At first this confirmed my anti-Catholicism, but it never sat right with me."

The nun laughed. "I've read that book, too. I want to believe their sincerity, but what they claim borders on the absurd. It only proves that anyone can attend Mass regularly, read Scripture, and pray the prayers of the Church, but never *listen*, and consequently never receive."

"That's true of non-Catholics, too," Sara said with a smile. "Secretly, I just kept reading, especially conversion stories of men and women who had become Catholic. I frequented Catholic websites, and read and read, comparing every doctrine. I even joined an online discussion group. At first I wanted to understand what was drawing my husband away from our Protestant faith and out of the pastorate. I wanted to stop him, but eventually, I came to understand and had no further arguments. I so wanted to tell Stephen, for I knew that this was what he was hoping for—it would bring us together. It would open every door, except of course, the pastorate for Stephen. But I couldn't tell him, because I've been paralyzed by my stubbornness and my secret."

"But you don't feel paralyzed anymore?"

"No, I don't, and Lord willing, I can tell him—" but her words were cut short by the shrill wail of an emergency vehicle. Both turned to watch as it sped into town, Sister Agatha crossing herself in prayer for its unknown passenger. Then, with the bright sun outside that small blue sports car reflecting a brilliance no greater than the joy shared within, the nun and the ex–pastor's wife embraced and together wept tears of joy.

 **32**

Scott Turner's Narrative

I've reached the point in this narrative where I must describe something that is beyond words, or at least my own ability to do so. As I mentioned earlier, I'm no philosopher, theologian, academic, or mystic, just an old football jock who went to seminary and became a minister. But what happened to me in the course of one hour, in the confined private space of that hotel room, changed my life, to this day—though I am still very much on the journey.

I suppose authentic spiritual conversion has been the main theme of my life and ministry, at least since my own adult conversion:

helping others experience what God wants for everyone. My Calvinist buddies didn't always agree, but I took seriously the verse that God "desires all men to be saved and to come to the knowledge of the truth."[25] For years, I pursued that mission through what you might call intellectual persuasion. In my preaching, teaching, and occasional writing, I exhorted my audience through scriptural exposition to "turn from their wicked ways" and surrender to Christ. And by God's grace, enough responded to convince me that my efforts were being blessed. My church in Maine grew in numbers and attendance, and the quality of the regular "atta-boy" backslapping was quite fulfilling. On Sunday afternoons, when I'd kick back and relax to watch some of my old NFL friends beat each other senseless, I did so with the contented feeling that I, too, had been a faithful warrior, fighting God's battle from the pulpit with the sword of the Spirit.

In time, though, I grew, in spiritual maturity and especially humility, partially from my devotional reading, partially from my own failing, shallow, hypocritical spiritual life, but mostly from what I was learning from this priest during that brief stay in New Hampshire. What I discovered was not new. We preached it all the time. But as they always say, we—or more correctly, I—didn't practice what I preached.

Conversion is a free gift of grace, not something we can do or cause or force, though, of course, we can nurture and prepare. But even so, the turning of our hearts away from ourselves, our peers, or our things, into God's direction is the work of His love, His Spirit. He doesn't force us. We aren't puppets, automatically programmed from all eternity either toward or away from heaven, as my old Calvinist buddies and I used to preach. We are free to respond to God's offer and turn in His direction, yet still, in the mystery of God's grace, even our ability to turn is a gift; our ability to believe in the unseen God is a gift of His grace.

But again I'm no theologian. All this is to say that what happened to me that afternoon in that room was far more than the result of an intellectual exercise, an argument well structured, heard, and then accepted. Rather, with hindsight, I'd almost say the intellectual side was nothing more than the road signs that guided me to the place where my heart and mind were touched by God's love and truth.

What I am going to tell you may have no effect on you whatsoever. That's okay. I'm just telling you what happened to me.

The truth is that God can use anything to get our attention. Lots of time, talent, and money are invested every year in developing the most effective worship environments, techniques, and programs for evangelization, but in the end, God can use the mere plop of a random cow pie to catch a passing motorist's attention, to remind him that without God's grace and love he is nothing but an unworthy sinner, that everything he is trying to accomplish for his own glory is equivalent to that pile of splat, and that unless he turns his attention back to his family and surrenders to God, he's a goner!

Well, in my case, God didn't use a cow splat, but He sure could have.

After Raeph and I wore ourselves out at the gym—our fear of being shown up by the other forced us both to overwork our aging frames—I was ready to veg out, so I retreated to my room with a fast-food combo that I nearly swallowed in one gulp. My afternoon was now amazingly free. Raeph had a lunch date with the woman he'd met the day before, and I assumed that Sara was isolated in her room for the afternoon on her self-imposed private retreat. Diane, Deborah, and Eddy had made their clean escape from Rowsville and were safely ensconced at her mother's until their Thursday flights to Boston. Stephen was somewhere up in Québec for some unknown reason, though Father Bourque hoped to get some news by morning. And to top it all off, as of Monday night, I was free as a bird: no church, no job, no responsibilities except for my family.

So there I was, lounging back in my hotel room recliner, remote control in one hand, a diet cola in the other, flipping through the channels looking for something worthy of this unexpected stretch of rare free time. But no programs were worth anyone's time, so I did something that I consider to be near miraculous—I switched the television off! That's right. I didn't merely settle for the least of the television drivel, but showed some muscle, some grit, and switched the dang thing off!

But now what? There were my sermon prep folder and materials laid out on the desk, but why? My preaching ticket was obviously empty, and who knows when I'd preach next. By my bed was the half-read copy of the latest magazine for runners, but it only made me feel guilty and over-the-hill anyway. I reached for the novel I'd tried to start the night before, but after several more tries on the same opening chapters I gave up. I was strangely restless, distracted; something else, unidentifiable, was vying for my attention.

For several minutes, I just sat there sipping my fake cola, staring blankly at the room, my mind a crowded intersection of conflicting ideas, until my eyes refocused on my sport coat, thrown carelessly across the bed, and not just the coat but specifically upon the right-hand pocket.

"Yes!" I said aloud, and retrieved the note. Back in the chair, I unfolded it and read. Father Bourque had obviously written hurriedly, but his scrawl was legible:

> Dear Scott:
>
> We both believe that Jesus sent His disciples to go forth and convert the world through the preaching of the Gospel. Consider this: how did Christ ensure that His Gospel message would remain true and trustworthy for all time? With a book or with a Church?
>
> In Christ,
> Fr. Bourque

My first knee-jerk response was that Father Bourque missed the most obvious answer: the Holy Spirit! In John's Gospel, Jesus promised to send the Holy Spirit to guide His followers into all truth and help them remember all that He had taught them. In Matthew's Gospel, Jesus promised that He Himself would always be with His followers, forever guiding and guarding them.

For a moment I gloated, rehearsing in my mind how, when the priest and I got together again, maybe tomorrow, I'd quickly and decisively point out his blatant oversight. But how would he respond? He surely wasn't so stupid as to miss such obvious scriptural promises.

I sat and sipped, then considered: *Has the promise of the Holy Spirit worked?* At Pentecost, the Holy Spirit came, empowering and inspiring the first preachers, reaping the first batches of converts. And the Church grew and grew. So what happened? Has the gift of the Holy Spirit ensured the integrity of the Gospel preached by those preachers and believed by those converts?

Then I remembered. The primary reason that the apostle Paul wrote what was possibly one of the earliest New Testament letters, Galatians, was because "born-again" Christians were wandering off after different gospels. With obvious frustration, maybe horror, Paul wrote: "I am astonished that you are so quickly deserting him who called you in the grace of Christ and turning to a different gospel."[26] Those who were teaching this alternative gospel may never have been Christians, but the key is that Paul was admitting that the mere reception of the Holy Spirit did not guarantee the integrity of the Gospel.

But then I recalled John's First Letter where he states, "the anointing which you received from him abides in you, and you have no need that any one should teach you; as his anointing teaches you about everything, and is true, and is no lie."[27] Here John seemed to be insisting that anyone anointed by the Holy Spirit knows the truth and needs no teacher! I knew Fundamentalists who used this verse to "prove" that all any individual believer needed, to know what was true, was the Bible and the indwelling Holy Ghost.

So which was it? And was the apostle John contradicting the apostle Paul? What does the indwelling Holy Spirit guarantee?

As I considered this, I realized something that proved to be the first of the scales that afternoon to fall from my eyes—the realization of what the very existence of those New Testament letters proved: whatever John may have meant in his letter, being anointed by the Holy Spirit was not enough to ensure that every single Christian knew the truth. Rather, the existence of apostolic letters proved that authoritative, Spirit-guided teachers were necessary. If all that was needed, to ensure that every Christian received and believed the true Gospel, was the indwelling of the Holy Spirit, then every New Testament letter would have been superfluous. There would have been no problems to correct, no heresies to warn against. But any reading of Church history proves that either the Holy Spirit Himself was mighty confused or His mere presence in individuals or random groups of Christians guaranteed nothing. Since the beginning of Christianity, there has never been a time without false teachers and alternative gospels, coming not just from outside the Church but from the lips of confessed believers. (Later, I would learn that John's use of the plural "you" indicates that he was emphasizing what has traditionally been called the "*sensus fidei*", that the Holy Spirit guarantees that the "whole body of the faithful … cannot err in matters of belief."[28] Individuals, however, can err gravely!)

So, I at least conceded that maybe Father Bourque had correctly narrowed down the field, but, assuming the assistance of the indwelling Holy Spirit, how was a person, a group, or Christian leader to know—to identify—which of the many gospel permutations was the true Gospel?

My second knee-jerk response was to opt for the priest's first option: a book. I believed and have always taught that after a period of oral tradition, the authentic letters and gospels, written by the apostles and their disciples, inspired by the Holy Spirit, were collected and established as the rule of faith. As Paul declared in his Second Letter to Timothy, "All Scripture is inspired by God and profitable for teaching, for reproof, for correction, and for training in righteousness, that the man of God may be complete, equipped for every good work."[29] This was the firm foundation upon which my faith and ministry had always rested.

But as I noted earlier, my faith in this "firm foundation" had already crumbled through the challenges raised by my now lost friend Stephen. It wasn't that he or I believed any less in the inspiration of the Bible; it's just that we recognized that the Bible *alone* is not sufficient to ensure that the Gospel will remain intact.

Besides, in addition to what Stephen had brought to our attention, I had seen for myself through my reading of Church history that all the early heresies—twisted or incomplete reformulations of the Gospel message—were proclaimed by Christian leaders promoting their own individual interpretations of the Bible. The Arians, the Novationists, the Donatists, Montanists, and all the rest were essentially "Bible-only" believers who merely said they had discovered a "more accurate" interpretation of the Scriptures. And one doesn't need to look very far today to see that the Bible alone does not guarantee a unified, clear understanding of the Gospel. The existence of thousands of Bible-only churches who disagree with one another over even the most universal of Christian doctrines—the Trinity—proves this.

And besides, nowhere do we hear Jesus tell His disciples anything about writing a book!

Now please understand, at this point, I was not ready to opt for the priest's second option. I knew fully where he was going with this. The things he had said the night before, about the continuity of the Church with the Old Testament People of God, had made their mark, but the implications were just too devastating: for my life, my ministry, and perhaps even my marriage.

But what if it was true?

I knew then why God had given me that free afternoon. I cleared the desk, got out my Bible and concordance, as well as a two-volume edition of the writings of the apostolic Fathers I had brought along, and set out to answer the question: *Did Jesus establish a Church?* Not merely a Spirit-guided free-for-all with every apostle going forth to evangelize and start independent churches (the Congregational theory), nor groups of loosely or tightly connected churches (the other non-Catholic theories), but one, united, worldwide, universal or "catholic" Church.

After an hour of skimming and searching hundreds of pages, two key quotes stood out, summarizing and congealing all the rest, one from Scripture, one from an early Christian writer.

The Scripture was from Ephesians. The apostle Paul, writing from prison, was describing the "mystery" which had been revealed to him by revelation. This mystery he equated with the Gospel that Jesus had commissioned him to preach and for which he "was made a minister according to the gift of God's grace."[30] But what was this mystery, this "plan" of which had been "hidden for ages" and had not been made "known to the sons of men in other generations"? It was in here "that my heart" began to be "strangely warmed," as John Wesley once admitted. Listen carefully: in 3:4–5, Paul writes of his "insight into the mystery of Christ", namely, "how the Gentiles are fellow heirs, *members of the same body*, and partakers of the promise in Christ Jesus through the gospel."

Far too often, the Gospel is seen merely as the message of redemption to all through the death and Resurrection of Jesus, but the point of the "mystery" is that this redemption is for *all*. Per Father Bourque's presentation, the Old Testament believers were not "saved" as individuals but as members of the family of Israel. They received the blessings of God in and through being part of the People of God. After Jesus Christ, the Gospel—or "Good News"—is that this Body is now open to everyone. Elsewhere in Ephesians as well as in Colossians, Paul equates the Body of Christ with the Church. These terms are interchangeable, and this is particularly clear in the verse from Ephesians, resting front and center on the top of my pile of research, that turned my tide. In this verse, Paul most clearly described the "plan of the mystery": "… that through *the* CHURCH the manifold wisdom of God might now be made known to the principalities and powers in the heavenly places."[31]

Through the Church. Jesus had entrusted the protection, preservation, and proclamation of His Gospel not merely to well-meaning individuals "filled with the Spirit," but to the Church, the new, wider, yet contiguous Body of God's Chosen People. Earlier in Ephesians, addressing the Gentiles who were now fully "fellow citizens with the saints," he said that they were also fully "members of the household of God."[32]

Jesus had not merely given the Holy Spirit nor a book, but the Church. My heart was getting strangely warmer.

Beneath this, I had copied the following opening greeting of a second-century letter, the *Martyrdom of Polycarp*: "The church of God sojourning at Smyrna to the church of God sojourning at Philomelium and to all those sojourners of the holy and catholic church in every place."[33]

Though my notes were filled with dozens of convincing if not shocking quotes, it was the simplicity of this unassuming greeting that most startled my assumptions: there were many churches, many communities, but yet all together one Church. All together one, and as the Nicene Creed would declare, one holy, catholic, and apostolic Church. My heart was burning!

My reverie was broken by the telephone.

"Hey, what'cha doing?"

It was Raeph.

"Just a little studying. How was lunch?"

"Great! Doing dinner?"

"It's a little early yet, but yes, of course. Seen Sara?"

"Not yet."

"Well, I'll be down there in a bit, and we can relax 'til she comes."

I hung up the phone, grabbed my coat, switched off the light, and burst from the room with unbridled enthusiasm, that I knew, given my audience, would certainly need to be bridled.

33

Scott Turner's Narrative

Our dinner together had gone quite pleasantly. I didn't appreciate until later, however, to what extent each of us was beside himself, or herself, with bursting enthusiasm to tell all, yet each was equally restrained by unique but similar fears. Given our guarded reasons for celebrating, we agreed to dine, not in the usual hotel diner, but in the more exotic, sportsmen's hangout next door, Burson's Tavern.

From personal experience, I knew that the food was good—we used to slip down to Burson's from the Mite as a break from the good but rich French Canadian cuisine—but I warned them to stick with familiar entrées. The locals were known to slip in wild game, especially on unsuspecting newbies like us. But, when the menus came, caution was thrown to the wind.

Glimpses of our hidden joys escaped, but only within calculated constraint. Much laughing and gaiety was observed by the few other patrons, who presumed that we were nothing but the best of old friends. And when the desserts and decaf were complete, I passed my card along to pay the bill.

"Raeph," I asked cautiously, "I've been meaning to ask you, what'cha doing tonight? Special plans?"

"No, unfortunately."

"Well, yesterday morning, you showed yourself a coward," I said with a taunting smile, "but today in the gym you proved you have some grit."

"So, want to go back to the gym and wrestle? You know, we didn't finish that match back at the Mite."

"Actually, I've got in mind something a whole lot more challenging. How about—now don't go berserk on me—going with me to Ash Wednesday mass over at St. Francis Church?"

"You've got to be kidding!"

I couldn't tell whether the look in his eyes was mock or true horror. I also noticed that Sara's raised eyes betrayed an unfathomable interest.

"No, really. Reverend Bourque invited me, and I'm actually intrigued on many levels. For years, I've fought with secretaries, music directors, and well-meaning but opinionated board members about how worship ought to be structured. I'm sure in all the churches you've visited you've experienced a wide breadth of worship styles. Well, I'm curious how the more liturgical, regimented, traditional Catholics do it."

"You've never been?" Raeph asked, with a curious receptivity.

"Only to a wedding, and that was weird."

"Weird?" Raeph inquired, eyebrows raised.

"Certainly not the usual stuff. One of those '70s, write-your-own-vows kind of weddings where everything was designed deliberately to contradict the usual. A priest in a tie-dyed stole and jeans asked the two to make no unbreakable vows—neither was to obey or honor or promise anything except to be husband and wife as long as they both should love. As you might expect, the marriage lasted about a month. What about you?"

Raeph laughed. "Wouldn't be caught dead!"

"Hey, come one, it's got to be interesting! What can it hurt?"

"I really don't know."

"I double-dog-dare you!"

He cracked a smile. "I haven't fallen for that in years."

"Tell you what, afterwards, I'll buy you the biggest hot fudge sundae in town."

Raeph's smile widened. "You know my weak spot."

"Would you consider joining us, Sara?"

She looked at me for a moment, then slowly, "I don't think so, but thanks for asking."

Raeph quipped, "It certainly can't be any more foreign to you than it is to me. I'm only going because Scott dared to drop the infamous double-dog-dare on me! But who knows," he added with a more serious tone, "if all the signs are pointing to Stephen coming back to that place, then why not tonight?"

She waited silently, then answered, "I'm sure you or Father Bourque will let me know soon enough."

So after the short walk back to the hotel, we broke company: Sara to her room for an evening of relaxing, mindless channel-surfing, and Raeph and I to get ready for an evening of ashes.

As I look back now on what we were about to face, a quote comes to mind from what many consider the greatest novel of the twentieth century: "Thus began our longest journey together."[34] I'm hesitant to use this because it might lead you to anticipate something akin to Scout and her brother Jem being attacked in the woods and then rescued by Boo. But, nonetheless, what we experienced that night and the next morning, changed our thinking forever.

Raeph met me at the van. "Are you looking forward to this as little as I am?" he quipped.

I smiled as I fought with one lock of the van after another. The afternoon thaw followed by the descending chill of evening had frozen them shut. Eventually, we forced our way in, and, as if God felt one obstacle was enough, the van started immediately.

"By the way, you got plans to meet your new sweetie later?"

"She ain't my 'sweetie,'" he said, but then added with a side-glance, "at least not yet. No, she said she was busy tonight, but I don't know with what." Raeph went quiet and stared out the window.

I was hesitant at first to push, but, then, Raeph seemed in the mood to be pushable. "Worried there might be someone else?"

Raeph brought his attention back inside, his body claiming a casual pose. "No, I don't think so. We pretty much cleared that up the first night. But there is something else, something she's hesitant to mention, something she's hiding from me." His face moved back toward the passing store windows that already showed signs of jumping the gun on Easter.

A block from the church, the parking spaces along the curb were already full. A stream of cars was pulling into the alley, presumably to some back lot, so I followed. Teenagers were directing traffic, so like an obedient sardine, the van found a place between a well-maintained classic Mercedes and a rusty pale-green Nova.

We melded into the parade of parishioners, which processed along almost silently, with only minimal greetings, down the walkway between the church and the parish offices, around to the front, and then up the three staircases into the church. The intricate stained-glass windows were ablaze from the internal lighting, casting a surreal rainbow of shadows onto the smooth white lawn. A plaque on the massive door before us consisted of a set of crossed keys that reminded me of a skull and crossbones.

I glanced over at Raeph, whose eyes were as big as Frisbees.

"Now Raeph, you aren't going to bolt again are you?"

"I was thinking about it," he said, with a nervous laugh, "but I guess God's got me locked in by this crowd. No, I'm with you all the way, but just don't expect me to like anything I see."

"Me neither," I said in a sympathetic, though less-than-genuine, tone.

We passed through a dimly lit outer hall. Upon entering the worship space, I almost lost my breath. My heart began racing noticeably. The place was brilliantly aglow with hundreds of candles besides the multiple candelabras. The entire structure was of tall vertical stone interspersed by the bright, story-telling windows we'd seen from outside and every conceivable reminder that we had entered into a Roman Catholic church, especially statues upon statues and paintings of saints and biblical scenes.

Ushers were actively trying to distribute the crowd to all corners of the long structure (the area I now know to be called the "nave"). One tapped me on the arm. After holding up two fingers questioningly and receiving a confirming nod, he began leading us down the center aisle toward the front.

"No, thank you," I whispered, shaking my head, as Raeph and I quickly dove toward the back left. I indicated to a woman sitting on the very end of a pew that we wanted to enter. With a look that screamed she wasn't happy about this, she moved her knees to the side and let us pass. It made me wonder if there was some Catholic protocol of which we were obviously ignorant, so once seated, I slunk down to be less noticeable. As I did so, almost as if my action were the awaited cue, the organist began playing and everyone stood. Raeph and I lagged behind but like lemmings we arose.

Strangely enough, they sang a familiar hymn, "Faith of Our Fathers," so it was easy to join in, though it sounded like Raeph and I were the only ones singing harmony. A procession then split the throng, boys in white robes, one carrying a crucifix on a pole, another holding high a gilded book, followed by several similarly clad adults, and finally an ornately robed Father Bourque. At the front, before a large stone table covered with linen, each person in the procession bowed and then proceeded to their seats. The priest, however, walked around to the back of the table, kissed it, and then moved over to stand before his chair, which admittedly looked like a throne.

After two verses, the opening hymn ended abruptly. Father Bourque stepped forward and, while crossing himself, addressed the congregation: "In the name of the Father and the Son and the Holy Spirit, amen."

Every single person around us, filling every pew, followed suit, some in deliberately paced imitation, others freely and even flippantly to their own drummer. I started to follow mindlessly but caught myself. Raeph put his hand to his mouth as if in a cough. We looked at each other, and simultaneously made shocked faces, which sent us into a laughing jag. The woman whose pew we had violated turned and glared until we became good, obedient boys.

Father Bourque announced, "Let us pray," and began fidgeting with a large book held before him by one of the robed boys, turning pages and transferring ribbons, but what I most noticed was that few in the congregation were doing what I would normally have expected: bowing their heads. Instead, most merely gazed blankly forward. Raeph looked up at me, apparently from the same observation, and with shrugged shoulders, together we bowed our heads and closed our eyes—though, admittedly, I peeked out of precaution.

"Father," the priest began, projecting his voice out and up presumably to the God who reigns above, reading a short liturgical prayer which ended in a benediction to Christ our Lord.

And in muffled response the congregation said, "Amen," and then all sat down.

After a moment's pause, a man rose from a middle pew, walked to the front, bowed before the table, and proceeded up to the pulpit.

"A Reading from the Prophecy of Joel," and that's what he did, a reading about coming back to God with all our hearts. When done he said something I didn't catch, but to which the congregation responded in unison, "Thanks be to God." He left the pulpit, turned to bow before the table again, and returned to his pew.

Another long silent pause ensued, until a woman rose from somewhere up front left and followed the same ritual as the first reader, only this time she led the congregation in the liturgical reading of a psalm. After she was seated, an even longer pause followed until, of all people, the woman at the end of our pew exited and walked slowly forward as if she were a bridesmaid at a wedding. Her bow at the table was so extreme I feared she might either fall forward or split her slacks asunder, but she made it safely up to the altar and proclaimed dramatically, "A Reading from the Second Letter of St. Paul to the Corinthians," and this she did just as dramatically. She reminded me of Clarence Darrow defending the trustworthiness of the Scriptures, especially when she read after the final verse: "THIS is the day of salvation! This IS the word of the Lord."

The congregation, however, responded in the same mumbled tone, "Thanks be to God," as she proceeded back to reclaim her pew, slowly and with theatrical pomp.

Raeph and I shared glances but restrained ourselves.

Father Bourque then rose, which apparently was the cue for the rest of us to follow suit. He walked to the table, removed the gilded book from its stand, and processed to the pulpit. With arms raised, he proclaimed, "The Lord be with you," and from the congregation came a united "And also with you."

When he announced "A Reading from the Holy Gospel according to Matthew," everyone in the massive nave, except Raeph and me of course, began touching their faces and chests. I was oblivious to what they were doing, but gave a quick semblance of an imitation, just to fit in.

The reading began: "Jesus said to his disciples: 'Beware of practicing your piety before men in order to be seen by them; for then you will have no reward from your Father who is in heaven—'"

Oops, I thought.

" 'Thus, when you give alms, sound no trumpet before you, as the hypocrites do—'"

I glanced over at the lady who owned our pew, but she just stared forward. Father Bourque read Jesus' instructions about almsgiving, prayer, and fasting, ending with, "'so that no one will know you are fasting except your Father who sees all that is done in secret.'" Raising the book once again before him, he announced, "The Gospel of the Lord."

Figuring the third time was a charm, I began, "Thanks be to—" only this time the congregation was saying, "Praise to You, Lord Jesus Christ."

All sat, so Raeph and I complied gladly. I wish I had a word-for-word transcript of Father Bourque's brief sermon because my summary cannot do him justice, and though we long-winded Evangelicals tend to look down our noses at preachers who deliver a less-than-twenty-minute, exegetical "three points and a poem" sermon, the priest's message was really quite good. And, I daresay, an uncomfortable shot in the arm to many there.

He began with creative silence, surveying his audience so all could see the dark gray smudge on his forehead, reminiscent of Tom Hanks' sole friend Wilson in *Castaway*. Then with a sly, devil's-advocate smile, he asked rhetorically, "So tell me, how is it that having a barely discernible cross on your forehead, which you yourself can't see or feel and which most of us forget about fifteen minutes after we leave, how is this not a gross contradiction of what Jesus just commanded us not to do? Jesus said, 'Beware of practicing your piety before men to be seen by them.' Excuse me, but isn't this exactly what we are doing?" He looked around at the congregation he apparently knew quite well.

"And parents, when you kneel beside your child's bed at night to pray, or make sure they cross themselves with you before and after the dinner blessing, or when you give your children a few dollars to plop into the offering basket, isn't part of this so that they'll see your piety and almsgiving? 'Yes, but we're doing this to teach them,' you might say, 'to show them how a Catholic ought to pray, and give alms, and fast. And as far as the smudgy cross on our foreheads, why, this is both a silent sign to help us evangelize as well as a sacrifice of humility. Others see the sign and if they ask, we can witness to them about our faith. And even if they don't ask, the Holy Spirit can use the smudgy cross to prick their hearts.'" This he had said with an affected voice that brought laughs from some in the congregation—but not the woman who owned our pew.

"All these answers are true and good, but how do we keep from forgetting these good motives and turning toward those bad, self-centered, prideful motives that are always trying to distract our thinking away from God and onto ourselves?

"First and foremost, we must remember what this cross symbolizes," he said, pointing to his own smudge. "It is first and foremost a mark of our repentance, but at the core it reminds us that apart from Him we can do nothing. We are freed from sin and death because and only because of what Jesus did for us on the Cross. We have no claim to our salvation. Everything we have in life is a gift of His grace, and this sign is a reminder to others as well as to ourselves that we accept this fact, this gift. At its core, it is a sign of thankfulness, or, if you will, in the words of the Old Testament, a sacrifice of thanksgiving.

"This is the kind of attitude we ought to have, not only as we come forward to receive the cross of Christ on our foreheads, but as we place our gifts in the offering, as we fast, and especially as we receive the Body and Blood of our Lord in the Eucharist."

Silently, Father Bourque left the pulpit, bowed as he passed the altar, and took his seat. People around us were crossing themselves, I guessed as one of those many unfamiliar rituals Catholics do at this point in mass. Raeph and I glanced around as everyone else just sat there, quiet, motionless, presumably in prayer. It reminded me of a Quaker meeting I had once visited.

Then Father Bourque rose and moved to the center, on this side of the table, where two white-robed boys were standing with small bowls. He said a prayer and did something I'd never seen before: with a wand kind of thing he sprinkled water on each bowl. Then he invited the congregation forward.

The organist and choir commenced with some unfamiliar hymn, and the pews began emptying in a quasi-orderly manner, starting in the front. Two lines formed, one before each bowl, where each person in turn bowed slightly, received their own private smudge, and then solemnly returned to their seats.

Raeph watched, eyes wide, wondering, I assumed, the same as I was: when it was our turn, would we go forward? Men and women, old and young, babies, children, parents, and grandparents, all processed up, around, and back, each receiving their sign of repentance and thanksgiving.

"Scott!" Raeph exclaimed with a loud whisper, sitting up stiff and pointing foreword. The people around us glared over sharply, but then returned their attention forward. I followed the trajectory of his finger to a woman walking back to her pew.

"Scott, that's Helen, Walter's wife."

"Walter? Oh yeah, Walter."

Helen, processing behind her daughter, was wearing a black lace head covering, partially blocking the newly applied cross of ashes.

"She must still be in mourning." Raeph commented.

"Guess so."

"I'd completely forgotten that I'd heard she was going here, or I woulda been watching out for her. And the teenage girl walking in front is her daughter, Stacy."

The two of them, both amazingly pretty, the mother a more mature image of the daughter, scooted back down their pew.

Raeph sneered. "Well, looks like she's surrendered to all the Catholic pompous protocol. Walter would puke, if he isn't already revolving in his grave."

"Shhh!" The lady at the end of our pew glowered.

"Sorry," I said, sheepishly.

The lines of people continued processing, going forward clean, returning smudged, tinctured with self-conscious smiles.

"Scott!" Raeph once again exclaimed—in a whisper, even more stiff and ashen.

"Now what?" I first glanced nervously at the lady down the pew, and then once again followed the direction of his finger to another woman returning to her pew. Her face also was partially blocked by a black lace scarf until she turned full in our direction.

Raeph was breathless. "That's ... Maeda!"

She too scooted down her pew.

"You didn't know?"

Raeph's mouth lay open like a trout. "I guess I could have guessed. She's from Ireland, duh! She insisted she wasn't a member of the Bible Fellowship but was always evasive about where she worshipped. I know she is a strong believer from everything else she said—but a Catholic!"

As he spoke, I happened to be glancing up past him, at a large stained-glass window of some woman saint. The windows were stone black in the absence of natural backlighting, but the leaded portrayal of her face reminded me of the Wicked Witch of the West.

Suddenly, surreally, directly through her face, shattering the image, came a projectile. As if in slow motion I watched the window buckle inward and explode into a rainbow of shards, spewing out over the people, whose arms rose up in instinctive protection.

"Look out!" I exclaimed needlessly above the din of other screams, as the projectile landed in a screaming hodgepodge of people several pews ahead. As sulfurous black smoke churned out, the congregation panicked, crowding forcefully toward every exit. Raeph and I were swept into the melee. He attempted to move against the flow toward Maeda, but being in the backmost pew, we were unable to free ourselves from the crowd's mindless momentum until our feet hit the pavement outside.

We then held our ground, turned, and saw. The smoke bomb was only a portion of the damage. Anti-Catholic graffiti had been painted in fluorescent green across all three doors. The papal emblem was obliterated and above was scrawled, "Papists go to hell!"

The first thing that crossed my mind was a question: *Was this a vulgar curse or someone's matter-of-fact conviction?* My musing was interrupted by Raeph's yelling, "Maeda!" Then, with his short stature, he was lost in the crowd. I turned toward the street to see whether anyone had caught the vandals, but other than the logjam of cars as people stopped to gawk, nothing appeared suspicious.

"Please, everyone, in the name of Jesus Christ, be orderly. Please calm down." The familiar yet sad voice of Father Bourque rose above the clamor of the parishioners as they careened down the front entrance, exiting, milling, pushing, and demanding answers in all directions.

An elderly man named Fred with an usher's badge pushed through the crowd. Father Bourque asked, "Did anyone see who did this?"

"As far as I know, every one of us was inside, ready to get our ashes. I was in back and probably the first man out, but I saw nothing: no one was running away, and the street was full of traffic."

I then realized that Father Bourque, facing the street and looking for the culprits, had not seen the full extent of the damage, so I pointed, nodding. He turned, and as his arms went up, he sank to his knees in a snowdrift.

"Fred!" I beckoned, and together we helped the priest up. "Give us some room," Fred ordered, as we moved Father to the front step.

"I never thought they would go this far," he confessed aloud to no one in particular.

At that moment, Raeph emerged from the thinning crowd, guiding Maeda who was coughing violently. She sat down beside Father Bourque, who turned to comfort her.

"Father!" A thin, casually dressed man pushed past me. "Father, I think I saw who did it."

"Who was it, Tom?" the priest asked.

"Oh, I don't mean I saw them. I happened to be, well, I'm sorry, Father, but I had slipped out for a smoke."

"Tom, that's okay. We'll talk about that later. What'd you see?"

"I was on the far side of the church, you know over by those bushes over around to the right."

"Tom, please, condense it."

"Yes, Father, sorry, Father. You see, I heard something from the front of the church, like feet scrambling across pavement. I wasn't expecting no violence, so I thought I'd finish my smoke first before I went to investigate. Then I heard some strange laughter and knew this wasn't normal, so I threw down my smoke and walked around to the front, and saw the writing, and kind of froze. Then from within the church, I heard a crash. I turned and saw a man jump into a van, and the van screeched out into traffic. It was gone 'fore anyone came out."

"What did the van look like, Tom?"

"I don't know what make it was, but it was yellow with bumper stickers all over it."

Raeph shot forward. "What'd you say?"

Tom repeated the description, and Raeph backed away.

Father Bourque asked, "Excuse me, but do I know you?"

"This is Raeph Timmons," I answered.

"Ah yes," the priest added. "You know, I've seen that van around town. What about you, Mr. Timmons?"

Raeph stood statue silent.

The piercing squeal of sirens cut through the crowd noise. Soon a patrolman was seen racing through the stalled traffic, motioning the drivers to move on and make way. In time, an ambulance pulled up onto the curb.

"Was anyone hurt?" Father Bourque demanded into the crowd, and a familiar female voice answered, approaching, "Yes, Father," Sister Agatha said. "Mrs. Tinsly. The smoke bomb landed directly in her lap of all things, Lord have mercy, and the explosion set her dress briefly on fire. She's not doing well."

"Good God!" exclaimed the priest, who rose immediately and entered the church.

I turned to Raeph. "You know something, don't you? You're acting like you recognized that van."

He looked first at Maeda and then up at me. "Yes, I think I do. It sounds like the van I've seen parked outside Jamesfield Bible Fellowship Church. It was there last night, and I saw it driving away this morning. The bumper stickers were mostly End of the World/Rapture–type slogans, and a few were clearly anti-Catholic." He hesitated then asked, "Maeda, can you guess whose van that might be?"

"I know that Pastor Guilford doesn't own any such van and, besides, I'm sure he wouldn't do such a thing, regardless of his crazy sentiments. But I also have seen that van."

"Well, I might be able to help the police identify them. Excuse me. Scott, can you take care of her?"

"Sure, Raeph," I said, as he moved toward a policeman who was trying to encourage everyone to go home.

"So, how're you feeling?" I asked Raeph's new friend.

"Better. The smoke—I couldn't breathe. Poor Mrs. Tinsly. She was right behind me. She's quite elderly, you know, and we've been praying about her anyway. Her sciatica." Her Irish accent was warm and lovely, and it was easy to see why Raeph was so drawn to her.

"Don't worry. The squad will take good care of her." At that moment, I turned to watch paramedics wheel Mrs. Tinsly out on a stretcher, place her gingerly into the rescue vehicle, and speed hurriedly away.

"I'm sure she'll be—" but as I turned my attention back to Maeda, she was gone. I scanned over and through the panic-stricken crowd, but she was nowhere.

An officious patrolman and the badged usher named Fred were shooing the masses onward. In the clearing, I spied Father Bourque again, standing before the desecration, his hair disheveled, brows clenched. He dropped his gaze, seeming on the verge of tears. When he looked up again, he noticed me and beckoned me over. Easing himself down onto the steps, he asked, "So, what do you make of this, Reverend Scott?"

"Actually, I do know anti-Catholics who might think that this was some kind of brave act in the name of God's justice. I'm truly sorry, Father."

"Oh, I know you had nothing to do with this, my friend."

"Do you have any idea who might have?"

"Well, sadly, I can guess. I visited a new member of our church yesterday whose house was vandalized this morning. They painted 'PAPIST' on his front door. I can think of a few in the community who have made threats; I guess I should have known this might happen, but I never really believed they'd do such a thing."

For a few moments, we sat together on the church steps in silence. Most of the parishioners had left for home, at the encouragement of the police. "Scott, I didn't have the chance to tell you or Sara, I spoke with my friend at the shrine in Québec. He said that Stephen had been there for several weeks, but Monday was his last day. He left the area without giving a forwarding address.

"So he might be coming here?"

"Possibly, but my friend didn't know, and frankly he wasn't that encouraging. He and Stephen had often talked about the Church, and he was concerned that Stephen had become overburdened with fear."

"Fear?"

"Stephen has apparently lost so much confidence in his ability to discern what is true, that he's spinning downward in doubt. We must pray for him."

Raeph returned, hands in pockets. "So, where's Maeda?" he demanded.

"I don't know."

"You don't know! What's happened to her?" He began searching through the remaining cliques of parishioners until, unsuccessful, he returned. "Didn't she say anything before she left?"

"No, Raeph, I'm sorry. I turned away for just a second, and she was gone."

Raeph dropped down on the step, a cautious distance from the priest.

"What did the police say?" Father Bourque asked.

"They want me to come in tomorrow for a full statement. I hate to put a finger on any of those who were at that meeting, but dang it, this must have been what that deacon was alluding to."

"What meeting?" asked the priest.

Raeph looked away, I interpreted, with shame, but then described his experience of the night before, including the threats of the two deacons.

"But Mr. Timmons, what were you doing there? I thought you were new in town," he demanded, looking at Raeph then at me. "How did you get involved?"

Raeph glanced at me, then away. "Reverend Bourque, it's a long story, but please believe me, I had nothing whatsoever to do with what happened here tonight."

"Then Raeph, can you and I talk tomorrow afternoon, say around three?"

Raeph shot him a questioning glare. "Why?"

"My church has been attacked by anti-Catholic vandals, whom you admit you know. I'd like to hear your story."

A strident woman's voice brought us all to attention. "What are *you* doing here?"

"Oh hello, Helen," Raeph said, slowly getting to his feet.

"Did you have anything to do with this?" she barked, moving in on him with her finger aimed at his chest like a jousting pole.

"Of course not," he exclaimed, knocking her hand away. He grabbed her by the shoulders at arm's length. "Helen, I had nothing to do with this."

"Then what are you doing here?"

Raeph released his grip. "That's a long story," glancing back at Father Bourque.

The woman kept glaring in disbelief.

"Helen," the priest said softly, "do you know this man?"

"Yes, he was a close friend of my husband."

"Oh."

"Helen, maybe you and I need to go somewhere and talk," Raeph said, grabbing her arm and leading her away. He turned and said to me in a whisper, "If Maeda comes back, tell her I was looking for her and will call her tomorrow." He then led Helen out to the sidewalk.

"Come, Father," Sister Agatha said, appearing beside at his elbow. "The police are waiting in your office."

"Yes, of course," he responded, as he was helped up. "Scott, will you promise to make sure that Raeph doesn't leave Jamesfield tomorrow without calling me first? It's very important."

The nun led Father Bourque away, and after a final glance at the desecration, I walked toward my van in the back lot. Passing the few remaining parishioners, chatting in hushed, conspiratorial tones, I felt as if all the joy of my afternoon had been sucked dry.

34

Once they had traveled sufficiently out of sight of the priest, the nun, and the few remaining parishioners, Helen ripped her arm out of Raeph's grasp, and with a lunge shoved him backward into a snowdrift.

"So, what are you doing here!" she shouted.

After two unsuccessful attempts to extricate himself, Raeph splayed open his arms and shot back a look of pleading helplessness.

"All right," she said reluctantly, extending her hand.

Cautiously, not wanting to pull her in with him, he popped free. Brushing away the residue, he responded. "First, let me say a few things. Number one, I repeat, I had nothing whatsoever to do with what happened tonight at your church, though I may know who did."

"How can you know anything about what happens here in Jamesfield? What are you doing here?"

"Look. That coffee shop is still open. Can you stop in there for a moment with me, for a warm-up, so we can talk?"

With a shrug, she went.

"Evening, Helen."

"Steve," she said to the man behind the counter.

"What happened at the parish? Were you there?"

"Yes, I was. Someone vandalized it and threw a smoke bomb or something through the stained glass window of St. Anne. Poor Mrs. Tinsly was burned, badly."

"But who could have done such a vicious thing?"

"We don't know yet." The last word was directed at her companion.

"That's unbelievable. Here, have some coffees on me." Steve brought over two coffees to the booth in the front window where they were seated.

"Thanks, Steve."

"Don't mention it," he said, walking away with an inquisitive glance at the stranger beside her.

"Helen, like I said, let me say a few things first. It's a long, complicated story, but it really is good to see you. I've thought about you and Stacy so many times during the past year, wondering how you were doing. I'd heard you were here in Jamesfield, but it slipped my mind when I came here a few days ago. I guess I also knew that you and Stacy were attending that church."

"Father Bourque was the only one, the only person that showed any concern for Stacy and me. Everyone else included us in Walter's craziness."

"I'm sorry, Helen. Patty and I, we had moved so far away, and—"

"Oh, Raeph," she said, as she reached out, and they embraced, long and tight. "You know I couldn't stay mad at you for long."

"I know, Helen. We go back a long way. I sometimes wonder whether you blame me for introducing you to Walter."

"What you don't understand is that even through all his fanatical craziness, even when his anger sometimes overflowed into violence, even to the very end, I loved him. I still do and always will. He was a good husband and father. What he did to Reverend LaPointe was wrong and wrong-minded, but his motives were pure. If he only knew then what I know now. Anyway, I've heard that things have changed a lot for you, too."

For the next fifteen minutes, the two talked, sometimes with tears but always with their hands clasped like the lifelong friends they were. They talked mostly about their losses, but yet also how each was growing to see, through the darkness, the constant hand of God.

"But then, what brings you here to Jamesfield?" she asked.

"Well, last Sunday, I visited Walter's grave."

She squeezed his hand.

"As I sat beside his grave, I realized how much I'd fed his fanaticism, sometimes with my silence, so, given everything else in my life, I decided to find Reverend LaPointe to determine whether Walter's conclusions had been right or wrong. I wanted to make sure the sacrifice of his life wasn't a mistake."

"But it was, Raeph. A terrible mistake."

"Well, in a way, yes, but he was at least right in seeing that LaPointe was leaning toward the Catholic Church, as are some of his friends. And they were all lured away by your priest. He may have been kind to you, but Helen, he's a Catholic priest. How can you trust him?"

"Raeph, I hate to tell you this, but Stacy and I are both in classes to be received into the Catholic Church this Easter."

Raeph sat back hard in the booth. "How can you? You know better than that!"

"Actually, it is specifically because of what I now know—what Stacy and I both now know—that we are doing this, with great joy and anticipation. And it isn't just because Father Bourque has been so caring, but—yes, it *was* his demonstration of love to Stacy and me, both Protestants, in comparison to the hatred for Catholics expressed by Walter and you and Ben and others. After Walter's death, he continued to care, to forgive, not once trying to convert us, while all our Protestant friends turned a cold shoulder to us; they were ashamed to be seen with us. This didn't convince us to become Catholics, but it did begin the process. With all the verses you 'Three Musketeers' used to quote against the Catholics, you seem to have missed one of the most important ones: 'If anyone says, "I love God," and hates his brother, he is a liar.'"[35]

"But a Catholic isn't my brother."

"Raeph, you fool, listen to yourself. Are you telling me that that gentle priest out there—mourning over his desecrated church and parishioners, who loves Jesus Christ and proclaims Him every single day, who spends hours each day praying to Him—are you saying he isn't your brother? Remember, Jesus said, 'By this all men will know that you are my disciples, if you have love for one another.'[36] Father Bourque, Sister Agatha, the parishioners of St. Francis showed us Protestants far more unconditional love than any of you who were supposedly our Christian brothers."

"Love doesn't prove anything," Raeph shot back. "Mormons love; Jews love; atheists love. Just because a Catholic loves doesn't prove that their beliefs are true anymore than it does Mormons, Jews, or atheists."

"Excuse me, Raeph. For years you three preached at me without allowing me one word of comment, so you listen to me preach for a moment. Besides, you got that free coffee because I'm friends with Steve there, so this is on my nickel."

Raeph smiled. "The podium's yours, my dear."

"Lots of people can love people they like or who like them or who are like them. But the kind of love the apostle John was talking about is a special kind of love. The kind of love that loves someone you don't like, someone you hate, or who hates you, or is so different you can't stand being with them. You know the Bible better than me. This is the kind of love that was meant by the verse, 'We love because he first loved us.'[37] The kind that loves a sinner before he repents. The kind of love that comes only by grace. The kind of perfect love that casts out fear, as St. John wrote. This is the kind of love Father Bourque showed Stephen, and Stacy, and me, and, Raeph, even Walter. Raeph, the problem is, your fear has cast out love."

"Walter?" Raeph said, sitting up.

"Yes, Walter. Father went in with me to see Walter the day he died. Walter was only showing minimal heart functions, and we assumed he was either asleep or sedated. The priest blessed him, anointed him with oil, read a few psalms, and then said a prayer for Walter and us.

Then all of a sudden, Walter opened his eyes. I thought for a second he was going to explode at the sight of Father and his priestly garb, but he didn't. He silently moved his hand, which was all entangled with tubes, closer toward the priest, and Father Bourque reached out and held it, and then Walter whispered something so soft. Father and I leaned over, and I asked, 'Walter, what did you say?' and this time we both heard him. He said, 'I'm so sorry.' Father extended his hand onto Walter's forehead and began praying softly, asking for God's forgiveness and grace and mercy, and then Walter fell back into unconsciousness." Tears began to fill her eyes, and then a few spilled over.

"I didn't know that," Raeph said, taking her hands.

"No one does. Father Bourque wanted it that way, because he knew that none of Walter's friends or family would understand. Raeph, this didn't make me a Catholic, but it opened my heart. It began my journey. It proved to me that Father Bourque is a true disciple, a brother in Jesus Christ, and so I began to listen to him, to read, and especially to pray. And I know you won't understand, you can't understand, but the most peaceful time I have ever spent in my life I now spend in prayer every morning in that church before the Blessed Sacrament. Just as Jesus promised, He is truly present there in the Eucharist, He is very near, and never before have I been more certain that He loves me."

"You two need a warm-up?"

"No thanks, Steve. I should be getting home." She made a move to rise.

"Helen, what do you mean my fear has driven out my love? You've known me a long time. I'm certainly not perfect, but I've always tried to be a loving person, to imitate my Lord."

"In our ignorance, we made the Catholic Church and her priests into bogeymen. And what we didn't understand, we feared, and eventually hated. But just as Jesus promised, the truth will set you free. It has for me."

A woman huddled against the weather walked swiftly past the window.

"Maeda," Raeph exclaimed.

"You know Maeda?" Helen asked.

"I met her yesterday, and we had lunch together today."

"Raeph, you're playing with fire."

"What do you mean?"

"Besides Father Bourque and Sister Agatha, she's the Catholic that most welcomed us into the parish. She has sat with me for hours talking about Walter and about her love for her Catholic faith. She's my sponsor," she said, with a broad, ironic smile.

Raeph stared into the eyes of his old friend. Then he pushed out of the booth. "I've gotta go. How can I reach you?"

"I'm in the phonebook."

"Okay, Helen, thanks." He hugged her and rushed out into the street.

Maeda was making her way toward her apartment. As he ran cautiously along the icy pavement, the trees and buildings flickered from the lights of the patrol cars parked behind him in front of St. Francis Parish.

"Maeda!"

She turned and stopped. The closer he got, the more his anxiety grew. Should he embrace her? Or did she assume he was somehow connected with the attack? Had she run away from him?

But as he approached, she extended her hand.

"Maeda, where'd you go? I looked everywhere." He took her arm in his and then walked along with her.

"There were a couple of elderly widows I needed to comfort, who were surely frightened by the cruel attack. Then I took a taxi to the hospital to visit and pray with Mrs. Tinsly. She's not doing well at all. I then came back to the church, to pray for a spell. I wasn't running away from you. I looked for you when I returned, but finding you gone, I figured I'd see you tomorrow."

She paused for a breath, and then, "Raeph, I certainly didn't expect to see you at St. Francis' tonight."

"Nor I you. I guess I should have guessed, though, you being from Ireland."

"Not all from Ireland are Catholic anymore. Not only are there lots of Protestants, but too many Catholics have lost their faith. There's a grave crisis within the Church in Ireland that I fear will soon explode. That was one of my reasons for leaving. All my friends were running wild bedazzled by the anti-Catholic media. I, well, was engaged to a man, my childhood sweetheart you might say, but he had lost the faith, and was pressing me to leave it, too. That's why I left."

"Do you miss him?"

She looked to him with a smile. "No, Raeph. My heart has been healed. Jesus did that. I'm happy here, and happy to have met you."

"But, Maeda, I'm not Catholic. I was only at your church tonight on a whim, hoping to find Reverend LaPointe."

"I know, Raeph," she said, holding his arm tighter as they walked on. "But I also know how much Jesus means to you."

After a pause, Raeph remarked, "It seems we have some mutual friends."

"Oh yes? Who might that be?"

"Helen and Stacy Horscht."

"Helen and Stacy? How do you know them?"

"I've known Helen all my life. We grew up together. She became my best friend's wife."

"So you knew Walter."

"I guess you could say I, well, as Helen might say, fed the fear that killed him. I certainly didn't mean to, but I guess Walter believed that I agreed with what he did to Reverend LaPointe. Sometimes my silence fed his fear and hatred."

They had reached her apartment building. "Would you like to come in for a bit? Sounds like we have a lot to talk about."

"I probably shouldn't."

"Raeph, I believe I can trust you, and you can trust me. I also believe that neither of us wants to displease Him."

"Thanks, I'd love to," he accepted, and with that she led him in.

The lights in the corridors of Jamesfield Memorial Hospital were dim. The gift shop was long since closed. A sign on the receptionist's desk directed all visitors to the north corridor nurses station. The cafeteria was closed, but vending machines galore awaited the onslaught of any late-night snack attacks. An occasional spurt of busyness from the emergency room denoted active doctoring, but otherwise the aging regional healthcare facility had downshifted into autopilot, fingers crossed that overworked and understaffed caregivers could steal a peaceful evening at home with family or out enjoying rarely seen friends.

Except, that is, for the sixth floor critical care unit. The night shift was in full gear and overdrive, two doctors, nine nurses, and support staff keeping close watch on fifteen patients, each hovering precariously on the brink of life and death.

"Katie," said one elderly, far-too-many-years-under-her-belt nurse down to another sitting behind the desk, "what's going on out there in those backwoods? I can't remember the last time this ward was so full of critical care patients. And this note says there's two more in emergency that need to come up here, but there's no room."

"I know, Irene. Mark it off to the prolonged winter."

"Or just cabin fever. Five of these are from some form of spousal or family violence."

"Guess they shouldn't have closed North Side Bowling."

"Evening ladies." The soft voice of a regular visitor interrupted their banter.

"Father!" Irene exclaimed. "I certainly didn't expect to see you tonight. I can't believe what we heard!"

"Yes, Irene, it was quite unbelievable, but sadly, very real. I would have preferred staying in the rectory tonight," he said, shaking his head, "but I've got a few parishioners here who are especially needy."

"You all right?"

"Yes, fine. I saw Mrs. Tinsly down in room 12. Can you tell me her status? She doesn't look good."

From amongst a regiment of clipboards on the wall, Katie pulled one down, handed it across to Irene, who began perusing through several sheets of scribbled notes. "She was brought in and sedated before my shift, so I apologize for not knowing too much about her condition. I think Nurse Higgins was here and may know more. It says here that Mrs. Tinsly received second-degree burns to her front torso, but her biggest problem involves extensive smoke inhalation. A specialist from Concord is coming first thing in the morning to examine her burns and to determine the extent of lung damage. I will say, Father, that I've worked with Doc Barnstable for years—he admitted her—and the tone of the notes seems to suggest that he doesn't hold much hope for her recovery. She was quite frail to begin with."

"Yes, I know. That confirms what I suspected. I gave her last rites, just in case."

The other nurse rose and walked away from the conversation, face buried in a pile of paperwork.

"Don't mind her, Father. Ever since her husband ran away with a good Catholic woman from Manchester, she's blamed it all on the Church."

"Sounds like you're being a bit free with the label 'good.' And besides," he said, leaning forward on the counter, "I haven't seen much of you lately around the parish."

She smiled, shaking her head. "You got me there, Father. I could make excuses, but you'd only see through me. Turns out, starting yesterday, I'm on nights, so you'll see me Sunday."

"Just remember the doors to the Church are always open, as are the doors to my study. We need to talk about you and Bill."

Her eyes dropped slightly, and her hands clenched into fists. "I know, Father Bourque, I'm sorry."

"Don't apologize to me. It's yourself you're hurting, not me." He tentatively touched her fist. She relaxed, and a tear glazed her cheek.

"I'll call for an appointment this week." She rose, cradling his hand in hers. "I promise."

"And since I'll probably be here every day for a while, I'll hold you to it." He blessed her and left her to her work.

At the elevators, he pressed DOWN and waited. There were a few others he could look in on, but it was getting late and the unanticipated attack and aftermath at the parish had exhausted him, physically as well as emotionally. When the elevator came, he pushed the button marked LOBBY, but when the doors closed guilt won out. He pushed the button for the third floor.

The corridor was subdued and strangely empty. One young nurse sat behind her station, leaning back on two chair legs and reading a glamour magazine.

"Everything quiet tonight, Marge?" Father asked, praying silently for an affirmative response.

"Yup, Father. Nothing to do but read this mindless waiting-room drivel until the top of the hour. Then I'll make sure they're either all sleeping soundly or in dire need of something that just can't wait 'til morning."

"Sound a tad edgy tonight. Even a tad cynical. I could certainly recommend something a bit more uplifting for your reading pleasure."

"No, I'm fine, Father. Just tired."

"Okay, I believe you. Mind if I glance down your list to make sure I haven't missed someone?"

"Of course not," she said, handing him a clipboard, then leaning her chair back once again, she returned her attention to the world of glamour.

The priest turned around and rested his weary bones against the counter. His tired eyes began skimming through the long list of names, glazing over in anticipation of his soft, comfortable bed. He assumed that most of the patients were strangers, whom he would greet maybe tomorrow when he had more energy, to make sure each were receiving some pastoral care. Some of the names were familiar, though not parishioners. Near the middle he read silently Steve Cornish, Mary Ellen Townsend, Jonathan Grable, Eileen Biggend, Richard C. Wildman, Stephen LaPointe, Valerie Anderson, Horatio Gona …

"What!"

The sound of a crash turned him quickly around.

"Marge, you all right?" He moved to help her up.

"I'm fine, but you can't be yelling like that around here this time of night. You need to let sleeping dogs lie."

"Sorry, but this lists a Stephen LaPointe."

"Yes, he was brought in this morning. He's down in room 5. Apparently—"

"Good God!" he said, rushing away at a gallop.

"But, Father Bourque—" she called out, but he wasn't listening, so she joined the chase.

PART 5

MY CUP OVERFLOWS

35

Scott Turner's Narrative

On the morning after, I was the first one down to breakfast.

"Coffee, please."

"By your lonesome?" asked Tilly, with little interest in my answer.

"Guess we'll see." I scooted back into the comfortable corner of my booth. Tilly returned with the coffee without comment. After four lonesome sips, I was joined by a welcome companion.

"Morning, Scott," Sara said, as she entered the booth, sitting opposite me.

"Good morning." I reached across to greet her, and she accepted my hand warmly. "Have a nice evening?"

"Coffee?" Tilly had returned.

"Yes, please. And cream."

"Expect any more?" again with minimal interest.

"Guess we'll see," I said with a smile.

"Yes, a very nice, quiet evening." She also accepted her coffee with a smile that was wasted on our waitress.

"I presume you heard about what happened last night?"

"Last night? I don't know what you mean."

"You didn't hear about the attack on St. Francis Church?"

"No, nothing. I purposely avoid the news channels. What kind of attack?"

"Last evening, during the crowded Ash Wednesday mass, some thugs spray-painted anti-Catholic graffiti on the front doors and threw a smoke bomb through a window, directly into the congregation, causing an elderly woman's dress to catch fire, and driving the entire congregation out in terror."

"You must be kidding!" She looked somewhat stunned. After a pause, she added, "Then you did go."

"Yes, Raeph and I were sitting in the back. I saw the projectile smash through the window and land only a few pews in front of me."

"Raeph," she said, as if everything were adding up, "was he—?"

"No, positively. He had nothing to do with this."

"But he and Walter. This sounds like what—"

"No, Sara. No. Raeph was with me, and it was obvious he was as startled as everyone else. And besides," I paused to be certain of my words, "I'm sure he would never do this, regardless of his prejudice. He was the one who told the police the possible identities of the vandals."

"But he's only been here as long as we have. If he's so innocent, how could he know anyone in this town?"

I didn't know the answer to that.

"Then where is he?"

"Don't know. He left the crowd last night with someone you might know, Helen Horscht?"

"Helen Horscht? She was there when all this happened? Scott, this is all too bizarre, too coincidental."

Sara sipped her coffee, her eyes clenched in confusion.

"Morning." Our third companion had arrived, catching Tilly who was on her way. "Oh, and coffee please."

"Any more?" she demanded, filling his cup.

"Guess we'll see," I smiled.

"Hey, this isn't Starbucks. You three going to eat anything?" Tilly was at her finest.

"This ain't no drive-through either," Raeph barked back.

"Raeph," I said, grabbing his arm. "Sorry, give us a minute."

She folded her arms and waited insolently. We quickly opened the menus and ordered.

"So, Raeph, you all right?" I asked Raeph after Tilly had stomped away.

"Sure, what's wrong?"

"Well," I said cautiously, "let's just say you don't look yourself."

He gave me a quick nervous side-glance and then one across at Sara. "Last night shook me up." He sipped his coffee. "I had a good talk last night with Helen Horscht, after the, well, the attack. She and Stacy are here. She wanted me to tell you how sorry she was for what her husband did."

"They're Catholics?" Sara asked.

"They're in the process. This Easter."

"Did you ever find Maeda?"

"Maeda?" Sara queried.

"Yes, I did, as a matter of fact," he said, with the hint of a smile. "We also had a nice talk long into the night."

"But Raeph, she must be a Catholic. Doesn't that kind of throw a wrench into things?"

"I don't understand," Sara asked. "What's been happening while I've been holed up?"

"Well, it seems our friend here has found a new love interest."

Raeph began to correct me, but was interrupted.

"Again, I don't understand, Raeph. You're married with two sons. What more don't I know?"

Raeph was about to answer, but Tilly arrived with our food. After a short grace, we commenced eating.

After a bite of hash, Raeph finally spoke. "Sorry, Mrs. LaPointe, the last few days have gone by fast." Raeph then summarized the steady downturn of his life. "You surely remember Ted, my youngest son. He left home, and I've not heard from him in years. I've spent many a night wondering what I did to drive him away."

"I'm so sorry, Raeph," Sara said.

"All a part of the great mystery of God's plan, I guess."

"Speaking of plans, what's yours today, Sara?" I asked. "More of the same?"

"I was going to make another visit with Sister Agatha," this got Raeph's attention, "to another unwed mother, but given last night, I don't know. Did they catch the vandals?" This she said to Raeph, in answer to his interest.

"I don't know," he responded, and returned to his breakfast.

"That was really something, last night," I began, when we were interrupted by another guest.

"Good morning, can I join you?"

"Reverend Bourque." I awkwardly tried to stand up in the confined crevice of the booth, with Raeph following suit. "Please do," I said, gesturing to the space beside Sara.

"Thank you."

"Here's your coffee, Fathah," our waitress said, with far more respect than she'd given the three of us.

"Thanks, Tilly. Harold's gout any better?"

"If you mean has he stopped complaining, hardly, but thanks for asking," she said and left us, with a smile to the priest.

"How are things at the church? Is Mrs. Tinsly okay?" I asked.

"Let's just say things are as well as can be expected. I must say it was quite shocking to see the shattered window in the morning light, and that foul graffiti: 'Papists go to hell!'" Humorously, he added, "I wanted to yell, 'Yes, indeed, some of us may join you there!' But, of course, God calls us to forgive, and what was done was done out of fear and ignorance. Fortunately, only one person was hurt. Windows and doors can be replaced, but now we need to reach out in love even to those who hate us."

Raeph was studying the priest. He started to say something, but didn't.

"The reason I'm here so early is because I have some very important news for all three of you, especially you, Mrs. LaPointe. But I need you to stay calm."

"What is it, Father?" Sara inquired anxiously. "Is it news about Stephen?"

"Yes. He has returned. In fact, he's only a mile away and anxious to see you, to see you all."

"Then let's go," she exclaimed, making to leave.

"Please, Mrs. LaPointe, sit a moment," he answered, checking her. "There's more. He's in the hospital."

"What?"

"I discovered him there late last night, unexpectedly, when I went in to visit Mrs. Tinsly. Apparently, he was in an automobile accident leaving the Widow's Mite yesterday morning. He was on his way here, in a hurry, because he'd heard that all three of you were here looking for him. Miraculously, he is all right. A bit dazed and bruised, with a nasty gash on his forehead, but, if all goes well, he should be released this afternoon. He insisted that I not call you last night. He wanted to rest up first. He has much to tell you."

"Can he see me now?" Sara demanded with tears. "Does he really want—"

"Yes, of course. I've arranged for Sister Agatha to pick you up in fifteen minutes to take you to him."

"Thank you, Father."

"I also have something to tell you, Raeph. A detective from the local police department contacted me this morning. Keith Torrance. He's a friend and what you might call a floundering church member. He said they've rounded up most of the suspects you mentioned last night, and they want you to come down and identify them. However—and this is why he gave me a heads-up—the suspects seem to be implicating you as a co-conspirator."

"What!" Raeph gasped.

"They're claiming that when you met with them on Tuesday night, you gave them the idea for the attack."

"I did no such thing! As I explained last night, Pastor Guilford asked me to come to meet with them, but I had nothing to do with their plans. Honest, Reverend Bourque."

"I believe you, my friend, but it's the police you need to convince. I was thinking, Scott, that you ought to take Raeph down there right away, to Detective Torrance. He's a good man. He'll listen to reason."

"Thanks, Father Bourque. Come on, Raeph, let's get it over with, and then can we also visit Stephen?"

"Yes, of course. Third floor, room 5."

Leaving Father Bourque and Sara to continue their discussion unhindered, Raeph and I exited for our appointment with the police.

"Scott, give me a few minutes first," Raeph requested. "I need to clean up a bit."

"Raeph, you all right?"

He dropped his head, pushing his hair back with a hand. "Just when I thought things might be turning around, it seems like God is punishing me for my past."

"If you had nothing to do with it, then you have nothing to fear."

He gave me a strange, distant gaze. "Fear. Come on, let's get this over with, and then on to see Stephen."

ONE of the things I most love about New England is the pervasive historic architecture. Every city, town, or village has its fair share of old buildings, some that retain only a portion of their former selves, improved (or, as some think, defiled) in stages over the centuries. Granted, the centuries here only number three or four, compared to the dozen or more of the architecture in the mother countries, but still, every old New England building, especially those that have preserved sections of their original hand-hewn log structure, is a whisper from our colonial ancestors.

Yes, I know I'm a transplant to New England from Michigan, but I've been told my family descends from good New England stock. Apparently, we're somehow related to a Captain William Turner who fought and died in King Philip's War, a bloody war between the English colonials and the American Indians during the late seventeenth century. Turner Falls, Massachusetts, was named after him, so if the rumor's true, I have deep ancestral roots here.

But regardless, I love walking around historic New England buildings, and the Jamesfield Police station was one. An aging bronze sign on the front lawn stated it was the oldest standing structure in the county. Somewhere in its core are the remains of a log cabin, erected from scratch by one of Jamesfield's founding families. Then, during the Revolutionary period, this small humble structure was transmogrified into an immense castlelike stone armory. It looks like four rooks from a chess set interconnected by insurmountable stone walls. Sometime in the late nineteenth century the aging armory was restored and converted into the town jail. Since then, the structure has been expanded and modernized, but even so, the imposing character of this Revolutionary stone armory still dominates the main thoroughfare of Jamesfield.

The original stone entryway was large enough to allow the passage of horse-drawn ammunition wagons, but it had been filled in with brick and glass. Admittance required buzzing the front desk. I looked at Raeph, and could tell he was not eager for this encounter, so I took the lead and buzzed. The door unlatched, and we entered.

"Can I help you?" asked a uniformed woman behind a desk.

"I'm Scott Turner, and this is Raeph Timmons. He's been asked—"

"Yes, of course, please be seated." We sat on two yellow molded chairs, while she made a call. "Detective Torrance? Mr. Timmons is here. All right." Hanging up, she said, "He'll be out directly."

"You doing all right?" I asked.

"Yeah, sure. What have I to worry about?" He sat pressing his palms, staring at the floor.

"I don't know, but you're acting kind of nervous."

"Guess I don't particularly like police stations."

"Well, this one's quite interesting. I feel like we're in an old Norman castle."

"Yeah. Wonder if there's a dungeon."

A strong, midsized man in a brown suit, tie loosened to one side, entered and extended his hand to me. "Mr. Raeph Timmons?"

"No," I said, rising, "I'm his friend, Scott Turner. This is Raeph."

"Scott Turner, of football fame?"

"Well, I suppose, but far less fame than aches and pains."

"Sounds like your pat answer," he smiled and re-shook my hand.

"I've moved on."

"Good to meet you; I remember you well."

"Thanks. This is Raeph Timmons."

Changing his focus, he greeted Raeph, who also had risen. "Mr. Timmons, I'm Detective Keith Torrance. Could you both follow me?" He led us through a pair of glass security doors, into a waiting room that was already crowded with guests.

"That's him," said a man in handcuffs, standing up and pointing with both hands.

"Sit down, Mr. Jonas."

Another man, also in handcuffs, pulled Mr. Jonas back into his seat.

Besides the detective and the two of us, there were nine people in the room: all men except for one woman. Most were dressed in suits or business attire, except two in laborers' dungarees, who also wore the additional steel bracelets.

"Mr. Timmons, do you recognize any of these people?" the detective asked, directing our focus from left to right. Raeph needed little time to make up his mind. With a side-glance to the detective, he said softly, "Yes."

"I'm sorry, we didn't hear you," with a less friendly tone than before.

With a puzzled glare, Raeph responded, "Yes, these are the pastors and others who were at that meeting where I saw the yellow van. Two are missing: Pastor Guilford and there was a woman, I can't remember her name."

"Detecteif Torrance," said a man with a pointed gray beard, "I am very busy. Most uf us are. I haf a meetink zeis mornink, unt Reverent Prescott, I zink you are joinink me in zat. I undershtant yer responsibility to solve zeis crime, unt our suppos't guilt at beink togezer at zat meetink, but, if you pleazed, you haf zee guilty vuns," pointing at the two handcuffed men, "unt zee rest of us aren't goink anyvere. Can vee return to our vurk?"

"Please, be patient, Dr. Steinitz, I'll let you go in a minute. Now, Mr. Timmons, so you admit that you were a part of that clandestine meeting?"

"Pastor Guilford asked me to attend. I'd never seen any of these people before, and I left when they started talking crazy."

"Several of them give the impression that the meeting was called specifically to meet and hear you. That you were new in town and had the information that sealed their decision to finally act. They say you may not have been there at the church last night, but you were their inspiration."

I interrupted. "If I may ask, Detective Torrance, are you saying that one of these men owns the yellow van that is plastered with anti-Catholic slogans and was seen escaping from the vandalism and the smoke bomb? Why are you taking their accusations against Raeph seriously—since he's the one who gave you the information you needed to catch them?"

"Yes, Mr. Turner, but this isn't the first of these incidents; I just want it to be the last. The information I have from you, Mr. Timmons, and from Curt Jonas and Bortlan Cordley, supports the idea that this involves far more people than the two or three who defaced St. Francis Parish last night. And if the group is bringing in outsiders—organizers—then we need to 'nip this in the bud,' as old Barney Fife would say."

"I had nothing to do with last night's attack," Raeph yelled, stepping back. "I'm not an organizer brought in by anyone to instigate trouble."

"Then why are you here?" Torrance asked, remaining calm. "What brought you to Jamesfield? Mr. Jonas and Reverend Thomas say that you are here specifically to stop the priest from luring your friends into the Catholic Church. How did you plan to stop him? They also say that you were a close friend of the man who shot that minister in Vermont last year because he thought the minister was secretly a Catholic—I remember hearing about that case. This is what doesn't make sense: if you are in the same camp as these, then what were you doing there at St. Francis Parish last night?"

"I ... I ..." Raeph's body and hands were speaking far more than his lips, rustling his hair, wiping his brow, shaking his head, turning away.

"Excuse me, Detective Torrance?" The receptionist had entered.

"Yes?"

"Father Bourque is here."

"Please, bring him in."

The seated co-defendants exchanged glances. The two in police bracelets began to rise, but were pulled back down by their neighbors. Reverend Thomas leaned over and spoke to the two in a hushed huddle.

"Hello, Keith," said the priest as he entered.

"Father. Long time no see."

"Is that a confession?"

"My mother would hope so."

"You are a Catholic, detective?!"

"Please sit down, Reverend Tyree."

Father Bourque continued. "Oh, and thanks for responding to my request 'for a favor,' though I'd rather we not talk about it now," he said, nodding toward Raeph.

"That's what I don't understand, Father. It doesn't make sense given what happened last night and his supposed part in it."

"Keith, trust me; Mr. Timmons was not directly involved. He was as shocked by what happened as the rest of us. He was inside the church when it happened and could just as easily have been harmed by the bomb as anyone."

"Okay, but I'm concerned that this hatred is more widespread and becoming more organized than this one incident of vandalism."

"So, do we know who the guilty ones are?" said the priest, looking over the array of characters.

"We have physical evidence and several witnesses who put the two with handcuffs at the scene."

"But you can't prove we did anything," yelled Curt Jonas. "Sure we hate this priest. He and his mistress nun have ruined my family; they're perverting our community."

"Mr. Jonas, be quiet! We also know who owns the yellow van that was seen driving away from the scene."

"Which of the two?" asked the priest.

"Neither. The van is owned by Reverend Thomas."

"Dick," the priest responded with a hushed surprise. "You and I've shared lunch together; we've served on committees together; we even bowled together last year in that fundraiser for the soup kitchen."

The minister just sat, glaring at the floor.

"What about the rest?" Bourque asked.

"Just here for questioning, in relation to that Tuesday night meeting."

The priest stood silent, examining the faces of his fellow clergy, and receiving the less-guarded hatred of the two in chains.

"What would you like us to do, Father?" Detective Torrance asked.

"Can we do what I asked you on the phone this morning?"

"Yes, I think so."

"Very well, then could you bring them over to the church? Now?"

"But vee haf utter zinks vee neet to do!" Dr. Steinitz insisted. Several of the others chimed in their concurrence, while a few just sat silently, nodding.

"We can arrange that, Father," said the detective. "Curt Jonas, Bortlan Cordley, and Reverend Thomas, you're coming with me. The rest of you, I'll see you at St. Francis Parish in fifteen minutes. If you have to cancel anything or make other arrangements, there's a pay phone in the lobby. But there will be no excuses," he said, glaring at a few who were beginning to make some. "Whether you were directly guilty for last night is irrelevant; if you were at the meeting Tuesday night, you were involved. We will all be together in fifteen minutes at St. Francis Parish. Anyone not showing up will be assumed to be a co-conspirator in this crime. See you in fifteen minutes."

The detective and another officer collected the two handcuffed prisoners and Reverend Thomas and led them out a different door, into the former arsenal. The rest moved slowly, exchanging muffled comments, while Father Bourque, Raeph, and I retraced our steps to the front lobby.

"Thanks, Reverend Bourque," Raeph said, awkwardly, as we descended the front steps. "And I'm sorry if I had any part in instigating this attack. Pastor Guilford invited me to that meeting. They'd gathered to hear me and to talk about what to do with you. I had no idea—"

"That's all right, Raeph. Some of my best friends are anti-Catholic," he said, motioning toward Reverend Thomas. "We can talk more about this later. Remember, you're to visit with me this afternoon at three?"

"Yes, I'll be there, but—"

"Good. Now, I'll meet you two over at the church." He left for his car with a wave.

"That was pretty wild, Raeph," I said, as we got into my van.

"Scott," he started, but then paused to stare out the window. The winter clouds had rolled back in, much darker to the northwest. Pedestrians were hurrying past, holding their collars up against the chilling wind. "Hatred and fear. Helen was very, very right. I've been so blinded by hatred and ignorant fear. They also were right, you know. I wasn't a part of their scheme last night, but I shared and fed their hatred. And I didn't pull the trigger that shot Reverend LaPointe, but I shared and fed Walter's hatred. And it was all from fear, based on ignorance. I was so wrong, and still am."

He returned to silence, and I did likewise. I understood. "Been there, done that," as they say, though to a lesser degree. What was reassuring was that we were on our way to meet with a priest whom I felt also understood, whose compassion seemed to far outweigh our hatred and fear.

36

It was not a long drive from the hotel down Main Street across town to Jamesfield Memorial Hospital. With but a day and a half until the weekend, the traffic heading north toward the ski slopes significantly outnumbered those returning south. What was surprising to Sara was the high number of motorcycles.

"They're probably heading north to visit the shrine in Colebrook," Sister Agatha said.

"Motorcyclists going to a shrine?"

"I know, it does run against the grain of the bikers' usual image, with their black leather, tattoos, and tough independence. But like most of us, the exterior public shell is rarely more than a façade to hide an insecure inner self. If anything, that's precisely why the Shrine of Our Lady of Grace has been such a magnet for bikers."

The main intersection of Jamesfield, where a north-south, two-lane highway, which threads its way along and through the breathtaking White Mountains, crosses one of the few east-west thoroughfares, was at that moment jammed with Harleys, Hondas, BMWs, and other brands of choice.

"Every June for nearly thirty years," Sister explained, "bikers from all across the U.S. and Canada take part in what has become the Annual Great North Woods Ride-In. The shrine boasts around fifty carved granite and marble monuments, including a life-sized tableau of two cyclists kneeling in prayer beside their motorcycle. The ride-in culminates with the annual 'Blessing of the Bikes' when thousands of bikers set aside the persona, kneel, ask God for forgiveness, and receive the blessing of the local bishop."

"But this is the middle of February. Besides the treacherous roads, it's freezing."

"Sometimes there's just no asking why."

"Excuse my doing so, but why is it called Our Lady of Grace?"

"Actually, I've always considered this one of the most Protestant-friendly titles of our Blessed Mother. She is who she is precisely because she was full of grace, not because she was strong-willed or because God kept her from temptation, but because she was given the full complement of God's grace. I guess you could say this brought a unique clarity and control to her intellect and conscience, so she could respond fully and faithfully to the will of God."

The confusion at the light had cleared, with the flow of bikers, trucks, and other vehicles from the west, south, and east melding into one unified stream heading north. For the next few blocks, the sister's Miata would be at the mercy of the parade's pace.

The lull in the conversation provided Sara ample opportunity to ask this new friend any of the myriad questions that plagued her conscience, but instead, she sat tensely forward, pressing toward the pending encounter with her long-lost beloved.

"Mrs. LaPointe—"

"Please, call me Sara. That formality was always linked with my position as a pastor's wife, which I guess I'll never be again."

"Sara, if I could be so bold, are you bitter about that? Is that one of the reasons you left Stephen?"

The next bumper-to-bumper block was passed in silence. Sister began a gesture, which implied an apology for crossing uninvited into personal territory, but Sara responded, "No, that's okay. You're right. Self-centered bitterness describes me to a tee, but even more, I was a walking guilt complex."

They had reached the entrance to the hospital, a long circular drive that passed first the emergency room, then the expansive glass portal to the reception area, and finally emptied into the parking lot.

"Sara, I realize how awkward this might be, but how about a quick prayer to Our Lady of Grace, asking for her intercession, that God might grant you and Stephen a special portion of that grace that gave Mary the courage to do whatever God wanted her to do, regardless of the outcome?"

Sara hesitated a moment, but then, with a tiny smile and a slight nod, she bowed her head, praying silently along as Sister prayed aloud, ending with a Hail Mary. Sister Agatha led the way into the hospital reception area, which was alive with young moms and screaming toddlers, the elderly transporting themselves or being transported in wheelchairs, a young family huddled in tearful shock, a maintenance man fixing a drinking fountain, and a deliveryman with a dolly full of toilet paper. Sara and her new friend weaved their way through to the row of elevators. Several heads turned to examine the passing young woman in her black-and-white habit.

"Father said third floor, room 5."

The gift shop doors were flung open as they passed, getting Sara's attention. Inside was a minimal assortment of snacks, toiletries, magazines, books, and of course gifts for last-minute signs of affection.

"Maybe I ought to get him something?"

"Come, Sara. I'm quite sure there's only one gift he's hoping to receive this morning."

Sara smiled, and they moved on. Sister Agatha pressed the up button, and Sara nervously watched the counters as the two elevators raced downward. But then, to Sara's dismay, both elevators stalled. She pushed the button again, then again, until finally the right-hand elevator began moving. It passed the third floor, but then seemed to take forever to reach the second, where they were waiting. Finally, the doors opened.

A family of six exited, parents and children, surrounding a grandfather in a wheelchair, pushed by a nurse's aide. Everyone, except the grandfather, was beaming. His was the bewildered look of an impatient outpatient returning to a real world.

"Morning, Sister Agatha," said the nurse's aide.

"Good morning, Alicia." The family troop passed on toward the front entrance.

Once inside the elevator, Sister asked, "You doing okay, Sara?"

Sara was fidgeting with her hair. After hearing the startling news from Father Bourque at breakfast, she had raced back to her room. There she tried to follow her usual routine before the mirror, but frantically kept correcting, then overcorrecting, then starting over with her makeup. To anyone else, she looked perfect, impressive, but she could not satisfy herself. After some spilled cover-up and a thrown mascara pencil, she had closed her eyes, regained composure, finished, and moved on to work on her wardrobe. She was preparing to present herself to the husband she had not seen for over eight months, and changed her mind a dozen times. Again she had paused. *If he is still the Stephen I married twenty years before, he will not care in the least whether my makeup is exact or what I am wearing. But is he the same Stephen?*

Pulling on her leather boots and grabbing her long camel-hair coat, she then remembered. *Twenty years. In two weeks it will be our twentieth anniversary.* With a final return and glance into the bathroom mirror, she had departed to join Father Bourque in the lobby and wait for Sister Agatha. Now in the elevator with yet a floor to go before reaching her husband, she was revisiting the condition of her makeup and her choice of clothes.

Sister Agatha reached over and touched her arm. "Sara, you look wonderful. It will be fine."

Sara turned with a smile, her mascara running slightly. Sister gave her a tissue.

The elevator doors opened to a busy ward. A nurse, her patient, and a stainless-steel tree of life-support tubes were waiting to enter. Another nurse's aide was walking another patient with his own private tree of tubes. Behind them strolled a corps of white-robed doctors, each with a clipboard, their stethoscopes arranged to denote their office like the pectoral cross of a bishop.

"Room 5 is this way," the sister motioned to their right. The doctors parted to let them pass, most nodding greetings to the habited nun.

The door to the room was partially open. Sara hesitated, then started to push the door, when it opened suddenly.

"Everything looks fine, Mr. LaPointe," the exiting doctor said matter-of-factly. "I'll stop by again after lunch to look you over one last time. You just rest." He turned and seeing the two women, backed aside to let them enter. "Oh, excuse me."

But they backed out into the hall with him. He pulled the door closed.

"How is he, Doctor?" Sister asked. "This is Mrs. LaPointe."

"Oh, hello," he said, shaking her hand. "He's doing amazingly—or should I say, miraculously—well. Other than a mild concussion and some bruising, he's inexplicably fine. It could have been much worse, but if all goes well today, he can go home later this afternoon."

"Thank you, Doctor. Can we see him?" Sara asked.

"Yes, of course," he said, reopening the door to let them pass.

Sara hesitated. She stepped back to allow Sister Agatha to pass, but the nun smiled and shook her head. "No, Sara, you need to go in first alone. I'll wait out here if you need me." Sara nodded, then entered.

The beds were to her left. The first was occupied by a sleeping elderly man. Tubes passed into his nose and arms, and the pulsating rhythms of various multi-lit control units were joining chorus to his peaceful snoring.

The curtains separating the two units were closed, following the contoured ceiling track, shutting off any view to the bed nearest the window. Glancing around the curtains, she saw her husband, dressed in a typical hospital gown, sitting on the side of his bed, staring out the window. The view was north, over the wintry hospital grounds, to the expansive northern woods, with the peaks of the white mountains above. It was a beautiful panorama. Stephen was just sitting still, staring out, cradling a Styrofoam cup of coffee. Sara watched unnoticed for a moment, studying her husband. His graying, receding hair was expectedly unkempt, but what most caught her eye was his close-cropped winter beard. He had never liked growing a beard, because it was too itchy. And besides, he said he never recognized the man in the mirror upon his first startled glance in the morning. But regardless, he often grew it in the winter because she liked it, so the very sight of his beard was a visible whisper of his love for her. He would never have done this if he hadn't been thinking of her.

"Stephen?" she blurted out.

He turned his head quickly, then sliding his feet to the floor, he rose slowly, walked cautiously to her, and they embraced.

37

Scott Turner's Narrative

I parked the van in the identical spot across from the church that we'd used for our first rendezvous with Father Bourque. Well, that is, Sara and I.

Raeph remained stone still, strapped by his seat belt into the passenger seat.

"I don't think you can remain here in the van," I hinted, trying to lighten things up.

Father Bourque had arrived before us and was standing alone, hands in his overcoat pockets, outside the church before the fluorescent-green graffiti.

"Scott, I need to say something. I'm not going to run away or stay in the van. I'm ready to go in, but not because of any police order. I don't know how to explain it, but somehow I'm feeling that this is one of the most important things I've ever been called to do, in my entire life."

He unshackled himself so he could more fully face me.

"All along I was thinking that God was sending me on this quest to confront Reverend LaPointe, to complete what Walter had started. At first, I even wondered whether it might require some form of violence, just like Walter had thought. But then, after all that happened with you at the Widow's Mite and our discussions and my meeting with Reverend Guilford and those crazies, I thought I knew what God was really calling me to do: to make sure that LaPointe and even you were not lured away into the Catholic Church. I just wanted to serve and defend my Lord.

"But then after all that happened yesterday, I'm thinking that the reason God called me on this journey had nothing to do with Walter or LaPointe or even you; it's all about me."

He sat back, his clenched fists resting on his knees.

"I've just never realized how much my faith has been poisoned by hatred and fear, and ignorance. Like you said yesterday, a lot of things I thought I *knew* to be true are just not true.

"And that confrontation there at the jail nailed it. God made me see what hatred, fear, and ignorance look like, and what it causes—what I caused. In the name of Jesus, I fueled Walter's hatred and also what happened there," he said, pointing across the street at the damage to the church. "And I don't just mean the vandalism and violence, but to the sorrow there of that good priest who, it's obvious, loves Jesus. Scott, I'm sorry." He turned his face away.

I was wrestling with how to respond, when I saw in the rearview mirror the caravan of vehicles. Led by two police cruisers, it passed us, then turned left into the drive leading to the parking lot behind the church. Other than the absence of those magnetic black flags and a hearse, it would have appeared to any bystander like your typical funeral procession. Father Bourque had passed out of sight behind the church to meet them, so I turned to my new friend: "Listen, Raeph. Jesus knows your heart. That's all that matters. Come on, we better go."

He nodded and exited the van. We walked in silence across the street, and paused for a second before the desecration.

"Maybe we better follow Reverend Bourque around to the back," Raeph said, "instead of going right into the church, I mean. He may have other plans for us."

I nodded and followed. In a sense, I was an outsider to all of this. They had not required that I be there; I was merely transporting Raeph in obedience to Detective Torrance. But I wasn't about to leave. Raeph not only needed my brotherly support, but it appeared that God was doing something momentous in his life. I was anxious to find out what it was.

Out back, the cars were unloading, and the occupants were wending their way in the direction of the priest. The ministers were pairing up, talking softly, while the two in cuffs and Reverend Thomas were pushed forward by their personal police escorts. Raeph and I moved up and stood behind Father Bourque, while Detective Torrance took his place beside him. I overheard their presumed private conversation.

"Been a while, Keith," the priest said.

"I know, but ever since Judy's murder, it's just been hard."

"I understand, Keith, but don't you think she would want you to return? Don't you think she would want you to have the reassurance of the faith and the strength of the sacraments?"

"Father, I just don't understand why God let it happen. She was so dedicated. She spent too much time down at the church, as far as I was concerned; she was always giving everything of herself to some church benefit or charity, and then she was murdered for no apparent reason, and with no clues as to who did it or why. I just don't understand."

"Then why haven't you come in to talk with me? We used to talk all the time."

"What can I say, Father? I'm angry, spitting angry and bitter."

The crowd had formed before us.

The reassurance of the faith and the strength of the sacraments. Those words seem to sum everything up.

"Come, please, around to the front." The priest turned and led us down the recently shoveled walk. The midmorning sky was clear, but the temperature had taken a February plunge. We all followed, mostly in pairs, huddled for warmth, and silent.

Around in front, the priest stopped on the first step, turned, and said, "I want us to stop here for a moment. I'm assuming that most of you may not have seen this yet. Please read carefully what was painted on the doors, and in a moment we'll go inside." Father then turned back around to study the words himself.

We stood, mostly in silence, there before the church, in the cold, for almost four minutes. It seemed like forever, and every time a voice within me wanted to utter a complaint, to give some kind of visual expression of impatience, I saw the words scrawled across the doors. It seemed that my lack of comfort was minor compared to this violent public act of, as Raeph was discovering, hatred, fear, and ignorance. I remembered the horror and panic of the Catholic parishioners the night before, their feelings of having been violated. And the shock that seemed to sap everything out of Father Bourque, driving him to his knees in the snowbank. But there he was this morning, standing firm with a calm composure, without any sense of demanding retribution.

Finally, without turning, he said, "Please, come now inside," and led the way. He grasped the handle on the large wooden door that had been defaced with the words "Papists go to hell!" and held it open as we each passed through. "Reverend Turner," he asked, as I passed, "could you direct them to sit in the area where the bomb landed on Mrs. Tinsly, in front of the broken window?"

"Yes, of course."

Not unlike Raeph and I had done, and probably for the same reasons, the crowd was gravitating to the back pews.

"Come," I instructed, "Reverend Bourque wants us to sit further forward, over there." I pointed. "Raeph?" I motioned. He nodded, and began "helping" them respond accordingly. Most complied, but a few, including the two policemen and their cuffed companions, held back.

"This is his house," Raeph told them, "so let's just obey like good little children." One of the policemen glared at him, but Raeph insisted with a broad, taunting grin, bowing and motioning forward, "Will we process nicely, or must I find a ruler for your knuckles?"

"Thanks, Mr. Timmons, but that won't be necessary," Father Bourque said, waiting beside those few holding back until they submitted and moved forward.

The pews and floorboards beneath the shattered glass window were strewn with colored shards. The spent canister of the smoke bomb still lay against the kneeler in front of the spot where Mrs. Tinsly had been sitting. A torn, charred fragment of her dress was draped across the back of the pew.

"I had nothing to do with any of this," the lone black minister uttered softly.

"Nor I," said several others.

"And you cannot prove we did," said Curt Jonas.

"Please," Father Bourque started, "gentlemen, fellow ministers, Mrs. Denard—"

"Reverend Templeton-Denard," she insisted severely.

"Yes, of course. Now, I don't think there is any question which of you actually did this. If we have to examine all the evidence and eyewitnesses, including some who called the parish late last night— some of your friends who were shocked by what you did," he said directly to the two in cuffs, "I don't think there is any question who is guilty."

"But you can't prove I—"

"Please, Mr. Cordley, not here and not now," he said, motioning the man to remain seated. "Let's suppose for the moment, that none of you did this. Why, then, might someone do this? Why deface the front doors with hate speech or throw the smoke bomb through the glass window into a sanctuary full of innocent people?"

"Well, you can't prove I did anything," Cordley answered, "but if I did, maybe it was because you are stealing our families and our children from us, and taking them to hell!"

"Reverend Thomas?" the priest asked. This minister had claimed the furthest pew behind the group, sitting alone, so upon the priest's direct challenge, the rest all turned and stared. He sank down into his pew, his face darting back and forth, looking for support.

"I ... well, I ... dang it, Reverend Bourque, you and I have talked about this. Sure, we've bowled together, but you know where I stand.

You know because you used to believe the same thing, before you poped. I just haven't heard anything yet to convince me otherwise."

"Reverend Bourque," from the only woman in their midst, "you know my background, so you know I have no sympathy for this godforsaken church. It is a sham perpetrated by power-hungry men who make God in their own image with the one goal of keeping all women in their place. I don't agree with what was done last night—I don't hold to any kind of violence—but I understand the reasons and the convictions behind it."

The tall, lanky minister sitting beside her nodded in anxious agreement.

"Anyone else?"

The short minister whom the detective at the station had called Pastor Tyree stood up and spoke with a calm resolve: "Reverend Bourque, I don't condone what was done. But understand, what you believe and teach in this church is contradictory to everything we believe and teach. Just look around us. The statues and paintings, the altar and candles. We believe, 'For by grace are ye saved through faith, and that not of yourselves: it is the gift of God: not of works, lest any man should boast.'[38] You teach works righteousness and superstitions and allegiance to a mere man in Rome instead of sole allegiance to Jesus Christ our Lord. I don't believe in violence, but I can't agree with you either. I can't compromise with you, and I can't stand for your luring away members of my congregation; not because I'm jealous for your success, but because I'm afraid for their souls, for their salvation!"

"Anyone else?"

Slowly, as with magisterial authority, the minister with the Freudian beard rose, removed his Tyrolean hat, and, with his head held high, began speaking. "Jusht as I tolt yee Teuschtay nicht, zee great Ludter, fife hundert years ago, inschpired by Got, tsaw Rome and zee pope for vat zey vere. He varnedt us to be vigilent, unt even tzo dis priescht iz kindt unt vinsome does nacht prove anyzincht! Remember: Simon Peter varnedt, 'zee devil alvays prowleth aroundst seekink somevun to devour.' Six members of mine church haf vallen into zee handts of dis mezzenger of Zatan. I do nacht like vat vas done here last nicht, but, Vadder Bourque, I schtil belief zat you must be schtopped!"

The black pastor got up and with a smirk said, "Thank you, Dr. Steinitz. I'd like to say that you speak for all of us, but, honestly, I still don't understand a word you say." With this, Dr. Steinitz replaced his hat and sat down. "Father Bourque, I'm the new pastor of Zion Apostolic Temple on the south side of town. We've not met yet. My name's Eddy Collins, and I attended the meeting on Tuesday night mostly out of curiosity. I wanted to better understand the lay of the religious land of this town. I assume most of y'all assume I'm a black Southerner come north to spread Bible-Belt Fundamentalism, but actually I'm a lifelong New Englander who had a life-changing conversion to Jesus in college. I'm an Evangelical who loves to preach the Scriptures, and I have only one goal for my congregation: that they surrender to Jesus Christ and follow Him in holiness."

He stepped out of the pew and moved forward so he could speak to their faces rather than the back of their heads.

"But there is one other thing I must insist: I do not hate Catholics and especially not Father Bourque. And I do not hate Pope John Paul the Second. I may not agree with how Father Bourque sees him, and I may not agree with other things he teaches, but I also don't agree with what most of you teach! But that doesn't mean I hate you or want to fight you. My Lord Jesus called me to love and pray even for my enemies—but Catholics are not my enemies. Regardless of what our Protestant history books might say, Catholics have done far more to help the poor and underprivileged, the persecuted, than any of our denominations—or even all of them put together.

"See that statue over there?" He was directing our attention to the large statue of Mary in the left corner. Her arms were reaching forward, and upon one wrist hung a black rosary. "Catholics do not worship that statue. I learned long ago in my studies—and any of you could do the same if you set your idiotic hatred aside and did your homework—that the Catholic Church has always warned that worshipping statues is idolatry. Catholics treat statues and icons just like you and I use portraits to remember our departed family members or to honor our heroes. That statue of the Mother of Jesus reminds us of her willingness to trust and obey God. And Catholics believe that she—not the statue—but she, alive with her Son and our

Lord in heaven, can pray for us, intercede for us to God our Father, Hallelujah!" This he said with the rise of a preacher's zeal.

"I'm sorry, Father Bourque," he said, with a bow of humility. "I didn't intend to preach. But I'm ashamed with what my brothers have done to your church, and I will help raise funds to repair the damage." He then sat down.

"But where is Pastor Guilford?" demanded the man called Cordley. "He's the one who instigated the meeting last Tuesday."

"I told him he didn't have to come," answered Father Bourque, moving around to the front of the crowd. "And I told this to Detective Torrance, who agreed. Pastor Guilford stopped by to see me late last night, after midnight, after I'd returned from my hospital calls. We talked a long time, and even though he agrees with what most of you believe about the Catholic Church, he was shocked and appalled by what was done. He admitted that he had called the meeting, but he insisted he did everything he could to dissuade you two from carrying out your plan of violence. He gave me a signed promise to raise enough money to pay for the damages." With this, he held up the document. "He had a funeral this morning, so Detective Torrance excused him, otherwise Reverend Guilford said he would gladly have been here to take his share of the blame."

The group sat in silence, listening to the rising howl of a winter wind coming in through the gaping hole of the shattered glass window.

"Gentlemen, and Reverend Templeton-Denard, I've kept you long enough. I'm sure you are all as busy as I am, especially in these weeks leading up to Easter. But—"

"Reverend Bourque."

"Yes, Mr. Timmons."

"I need to say something."

The priest gestured that he take the floor.

"I don't want to say much. I said too much Tuesday night." Raeph moved out of the pew beside me and walked down to stand directly in front of the two men in handcuffs. Looking them straight in the face, almost as a taunt, yet with a controlled, determined voice, he burst out, "We were wrong! What, if anything, done here last night shows the love of Christ? It reeks only of fear, hatred, and ignorance. We were wrong! I was wrong. And Reverend Bourque," he said turning, "I'm sorry, and I only pray that our Lord can forgive me." Raeph turned to stare again challengingly for a moment at the pair, but then raised his gaze to catch everyone else in the crowd one at a time, holding their eyes until each flinched or turned away, and then he returned to his seat beside me.

I reached over and grabbed his knee with a good hefty squeeze, and he grabbed my hand in such a way that has solidified our friendship forever.

"Thank you, Raeph." Father Bourque responded softly. "As I was about to say, I already told Detective Torrance, before we left the police station, that I am not going to press any charges."

"What?" Curt Jonas said, his face jerking toward the priest.

"I have no intention of pursuing any form of retribution for what was done last night. See that large crucifix beside the altar?" He was pointing to a tall, ornately carved, wooden crucifix atop a tall pole. "I take very seriously what Jesus said from His Cross: 'Father, forgive them for they know not what they do.' I realize that some of you may think I'm patronizing you, but I know, from my own background, that much of what you believe about the Catholic Church, what you believe about me and my parishioners, and what you did to that beautiful window and wrote on the front doors, you did out of ignorance. I'm not saying that you're stupid, because I know that some of you are far more intelligent than I. But you just don't know the data, as Reverend Collins has stated. You just haven't taken time to do the homework.

Here's what I suggest: rather than my pressing charges, I'd like to invite you all to join me, next Tuesday evening, in that same room at Pastor Guilford's church where you had Tuesday night's meeting, at his invitation. I will come, willing to answer any questions or charges you might have against the Catholic Church. I'm not requiring that you come; I'm just extending this as an invitation. Is that agreed?"

"You really aren't going to press charges?" demanded Bortlan Cordley.

"Well, let's say that's partially true," Detective Torrance spoke up. "There will be no charges filed for the damages to the church building. However, there is a critically injured woman in the hospital, and that crime will be prosecuted. So officer, if you would please remove the two in cuffs."

"But you can't prove anything! You'll pay for this, priest!" Curt Jonas yelled as he and Bortlan Cordley were led out.

"Reverend Thomas," Torrance added, "I don't know what part you played in this, but you'll need to come also."

He rose and answered, "I understand." As he exited the pew, he turned to Father Bourque, "And William, I'm sorry for all this. Please know, I did not know what those two planned to do with my van, but that's no excuse."

"Dick, you owe me a private conversation."

"Will do," he said as he followed the police officer and his prisoners out.

"As for the rest of you," said Detective Torrance, "you're free to go, quietly and reverently."

The crowd dispersed. I'd like to report that they all left like dogs with their tails between their legs, but some of the mumbles I heard indicated that for a few what was said had made nary a dent. Father Bourque motioned for Raeph and me to hold back.

"So Keith, when can we talk?" Father Bourque asked the detective.

"I'll call you."

"No you won't."

The detective hesitated. "You're right. When do you suggest?"

"How about this Sunday, after Mass, you join me for lunch. Sister Agatha will gladly treat us."

"Okay, but I'm not sure my mother's heart can stand it."

"You'll make her the happiest mom since St. Monica."

"St. Monica?"

"Look it up. See you Sunday." The detective smiled and left.

Father Bourque then turned to Raeph. "Now, are we still on for three this afternoon?"

"Yes, I'll be here."

"Good. Before you go, how about a prayer?"

Raeph glanced up at me, and I smiled, "Please do."

Turning and kneeling toward the altar, the priest crossed himself. We just stood behind him, with bowed heads, as he prayed: "In the name of the Father and the Son and the Holy Spirit, amen. Lord Jesus, You know the suffering of ignorance, but as Scripture teaches that, in Your humanity, You learned obedience through suffering, help us by

Your grace to learn the obedience of forgiveness and love. Thank You for these two men in Christ. May You guide each of them to hear and follow Your will, and may I be to them a brother in Your name. Hail Mary, full of grace ..." He began praying the prayer that surely Raeph previously would have been appalled to hear, but I wondered if this time, after all he'd heard and experienced, especially with his budding relationship with a woman who herself was a faithful Catholic, he may have been listening to it for the first time.

When the priest finished, he crossed himself and rose.

As Raeph and I turned to leave, I said, motioning him forward, "Raeph, I'll be with you in a second."

"Sure," he said, making his way toward the front doors.

"Reverend Bourque," I asked softly to the priest, "I realize all this has certainly put a strain on you, but are you and I still scheduled for one thirty?"

"Yes, of course. I haven't forgotten."

"Thanks." We shook hands, and while I left by the way we had entered, the priest retreated to the front. With one last glance, I noticed him kneeling before the tabernacle.

Raeph was out on the front steps waiting.

"The good Lord never ceases to amaze me, Raeph," I said as we descended together. "Come, let's go finish our quest and visit Stephen."

"Scott, you go ahead without me."

"What? You've got to be kidding. After all we've been through these past few days? I was about ready to burst in there just knowing he was only a few blocks away."

"I know, but my motives for wanting to confront him are all gone. Sure, he's my old minister, and I'm glad he's okay, and yes, someday I'll apologize for whatever I did to influence Walter's frenzy, but he's really your old friend. Besides, I'm supposed to meet Maeda for lunch in a half hour, so, if you don't mind, I'll just walk a bit until then."

"I'll greet him for you."

Raeph lifted his collar up around his neck, and turned to walk away, but stopped. "Thanks, Scott, for being there for me."

"That's what friends do. See you later?"

Raeph nodded, and walk away with his back to the wind. I stood watching him for a moment, then glanced back at the desecration.

Someone had taped a sign over the defiled papal seal that declared, "Forgive us our trespasses …"

Out loud, I responded, "Amen," and turned away, remembering, *but for the grace of God go I.*

The elevator opened to the third floor, and to the rear of a knot of visitors, nurses, and an aide pushing an empty gurney exited the local priest. His black clothes bore a stark contrast to the more earthy tones of the visitors in their winter garb and the staff in their institutional white. He stopped at the nurse's station.

"Is Stephen LaPointe okay for a visit?"

"I was hoping he could rest after the visits he had this morning, but I think he's too excited to sleep."

"Thank you, Nurse."

The priest set off down the hall, greeting the few he passed, then turned into room number 5.

The man in the first bed was a parishioner, a Mr. Christopher Ratlin, a beloved pillar of St. Francis Parish, whose extensive family filled two pews when they were all in attendance. The priest assumed he was heavily sedated because every time Father previously had stopped for a visit, even before Stephen had become Mr. Ratlin's roommate, the latter was sound asleep. And *sound* was the right term, for as usual his snores were the sign of a man without inhibitions.

The curtains around Stephen's bed were fully drawn, dividing him from view. The priest walked past to the side open to the window. Stephen was sitting up in bed, reading what the priest recognized as the Liturgy of the Hours.

"May I bother you?" asked the priest.

"Of course, Father Bourque," he answered, setting aside the books of psalms and prayers. "Please, please do. Here pull up a chair."

The priest did. "Finally finding solace in the Divine Office?"

"You remembered. Let's just say it's getting better. I still feel more comfortable praying directly from the Bible, but, per your admonition, I'm submitting my preferences to the wisdom of the Church."

"Besides the many benefits and blessings of the Divine Office, it also gets you in liturgical rhythm with Christians around the world and throughout history. Though the arrangement of the psalms and readings has gone through various revisions over the centuries, the selections represent the wisdom and spiritual insight of some of the greatest saints of the Church. Remember your favorite 'life verse,' as you called it? 'Trust in the Lord with all your heart, and do not rely on your own insight'? Accepting the discipline of the Divine Office, or Liturgy of the Hours as it's now called, is a practical means of trusting God and of self-effacement."

"I know, Father, and per your encouragement, I've tried to follow your advice every day of my absence."

"Stephen, I haven't a lot of time right now. I'm meeting in a little while with your good friend, Scott Turner."

"I'm floored to hear he's been seeing you."

"It all began for him with what you divulged at your retreat last year. Like a burr in his bonnet, he couldn't escape the implications of what you said."

"Is he going to enter the Church?"

"Oh, he's not that far along. Like you and the rest, there are always a few major hurdles to vault. Last night, after you described your excursion into Québec and just before Nurse Marge forced me to leave, you said you had one last thing you needed to vent. Is now a good time?"

"I suppose, Father, but first there's something else I just realized this morning. I know why I miraculously survived that crash, in fact, why the Lord used a crash to get my attention: the prayers of St. Brigitte."

"St. Brigitte? But of course," he responded with a grin.

"She and I talked about my Protestant reticence to accept modern miracles. So God used the same kind of accident—one in which I was totally airborne and without control—to help me see how powerful He still is to heal and protect and to save. I walked away with hardly a scratch, I'm sure, because of her prayers."

"I wouldn't doubt that for a moment, my friend."

"Please tell her thanks the next time you speak with her."

"I will, of course. She will be thrilled to know. It will give additional precious meaning to her own tragic experience."

"Oh, and another thing I forgot to mention last night. Suzette Cousineau conveniently planted a copy of your book on marriage in my bedroom at the Mite."

"Suzette can be a bit bold in her subtleties."

"I didn't have time to read the entire book, but your discussion of that verse from First Peter was a godsend: 'You husbands, live considerately with your wives … in order that your prayers may not be hindered.'[39] It confirmed everything I'd concluded from my time away, and maybe explains why for so long I've felt out of touch with God."

"I'm always hesitant to make a direct connect between good and bad experiences with God's pleasure or displeasure, but, as the saying goes, if the shoe fits—," Father replied with a wink and a smile. "Now, about your other concern?"

"Juxtaposed to the mercy I've just received, I shouldn't even mention it. And besides, I'm sure there's an easy answer."

"Sometimes the seemingly simple questions uncover the deepest truths."

"Well, in this case it will probably just reveal my stubborn stupidity, but frankly, it's an intellectual conundrum that has ground my wheels to a halt. Like so many converts, I was drawn to the Church because of issues of truth. The problems of too many gospels, denominations, contradictory and conflicting voices, all claiming to be the truest interpretation of Scripture. In the process, I realized, mostly with your help, that *sola Scriptura* isn't scriptural and that the 'pillar and bulwark of the truth' is not the Bible but the Church."

"I think you discovered most of that on your own."

"Well, I certainly could not have put the pieces together without your help. But as you remember, my next long hurdle was *which* Church, and, again with your help and my other readings, I discovered the continuity between the Old Testament People of God and the Church Jesus established upon His apostles, centered around the leadership of Simon Peter. And my reading of Church history convinced me that the Catholic Church is this Church. And the historical problems we Protestants insist on pointing out take nothing away from the claims of this Church. Bad popes, bishops, priests, and the like were not hidden away or excised from the records by a Church trying to pass along a pure image. It's all out there for anyone to read.

"But history is a two-edged sword, and therein lies my conundrum."

The other conundrum he presently faced was the continual rhythm of Mr. Ratlin's incessant snoring, particularly the occasional rise to an abrupt exclamation, which then reverted to the appointed cadence. But Stephen pressed on.

"Again, it's probably nothing, but I can't shake a problem I have with the uncensored records of those bad popes, bishops, priests, monks, and nuns. Other than the issue of authority to determine, preserve, and proclaim the truth of the Gospel, the key reason I questioned my ordination and resigned from the ministry was the sacraments. I recognized that my Congregationalist sacraments were empty shams and carried no guarantee that they accomplished anything, including giving grace. Most Protestants, of course, don't claim that they are anything more than mere symbols, signs of the grace already received by faith.

"The Catholic Church, however, claims that her sacraments convey grace, and that only her sacraments, and the Eastern Orthodox, do this; others might convey grace, by God's mercy, but outside the Catholic Church, and the Orthodox Church, no one can be certain of this."

"That's correct, Stephen, except that the Church accepts the validity of baptism, if done correctly."

"Yes, of course, but my concern is this: where is the objective historical evidence that Catholic sacraments make any difference? I realize I may be asking too much, but seriously, if Catholic sacraments convey, to the worthy recipient, grace, the very Divine Life of God, whereas others' don't, then why shouldn't we expect there to be some objective evidence over time? For two thousand years, the Catholic sacraments have been received; for hundreds of years non-Catholics have either received only their sacraments or none at all: where is the objective, measurable difference?"

Father said with a wry smile, "Well, what about the saints? Can't the Catholic Church point to them as her objective, measurable proofs?"

"But that's comparing apples and oranges. Only the Catholic Church, the Orthodox, and maybe the Anglicans declare their own departed members as saints; none of the other Christian traditions are so presumptuous. Yet, history is full of good and faithful non-Catholic laity, ministers, missionaries, et cetera. All my life I've known very faithful men and women who love Jesus Christ and live holy lives, yet they never received any Catholic sacraments, except, of course, baptism.

"And besides, history provides far too many negative Catholic examples, and this is the fly in the ointment: the Catholics throughout history who caused the most problems for the Church were those who had received the most sacraments! All the major heretics and schismatics were not laymen, nor were they 'Protestants,' but Catholic cardinals, bishops, priests, monks, and even a pope or two. And the modern priest scandal just adds an exclamation point to this.

"I guess my question is, 'Where's the beef?'—at the local or national or worldwide level—where's the evidence that receiving Catholic sacraments makes any difference?"

Stephen then repeated the question he had earlier posed to Cliff on the phone: "Are the high-sounding theological and philosophical claims concerning Catholic sacraments as channels of divine life and grace no more than just that: high-sounding theological and philosophical claims?"

"Maybe I better take my coat off for this one," the priest said, doing so and then retaking his seat. "I suppose I could begin by pointing out that most of the good non-Catholic people to whom you refer were baptized, and therefore were cleansed of original sin, and received the gift of the Holy Spirit and sacramental grace. So, from an empirical standpoint, it's near impossible to do a blind study.

"But the true problem with your conundrum is that you're trying to compare the state of people's souls, their salvation, their present and eternal union with Christ, none of which can be measured empirically in this life."

A snort from the other bed seemed to indicate agreement and brought smiles to their faces. The priest continued.

"Yes, Jesus said it was 'by their fruit' that His followers 'will know' their less-than-perfect religious leaders, the scribes and Pharisees, but

337

He also warned them, for a very important reason, not to judge lest they be judged. We can never in this life know the spiritual condition of anyone else's heart, and for that matter, hardly our own; only God sees and knows. Trying to make some kind of empirical spiritual analysis of the effect of sacramental grace throughout history is rife with complications, precisely because we are limited to the reports of secondary sources. No person's exterior is a pure window to their interior, whether we are talking of an arch-heretic or a glowing saint. This is why the Church goes through seemingly endless examinations, from every angle, before she declares even the most unanimously holy people to be saints."

"And, I suppose," Stephen added, "why the Church has never specifically declared anyone in hell, even the most unanimously evil tyrant."

"That's correct. One of the reasons for this is the recognition of the ever-pervasive spiritual battle that rages against the heart and mind of every believer, but particularly those who have accepted positions of leadership. Does the fact that the heretics and schismatics were the ones who received the most sacraments prove that the sacraments don't work, or that the more graces one receives, the more temptations there will be to misuse them? As Jesus warned, 'Every one to whom much is given, of him will much be required, and of him to whom men commit much they will demand the more.'"[40]

Outside, the sun had just broken through the winter overcast, bringing renewed light into the room, but a bit too much into the patient's eyes.

"Do you mind?" Father Bourque asked, ready to close the blinds.

"No, please do, thanks."

"Stephen, I do see your point," he said as he fixed the blinds and then retook his seat, "and like all Catholics, I'm saddened by the stains given to the record of history by some of our leaders. But I believe that the reason the Church has not whitewashed or purged the records of these failures is to serve as a warning, not just to all but specifically to anyone who would consider accepting the cloak of leadership. And as for all those good, faithful believers outside the Catholic Church, she has always recognized what Scripture teaches, 'the prayer of a righteous man has great power in its effects.' God can give His grace and blessings outside the Catholic Church and her sacraments, to anyone He wants, because He sees and responds to the hearts of men. History has likely been full of people who looked good and holy on the outside but on the inside had cold, empty, loveless hearts, while there were perhaps more people with rough, uncouth, undisciplined exteriors, yet on the inside had selfless, humble, repentant hearts.

"In the end, we can only look at ourselves. If we are not better Christians, is it because the sacraments we received conveyed no graces, or because in our sinfulness we failed to act on the graces we received? Was it the sacrament's fault, or my own?"

The priest took up Stephen's closed volume of the prayers of the Church and turned to the inside cover. "Remember what I wrote in here?"

"Of course."

The priest read, "'John Henry Cardinal Newman, the great Anglican convert, once said, "Ten thousand difficulties do not make one doubt."' Newman meant this as a point of fact, Stephen. However, if we push your difficulties too far, if we obsess on them, we can end up with nothing. If one pushes *sola Scriptura* and the right of private interpretation to the limit, one ends up with relativism, agnosticism, even atheism, because one can grow blind to the inner influence of the spiritual battle. If you push your concerns over the Church's teaching on sacramental graces too far, seeing them as mere fictional power grabs by clericalist popes, bishops, and priests, you will end up questioning all other levels of the Church's teachings, traditions, and doctrines. We know from historical records that we have the New Testament solely because the ordained bishops of the Catholic Church, in fourth-century councils, declared which of the hundreds of highly valued books were to be included in the canon of Sacred Scripture. Their decision was accepted because the Church believed they had this authority, and the guidance and protection of the promised Holy Spirit, due to their sacramental ordinations. Question their sacramental ordinations, question their authority, question the validity of the Church, and eventually you have no option but to reject the authenticity of the New Testament. You have no Bible. You have no Gospels. You have no Savior."

The priest glanced over at the wall clock, and stood. "I'm sorry, Stephen, I'm late for an appointment, so we'll need to continue this another time. I guess all I can say, in conclusion, which frankly, my friend, I know you already know, is this: one, we must walk by faith and not by sight, not by empirical evidence; two, the sacraments convey grace to the soul, without any necessary evidence in the senses; three, to have any effect in our lives, this grace must be acted upon; four, those given much are required much, and receive the greatest resistance from the devil; and five, I guess I can add that there are many reported miracles associated with the sacraments, with empirical confirmation, but our skeptical nature denies this. See you maybe tomorrow?"

"Of course, Father, and thanks."

"Oh, one last thing. I'm assuming we're putting off our long-scheduled meeting with the bishop this afternoon?" he said with a grin.

"I'd say that's a safe bet, but not just because I'm laid up. I'm placing the issue of dispensation from celibacy and priestly ordination on a far back burner. I need to rebuild my marriage and family first. Then, if Sara enters the Church with me, and after I've learned how to be a good, faithful layman, and an even better husband, maybe then you and I can reopen the subject."

"So, you're ready to enter?"

"I'm ready, but I need to discuss this with my better half."

"Understood. Then blessings, my friend," the priest said, making the Sign of the Cross in the air above his patient; then he left the room.

Stephen picked up the prayer book to resume where he had left off, but then set it back down. He left the bed and reopened the blinds to examine the world outside his window. The weather appeared deceptively pleasant and clear, but the huddled nature of the pedestrians accented by the vapor trails of their breaths and conversations told a different story. Eyes indeed can deceive.

"Lord," he said softly, "I wonder, when people look at me, especially when they consider my past eight months of separation, do they see a man touched by grace?"

For a few moments, he watched the pedestrians passing outside, each one a person for whom Christ had died; each a recipient of some level of grace, and responsible for how they used it.

"Lord, help them ... and help me."

He closed the blinds, returned to his bed, turned off the overhead light, and tried unsuccessfully to sleep.

39

The diner was busier than usual. As Raeph sipped his soda, the buzz around him was about the attack on the only Catholic church in town. An opinionated discussion to his right was aghast at the violence reminiscent of the "early days when the Ku Klux Klan persecuted Catholics before the robed hoodlums turned their attention to blacks." To his left, an alternate discussion, in a softer, more guarded tone, gave tribute to "the brave souls who took steps against the rise of popery in this community." He was surprised to hear both groups, unbeknownst to the other, remark how "no Catholics were allowed in New England before the American Revolution," the only difference being that the discussion to his right bemoaned the fact, while those to his left lamented the repeal of those penal laws.

Raeph just sat quietly, sipping his drink, praying she'd come soon.

And she did with her face abeam, through the front door, the brass bell ringing, catching the attention of the waitress behind the counter, as it was intended.

"Boy, you look chipper," Raeph said as she joined him. "What could make you so happy this morning?"

"I quit!" Maeda tossed her coat into a vacant chair.

"You quit? Quit what?"

"I walked right in, didn't even wait to knock but burst open Pastor Guilford's door, and dropped my letter of resignation right down in front of his face."

"Whoa, what did he say? What'd he do?"

"You wouldn't believe me, Raeph." She stopped as the waitress interrupted. "I'll have a bowl of the chowder and a grilled cheese. Raeph, I'm buying!"

"Well, in that case, I'll splurge! Bring me the same." They both laughed.

"So what won't I believe?"

"He picked up my letter, read it, then, taking off his cheaters, he asked me to sit a moment. I did, reluctantly, assuming he was going to make some attempt to talk me into staying or at least make me feel guilty for leaving him in the lurch. But he didn't; he just sat looking at the letter for a moment, then said, 'Maeda, I totally understand and am sorry.' He told me that he met with Father Bourque to apologize for anything he might have done to cause last night's attack! And, get this, he promised to raise the money to cover all the damages!"

"Actually, Reverend Bourque told us about this in our meeting this morning."

"Your meeting?" She asked, her joyful countenance diminishing a bit into puzzlement.

"I'll tell you about that in a moment, but what happened? Did Guilford try to talk you out of leaving?"

She studied him first, then continued, "He said he wished I'd reconsider, but that he understood my decision. Honestly, I think he was kind of glad to see me go. Many in his church know that I belong to St. Francis, and besides, I certainly haven't fulfilled his expectations for a secretary anyway."

"But what are you going to do? You," Raeph paused, shifting his glance to the newly arrived food, "didn't mention anything about this last night. I kind of got the impression that you saw your position there as a Catholic witness in the midst of infidels."

" 'Tis true, but the more we talked into the night, the more my mind began seeing other options for my future." She sampled her food, then asked, "So, tell me about this meeting you had this morning?"

Raeph related his long morning, first at breakfast, then at the ancient armory, and finally the gathering in the damaged nave of St. Francis Parish.

"You mean he let them go? Without any punishment? What about what happened to Mrs. Tinsly!" Her voice garnered the attention of the surrounding tables.

Raeph calmed her down with a lift of his palms, and with pointed glances to the adjacent tables, regained their privacy. "Detective

Torrance said there'd be prosecution for what they did to her, but just not for the damage to the church. I think your priest was playing a bit of poker. He knew that, short of a miracle, no explanation could break through their prejudice—their fear, hatred, and ignorance. So prosecuting them would only make the problem worse, fueling the fire of their hatred and of those who applauded their actions." At this, he nodded to his left.

"Huh?" she asked, turning.

In a whispered tone, he informed her, "That table thinks the vandals are heroes."

"Hmm," she responded with a look to kill.

"Now calm, calm. By showing unconditional forgiveness," Raeph said, gently nudging her face back in his direction with his hand. "Reverend Bourque modeled Christ and took the high ground. To the ignorant this may prove a sign of weakness, but to the Spirit-filled and even to those who once applauded the action, this priest will prove a sign of contradiction, not unlike Jesus Himself."

"So how are you feeling today?" she asked, reaching across the table to take his hand.

He gave her hand an affectionate squeeze. "Well, I think God's barrage has got my goat."

"What does that mean?" she asked with a puzzled squint.

"All week God's been trying to break through. Last year, I was shocked by what Walter did, blaming it on his fanaticism. Then at that meeting Tuesday night, I saw it, and especially last night, I saw it and was shocked and angry. But it wasn't until Helen confronted me, and then you, last night—all of this helped me see."

"See what?" she asked, reaching now to claim his other hand.

"How much my faith, my whole life, has been tainted by ignorance, fear, and hatred." He held her hands, still not believing he was sitting in this diner in New Hampshire with this kind woman from Ireland.

"But it was really this morning that it all came home. At the police station, I found out that the vandals were blaming me—my witness at the meeting on Tuesday night—for instigating their actions."

"You?"

"Detective Torrance didn't buy it, nor did Reverend Bourque, but I knew, down deep, that they were right. I didn't tell Jonas and Cordley to write their vulgarities or throw the smoke bomb, but everything I said fed their suspicions."

With these words, he noticed that the discussions on either side had stopped. Both groups were listening to his account, his confession. Alternately, he leaned to glare back at each party until they returned to their own respective business.

He then returned his attention to the one person in that room who truly mattered to him. "Maeda, I'll just say this: I think God did some kind of miracle inside of me. I don't know anything more about your Catholic faith than I did before—except, that is, for a few new clarifications I've picked up along the way this week." He gave Maeda a smile. "But, by His loving, merciful grace, He has taken the fear and hatred from my heart. As Helen reminded me last night, 'If any one says, "I love God," and hates his brother, he is a liar.'[41] For years, I have been a liar. I excused my actions by claiming, 'Papists aren't my brothers,' but I know that Reverend Bourque loves Jesus and is a true man of God, therefore, he's my brother. I've always known that Reverend LaPointe loved Jesus and was a man of God, and so, he also is my brother. And Maeda, I know you love Jesus, I know that you are a woman of God, and, though you may not be my brother," he said with a smile, "I certainly can't hate you just because you're a Catholic!"

"Well, t'ain't that good of you," she said with a mock withdrawal.

Still holding her hands, he drew her back. "It's hard for me to say this, after all I've been through this past year, but, Maeda, I think I'm falling in love with you." She smiled, then a movement by the door caught her eye.

"Raeph, your friend is here," she said, releasing her grip and pulling back.

Raeph turned and saw Scott Turner at the door. He waved to get his attention.

"Hi, Raeph. And Maeda, good to see you're doing well after last night. I lost track of you when I was told to keep you in sight."

"I know, he scolded me for that. But I needed to take care of some widows in distress. Want to join us?" She looked over at Raeph to make sure her bold invitation met his approval, which it did.

"If you don't mind?"

"No, please do," Raeph said, removing their coats from a chair. "Did you get to see Reverend LaPointe?"

"No, I didn't. The nurse said he had a visitor, and once the visitor left, she insisted that Stephen have no more visitors for a couple of hours so he could rest. They want to release him later this afternoon."

"That's awfully quick," Maeda said.

"Chalk it off to hospital and insurance company economics, as well as God's mercy."

When the waitress arrived, Scott placed his order. With all that the three had been through over the past two days, it was good for them to talk about lighter subjects. Maeda shared nostalgic memories of growing up in Ireland. Raeph talked about his sons, for whom his pride and longing was obvious. Scott reminisced on his days in the trenches and the struggles of bringing up a family in the ministry.

"So," Raeph asked, "now that Reverend LaPointe has returned, and you're as unemployed as me, what are your plans? I do have a red Camaro sitting snowbound in the Mite's parking lot."

"Well, maybe tomorrow morning after—oh, shoot, excuse me," Scott said, getting up, "I've got … ah … I'm sorry I need to go. I'll see you both later." With but a few bites out of his sandwich, Scott threw down a ten and left the diner.

"Wonder what that was about?" Raeph mumbled.

"Not sure. So," Maeda asked hesitantly, "may I ask you the question you just asked Scott? Once you get your red Camaro started, where are you going to drive?"

He chewed the last bite of his grilled cheese, washed it down with coffee, then looked cautiously across at Maeda, who sat quietly staring into her food. Could he dare share his thoughts? "I don't really have any place to go. Sure, I still have a lease on an apartment down in Massachusetts that I'm not using, but I have no reason to go back there or a job to pay the rent. When I left, I wasn't thinking any further than finding Reverend LaPointe. I guess I was counting on God helping me figure out the rest."

He watched her, wondering what was behind her evasive smile, when she said softly, "I guess it looks like God has made us both unemployed and unattached at the same time."

"Maeda," Raeph leaned cautiously forward in his seat, planting his elbows on the table, his hands nervously together, "are you also thinking that maybe God has, well, somehow brought us together?"

"Raeph," she said looking up, "my meeting you is the first thing that makes sense out of why I came here to Jamesfield, why I came all the way from Ireland. I do think that, maybe, God has led us here."

Raeph was about to respond, when his moment was taken away.

"Anything else?" the waitress asked.

"No, I don't think so," Raeph answered, sitting back in his chair.

"Me neither," Maeda said, folding and placing her napkin on the table.

"Then here's your bill. Please come again." The waitress left.

Maeda paid, then the two slowly rose, grabbed their coats, and made their way out of the crowded diner into the cold winter air. The sun was shining through the cloudless sky, causing the snow on the sidewalks to melt, even though the temperature outside was still below freezing.

With the momentum of their tête-à-tête lost, Raeph walked behind her, hands in his coat pockets. "So," Raeph started awkwardly, "you going to your apartment?"

"No, I need to return to the church and clean out my desk." Her focus was on getting her fingers into her gloves. "Thankfully, Pastor Guilford will be out all afternoon, so I won't have to confront him again. After that, I was planning to go to the hospital to see how Mrs. Tinsly was doing. What about you?" She glanced shyly into his eyes.

"I have that meeting with Reverend Bourque. I'll probably go back to the hotel for a while, maybe punish myself at that gym down the street. Are you free tonight for dinner, maybe?"

"Yes." This brought more of a smile, "No Mass of obligation this evening."

"Then how about meeting me over at Burson's, say, at seven?"

"Okay," she said, "see you later," and with this she turned and walked away. Raeph stood watching, and as she receded into the distance, he felt his heart going with her.

"Maeda, wait, please." He hurried to her as she stopped and turned. "I feel the same way, that somehow meeting you was the very reason God brought me here."

"Oh, Raeph," she said, as they grasped each other in a big wintry hug. The problem was he had stopped her in the middle of an intersection. Their embrace was interrupted when the light changed and three drivers laid on their horns, providing comic relief.

Raeph and Maeda separated, laughing, to opposite sides of the street, divided by the passing traffic.

"See you at seven?" Raeph yelled.

She nodded and turned in the direction of Jamesfield Bible Fellowship.

Raeph remained planted by the roadside. When she reached the church's front walk, he watched her turn left, glance in his direction, and stop. She put her hands on her waist and cocked her head with an expression of "What are you doing?!"

He waved, smiled, and nodding good-bye, turned for the hotel.

"Lord," he asked, "is this all really happening? To me?"

40

Scott Turner's Narrative

After leaving Father Bourque and Raeph—after our meeting at St. Francis church—I drove to the local hospital, anxious to finally see my long lost friend. My list of questions was nearly endless, but I knew this would have to wait, given his physical condition. The hospital gatekeeper, however, said he already had a visitor and, after that, they wanted him to rest uninterrupted for a few hours.

So, relegated once again to waiting, I headed back toward the hotel, but, passing a small diner, I decided to stop in for a quick lunch. As I walked through the front entrance, I remembered too late Raeph's plans, for there, directly in my path, he sat with his new friend, Maeda. I considered, for his sake, backing out or taking a seat at the counter, but they beckoned me over.

For a half hour or so we sat, the three of us each sharing a bit from our past, but now as I look back, I think it was then that I first noticed the radical change in Raeph. It wasn't what he said or how, it was his smile; but then again it wasn't just his smile, it was his entire demeanor. I guess with hindsight I can say that what I saw in Raeph was the grace of hope.

But then I had to cut the encounter short, because I remembered I was late for my meeting with Father Bourque. So awkwardly, I excused myself without explanation and left.

Once I'd extracted my bulk from the crowded diner, out into the below-zero winter, and precariously walked down the icy sidewalks to my van, I hopped in and did a U-turn, once the traffic had cleared—hoping a local cop didn't mind—and sped back down toward St. Francis church. With no parking space free along the curb, I drove around into the rear parking lot.

Even though I was running late I needed to make a call, because at that very moment, the plane carrying my family was probably on its descent into Boston's Logan International Airport. My original plan had been to be there to meet them, but the recent events had made that impossible—and I didn't want to miss the opportunity to talk with Stephen.

After only one ring to her cell phone, Diane answered. "Hello, darling. We're just in the process of unloading the plane. It's a bit— *Eddy, check in the seat pocket in front of you to make sure you haven't forgotten anything. No, leave the magazine there. I know, but we don't need it. Yes, Deborah, one of our carry-ons is back there, behind us. I don't know, but see if … oh, thank you, that's very kind of you. Now here, take this, and—Eddy, you're on that woman's purse. I'm so sorry …"*

"Diane?"

"Yes, dear, I'm sorry, can you call me back in a few minutes?"

"Yes, I guess—"

"Thanks." And the call was dropped. This all made me even less confident she would take to the new arrangements, but my hands were tied.

I exited the van once again out into the bitter cold and walked gingerly around to the front door of the church annex.

After a few rings, Sister Agatha casually opened the door.

"Hello, Reverend Turner. Please come in." She seemed unconcerned that I was late.

"Father Bourque has not returned yet from his hospital visits"—
which explained everything—"but I expect him anytime. Would you
like to wait for him in his study, and would you like a coffee?"

"Yes, to both if you don't mind."

I walked down to the study, and entered what, once again, seemed
like a passageway into a different world. The fire had been prepared,
and the glimmer of the flames, teaming with the one soft reading lamp
beside the priest's rocker, gave the small enclosed library the welcome
feel of the inner sanctum of a wizard—a good and trustworthy wizard,
like Gandalf or Merlin. Or more appropriately, the private den of an
Augustine or a Thomas Aquinas.

"Here, Reverend Turner," the sister said, as she placed my coffee
beside the other rocker. Seeing me eye the books, she added with a
knowing smile as she departed, "Please make yourself at home."

"Thanks. Appreciate it."

With coffee in hand, I once again perused the priest's shelves,
which I had only begun to scan on my earlier visits. Lots of great titles,
many familiar authors mixed among the new ones. It was obvious
he wanted to understand the thinking of those who considered his
Catholic theology "of the devil."

Minutes passed as I awaited the priest's return, and then my eye
passed a book I had to pull down and read. The spine gave only the
author's last name, but the title page told the whole story: *Discerning
the Will of God* by Father William A. Bourque.

I absconded with the book and my coffee to the extra rocker
by the fire and began a hurried skimming of the contents. The first
chapters covered problems of discernment, subjectivism, illuminism,
enthusiasm, even psychosis, and how all of these and other things
affect our ability to discern whether we are hearing God, or just
ourselves, or even the devil. He then addressed a long list of various
things, such as how and when God speaks, the conditions for our
receptivity, the signs of the Holy Spirit, and the necessity of listening
to the Church.

I was just turning to the first chapter, when I heard the front door
slam. I quickly extracted myself from the comfortable rocker, careful
not to spill coffee everywhere, to replace the book in its place, but he
beat me.

The door opened, and Father Bourque entered, looking for me. "Scott? Oh good, you're still here. Please be seated. I'm so sorry. I was visiting with Stephen and lost track of time. Sister Agatha," he called across the hall.

"Coming, with your coffee, Father," she said, as she followed him in.

Once we were situated together comfortably before the fire, he said, "I see you found one of my books."

"Yes, I didn't know you were published. This one looks particularly interesting," I said, putting it back in its place.

"I won't pretend it's the last word on the subject. If you search online, you'll find dozens of books on discernment, but actually my short treatise may be the perfect book for you, and for Stephen, for that matter," he said, jotting a note to himself on the pad next to him. "In that modest treatment, I'm writing as a convert, so it's really a biblical study of the subject of discernment, and I was particularly sensitive to the different ways Protestants and Catholics discern the will of God. They are radically different."

"How so?"

"Before we get to that, is there anything else you wanted to talk about first? I gave you a little note when you left on Tuesday. I didn't mean for it to be an assignment, but, just a second—"

The afternoon sun was beaming unhindered into the room, over my shoulder, and into his eyes, so he paused to close the drapes. Once again in his seat, with pipe in hand, he said, "So, I was just wondering whether you'd had time to tackle my question?"

"Yes, I spent all Wednesday afternoon locked in my room, determined to return with an answer that would charitably trump your intentions. But in the end, your strategy worked. To make sure I understood you correctly, the night before you pointed out how Old Testament believers were not 'saved' merely as individuals but by being faithful members of the People of God. After the coming of Christ, the mystery of the Gospel is that this New Covenant People of God, called His Body, is now open to everyone. Paul constantly equates the Body of Christ with the Church, using these terms interchangeably. It was here where I got 'zapped,' you might say."

Father Bourque was rocking back and forth, puffing his pipe, and I could tell enjoying my revelations immensely.

"It's not that I never saw this before; it's just that I never *heard* it. I never really noticed what St. Paul was trying to say. In Ephesians, he wrote that it was 'through *the Church*' that 'the manifold wisdom of God' was to 'be made known to the principalities and powers in the heavenly places.' Jesus had not merely given the Holy Spirit to every believer so they might 'know' or discern what was true. If that were the case, it hasn't worked, for which group of Christians or which individual Spirit-filled Christian has a corner on the truth?

"Nor did Jesus merely give an inspired book so that everything needed for salvation could be passed along without error, for again this has not prevented confusion and conflict amongst Christians. Rather, Jesus gave us the Church, the new contiguous Body of God's Chosen People, 'the household of God.'"

"Which Paul said, in his Second Letter to Timothy," the priest added, accenting his words with his pipe, "is the 'pillar and bulwark of the truth.'"

"There's that 'verse I never saw' again," I responded with a laugh. "But what really convinced me—of what, I think, you were trying to get across to me—was a quote from the *Martyrdom of Polycarp*. Living long before any of the major controversies of the Church, any of the schisms, divisions, and thousands of denominations, this second-century author startled me by his matter-of-fact recognition that, though there were many churches or communities, they were altogether one Church. This is far from the Congregationalism I know, and to which I was ordained. This is contrary to any Protestant Church I know."

After a quick sip of coffee, I added with a nervous laugh, "But Reverend Bourque, please, I'm not ready to become Catholic!"

"Scott, I fully realize the difficulties of this decision. Remember, I made it myself, but I no longer had a wife and family. That reminds me ... just a second."

He went to door, and asked across the hall, "Sister Agatha, have you heard anything about the arrival of our visitor yet?"

"No, not yet, Father," her voice came softly from the dining room. "Let me call the airport to see if there's any news."

"Thank you."

"Airport!" I exclaimed, almost leaping from my seat, "Excuse me, please, I also need to make a quick call."

"Go ahead, Scott. I'll leave you alone," he said, closing the door behind him.

I dialed Diane's cell, and she picked up immediately. "Hello, darling, where are you? Are you outside somewhere? We're here waiting near baggage claim, I think … *Deborah, what's that door letter?* … Door Letter G."

"Well, yes and no. I'm actually not there to meet you."

"What? What do you mean? Are you delayed?"

"Well, again, yes and no. There's so much to tell you, but I'm still up here in Jamesfield."

"Jamesfield? You're no longer at the Widow's Mite?"

"Honey, it's a real long, long story, which I'll gladly tell you when I see you, but I can't leave until tomorrow morning."

"Are you doing all right?"

"Yes, just fine. My delay has to do with Stephen LaPointe. He was in a car accident—"

"What! Was he hurt badly?"

"No, calm down. He's just fine and should be released from the hospital this afternoon."

There was a long pause on the phone, then, "Is what we heard true? Did he really resign the ministry to join the Catholic Church?"

"I haven't been able to see him yet," I replied, leaving the answers for later. "I do want to see him, though, so here's what I'd like you to do. Somewhere near you there should be a large display of hotels and shuttles. The three of you choose whichever hotel you want, right in downtown Boston. Get situated, enjoy walking the Freedom Trail or whatever, have dinner on me at Anthony's Pier Four, and then I'll get there as soon as I can in the morning."

"The adventure continues."

"I know, honey, I'm sorry. You've had to shoulder a lot, especially alone with the kids, but we'll be together tomorrow."

"Have you figured out what you're going to do, now that you're unemployed?"

"Not really, but we can talk about that later. Are you all right?"

"Yes, dear, I'm fine. Wish you were here, though, and so do the kids. They're anxious to see you, and Deborah is especially confused about what has happened. She had just made a whole batch of new friends, and hardly had a chance to say good-bye. I'm thinking we could have done this a little better for her sake."

"You're probably right, but at the time I thought it was the best decision. I'm sure in time she'll understand."

"I agree. I'm looking at the list of hotels. Most of them are pretty swanky. Can we afford it?"

"Just pick whichever one you want, especially one conveniently downtown with an indoor pool. This might help the kids weather the transition."

"All right. I love you and miss you."

"Love and miss you, too. See you sometime tomorrow."

After I hung up, I went to the door. Father Bourque was not out in the hall.

"Done with your call?" Sister Agatha asked from the kitchen. "I'll get Father; he's in his chapel."

I returned to my rocker. The fire was still burning bright and warm in the woodstove when the priest entered and reclaimed his seat. "Everything all right, Scott?"

"Yes, thank God. My wife and kids just arrived at the Boston airport. We're going to rendezvous tomorrow and then drive up to our cabin in Maine."

"That's right, you're now an unemployed clergyman, which frankly makes you conveniently free. But Scott, as I said, I understand the difficulties you're facing, so I never push, pull, or prod anyone to convert, though I fully believe all non-Catholics need to come home to the fullness of the Church."

"This touches on one of my key stumbling blocks. Over the years, I've known many Catholic football players who were anything but holy. I've also known a few Catholic priests, through ministerial associations, and again I've not been particularly impressed, present company excluded."

"You haven't played against me in football yet," he said smiling.

"On the other hand, I've known many very holy non-Catholic Christians, clergy and laity, who love Jesus and try to live holy lives.

Given all we've said before, that Christ intended salvation to come through His Church, I still struggle with the idea that there is a mandate for all Christians to become Roman Catholics. I've read that the Catholic Church still teaches 'no salvation outside the Church,' even though I've heard that many Catholics claim that the Second Vatican Council changed this. What is true, Reverend Bourque? What does the Church teach, and really, what difference does it make what's on a person membership form if it doesn't lead to holiness in real life?"

"It's interesting you ask this, because that's not far from a conversation I just had with Stephen. First. Let me set the foundation: *All* salvation, no matter how it comes, comes from Christ alone. As our Lord said, 'No one can come to the Father but by me.' At the same time—and Pope John Paul II makes this clear in his writings—that just as Christ redeemed the universe through His natural body alone, so now He continues His supernatural work, applying His redemption to human souls through His supernatural body alone, the Mystical Body of Christ. For this reason, therefore, all salvation that comes from Christ alone also comes through His Church.

"Now, there has always been two sides to the same coin on this matter of 'no salvation outside the Church,' though not always explained well or charitably. But rather than attempt a summary of the historical issues, let me basically explain what the Church means by this. First, this understanding of the Church as the one true channel of grace and salvation was never intended to be used as a cudgel of judgment. Catholics are never to pass judgment on whether someone else will or will not be saved. That is God's decision, based on His knowledge of a person's heart and His mercy."

"But I've found references in history books where Catholic popes and bishops have indeed used this as a cudgel of judgment."

"But in the context of that time period it was a warning to bring wandering Catholics back into the fold, not as a judgment against those outside the Church who had never been in the fold."

"What about those who have never heard? Are they condemned for not being in the Church even if they love Christ?"

"That's two different groups—non-Christians and non-Catholic Christians—but the answer is essentially the same for both: we don't judge anyone's salvation. We leave this to God, yet we have a responsibility to tell them the Gospel of Jesus Christ, to love them, pray for them, and invite them to come home to receive baptism and become adopted into the Body of Christ. This is why, for example, the great Catholic missionaries sacrificed their lives in bringing the good news to the invincibly ignorant Indians of North America.

"But there is something else which we Catholics believe that is crucially important," he said, once again accentuating his words with his pipe. "We believe that every single person has within their hearts the desire to know and love God. Remember the famous quote from St. Augustine's *Confessions*: 'Thou hast made us for Thyself, O Lord, and our hearts are restless until they find their rest in Thee'?[42] We believe that even the ignorant have in their hearts, in their consciences, a God-given seed of what is right and wrong, and God will hold them accountable and judge them according to how they live. Without baptism and the other sacramental graces, they are subject to the effects of original sin and lack the aid of grace and the Holy Spirit. They are on their own, and, as Jesus warned, 'Apart from me you can do nothing.' So the Church has always been committed to missions."

"But what about non-Catholic Christians who have been baptized and have surrendered their hearts to Jesus Christ? Who believe that by grace they have been born again?"

"We recognize that they are not held accountable for the schisms caused by the founders of their religious traditions, and, therefore, that God *can* by His mercy save them, according to the light they have received, accepted, and followed by grace. We cannot say, however, that God *does* save non-Catholic Christians, for to do this would mean to deny everything the Church has taught from the beginning about the meaning of the Church and her sacraments. To change 'God *can* save' to 'God *does* save every Christian, regardless of their Church tradition,' eventually leads us back to a "Jesus-and-me" individualism."

"So what about me, Reverend Bourque? I am a pastor—well, make that an unemployed pastor—with a family, and a wife who has no interest whatsoever in becoming Catholic!"

"May I ask how you know for certain where her heart is? Have you discussed this with her?"

My mind drifted to an image of Diane struggling on her own through Boston, dragging luggage, trying to keep Eddy and Deborah moving forward without getting distracted by all the gift shops. I felt a pang of guilt as I compared that frantic image with my present relaxed setting, and on top of it imagined how Diane would be reacting if she knew why I was meeting with this Catholic priest.

I brought myself back to the present. "My wife Diane was born and raised Catholic. I played pro ball with her brother Bruce who attended mass perfunctorily on the morning of big games. As she describes it, she *escaped* from her Catholic roots during high school like one being rescued from a fiery inferno. An interdenominational youth fellowship and its winsome, sandy-haired youth leader brought her not only to faith in Jesus but to an abhorrence for the church of her childhood. Once baptized again 'for the first time,'" I said, using my fingers to denote quotation marks, "she rejoiced in her new faith and freedom. It became her dream to be a pastor's wife, which she had to patiently keep on hold until my badly bruised football brain finally heard the call of God. She took to ministry quickly and loves it. I'm sure right now she's assuming this time of unemployment is merely temporary, that we'll regroup, start circulating my vitae, and soon be back in the pastoral saddle. I would be startled if she has any clue whatsoever of my leanings."

The priest nodded his head. "You know that I've met with many men in your situation, two of your best friends, and so you also know that there is no easy answer for this. Conversion can be difficult and complicated, as you know from what has happened to Jim Sarver, and possibly Stephen. Therefore, my main advice to you is to continue doing what you've always done: seek to follow Jesus faithfully, in everything you do; be uncompromising in your commitment to proclaim and live His truth; seek always to be obedient to how the Holy Spirit is leading you; and, most important of all, love your wife. I do believe that Christ is calling all of His children home to the Church, but I also believe He does this according to His own schedule, His own timetable. Conversion is always a work of grace, in which God opens our hearts and minds to His truth; it is not merely an intellectual awakening to new information."

The priest left his rocker, crossed to the shelf I had recently visited, and then returned.

"Therefore, Scott, I will pray for you and help you in any way I can. And, I will give you this."

"Oh, you don't have to do that. I was just—"

"Nonsense. I really can't think of a better book for you to read right now. Remember, regardless of all these theological and doctrinal gymnastics, you made a lifetime vow to God when you married your wife Diane. You may still be struggling with whether it's God's will for you to become Roman Catholic, but you and I know what God's will is concerning your marriage. Diane is God's gift to you. In your sacramental marriage—which I presume at this point—He made the two of you into one. I generally believe that He never desires that we flippantly set aside one covenant for another."

He crossed back to the window and opened the curtains. The winter sun was bright and warm through the glass, but the huddling pedestrians with their vapor trails told that the temperature was still below freezing.

"If I may give you a word of counsel, based on what you will read in that book of mine," he said as he returned to his seat. "You are now uniquely free. You are not in need of a job, due to your financial independence. So I would encourage you consider this firing as a providential gift from God. Take seriously the advice Jesus gave in His Sermon on the Mount: have no anxiety about tomorrow … be present in the now. Take this time to step back, to read, to pray, to discuss, to learn the fullness of faith protected, preserved, and proclaimed in the Catholic Church, and do it slowly. Don't be afraid to challenge everything, to compare. And in the process share what you learn with Diane. Since she may have some presumptions from her past that raise too many red flags for her to handle, you'll probably want to be cautious about where you are in your journey. On the other hand, you also may be surprised by how open she actually is, because grace may have been working on her heart, also. You might discuss with her, for example, the underlying problems of Congregationalism and Protestantism, and then, with her, step back into the Scriptures and the early Church Fathers to help her discover for herself the necessity of the Church, trusting the Spirit."

"Father Bourque?" The sister's voice came hesitantly through the door. "Your three o'clock appointment is here."

"Oh, yes, of course. Any news from the airport?"

The door opened. "His plane was delayed and is now scheduled to arrive around four o'clock. I've talked with Fred, who understands and is patiently waiting. He thinks, after they get through baggage claim, they should be here, barring traffic problems, between six thirty and seven."

"I see. That complicates everything." The priest paused to study the fire and puff his pipe. Then, "Sister Agatha, please come in." Once she was inside, standing beside me, he continued: "I have a very big favor to ask both of you. Sister Agatha, I hate to do this at such short notice, but could you get your helpers to provide a nice meal tonight here, say, around seven o'clock?"

"Glad to do it."

"For, say, seven people, for I'd like you to join us?"

"I better get started then," she exclaimed as she left.

"Scott, first are you free for dinner tonight?"

"Yes. I had hoped to find time to meet with Stephen."

"Stephen is to be released this afternoon from the hospital. Can you make every effort and insist that Sara bring Stephen here tonight for dinner?"

"I'll do my best."

"I'm quite sure they'll come, but most important of all, I need you to make sure Raeph comes. As you know, I have a meeting next with Raeph at three. I'll ask him myself to come, but I need you to promise to make sure, and I mean make sure, that he comes."

"May I ask why?"

"You'll need to trust me on this."

"Does that seven include a plate for Maeda, Raeph's newfound friend?"

"Maeda? Ah, that explains a few things. No, it doesn't. We'll need settings for eight," he yelled across the hall.

"Okay, I'll make sure he's here, but if he's your next appointment, maybe it's best I slip out a different way. He knows I met with you Tuesday night, but I'm not sure how he'll take seeing me leave just before you meet with him. Looks a bit too conspiratorial."

"Good idea. You can use the back entrance. First, let's pray."

I bowed my head, while he placed his hands on my shoulder. He prayed briefly, asking for God's guidance, especially for when Diane and I were reunited and had to deal with all this stuff. He then showed me the back door, and as I walked briskly out to the van, I was imagining a host of scenarios of what was about to happen back in that priest's study as former anti-Catholic zealot met, for the first time in private quarters, former-Lutheran-pastor-turned-Catholic-priest. I wished I could be eavesdropping. Given our newly developed friendship, however, I was quite certain that later I'd be getting the full skinny.

41

The overstuffed leather chairs, provided to ease his nervous impatience, were far more comfortable than the chrome and plastic ones at the church across the way. Raeph laughed at the contrast, fussing with the viselike grip of his collar. He had donned the best he had brought along: his sole navy blue blazer, last clean white shirt, and red tie, very patriotic. It clashed with his earthy brown pants, but it was the best he could do.

This time there was no life-sized mural of the resident pastor, but what hung in its place was far more disconcerting. A brightly colored portrait of a woman, he presumed the Virgin Mary, with a heart painted on her chest. The heart was pierced with many arrows, and Mary was pointing to it, as if to make sure you didn't miss the gore of her suffering. On another wall was a painting of Mary he recognized, called Our Lady of Guadalupe. Most of the Hispanic workers at the plant had one in their homes or lockers.

On the front wall between the windows was a large ornate crucifix. His crucified Lord was portrayed bent sideways, knees twisted, head fallen upon His chest. From the wound in His side, painted in vivid red, flowed the last of His lifeblood. Raeph had always assumed that the crucifix proved that Catholics only worshipped a dead Jesus, not a resurrected Lord, but Maeda had straightened him out the night before.

WHEN he asked her about the meaning of the crucifix that hung on her apartment wall, she explained the absurdity of what he had been taught. The one central underpinning belief of the Catholic faith, which they proclaim with gusto at Easter, is "He's alive! He is risen indeed!" To deny the Resurrection is to make a sham of everything else. Christianity and the Church would never have existed one day without a crucified and risen Savior.

"Then why so many crucifixes?" he inquired. "Every Catholic I've ever known had one in their living room."

"Because it reminds us of what He suffered for our sins and how we must accept suffering as our share in His suffering."

"What was that last part?" he asked, shrinking slightly as if afraid of what she might answer.

"Raeph, I'm sure you know your Bible far better than I. Don't you remember all those verses about how we are heirs of the Kingdom 'provided we suffer'? How St. Paul rejoiced in his sufferings because somehow in his flesh he was completing what was lacking in the afflictions of Christ Jesus, for the sake of the Church? Don't ask me to explain all this, but the Church calls it redemptive suffering. Remember when somewhere St. Paul talks about how when one member suffers we all suffer because we are together members of the one Body of Christ? Somehow when I suffer, if I prayerfully accept it as a gift of God and offer it back up to Him in union with the suffering of His Son our Savior, it helps others, it … well, that gets us into another topic I'm sure you take umbrage with, Purgatory."

"I don't understand any of this, Maeda," Raeph admitted, rising to pace. In the past, he would have ridiculed all of this, demanding that Christ's death on the Cross was sufficient and complete. *"It is finished!" Christ had said. What can our meaningless suffering add to the infinite worth of the sacrifice of Christ?* But he couldn't say that to this woman to whom he was losing his heart. He could see how much this meant to her. And besides, he had no alternate explanation for that verse in Colossians.

LONG into the night, the two had sat or paced in Maeda's living room discussing many of his questions and concerns about her Catholic faith. More than a dozen times, he'd been forced to restrain his knee-jerk tendency to attack anything Catholic—the first time in his life he'd ever been able to do this—but this, of course, was because he'd been with Maeda.

And then he remembered, as he sat there in the waiting area of the Catholic church offices, under the gaze of what he had always considered oppressive Catholic idolatry, that he had also restrained himself in the face of Scott's guarded and sometimes awkward attempts to introduce Catholic ideas into their breakfast conversations. *Something has been happening to me*, he reflected.

He glanced at his watch: 3:35. He got up and moved toward the front door, but pulled his hand back from the knob.

"I'm not running away this time," he muttered as he regained his seat. "For Maeda."

A door opened somewhere down the hall, followed by receding footsteps and the closing of another distant door. Then footsteps came in his direction. He straightened himself up, checking his tie and buttoning his coat. *I hate this monkey suit!*

"Mr. Timmons," said the nun he'd seen from a distance on the first day in town and last night in the crowd, "we're so sorry to keep you waiting, but Father Bourque can see you now."

"Thank you, but it was he that wanted to see me."

"I understand. Please come this way." She motioned for him to follow, then preceded him down the hall. Along both walls he was confronted by countless photographs of priests, nuns, and parishioners, elementary school children, basketball squads, all telling the history of St. Francis de Sales Parish. It was one particularly faded photo, however, showing the bearded, stiff profile of the first priest of the parish, that gave him pause. The priest did not appear happy or particularly friendly. *What am I getting myself into!*

"Can I get you a coffee?"

"No thank you, miss, I mean, Sister, ah, I mean—"

"That's okay," she said with a warm smile. "Father Bourque is inside waiting."

Raeph entered the dimly lit study. The priest was sitting in his rocker, smoking a pipe, staring into the flames of a wood-burning stove. When he noticed Raeph's entrance, he stood and motioned him over. "Come on in, Mr. Timmons. Can I call you Raeph?"

"Of course." He sat down in the other rocker, and then it struck him that for the first time in his life he was sitting alone in a small enclosed room with a Catholic priest—and unable to run. The flames dancing through the glass doors of the stove brought to mind the destiny of anyone caught in the clutches of the Antichrist pope of Rome, that is, as warned in those anti-Catholic, comic book tracts that had fed his ignorant prejudices. He had matured as through fire, however, and saw those flames now as a reminder of where anyone goes whose life is built on fear and ignorance.

"I want to thank you, Raeph, for helping out last night. Your quick action as well as your information to the police helped a lot of people. Are you doing all right after this morning's confrontation with the police and the accused?"

"Yes, I'm fine. I'm sorry, though, for any part I may have played in what they did." He found it difficult to find a comfortable position in the rocker. Leaning back felt too casual, sitting forward too intense, so he commenced to rock, which made him think of sitting on someone's front porch sipping lemonade. So he stopped himself, feet flat on the floor, board rigid.

"Raeph, I don't hold you responsible. I'm well aware of what many in this town feel about this Church, and about me. I understand because I was a Lutheran pastor before I converted and became a priest." Then with a smile he added, "But just because I was a Lutheran pastor doesn't mean I understand the Reverend Dr. Steinitz, either."

This brought a grin to Raeph's nervous expression.

"What I also don't understand, though, is what you were doing at Mass last night? Given your background and beliefs, I would have thought that that would be the last place you would have wanted to be seen. Unless, you were suspecting that something might happen."

Raeph relaxed back into the rocker before he responded, rocking slowly, studying the priest and then the fire. "I came last night half because Scott 'double-dog-dared' me, as we used to say as kids, and half because I was curious. I'd forgotten that Curt Jonas had mentioned Wednesday night until after everything happened." He looked back into the fire, then said, "I'm still a bit surprised myself that I came. So much has changed over just a few days."

"If you don't mind my asking, Raeph, if you've never been here in Jamesfield before, how did you end up at that meeting Tuesday night?"

A smile spread across Raeph's face before he answered. "Running away from you, I guess. I was supposed to be here with Reverend Turner and Mrs. LaPointe, you know, but, well, I chickened out and landed at the first Christian church I stumbled upon. One thing led to another, and Pastor Guilford invited me to attend his meeting."

"But why would he do that, a perfect stranger?"

"I had asked to see him. I … wanted his help … to help stop you from talking Scott into becoming Catholic the way you apparently did Reverend LaPointe and others. That's what I also told them at the meeting."

"So what do you think now, Raeph? Do you still think I'm the devil's advocate trying to lure good Christians to their doom?"

"No, of course not," he answered nervously, diverting his eyes.

"Raeph, I realize that you're here now because I pressured you. It turns out, however, that the main reason for my invitation is a bit delayed, so I have no particular agenda for our time at the moment. I suppose you can go if you're uncomfortable here. I only insist, if possible, that you come back tonight for dinner. Scott, Sara, and Stephen are all coming, kind of a celebration for Stephen's recovery. I'd really like you to be here, though. It's very important."

"Why is it so important?"

The priest fidgeted with his pipe, attempting to rekindle its flame. "I'm sure, with all that has happened this week, with why you came to Jamesfield, that all who are coming would want you here and would be disappointed if you weren't. Promise?"

"I suppose. I don't think—oh wait, I did make other plans." He paused to reconsider. "But, can I bring someone with me?"

"Miss Maeda McLeary?"

"How'd you know?" he said with a start.

"Let's just say I guessed. I saw you two together last night, and heard your concerns for her welfare. Of course, please bring her."

"Then I'm sure we can come."

"Good. Now, what would you like to do right now?"

Raeph rose from the rocker and started to pace.

"Maybe it's good that I talk with you. You see, my life is pretty much a mess right now. I'm unemployed. Since my youngest son left home, and my wife Patty and our oldest son both died, I have no connections anywhere. My primary commitment is to Jesus my Lord. I love Him and would do anything He tells me. The big problem is that I come from a strong anti-Catholic background—that's the primary reason I'm here in this town. I've come to realize, though, from all that's happened this week, that so much of my faith was built around my fear and hatred of the Catholic Church. I'm ashamed of this, but what's most complicated is that, well, I think I'm falling love with a devout Irish Catholic woman."

"Maeda is a fine woman, Raeph, and, yes, a very devout Catholic. I wouldn't be surprised if she hasn't considered becoming a nun."

"A nun? Maeda is thinking about becoming a nun?" Raeph yanked at his tie, loosening it considerably, and unbuttoned his collar.

"I'm not saying that this is what she is planning to do. She's never told me this. I just know, from our conversations and her service, especially to the widows of this parish, how devoted she is to our Lord. Do you know whether she returns your feelings?"

Raeph studied the priest to determine the tone of his question, then answered, "Things have moved much faster than either one of us could have expected. When I came here on Monday, the last thing on my mind was finding another wife. But then Tuesday, I met Maeda. We've only been together a few times, but, well, yes, it does seem like she feels the same way. We both think that God has led us together."

"So what about her Catholicism? I can assure you, my friend, that this is an essential part of who she is, and I would dread to see her married to someone who hates this part of her."

Raeph glanced at the books on the shelf and had a déjà vu feeling of being back in the library of the Widow's Mite. "I agree with you, completely. A week ago there was no opening in my heart for Catholics or the Catholic Church. But because of everything that has happened this week, getting to know Scott and Maeda and you, and seeing those strange anti-Catholics through new eyes, and especially being confronted by Walter's wife, Helen, I was able to see myself through new eyes. Reverend Bourque," he said, turning back, "I really am sorry for the hatred that for so long has filled my life."

Returning to his rocker, he went on, "After lunch today, before I came here, I stopped by my hotel room. I was going to work out at the gym, but instead I pulled out the good old Gideon's Bible. Like most Evangelicals, I'm a pretty good student of the Bible, but I don't always listen to what I read. I looked up all the verses I could remember where Jesus emphasizes the need to love and not fear or hate, and they hit me like a brick."

"Raeph, my friend, don't beat yourself up over this. We're all tainted by the same human condition. We all have the stain of hatred and sin in our hearts."

"I know, and thankfully I also looked up all those verses about forgiveness and starting over, about forgetting what lies behind, confessing our sins, and being a new creation in Christ. Reverend Bourque, on my walk over here from the hotel, it struck me: everything that has happened to me during this past year, and especially this past week, has been a gift from God to drive hatred from my heart, to help me love like I've never loved before, without prejudice, like Patty always wanted me to do." Raeph dropped his head into his hands. "She used to warn me about my anti-Catholic rants, but I never listened. She was right, and it was my hatred that drove Walter to his grave." Raeph ran his hands through his hair and then sat back in his rocker.

"What you've shared is the overflow of a truly contrite heart, my friend. All this has come to you by grace—through your love for Jesus. But you stand at the door of far more grace than you have ever imagined."

"I guess I don't know what you mean. What I do know is that meeting Maeda had a big part in changing my heart. I could have learned to love and treat Catholics with the equal respect I should give all people, regardless of race, color, or creed. But meeting Maeda— finding my heart drawn to someone who I discover is a devout Catholic, and who lovingly accepts me, knowing what I believe—that has changed me."

"I can assure you that her loving acceptance of you is a direct outpouring of her Catholic faith. She is who she is partially from her knowledge and practice of Catholic teachings and devotions, but mostly from the graces she receives through the sacraments. She is being saved by grace through her active faith. She confesses her sins regularly and strives to live in holiness by the graces she has received. She receives Christ in the Eucharist with great devotion and conviction, and again strives to live out the graces she has received. She comes often to pray before the Blessed Sacrament—in fact she comes twice a week at one in the morning for an hour of adoration. She often accompanies Sister Agatha on her visits, even to the daughter of that man who desecrated this beautiful church. All this and more gives Maeda what she's got; it's made her who she is; apart from this, she would be nothing. And it's through all these things that, by grace through faith, she has grown in union with Jesus."

Holding his hands aloft as if in surrender, Raeph admitted, eyes wide, "I don't understand any of that. It just all sounds to me like works righteousness."

"No, Raeph. I said what I said carefully. It's not for a result or reward that Maeda does these things, as if God now owes her a payment for her works. Rather, it's through these things that she lives her faith. Too often Protestants understand faith as only a mental assent to the truths about God: accept Jesus with your mind and heart for salvation, regardless of what one does with one's body. But this borders on a heresy called Gnosticism: the spirit is good, the body is bad. As Catholics, we recognize that as human persons created in the image of God, we are body and soul, one complete being, and faith must be an expression of our entire being: what we think and what we do. I'm sure you remember what St. James wrote: 'For as the body apart from the spirit is dead, so faith apart from works is dead.'[43] James wasn't merely giving a counter response to St. Paul's seeming emphasis against works. Rather, James was emphasizing the union of body and spirit, faith and works. Maeda freely gives everything in her life to God, her devotions, her service, her sufferings, freely without demanding anything in return. When a person does this, then they can grow in grace and in love."

Raeph stood again to pace. "I just don't know, Reverend Bourque. I really know so little about what Catholics believe. I've been corrected on a few things I'd learned wrong, by Scott, Helen, Maeda, and you this morning, but I've never, so far as I know, read anything by a Roman Catholic, just, I suppose, books by anti-Catholics or ex-Catholics, like Reverend Harmond—who actually just returned to the Catholic Church."

"I heard about that," the priest admitted. "I once debated him. He was quite the showman, but I'm not surprised to hear of his reversion."

Raeph slowly reclaimed his seat. "I'm not like Reverend LaPointe. I can't even imagine becoming Roman Catholic, but yet, now, frankly, I don't want to let Maeda slip through my grasp."

Father Bourque leaned forward in his rocker planting both feet on the floor and his elbows on his knees. "Raeph. It has always been my policy never to press anyone to become Catholic. I believe that the truth of the Catholic faith is convincing enough that once a person takes the time to examine it, prayerfully with an open heart, it will bring him home."

"But there are so many things that Catholics believe that, frankly, I can't stomach, especially that Jesus is truly present in the wafer of bread or that the wine truly becomes His blood."

"Raeph, you believe the Bible to be inspired and inerrant? Then, didn't Jesus say in the Last Supper, 'This is my body … this is my blood'?"

"But He also said elsewhere 'I am the door' or 'I am the vine.'"

"You're right, Raeph, He did, and many, many people believe this answer ends the discussion. But, for now—and I hope we can discuss this more thoroughly later—it's the contexts of these statements that make all the difference. I encourage you to look up all the 'I am' statements, and prayerfully consider: How did Jesus' hearers react to what He said? You will see that the point of John chapter six, where Jesus claims to be the Bread of Heaven and that we must eat His Body and drink His Blood, is that every one of His hearers took Him literally. Even some of His disciples were so offended that they left Him."

"But anyone can see that it remains just bread and wine."

"Raeph, this has been the constant charge since the beginning of the Church, that our senses are the measure of what is true. This is one of the reasons Jesus was nailed to the Cross because those who saw Him could not believe His words that He was also the divine Son of God.

"This, however, requires a much longer discussion," he said, slapping his pipe into his palm to loosen its contents before emptying it in the woodstove. "But only if you want it. Here's what I'm promising you, my friend. I will pray for you and be here for you whenever you want to talk, especially if you and Maeda want to talk with me together.

"Now, though, it sounds like you might need a job. I'm presuming that Stephen will be moving out East to rejoin his wife and sons, so I'm pretty sure his old job at the hardware is still vacant, if you're interested in at least starting there. As for Maeda, she caught me this morning before I came to meet with you at breakfast. She was on her way to Mass and told me of her decision to quit her job under Pastor Guilford. I'm guessing that Sister Agatha might be able to find something she can do to earn a little, at least until you two figure everything out." He offered Raeph the hand of friendship. Raeph at first hesitated, but then took it with a grin.

The priest rose cautiously due to the aches of age, and said, "Remember tonight. It's important that you come, and please, bring Maeda."

"We'll be here."

At the door, the priest asked, "Raeph, can I have a word of prayer with you before you go?"

"That would be fine."

The priest laid his left hand on Raeph's shoulder, and raising his right in the form of blessing, prayed aloud, "Heavenly Father, may You shower this man with Your mercy and forgiveness, help him by Your grace to love just as he has discovered he must, guide him and Maeda to know Your will for their lives together, and may You pour out a special measure of Your joy into his life this evening, we pray, in the name of the Father and of the Son and of the Holy Spirit. Amen."

But Raeph was not ready to quit. He raised his own right hand to hold the priest's. "And, Lord, thank You for this priest, this new friend. Help me to accept him fully as a brother in Christ, and cleanse my heart of all prejudice, in Jesus' name, Amen."

And the priest said, "A–*men!*"

ᘓ 42 ᘔ

U pon entering the hospital, Sara made her way through the lobby
toward the hall of elevators, but then sidetracked to the front
desk.

"Excuse me."

"Yes, dearie, how can I help you?" The elderly volunteer set aside
her book of crosswords.

"I'm here to pick up Stephen LaPointe. Is he still scheduled for
release and still in the same room?"

"Let me check." She focused for a few moments on the computer
monitor, her face aglow. Sara could almost read the answer in the
reflection on the woman's thick trifocals.

"Yes, room 5, third floor, and he's still scheduled for release."

"Thank you."

She resumed her path, which brought her past the gift shop.
She almost made it by, but changed her mind and ducked in. The
selection was not extensive. Shelves of stuffed animals, fake flower
arrangements, porcelain figurines, games, magazines, paperbacks,
plus a limited offering of over-the-counter drugs, toiletries, and candy.

"Excuse me," she asked the teenager behind the counter, who was
chewing with mouth half open a golfball-sized wad of gum. "I don't
see any gum for sale."

"Oh, yeah. Well, they decided not to sell gum anymore, 'cause
kids kept leaving wads everywhere, underneath tables and chairs, or
dropping it on the carpet. A bear to get out."

"But—?"

"Yes?" The girl waited attentively, looking every bit like a happy
cow enjoying the afternoon remnants of breakfast.

"Oh, nothing." Sara wandered slowly back out into the hall. Near
the elevators, a wall placard detailed the locations of everything
within the hospital, and Sara noticed particularly the cafeteria on the
first floor.

She had not eaten well at lunch. She had ordered a vegetable soup
and some kind of chicken salad pita sandwich, but had hardly touched
either. She was still hoping they could beg out of that dinner invitation

tonight at the parish. Sure, they had become friends, but she wanted more time alone with Stephen.

The left elevator door opened. Inside stood a white-clad woman with an armful of linen.

"Going up?" the woman said, with some kind of European accent.

"Ah, no, no, to the basement," Sara said, as she stepped back.

"Suit yourself."

Sara pushed the button again, and the same elevator door opened, revealing the same woman with her linen.

"You need to wait a moment, Miss, to let this one pass before you push the button."

"Oh, that's okay. I think I'm going up after all."

"Suit yourself."

Sara stepped inside.

"Which floor then, Miss?"

"Ah, the third, please."

"Okay," she pushed the button. "Case you didn't know, the main floor in this hospital is the second floor, not the first. Confusing, but hospitals are just that way, you know. Sometimes it's just easier to walk up those stairs over to the right than to wait for these slow elevators, don't you know?"

"Thank you, I'll remember that next time."

"It's a bit brisk outside, but still a fine, clear winter's day."

"Yes, it is."

"I was just telling me husband this morning ..."

The elevator door opened.

" ... how much like home it was feeling ..."

"Thank you, have a nice day," Sara said, as she escaped out into the hall.

" ... don't you know?" The voice faded as the doors closed.

Before her was the nurses' station. Down the hall to her left were patient rooms and a family waiting area. To her right more patient rooms, including that of her husband. She paused, stone still.

"May I help you?" the nurse behind the desk asked.

"What was that?"

"Do you need help?"

"Oh, no thank you, I'm sorry, I know where I'm going."

She walked down the hall to her left and entered the family lounge. Thankfully, she found it empty, for she wanted a moment to sit. The television had been left on with some afternoon soap. She searched the coffee table before her, strewn with magazines, for the remote. Once found, she returned the room to peaceful silence, so she could sit and reflect.

Their long-awaited reunion earlier that day had gone far better than either had expected. There was even a welcome aura of self-deprecating humor as they each shared the joys and mistakes of the past year. The grace-filled union of their marriage had not been broken, only temporarily parted by the island of their miscommunications, each projecting upon the other the weaknesses of their insecurities. This had all been fed by the inner voices of the spiritual battle, and to some extent each had failed; each had listened too long and hard, feeding their doubts with fantasies. But reunited that morning, they had sat, hand in hand, cheeks streaked with tears and aching for joy.

Yet, there were still barriers to overcome.

She found with embarrassment that on Tuesday evening, when he was driving south, he had called the apartment, and of all things, Frank had answered the phone.

"STEPHEN," she had said, so ashamed, angry at her own stupidity, "I'm so sorry that happened and how confusing it must have sounded. Yes, that was Frank, my first husband. It's all so complicated, but not what you might think."

"I wasn't sure what to think," he replied. "I could never get through or even leave a message." He slowly pulled his hand away to straighten the blanket covering his bare legs and take up his coffee. She wanted to scream with contrition, but instead tried to explain.

"Honey, I now see how the devil was using one coincidence after another to bring Frank back into my life, to muddy the waters of my despair. When I decided to go back to school, it made sense to go where William had been accepted, at North Shore University. The first day I stopped in to register, I bumped into Frank. I had forgotten that he was a chemistry professor there. He bought me coffee, and when he found out I was looking for an apartment where the boys and I could live together, he said there happened to be one vacant in the apartment building he and his wife owned along the ocean. It was hard to pass up. A really beautiful spot, convenient to the university, and he gave us a great deal."

She could tell that her husband wasn't taking this well, so she reached over, gathered his hands into hers, and said, "Please, honey, hear me out."

He nodded, giving her his attention.

She continued. "So, we moved in and all was fine, until I learned that he and his wife had recently split up. I don't know the reasons. But, needless to say, he and I at times fed on each other's sorrow. He started hanging around the apartment, playing chess with Daniel, and, I admit, it was getting confusing and awkward to William. There have been times, not knowing where you were or what you were thinking, that I felt tempted to seek his comfort, but honestly, Stephen," with this she leaned closer to look deep into his eyes, "I never gave in. Frank and I have no relationship, no tenderness, no intimacy, nothing. Even though there were many angry, bitter days, I never gave up on *us*."

He squeezed her hands and nodded with a smile. "I believe you, dear. Sure, the voices were working on me, also, during our separation. There were times I wondered what I would do if you refused to have me back, if you had already decided to move on, but I never really gave in. And it wasn't only that I wouldn't give up on God; I just couldn't believe that your heart could turn so quickly."

"It didn't, dear, and it never will. I love you."

"Me, too."

And once again they had embraced.

ON top of magazines strewn on the table before her now in the waiting room was one devoted to maternity. On the cover was the picture of a happy family, a father standing behind his wife who was holding their newborn baby boy. An empathetic smile conquered Sara's sad face.

"We'll be a happy family again," she said aloud. "We just have to!"

She rose and left the room. At the nurse's station, she asked, "I'm here to pick up my husband, Reverend, I mean, Mr. Stephen LaPointe."

"That would be room 5, down to your right. He's all ready, checked out, and waiting."

"Do you mean he's not in his room?" She asked, her face a panic.

"No, no, he's there, just waiting anxiously for your arrival."

"Oh, yes, of course. Thank you."

She turned slowly and began making her way down the hall to her right. The doors of most of the rooms she passed were open, each revealing its own unique glimpse of humanity. A family gathered, sitting and standing, around the bed of an unseen patient. A woman reclining, reading a book. Another angrily trying to get the television remote to work. A doctor attempting to calm a crying woman. A mother ushering her anxious child to the bathroom.

Then room 5. She paused outside. *Why do I feel like I'm on my way to the guillotine?*

Across the hall, recessed into the wall, was an encased fire extinguisher. BREAK GLASS IN CASE OF FIRE. She caught her reflection in the glass. She looked quite presentable, but worried. Her brow was creased and the lines of her frown told her age.

She forced herself to smile, and there saw the woman she knew her husband still loved. She turned and entered the room.

"Sara, thank God; I was getting afraid you'd changed your mind," he said with a smile.

"No, darling, just a few uncontrollable delays. Are you ready?"

"Is this your wife, Stephen?" said the patient in the other bed.

"Yes, of course, I'm sorry. Sara, meet Mr. Christopher Ratlin. He's a member of St. Francis de Sales Parish. I had no idea it was him snoring next to me until this afternoon."

"Sorry about that," he said laughing, "they've had me so sedated, my life has been nothing but dreams for three days."

"We've played cards together at a few K of C banquets."

"Well, Stephen, like I said, it's good to have you back. We were all wondering. Anyway, it's also good to see your injuries aren't keeping you in this place. I'm afraid my sentence is indefinite."

"I'll keep you in prayer, Chris, and if I'm still around, I'll stop back in to see you, maybe for a game of Rummy."

"Oh, are you leaving again?"

"I'm assuming I'm going out East to rejoin my family," Stephen said, with a glance at his wife.

"Then, we'll miss you, my friend."

"You take care." They shook hands.

"And nice to meet you, Mrs. LaPointe."

"Likewise, Mr. Ratlin."

"Ready to go, Mr. LaPointe?" The voice of an orderly pushing a wheelchair drew their attention.

"Yes, but I don't need that. As you can see, I'm walking just fine."

"Hospital rules."

"Oh, all right. Honey, can you get that bag? It's all I brought with me, I guess. I'm assuming all my luggage is still in the Wagoneer?"

"Sister Agatha said they got everything out, and it's waiting for you at the rectory."

"That was nice of them."

"They're that way, you know," said Mr. Ratlin, "Always looking out for the sheep. Even lost ones."

Stephen smiled back as he took his place in the unnecessary wheeled transport. "Take care, Chris."

"God bless. And you, too, Mrs. LaPointe."

She nodded as she followed the orderly and her husband down the hall and into the elevators. Stephen and the orderly were carrying on some conversation, but she was distracted. When they reached the main floor and exited, Sara lagged behind. She wanted to do this before they left. There was the cafeteria, or the front lobby, neither was the perfect setting, too many casual ears and prying eyes. But before she could decide, they were at the front revolving doors.

"Here you go, Mr. LaPointe."

"Thank you, Jeeves," Stephen said, with a haughty lilt, as he cautiously extracted himself from the wheelchair. "You can retrieve your tip at the front desk."

"And a good day to you, Mrs. LaPointe."

She nodded her response as the orderly turned and wheeled away out of sight.

"Why don't you wait while I go get the van for you," Stephen said. "Where are you parked?"

"Oh, no, please, Stephen, I know you're feeling better, but I'll get it. It will only take a moment."

Sara walked out into the cold, carrying her husband's small bag of belongings, out to the van. As she started it up and drove around to the front entrance, she berated herself, for still she had not told her husband.

The one-mile drive down Main to the hotel was unusually congested, but she and her husband had lots of small talk to fill the time, he about his genealogical discoveries in Canada and she about her studies. At the hotel, they went directly to their room. Once inside, they were in each other's arms.

LATER, while Stephen went to the vending area to retrieve some ice and buy a diet soda for Sara, she glanced at herself in the mirror. Priming her hair and straightening her robe, she berated herself, *So when will I tell him? Am I going to put it off one more time?!*

She sat back on the bed, propped up by pillows. Upon his return, Stephen made up some iced drinks, and asked, "What time is that dinner?"

"Seven."

"Sure you don't mind going? We don't have to if you prefer not to."

"No, it will be good. Especially since we've already had some 'quality' time together." She smiled, and he leaned over to kiss her once again.

Stephen grabbed the television remote and was about to surf the stations, when Sara said, "Honey, can we wait on that a minute? There's something else I want to talk to you about."

"Sure, Sara, what is it?" He sat down on the edge of the bed, turned in her direction, the bandages on his forehead creased with worry.

The moment she had wanted had come, but now how to begin? She cradled her soda.

"There is something I need to say to you, something that I did long ago, before I met you, that I should have told you years ago. I've often wanted to, but it seemed the longer I put it off, the more difficult it got. I guess I've always put it off because I was afraid, afraid you'd be ashamed of me, and reject me."

Stephen started to speak, but she raised her hand. "Please, dear, I need to get this out."

She set her soda aside, folded her hands in her lap, and then launched in. "When you and I were dating, I told you about my divorce from Frank, but I didn't tell you everything. I was afraid to, because of who you were and because you were training to become a minister. I'm still terribly ashamed to tell you, but before he and I got married, I became pregnant. When I first found out, I had conflicting feelings. You remember my radical feminist past. Part of me wanted nothing to stand in the way of my career. But another part, the mother in me, wanted to accept and love that baby. Everyone close to me, however, especially Frank and even my parents, insisted that I get an abortion," she paused in silence to study her husband's eyes and winsome smile, which had not altered throughout her story, "and I agreed—I didn't just relent or give in. Honey, I chose to do it."

She dropped her eyes to regain composure.

"Sara—"

Again she stopped him with her hand. "I was afraid to do it alone, though, so that's why Frank and I got married. I tried to love him; I even tried to change my mind about the baby growing in my womb. But after a few months, I gave in and gave up."

"Sara—"

"No, I need to finish this." With this, she got out of bed to sit in a chair facing him. "I went to a clinic in South Boston. All that I remember about my visit are the Catholic picketers, with their grotesque signs and rosaries." As she said this, she noticed his rosary lying on the dresser. She returned her attention to his welcoming eyes. "They called me a murderer, demanding that I change my mind. I now know that my impression of their actions was twisted by my self-centered feminist anger. I ignored them, and with even more nerve, went inside. Almost exactly a year to the day before I met you, I killed my first baby. Stephen, I'm so sorry, but I did it." She started to cry.

"Sara, darling—" he said, reaching out to her, but once again she stopped him with her raised hands.

"The procedure went like clockwork, I thought, but as you know it had repercussions. William's birth went fine, but over the years, I've seen various doctors for abnormal bleeding, though I never told you why. Then when Daniel was born, we were told I could never have any more children. The doctor said it was because of some previous procedure, of which I claimed ignorance. I lied. I always wanted to tell you, but I was ashamed, because, even though I knew that Jesus forgave me, I never really forgave myself."

She grabbed a tissue from the box on the nightstand, and after wiping her eyes, she continued, "This is the reason I ran away from you. I was afraid that if you insisted we become Catholic, I would have to revisit my divorce and admit the abortion. I couldn't face it."

"Sara, please, can I say something?" he said, grasping her hands. "Here, sit beside me." She rose to sit next to him on the bed, and he took her into his arms. After soothing her, he said, "I see now that I'm the one who really needs to apologize, for you see, I guessed all of this years ago."

"You did?!"

"Yes. There were bits of evidence that made me suspect, like your silence about why a radical feminist would get married in the first place. And then why your first marriage ended so quickly. But especially there was that charred receipt in the attic you were trying to hide years ago. Do you remember?"

"Yes, but I didn't think—"

"All that was left were the words, 'STON FAMILY CLIN', but I guessed almost instantly, because I knew the South Boston Family Clinic quite well. You see, darling, I used to go down there as a seminarian. I was one of those picketers, though I stayed way clear of those strange Catholics. You say you went there about a year before we met? Well, who knows, I may have been there in that crowd. I may have been one of those begging you to change your mind."

This brought a kind of tearful smile to her face.

"Then later when we got the news after Daniel's birth, I called the doctor."

"You did?" she said again, wiping her eyes.

"Yes, and he said the results were consistent with a woman who'd had an abortion, which confirmed my suspicions. You see, I thought I understood your hesitancy to tell: your sense of guilt counteracted by your growing understanding of forgiveness in Jesus Christ. I figured, even though you hadn't told me, that you had confessed all this to Jesus. If so, then your slate was clean, and if He forgave you, then who was I to dredge it all back up. I felt the best way for me to show my love to you, was to forget it, to just let it pass."

She grasped him in the tightest hug she had given in years. She was trying to speak but couldn't. After a moment, she relaxed her grip, and just leaned against him, dabbing her tears.

"Sara, I forgave you long ago for this. I'm sorry I didn't let you know. I just thought—"

"I know; I'm slowly realizing how difficult I can be. But Sister Agatha helped me."

"How was that?"

"Tuesday, she and I had a nice long talk. She answered a whole host of questions I had about Catholicism, but mainly she told me about, well, the mistakes of her past. When we were done talking, I knew there was no reason for me to fear becoming a Catholic, if that's what you've decided for us." She stopped, with a questioning glance up into his eyes.

"Sara, I know how confusing these last months must have been for you and the boys, and I'm so sorry. But these last few months have helped me see that there are two things I must do. I'm just not sure how to do them both: Yes, I'm convinced, I must become Catholic because Jesus Christ intended there to be only one Church, but I will not convert until either you convert with me—and only if you are equally convinced—or until you give me your complete, unconditional permission."

"What about your call to the ministry?" she asked, not with anxiety but love. "Your ordination? What will we do?"

"I'll explain more later, darling, but if and when I become a Catholic, I will enter the Church enthusiastically as a layman. I'll figure out how I can support us in some secular job, while you finish your schooling, if you like. I'll offer my services to the local parish, wherever we decide to live, but I'll only serve if asked by the priest or bishop. If in time a bishop discerns that I have a call to the priesthood, I will only consider it if you are equally open."

"But what about your being married? Aren't Catholic priests supposed to be celibate?"

"The Church allows some exception to the rule for married former non-Catholic ministers, but what I'm saying is that this is not my concern right now. The only important thing right now is that we are back together—that is, if you'll accept me back?"

"Of course, dear." And they were once again in each other's arms.

43

Scott Turner's Narrative

The sunset was particularly beautiful that evening. Though the winter's solstice had long since waned and the eve of spring was but a month away, the darkness of the night sky still rushed in far quicker than many an inhabitant of central New Hampshire cared to stomach. It had been a difficult winter. Maybe not as unbearable as some that many with gray hair bragged nostalgically about to their grandkids, but long, cold, and deep in snow nonetheless.

Jamesfield was bright with a festival of lights. The chamber of commerce, hoping to tempt those on their way north to tarry a bit for the benefit of the local merchants, had voted unanimously to invent, shall we say, an historic event to justify a lingering celebration. A fictitious Indian maiden with her fictitious pilgrim lover had plunged to their doom off a fictitious cliff along the nearby quite real river, three hundred years ago that very day. They were escaping the unyielding prejudice of both sets of parents into a better world, and the town would now celebrate this long-lost legend with a downtown festival, concerts, hayrides out to the only cliff that could fit the bill, and of course sales in every store.

Further from the town center, the lights that flooded the exterior of St. Francis de Sales Church shone no less brightly than any other night of the year. When we mortals wake up with a major blemish on our face, we do everything possible to hide it, and if nothing else works, we call in sick and stay at home, until we feel presentable. But St. Francis, with its shattered pane and degrading epithet, glowed without embarrassment. It wasn't parading its scars, just not hiding them.

In the bright light, on the front step of the building adjacent to the church, I stood alone, buffeting myself against the cold, my frozen breath hanging about me like an aura, enlarged by each seasonal cough. My focus was primarily toward the town, but occasionally I glanced around in all directions. I'd certainly been wrong before.

The door of the rectory opened, and Father Bourque stuck his head out and asked, "Any sign of them yet?"

"No, nothing, but he said they'd come."

"What about Fred?"

"No, not him neither."

"Well, you really don't need to stay out here, Scott. It's freezing."

"I know, but I wanted to greet them. I'll give them five more minutes, and if they're not here by then, you may need to come and carry me in to thaw out."

"Just don't overdo it, my friend."

The priest closed the door and left me to my lonesome. A car of revelers passed: a convertible Buick overflowing with summer-clad fraternity types, probably from the local branch college. Distorted by inebriation, they presumed anyone watching would admire their manly fortitude. Hopefully in the morning they would have the maturity to recognize their stupidity.

Standing in the freezing cold, waiting for those I'm sure would come, knowing that my waiting had no influence whatsoever on the time of their arrival, I wondered how different my stubbornness was to those bare-chested fools passing by, braced with liquor against the elements. I decided I could at least benefit from their example, so I abandoned my post and went inside for a glass of wine.

The rectory kitchen was a flurry of activity. I mentioned later to Father Bourque that it looked like the chaos of a dozen hamsters scurrying helter-skelter in a cramped cage, but he corrected me. To him the cadence, movements, and concatenation of the eight women was reminiscent of Knute Rockne's 1924 undefeated backfield. When Sister Agatha made the calls, she apparently had suggested "meal plan number seven," and within the hour the ingredients had been purchased, the volunteer cooks had huddled, and now in less than eight minutes the first course would be ready for consumption.

"Are you sure Father will want wine?" one of the ladies questioned. "It is Lent, you know."

"Betty, it's already been opened and served. Father and Reverend Turner are nearly through their first glass."

"Any word yet, Sister?" Father Bourque asked from the study.

"No, Father. Fred doesn't own a cell phone, and he's probably too anxious about being late to stop and call."

"It's almost seven, though. Well, nothing can be done."

I must say, the Merlot tasted especially good that evening. My limbs were nearly thawed from waiting outside for Raeph and his beloved, when, just like the proverbial watched pot that never boils, not long after I came in, they arrived.

A knock was heard at the front door. "Can someone get that?" Sister Agatha cried from the kitchen.

"Yes, of course." The priest left the study, his receding black hair as unruly as usual. He checked the peephole, and, turning away with an anxious look, opened the door.

"Good evening, Mr. Timmons, Miss McLeary, please come in."

"Thank you, Father," Maeda said, stamping her feet.

"Reverend Bourque." Raeph took her coat.

It was amazing how much life Maeda had brought to Raeph. He looked like what I presumed was his old self, laughing and abeam with contentment. This was certainly the true Raeph that had been held captive for so many years beneath the shroud of hatred and fear. *What was in store for him that night, however, was even more of a life-changer.*

"It's a zoo downtown," Maeda said, removing her overshoes. "Is Jamesfield always this busy this time of year?"

"No, and the city fathers may have released more demons than they can handle with this contrived midwinter festival," the priest replied. "When 'holy days' evolved into 'holidays,' the flesh won a victory over the spirit, especially when, like this one, a fictitious couple are being honored as martyrs to the wider cause of freedom: not freedom to live according to moral law, but freedom from all constraints in the name of 'love.'"

"You sound a bitter tone tonight, Reverend," I said with a smile. "Evening, Maeda. Raeph. I called your room, to offer you a ride."

"Appreciate it, Scott," Raeph said, now free of cloaks. "But Maeda helped me do a little last-minute shopping."

"I was going to say, I didn't remember you bringing that sharp tweed coat."

"She took me down to that Scottish shop. It's actually made in Ireland. The shop owner said he wasn't hindered by prejudice. It was, well, a gift," he said with a smile for Maeda.

"I just wanted him to look nice tonight. Besides," she glanced at Raeph first before saying, "even he was getting a bit tired of the old blue blazer."

He laughed. "Isn't she kind? That blazer has seen so many snowdrifts and slush puddles this past week, it looks like one of those old tie-dyed shirts from the '60s."

"Well, I want one of those for myself," I said. "You'll have to show me the shop."

"Are we all here?" Sister asked the priest from the door of the dining room.

"The LaPointes haven't arrived yet. Scott, they are coming?"

"They said they were."

Father Bourque answered with a worried look, "And, of course, our other—, ah, I guess we can give the LaPointes a few more minutes, and then we'll start. It may be that Stephen was just not up for company tonight. Understandable."

The women of the church had outdone themselves. Braised pork tenderloin and roast chicken, a potato-and-cheese casserole, mixed green and fruit salads, steamed vegetables, and, the starter, a homemade corn chowder to die for. The table was set and ready, when our last "announced" guests arrived.

"Stephen and Sara," the priest said, "we're so glad you could make it. I realize you probably would have preferred to spend the evening alone—"

"No, Father, we're very grateful for the invitation," Stephen said, hanging up their coats. "We both owe you so much."

"Yes, thank you," Sara said, kissing the priest on the cheek.

"Then all of you, come; dinner is ready."

We went into the dining room, and to our surprise found the seating prearranged with place names and gifts: hand-carved wooden rosaries for each, the labels indicating they were from Vatican City.

"I brought back a bushel of them on my last visit," remarked the priest.

Father Bourque was positioned to the far left, on the end, with Sister Agatha opposite him, nearest the kitchen. Sara, Stephen, and then I were positioned on the side with our backs to the door, while on the opposite were Maeda, next to Father, and then Raeph directly across from and facing the door. Next to him was an unmarked place, empty, yet fully set. In our family, we often left just such an empty place for our ever-present yet invisible Savior, so I guessed that was the reason.

"Would anyone like wine?" one of the volunteers asked. She responded accordingly to the *yesses, pleases* and *no, thank yous,* and then Father motioned for prayer. Crossing himself, with half the room following suit, he prayed, "Bless us, O Lord, and these Thy gifts, which we are about to receive from Thy bounty, through Christ our Lord," and together we gave our "Amen."

As the feast began, I noticed that the seating arrangement had positioned Raeph directly across from his quest. They had not as yet encountered one another, but for the moment they focused on their food.

Then Stephen lifted his attention. "Raeph, it's been a long time."

Raeph finished his mouthful before he answered, "It's good to see that you're doing well, Pastor."

"You don't need to address me as pastor anymore, for lots of reasons, but I appreciate it. Now it's just Stephen." He extended his hand across the table. Raeph hesitated then responded, and the two were friends.

"Scott told me about what has happened in your life, Raeph. I'm so sorry."

"I'm sure it's all for my own good. At least that's what I keep telling myself. Have you met Maeda?"

"Yes, I have, here at the parish. Hello, Maeda, have you met my wife, Sara?"

They greeted, a bit awkwardly in my opinion, but it could just have been me.

Various conversational threads wove intermittently between all gathered throughout the meal. Well into the meal, across the current of conversations, Father Bourque asked, "Sister?"

"Yes, Father?"

"Any sign of Fred?"

"I'll check. Excuse me," she said as she left the room. The table was being cleared for dessert and coffee when she returned, conveying to the priest an animated negative pantomime.

Father Bourque reluctantly rose. "I had not intended a speech for this evening, nothing more than a celebrative gathering of friends, but I came across something late last night that seems appropriate."

He reached inside his jacket and removed a slip of paper.

"After what happened here, and then discovering you, Stephen, at the hospital, and then meeting upon my return Pastor Guilford, who was completely remorseful for the vandalism, I couldn't sleep. I thought reading would help, so I picked up one of my favorite books, a novel about conversion by John Henry Cardinal Newman. He is considered one of the greatest of English writers, and his book *Apologia pro Vita sua*, in which he describes his own conversion, is listed amongst the greatest books of Western civilization. I, though, particularly enjoy his lesser known novel, *Loss and Gain*. I started rereading, almost at random, when I came across the following quote, which made me think about, well, all of you, all of us.

"The novel is about an Oxford student, named Charles, who is having a crisis with his Anglican faith. Newman writes, 'He had now come, in the course of a year, to one or two conclusions, not very novel, but very important: first, that there are a great many opinions in the world on the most momentous subjects; secondly, that all are not equally true; thirdly, that it is a duty to hold true opinions; and, fourthly, that it is uncommonly difficult to get hold of them.'"

The priest placed the paper on the table before him.

"Stephen and Sara, Scott, Raeph, I hear in this man's conclusions, the same convictions that have brought you to where you are today, though, Raeph, I didn't fully realize this about you until this afternoon. In your commitments to Jesus Christ, you each believe it is a duty to hold true opinions, to follow the truth wherever it leads. But how does one discover for certain what is true?

"In our conversations, most of you have indicated that, in your own way, you've wrestled with the same text of Scripture, where St. Paul describes 'the household of God, which is the church of the living God' as 'the pillar and bulwark of the truth.'[44] This can be a startling disclosure to those who believe that the Bible *alone* is 'the pillar and bulwark of the truth.' But not to bore you with a discourse on this tonight, I merely want to remind you that this search of yours is not a new or novel one. Newman wrote this statement that I quoted, 150 years ago, after his own struggle with truth, and the problem of his day remains: men and women continue to accept as truth whatever they happened to pick up along the way. They accept and even stubbornly defend what they were told by parents, pastors, teachers, politicians, journalists, and writers, all without taking the time to examine the trustworthiness of the source. I'm not saying that parents and pastors are always wrong," he said with a confirming smile to Stephen and Sara, "but only that many parents and pastors themselves are merely passing along what they themselves had accepted without examination. I know this to be true about myself, when I was a Lutheran pastor and husband." He glanced down at the paper before him.

"But Jesus promised that those who would follow Him without hesitation would know the truth, and the truth would set them free. I can only say, from personal experience, that I did not find this freedom until I accepted the truth of His Church."

A soft knock was heard, and through the opened door appeared the head of Fred, the parishioner who'd helped me Wednesday night with Father.

"Sister," he whispered, "we're here."

Sister Agatha jumped up, and with a wink at Father, left the room.

"I, well," continued Father Bourque, "was just saying that Jesus knew the spiritual battle that was ahead for His followers, how the world, the flesh, and the devil would fight against the truth, flooding the world with counterfeits. For this, He promised to send the Holy Spirit, who would teach His hand-chosen apostles all things—teach them the truth—and bring to their remembrance all that He had taught. This is the gift of the Church."

The door opened, and Sister stood there, smiling at Father.

He continued. "Friends, I did not invite you here tonight to hear me pontificate or proselytize, forgive me, but to have you present to share in a most wonderful surprise. Raeph, on Tuesday, Scott gave me a little information about your life, particularly about the hardships of the past year. One particular piece of information made me think of Detective Keith Torrance, whom you met this morning. He may be a small-town police detective, but he has some unique skills and contacts that at times have become handy, and since he owed me a favor anyway, I asked him for some help. Late Tuesday night, he told me the results of his work, and I was pleasantly surprised beyond belief. We followed up, made all the necessary arrangements, and now—Sister Agatha, if you will—Raeph, we have a present for you."

Sister backed out of the space in the doorway, and in entered a thin, brown-robed, bearded young man.

Raeph rose slowly. "Ted?"

"Hello, Dad."

"Ted!" Raeph said, as he ran around the table and buried his slightly taller son in a bear hug. Through sobs, he said, "I thought you were dead. I never heard from you after you left."

"Sister," Father Bourque suggested, "why don't you take them into my study." After they left the room, the priest continued. "That young Franciscan brother is Raeph's long-lost son, Ted."

"I remember him," Sara said, tears racing toward her smile. "I taught him in Sunday school, and, Stephen, you had him in the scout troop."

"I would certainly never have guessed that he'd choose the religious life," Stephen added. "He was always the biggest cutup and troublemaker. I heard he'd gotten caught up in drugs."

"That's what Raeph assumed," I added. "He'd run away from home before completing high school and never wrote back. He hadn't even returned for the funerals of his mother or his brother. Raeph assumed drugs had killed him. So, Reverend Bourque, what happened?"

"I don't know all the details. We'll have to find that out later. Detective Torrance located him through his channels, but when he told me that Ted had become a Franciscan brother I almost passed out. And from what I had learned about Raeph from you, Scott, I wasn't certain he would take this as better news than Ted's supposed death by drugs. But we arranged for his flights anyway. What I do know is that Ted had tried to contact his parents from California, but they had moved with no forwarding address or phone number. He learned of the deaths of both his mother and brother after the fact, and knowing his father's zealous hatred for Catholics, he procrastinated on contacting him. When he received the call from Detective Torrance, he asked leave to make the trip, which his superiors granted without hesitation."

Later that night, Raeph gave me the details of their reunion. Once in the study, seated in the rockers by the wood-burning stove, Raeph had spoken first …

"Ted, you can't imagine how good it is to see you, to know you're all right. But, the robe, I … I don't even know what to ask."

"Dad, I've always wondered how you'd react if you found out. I guess that's what I was afraid of—why I put off trying to contact you. But I wanted to; I wanted to tell you about how my life had changed, and really how it all happened because of you."

"Because of *me*?" Raeph said, moving his hand to his heart.

"It always looked like I wasn't listening, that none of your religious enthusiasm made a dent, but it did; I just refused to let you see. I need to say, though, that I was a bit afraid of your fanaticism. I don't know how much you realized it, but all my friends made fun of you and Mr. Horscht. Called you 'crazies.' That's why I distanced myself from you, rebelled."

"Son, your friends weren't all that wrong."

"Well, they were in lots of other things. Remember when we argued about the dent in Mom's car?"

"Yes, I do," Raeph said, turning toward the fire, "the day before you left."

"I was so frustrated. You wouldn't believe me when I said I had nothing to do with it, so when Kyle and Theo told me the next morning they were leaving town to hitchhike to California, I kissed Red Creek good-bye. I did a lot of bad things over the next few years, which I'd rather leave buried in the mercy of God's grace. Maybe I'll tell you the whole story another time, but one morning I woke up, my face lying in my own vomit, on the stone floor of a Catholic mission in southern California. I don't remember how I got there, but the brothers took me in, fed me, helped me regain control of my life, and in the process, I remembered. I remembered your love for Jesus, your convictions. At first, I was nervous about being with those Catholic monks in that Catholic mission, surrounded by Catholic stuff—statues, relics, rituals—but in the end, their love and acceptance won over my fear."

"Ted, you have no idea how much you are like me," Raeph said, reaching out and grasping his son's hands. "How much your experience is just like mine. The Lord used different means to break me, but He used the same thing, love, to drive out my anger and fear." He paused, then asked, "But the robe, are you now a Catholic *monk*?"

"I'm in discernment as a Franciscan novice. I'm living a life of prayer and service in a monastery in northern Minnesota, helping the friars serve the poor, many of whom are American Indians. Actually one of the things that stood in the way of my progress was my hesitancy to seek your forgiveness and approval. That's one of the reasons I came as soon as I was contacted, along with my desire for you and me to at least be friends again."

"Ted, it's so good to see you," Raeph said, squeezing his son's arms. "You know me. I don't know a whole lot about Catholic things, especially about the life of a Franciscan monk. But, believe it or not, I've come a long way."

Raeph studied his son, once lost but now found, then closed his eyes briefly to compose himself, before answering: "Yes, Ted, you not only have my forgiveness, but, if you really think this is what God is calling you to do, then you have my full approval too. I want nothing but the best God can give you!"

He could no longer hold himself back. He grabbed his son in an engulfing bear hug while tears poured forth unheeded. After a minute or so, he pulled himself away, and seeing his son also moved, wiping his eyes on the sleeve of his robe, Raeph said, standing, "We can talk more about all this later, but maybe we better join the rest for dessert."

After that, they rejoined us in the dining room, where we were anxiously waiting to hear of the reunion.

"Everyone," Father Bourque announced, "this is Brother Theodore Timmons of the Franciscan Friars in northern Minnesota, Raeph's youngest son."

We all rose to greet him, but the one who showed the most enthusiastic joy, who gave him the biggest hug, was the woman from Ireland.

EPILOGUE

AND I SHALL DWELL IN THE HOUSE OF THE LORD FOREVER

⟨ 44 ⟩

Scott Turner's Epilogue

After that great celebrative dinner, I finally had my long-awaited conversation with Stephen. I had hinted as we separated at the church for him to stop by if he was up for a late night, but I hadn't counted on it. But sure enough, around ten thirty, there was a knock at my door.

"Stephen, please come in. Have a seat," I motioned to the only chair in the room.

"Thanks, Scott. It sure is great to see you."

I took the edge of the bed, and for the next hour, with hardly a break, we revisited old times, compared our respective seminary days and pastoral experiences, seen now from a much different perspective. Our conversation began with slowly bringing each other up to date on our lives and families, then segued into a basic comparison of the journeys we'd separately trod the past year, and finally morphed into a mild and friendly apologetic debate. To most, the record of our dialogue would be a sleeper, a bantering of two middle-aged men quoting Scripture, early Christian writers, and Church doctrine. In the end, sometime after midnight, with a solemn joy, Stephen gave me the details of his recent journey, reconstructing the path of discernment he had taken from the Mite to the Canadian shrine and the cemetery of his ancestors. To him, though, the most precious miraculous work of grace had been the unanticipated receptiveness of Sara's heart. They were already talking about when they might be received into the Church.

As for the possibility of priesthood, Stephen said that for now he just wanted to be a good *Christifideles laici*, a good lay member of Christ's faithful people.

"Remember Jesus' warning against choosing places of honor?" Stephen asked. "How we are to chose the lowest place with contentment until someone of authority invites us to take a higher seat? Well, it took the humility of a young woman named Brigitte to help me see how entitled and deserving I'd come to feel. Since my ordination, by the mercy of God and the generosity of the congregations I've served, I'd been invited to rise from the lowest pew to the front seat of leadership. Now it's time for me to return with contentment to the pew. What about you, Scott?"

For our entire time together I had successfully kept the focus mostly on him, but I knew it would eventually come around to me. *Wasn't this the reason I had come searching for him in the first place?*

So, I reviewed everything, what his monologue at the Mite had done to my confidence, how all year long I'd questioned everything about my calling and my ability to know for certain that what I was preaching was true, and how I'd come here hoping he could help me make sense out of my confusion. But then, of course, I reviewed everything else that had happened that week, the highs and lows, my time with Father Bourque, but especially my new friendship with Raeph.

"What was the last straw, so to speak, for you, Scott?"

"Honestly, that hasn't dropped yet. I still need to present all this to Diane."

"Ah, yes," he said, running his hand back through his graying hair. "That will be a tough one."

He knew Diane, not that she was in any way a difficult wife, but her religious history—the wounds of her childhood left her even more set against the Catholic Church than Sara.

"But, so far, with all I've learned, and frankly unlearned," I said, shaking my head, "I think it was experiencing the transformation of Raeph. People say eyes are the windows of the soul. Well, in and through his eyes, I watched God transform a heart from hatred, through contrition, to love. It was a literal heart transplant, but it wasn't just because he had found a new love in Maeda. It was because what Jesus said literally came true: 'You will know the truth, and the truth will make you free.'"

Then I remembered. "Stephen, you know what was really strange, though? When I began this journey from Ohio to Jamesfield, I passed a graveyard and saw the strangest thing. A tombstone with our names on it."

"What? Our names? What do you mean?"

"A tombstone, denoting a family burial, had Stephen, the father, Sara, the mother, and Scott, the son. It was weird."

"Sounds like a plot line for a Stephen King novel."

"I know. I first wondered whether it was some kind of portent or omen, but now I think it was a different kind of sign from God. A graveyard is too often perceived as the endpoint of a person's life and dreams, a melancholic place. But on the contrary, it's actually a reminder that the dead have passed on to a fuller understanding of life. Now they know more clearly the truth about all the things in life they thought were important."

"As St. Paul said, 'For now we see in a mirror dimly, but then face to face. Now I know in part; then I shall understand fully, even as I have been fully understood.'"[45]

"Exactly. I have now come to see my faith and my call to ministry, my whole life, in an entirely different light, a truer light, because, as if for the first time, I am looking face to face with the Church Jesus established for our salvation. Not one of my own creation. And this is also true for you and Sara: 'Stephen, Sara, and Scott.'"

We ended that night with a prayer together, for each other and our families, and with a promise to get together as often as possible.

About six weeks later, I completed another round-trip drive out to Jamesfield, but this time from our cabin in Maine. The return leg seemed particularly long and lonely. I suppose this only shows my immaturity and ingratitude, but the Easter Vigil Mass, at least for me, was a mixed bag. A dozen or more Catholics had described the Easter Vigil as definitely the most impressive Mass of the liturgical season, and I understand how it probably is in the big picture, but it just did nothing for me. It only shows how much growing I still need to do.

The interior of St. Francis de Sales Parish, with its recently repaired stained glass portrayal of St. Anne, never looked so beautiful. And the dark, somber relighting of the church accompanying the procession of the cross was quite impressive. I laughed at the idea of trying to recreate this in one of my former Congregational churches; one candle and the lighting would be complete.

The congregation felt like old home week, for it seemed like I knew everyone there. Cliff Wilson sat with me in the second row, a pew reserved for family and friends of those being received. Cliff's marriage had been dissolved, having never been sacramental nor valid in the first place. He was now testing his fit as a Benedictine monk.

Father Gary Harmond, the ex-priest, ex-Baptist, reinstated-priest, was up front concelebrating the Mass beside Father Bourque. Immediately after his reception back into the Church that he had for so long berated in books, tracts, and debates, Harmond's bishop had sent him on a thirty-day retreat. Convinced of his sincere change of heart, the bishop restored his faculties, and this Vigil was his first public Mass.

Helen and Stacy Horscht also were sitting in the reserved pew. Beside Stacy sat a tall young man I didn't recognize at first, but then realized it was William, Stephen's oldest son. Apparently, they had begun corresponding not long after she'd returned to discover that her father had shot his. Working through the misunderstandings and the betrayal with the bikers—another story—took months, but they had emerged as friends, and this Vigil was to be their first face-to-face encounter.

Filling out the reserved pew were Raeph and Maeda. They had actually driven much further for this occasion, all the way from northern Minnesota, where they had both moved to live closer to Raeph's long-lost, Franciscan son Ted. Father Bourque had used some amazing connections to find Raeph a foreman's job not unlike his previous position. Maeda worked in a large department store, and rumors were that, though Raeph was still skittish about becoming a Roman Catholic, their relationship was progressing quite smoothly.

Halfway through the Mass, after what seemed like an hour of Scripture readings, came the reception of new members. Stephen and Sara, without any special notoriety, took their place with the other fifteen candidates. Not long after their leisurely drive from Jamesfield to her apartment on the North Shore, Sara had asked Father Bourque if she could be received with her husband at Easter. Through correspondence and several grilling, face-to-face meetings, he became convinced that she was equally as ready for reception as her husband.

Behind Sara stood Sister Agatha, her sponsor, and behind Stephen stood his sponsor, Jim Sarver, the long-time friend who had opened his heart to Christ and bravely paved the way for his discovery of the Church.

When the seventeen candidates had been duly received, Father Bourque bid them turn to greet the rest of their new family, and the loudest standing ovation came from Cliff, and a woman I'd never met, named Philomena.

As I made the return drive from Jamesfield to our cabin near the coast of Maine, I won't deny that I was overwhelmed with a sense of satisfaction, a joyful sense that God had poured the light of His grace into the lives of my friends and that all was right in the world.

So why was my drive back such a long and lonely one? Let's just say that the final straw still has not fallen, for, as suspected, Diane was far from keen about my new discoveries. She and the kids had had a wonderful time in Boston, and our reunion the next day had been hopeful. Neither of the kids understood why we had to leave Rowsville so quickly and definitively, but they were excited about living in our cabin. Up until then, we had only used the cabin for weekend visits; now they thought life was going to be one long vacation. Their excitement ended abruptly, however, once Diane reinstated in full force their previous homeschool routine.

After a week of settling in, I finally took the opportunity, over a quiet glass of wine—a pleasant new tradition for our marriage—to wean her into what I'd discovered during my week in Jamesfield. As soon as she got the slightest scent, however, of where I was headed, her face went stone cold; she stood up, threw her crystal into the fireplace, exclaimed, "Don't even think about following your friends down into the same cesspool," and left the room.

I sat paralyzed, speechless. I'd anticipated a strong reaction, as she matched my newfound joy against the trauma of her childhood in Catholic schools, but this was not like Diane. Many times, as the climax of her conversion testimony, she had shared how she had been "saved from the Whore of Babylon and into the arms of Christ!"

Never, however, for any reason had I experienced this kind of anger from her. I knew then that there must be something deeper, darker, that I realized could not be cured overnight. *This has caused me to wonder whether there was a significance in the absence of Diane's name on that tombstone.*

As a result, I now enjoy the beauty and peacefulness of our backwoods hideaway, but the trajectory of my spiritual life remains mostly private. We go to church together, with the kids, at a Presbyterian church in our coastal village. All the Catholic churches nearby have been closed down; the nearest open one is forty-five miles away. I continue to read Catholic writers, especially the early Church Fathers and nineteenth century English converts. I continue to look for cracks in Diane's armor, but for now, short of a direct jolt of God's grace, I must admit, it sometimes seems hopeless. She's not happy that I've given up the ministry. The local Presbyterian minister has asked if I'd like to teach a Bible study or help lead worship, but I've begged off gracefully.

Crazy as it sounds, I'm thinking of using some savings to buy a small lobster boat, something an old retired pastor friend of mine once tried. A few guys in town, who remember my football career with the typical Maine lack of enthusiasm, say they'll help me get started, but I don't know.

Some days I wonder whether I misheard God way back when I gave up football to become a minister. I knew (and still know) that God loves me and called me to live a holy life, to be a good and faithful husband and father, and to be a witness to others of His saving grace. But had He called me specifically to leave everything, to go to seminary, and to become an ordained Protestant minister? Twenty years ago, when I believed this, I also believed that the Bible was the sole foundation for faith and the "pillar and bulwark of the truth." And I believed that though others might confirm or challenge my call, in the end I was accountable to no one except Jesus Christ. He had "called me," and if I was certain of this, I was to let no one dissuade me.

I've now come to know differently. The "pillar and bulwark of the truth" is the Church, and not some invisible, vaporous, unknowable collection of true believers, but the Church established by Jesus Christ Himself in His apostles and built on the rock of St. Peter. And the call of anyone to a full-time religious vocation, whether as a priest, deacon, friar, or nun, is a call of the community for service in the community. I might believe I have a call, but if the Church decides not to confirm this, I must be willing to accept the possibility that I might be wrong. I must be willing to remain in the lower place, until invited to come higher.

No man is an island. We are members of the Body, and each with his own place. Like on a football team. Every player has an important role if the team is to compete, but the coach is the Coach, and I, just a defensive end.

So I'll steer my boat through the waves, pretending to fish for lobsters; I'll love my wife and kids; I'll jaw with the locals; and I'll worship my Lord in my wife's church. But in the privacy of my morning devotions, before anyone else in my family is awake, I will sit at this desk, before my icon of *Christ Pantocrator*; I will pray the prayers of the Church, asking for forgiveness and the ability to forgive, for mercy and the grace to be merciful, and for a heart willing to rejoice in my sufferings, "offering it up," as Father Bourque says.

And next Easter, Lord willing, I hope against hope to come home, for indeed, all things work together for good for those who love God and are called according to His purpose.

AFTERWORD

As with *How Firm a Foundation,* the first novel in this sequence, all of the main characters, names, places, and incidents in this story are fictitious. This is a novel, not a biographical conversion story. However, built upon what I have learned over the years, from interviewing converts on the *Journey Home* program as well as in my work with the Coming Home Network International, I have tried to express the actual reasoning and emotions that many ministers like myself have experienced, yet in a fictional format. This allows me to relate the psychological, emotional, and relational aspects of conversion, which are not always shared in condensed or detailed autobiographies. It is particularly important to note that the experiences of Sara LaPointe do not parallel those of my wife, Marilyn.

Besides those many friends acknowledged in the afterword of *How Firm a Foundation,* I particularly want to thank those on the present staff and board of the Coming Home Network International, who walked beside me during this composition, reading, critiquing, and encouraging—particularly Fr. Ray Ryland!

I especially want to thank Eleanor Donlon and Jeanette Flood for their superb editorial assistance. Any residual mistakes in the text are solely mine. Thanks also to Jennifer Bitler for this book's layout and design.

I want to thank "my three sons" for always making my life a joy, and especially my loving and patient wife, Marilyn. In the end, it was only through her encouragement that this book was able to reach fruition.

Please feel free to pass along any comments or questions, and may the Lord bless you as you seek to follow Him faithfully.

—Marcus Grodi

Endnotes

1. Rom 1:22.
2. Mt 18:20.
3. Mt 24:40-42.
4. 1 Tm 4:1-3.
5. 1 Thes 3:12–13.
6. Phil 1:9–10.
7. 1 Cor 15:1–2.
8. Lk 6:22–23.
9. 1 Cor 15:58.
10. Lk 6:41–42.
11. G. E. H. Palmer, Philip Sherrard, and Kallistos Ware, trans. and eds., *The Philokalia*, vol. 1 (London: Faber and Faber, 1983), p. 66.
12. Jn 8:31-32.
13. Phil 3:13b-14.
14. Eph 5:25.
15. Mk 9:24.
16. Phil 4:6-7.
17. Ez 36:26a.
18. Volume II (New York: Hurd and Houghton, 1868), pp. 99–102.
19. Ibid.
20. Prv 3:5-6.
21. Jn 8:31b-32.
22. Rom 8:16-17.
23. Matthew 18:15-17.
24. Rom 10:9.
25. 1 Tm 2:4.
26. Gal 1:6.
27. 1 Jn 2:27.
28. *Catechism of the Catholic Church*, no. 92.
29. 2 Tm 3:16-17.

[30] Eph 3:7.

[31] Eph 3:10.

[32] Eph 2:19.

[33] Kenneth J. Howell, trans. and ed., *Ignatius of Antioch and Polycarp of Smyrna* (Zanesville, OH: CHResources, 2009) p. 160.

[34] Harper Lee, *To Kill a Mockingbird* (London: Arrow Books, 2006), p. 280.

[35] 1 Jn 4:20a.

[36] Jn 13:35.

[37] 1 Jn 4:19.

[38] Eph 2:8-9.

[39] 1 Pt 3:7.

[40] Lk 12:48.

[41] 1 Jn 4:20.

[42] St. Augustine, *Confessions*, (c. a.d. 397), 1.

[43] Jas 2:26.

[44] 1 Tm 3:15.

[45] 1 Cor 13:12.

Author's Biography

 Marcus Grodi received a B.S. in Polymer Science and Engineering from Case Institute of Technology. After working as a Plastics Engineer, he attended Gordon-Conwell Theological Seminary, where he received a master's in divinity degree. After ordination, he served first as a Congregationalist and then eight years as a Presbyterian pastor. He is now the President / Founder of the Coming Home Network International. He hosts a live television program called *The Journey Home* and a radio program called *Deep in Scripture*, both on EWTN. Marcus, his wife, Marilyn, and their family live on their small farm near Zanesville, Ohio.

ALSO PUBLISHED
BY CHResources

For more information about the author and the Coming Home Network International, please write, phone, or visit their website:

The Coming Home Network International
PO Box 8290
Zanesville, OH 43702-8290
1-740-450-1175
http://www.chnetwork.org